Ellice Hopkins

Life and Letters of James Hinton

Ellice Hopkins

Life and Letters of James Hinton

ISBN/EAN: 9783744726375

Printed in Europe, USA, Canada, Australia, Japan

Cover: Foto ©Raphael Reischuk / pixelio.de

More available books at **www.hansebooks.com**

LIFE AND LETTERS

OF

JAMES HINTON,

EDITED BY

ELLICE HOPKINS.

WITH

AN INTRODUCTION BY SIR W. W. GULL.

FOURTH EDITION.

LONDON:

KEGAN PAUL, TRENCH & CO., 1 PATERNOSTER SQUARE.

1883.

INTRODUCTION.

It would be a pain to me that any Memoir of James Hinton should go forth without a word of affectionate regard for his memory from me. It is now near twenty years ago that our acquaintance began. Sympathies in common on the nearest subjects of human interest brought us much together. It was at this time that " Man and his Dwelling - Place " was projected and written. Every page bears witness to the workings of his intensely energetic mind. I recall vividly the earnest manner with which he would submit to me the different chapters of this work. Convinced as he was that the only deadness in nature, the only negative condition, was man's selfishness, his whole life and thought was to excite a reaction against it.

It was his favourite conception that the "phenomenal" was essentially antithetic to the "actual." He would illustrate in a hundred ways how this was equally true in relation to our moral sense. The same error which led man, from limited observation, to suppose the earth the *centre* and *at rest*, repeated itself under a new form in supposing himself to be a living centre surrounded by dead things.

Death to him was a purely human idea. All nature is living. The " Physiological Riddles " exemplified his thoughts on this point very fully. In these essays he was abreast of the best physiology of the time, and may be considered as having done good service in combating the narrow views that still prevail, even in high quarters, and which would raise a barrier in nature between organic and inorganic where none exists.

Hinton was not a man of science, but a philosopher. Science was to him the servant of philosophy. He felt himself to be an interpreter of nature; not in the Baconian sense by the collection and arrangement of facts, the sequences of causes and effects, but, like the Hebrew seer of old, penetrating through appearances to their central cause.

I remember one occasion when he came to me full of emotion, with tears in his eyes, at a glimpse he had caught of the universal relation of things to the Divine Cause. "What I see in nature," he said, "is the Divine power acting within an imposed limit. God, self-limited, is the universe. God is not the universe, but it flows from Him and becomes phenomenal by the laws of limitation."

I could not at the time but check him by quoting Goethe's words—

> "Oh ! glücklich wer noch hoffen kann,
> Aus diesem Meer des Irrthums aufzutauchen,'

laying severe stress upon hope, and urging on him that the poet did not seem to admit the likelihood that we should ever realise it by seeing truth as it is. Hinton would not, however, be brought back to our everyday views and imperfect ways of thinking, but insisted that we voluntarily hindered our vision by the mere scientific relation of facts, as opposed to a true philosophy of them.

How often he would repeat, "It is the sense and the intellect which raise us to a scientific appreciation, to the mechanical relations of things; but it is *genius* and *intuition* which enable us to penetrate to their higher meaning." To limit human knowledge to that which is scientific was a capital error against which Hinton combated with all his might. For Hinton Goethe was not a true poet; his view was limited to the scientific and phenomenal. No wonder, then, that Hinton scorned his supercilious doubts, and went on with the assurance that truth was still attainable by man.

I should give, however, a wrong impression of Hinton's mind, so far as I observed its workings, if I let it be supposed that he was a careless observer. He was not in the least indifferent to observation, nor had he a limited view of the range of science or of scientific methods; this is proved by his physiological and pathological work. It could hardly be otherwise, impressed as he was with the philosophy of his subject. Organic forms were not to him "manufactured articles." He was, I think I may say, from long conversations with him through many years, the truest believer in evolution. Form he saw was the product of growth under resistance, whether in the uncoiled frond of the fern, the symmetry of leaves, or the features of man. He would have endorsed the words of Milton—

> "One Almighty is, from whom
> All things proceed, ...
>   One first matter, all
> Endued with various forms, various degrees
> Of substance, and, in things that live, of life ;
> But more refined, more spirituous, and pure,
> As nearer to him placed, or nearer tending,
> Each in their several active spheres assigned,
> Till body up to spirit work, in bounds
> Proportioned to each kind. So from the root
> Springs lighter the green stalk ; from thence the leaves
> More airy ; last the bright consummate flower
> Spirits odorous breathes ; flowers and their fruit,
> Man's nourishment, by gradual scale sublimed,
> To vital spirits aspire, to animal,
> To intellectual ; give both life and sense,
> Fancy and understanding ; whence the soul
> Reason receives."

Suppression and reappearance in a new and higher form was to him the fundamental law of physiology.

Organisms in upward order, concoct, digest, assimilate, "and corporeal–to incorporeal turn."

Hinton's thoughts on moral subjects were of the same character as those on material. The miserable, despised, and abandoned outcasts of society, sacrificed to the selfishness of the well-to-do and respectable, was a glaring instance of the deception of the phenomenal. I think I am justified in saying, from my intercourse with him, that he thought such facts illustrated the object of Christ's work on earth, as showing us how contrary truth is to appearance. I do not, however, trust myself from reminiscences only, to enter largely into these subjects. Hinton's views on such matters appear fully in his writings, perhaps chiefly in the "Mystery of Pain."

To descend to lower matters, I may say that Hinton's physical energy always seemed to me as great and indomitable as that of his mind. Together they afforded an example of intellectual and bodily activity rarely surpassed. His feelings also were "finely touched," and to "fine issues." Our profession is proud of his name. The work he did in it was well done, and by it he laid stepping-stones for others to advance upon.

Hinton's life was not so full of incident as it was full of thought. Reminiscences of such a life are therefore everywhere embodied in and to be collected from his writings. The main object indeed of his practical life was, I may say, to afford him opportunity to pursue his philosophical speculations. Hence it was that he so early retired from professional work, according to the teaching of his own parable, that gold should be made to buy the more precious things. He was one of the pioneers of humanity through the obscure and dark ways of the sense to the region of truth.

W. W. GULL.

CONTENTS.

CHAPTER I.

PAGE

Birth and parentage—Home influences—Death of his eldest brother—School life—Family removes from Reading to London—Placed in a situation at Whitechapel—Distress of mind at the wrongs of women—Passion for knowledge—Early attachment—Letters to his eldest sister—Renewed distress and illness—Enters medical profession —Voyage to China as ship's surgeon—Returns to England —Takes out his diploma—practises at Newport . . 1

CHAPTER II.

Takes charge of Negro emigrants to Jamaica—Remains in Jamaica as assistant surgeon—Letters home—Religious difficulties—Visit to America on his homeward voyage— Change of religious views—Letter to his sister—Arrival home 19

CHAPTER III.

Engagement to Miss Margaret Haddon—Letters to her : On beginning London practice—The nature of love—Religious difficulties—Coleridge's "Aids to Reflection"—Practical proofs of Christianity—Medical quacks—Cure of his mother's deafness—Channing—Fault-finding—Nobility of his father's character, and plea for his own shortcomings—Faith in Christ 36

CHAPTER IV.

PAGE

First turns his attention to aural surgery—Friendship with
Mr. Toynbee—Studies physiology—Letters to Miss Margaret Haddon :—Neglect of health—Musical composition
—Intoxicating drinks—Moral drugging—Want of a fit
object in life—The wonder of the world—Attends
homœopathic hospital—Physical power of the emotions
—Physiology of blushing—Emotional cures—The use
of a tear—Allopaths and homœopaths—Difficulties—
Enthusiasm for knowledge—Rarity of scientific investigation—On the nature of the brain—Matter and spirit .   54

CHAPTER V.

Letters to Miss Margaret Haddon, continued :—Physiological
speculations—The doctrine of the Atonement—Limits of
knowledge—The trading spirit in professions—Emotional
therapeutics—The metaphysics of science—How to practise homœopathy—Aspirations—Incredible credulity—
Absorption in thinking—Increasing faith in Christianity
—Converts a homœopath—Different modes of service—
Proposed emigration—Limited income—Determination
to marry   83

CHAPTER VI.

Marriage with Miss Margaret Haddon—Birth of his children
—Friendship with Sir William Gull—Letter to Pro-
fessor Croom Robertson—His method and philosophy—
Historical sketch—Thoughts illustrative of his philosophy   108

CHAPTER VII.

Letters to a friend in religious difficulties :—Self-surrender—
The Bible and eternity—Love of God and man—Truth
an union of opposites—The spiritual unthinkable—Mis-
construction of Christ's teaching—Feeling good as evil—
Nature divine and spiritual—National communions—
Asceticism—Miracles—Prayer—Interpretation of error
—Self-tormenting—Practical puzzles—Intellectual pa-
tience—Mental depression—Feeling sure   .   .   .   130

CHAPTER VIII.

PAGE

First begins to publish—Assists Mr. Toynbee in aural practice—Paper on organic forms—Pecuniary difficulties—
Publication of "Man and His Dwelling-Place"—Its
success—Gives up practice for philosophy—Life at Tottenham—Publication of "Physiological Riddles," and
"Thoughts on Health," in Cornhill—"Mystery of Pain"
written—Letters on the subject—Involuntary sacrifice
—Source of his thoughts 154

CHAPTER IX.

Letters :—On the after-death state—"Man and His Dwelling-
Place"—Imagination—Lack of Dramatic power—German
—Relation to other thinkers and present thought—The
self—Failure of income—Birth of his youngest child—
Appointment as aural surgeon to Guy's Hospital—Gives
up philosophy and returns to practice—Letters on giving
up philosophy 175

CHAPTER X.

Residence at Tudor Lodge—Removes his family to Barnet
and Brighton—Letters to his wife and son—Letters :—
Indifference—Bereavement—Belief—How to treat the
Bible — Letters to his little boy — Succeeds to Mr.
Toynbee's practice—Happiness of his home life—Conversational powers—Character of his intellect—Love
for music and art—Social meetings—Personal influence
—Sympathy—Letters :—Adoption of Orphans—Divinity
of Christ—To his wife—Mental hibernation—The vision
of God—On what we can know—Relations of his philosophy to Kant and Fichte—Conversation with Mr.
Berry 207

CHAPTER XI.

Travels on the Continent—Letters home—Resumes philosophy
—Mental photography—Prints his early MSS.—Letters
to his family—Feeling towards the Established Church
—Pamphlet on nursing—Joins the Metaphysical Society
—Purchases a property in the Azores—Visits France
and Spain—Studies Asceticism—Altruism as held by Mr.
Hinton—Ethical thoughts 246

CHAPTER XII.

PAGE

Letters :—Giving up one's best—On the art of thinking—Project of living in the East End of London —Man as Christ reveals him—Nature of women—Joy in the world— Sadness of modern life—Sends his pictures to the East End of London—Letters :—Aspromonte—To his wife —Self-basis of modern life—Regard for others—Shrinking from antagonism—Sectarianism—Pleasure as a guide —Thoughts on genius 286

CHAPTER XIII.

Letters : — Book on aural surgery — The false law—Conscientious sacrifice—Jacob Böhme and modern theosophists—Social views—Apparent recklessness—Increased excitability and need of rest—Significant prescription —Letters :—Cruel idols—Dogmatic theology—Nothing seen in itself—The desire on good—Social changes— Inaugural lecture at Guy's—The place of the physician —Retires from practice—Publishes " Questions in Aural Surgery " and " Atlas of the Ear "—Death of his mother. 318

CHAPTER XIV.

Summer at Lulworth—Mrs. Hinton winters in the Azores— Letters to his son—the method of fluxions—His selflessness—Stored up force—Letters :—Right—Self-restraint —The liberty of art—The wonder of the world—The correction of the premiss—Falsity to fact—Dreamland— Degradation of women—Dynamic relations of evil . 334

CHAPTER XV.

Visit to South Wales—Letters :—Thinking by leaving out —How self came to be put first—Lewes' " Problem's of Life and Mind "—The fluxion—Visit to Brighton— Brilliancy of his intellect — Pain of life — Personal characteristics—Attitude towards death, and questions of the hereafter—Depression and nervous exhaustion— Sets sail for the Azores—Failure of property—Letters home—Inflammation of the brain—His death—Burial at Ponta Delgada, St. Michaels—Conclusion . . . 357

LIFE AND LETTERS

OF

JAMES HINTON.

———•———

CHAPTER I.

JAMES HINTON was the son of the well-known Baptist
minister, the Rev. Howard Hinton, and Eliza Birt, his
wife. He was born at Reading in 1822, and was the
third of a family of eleven children. On his father's
side, he sprang from the same stock as the Taylors of
Ongar, Mr. Howard Hinton's mother being Ann Taylor,
daughter of Josiah Taylor, the engraver, and aunt to Isaac
Taylor, the well-known author of the " History of Enthusiasm," and his sisters Ann and Jane Taylor.

At the time of his birth, his father was already known
as a powerful preacher, as the not altogether orthodox
exponent of a more moderate Calvinism than was then
in vogue among Baptists, and as a man of great energy of
character. Indeed, he bore the strong Taylor stamp of
individuality, which made him a leader in his own deno-
mination, both in thought and in active philanthropy.

He owed his name to the philanthropist John Howard,
who was an intimate friend of Josiah Taylor, the grandfather, and who, just before starting for Russia, whence

A

he was never to return, said to his friend's daughter, in sorrowful allusion to the blight which had fallen on his own happiness while seeking to alleviate the woes of others: "I have now no son of my own; if ever you have one, pray call him after me," a request which was held sacred.

His father, the Rev. James Hinton, had given him a liberal education at the University of Edinburgh, the two older universities being then closed against Dissenters; and he was distinguished not only for sound scholarship, but for the strong scientific tastes which his son afterwards inherited, being an excellent geologist and naturalist. Altogether his was one of those strong, clearly-defined personalities that impress themselves on the minds of men. "When," in the words of a contemporary, "he rose up in a public meeting to speak, six feet in height, of spare and severe form, with a countenance calm and thoughtful and touched with sadness, hardly lighted by eyes which seemed to turn inwards, as if they were more concerned to see truth than men, the first sentiment awakened was reverence bordering on dread. When the sentences began to come, clear and convincing in their logic, but uttered in the shrill tones of a nervous temperament, and sometimes flung defiantly at the audience, as if he intended to arouse rather than to conciliate, it was not surprising that he produced on some the impression of being a bitter and passionate disputant."

But those who knew him better, knew that under some apparent harshness of demeanour lay hidden a nature full of tenderness, with sympathies at once delicate and prompt, noble in forgiveness, and humble as a child in acknowledging the faults of temper into which the vehemence of his nature occasionally betrayed him.

Under the influence of the strong religious feelings which made it his habit for thirty years regularly to retire three times a day for prayer and communion with God, his character gradually mellowed and softened, a growth of years best embodied in his own touching words: "We are near home; may we be home-like."

But if James Hinton was thus closely related on his father's side to the Taylors, if from him he derived the intellectual thoroughness, the dislike of bad logic, and reverence for scientific methods which saved him from the otherwise visionary tendencies of his mind, it was not from his father but from his mother that he inherited most, despite the stress Mr. Francis Galton lays on his paternal pedigree in his book on "Heredity." Deep as was the reverence in which he held his father, he always spoke of himself as more especially his mother's child; and it was certainly her impress that he chiefly took.

She, too, was every way a woman of strong individuality of character; a fervent, lofty-souled woman, with a spring of sacred enthusiasm in her that seemed to remove her in a measure from the common concerns of life; beautiful to look upon in her early years, till she grew worn with much anxiety and ill-health, but always retaining the gracious dignity of manner which made her rule every one who belonged to her with a woman's mild but irresistible sway,—a sway tempered by deep womanly compassion that was ever ready to excuse an offender on her favourite plea of "poor human nature."

The home in which James Hinton received his early training was a very happy one. It was surrounded by a large garden, where the eldest children, Howard and Sarah, used occasionally to hide from their little brother, a small, toddling, sweet-tempered fellow, much given to disturb their play; even then showing a strong tendency to investigate everything, and re-arrange the game " as it ought to be."

As he grew older, all three used often to go out to tea together, the great delight being to spend the evening with a certain Miss Davis, who kept a drawer full of toys for their especial benefit, and acted the part of a beneficent fairy in their childish world. But, perhaps, what they grew to love best were the long walks they used to take with their father, which he made delightful to them by teaching them to observe the habits of birds and insects, the connection between the stone at their feet and the crust of the earth, the trees, the flowers, the mosses, the lichens ; all were made sources of pleasure to them. James, too, shared his father's taste for music, which subsequently made Mr. Howard Hinton's chapel noted for its exquisite singing.

But if the stern, upright, yet kindly father was the granite pillar on which that large family rested, the mother was pre-eminently its shaping influence, more especially as Mr. Hinton's studious character and professional duties led him to spend much of his time in his study. Consecration to God and to the higher interests of life was made the very life-breath of that home; and the children grew up under a religious pressure difficult to realise in these easy-going days. In the round, carefully-ruled copy-book handwriting of a little pinafored maiden, in a letter addressed on the outside " Brother James," one reads that the child on first going to school could not play, but, " when I went upstairs to learn my lessons, I used to fall down on my knees, and pray that God would keep me, and not let me prove treacherous ; " and afterwards she tells us that her aunt had given her the morning hour before breakfast, and the evening after tea "for retirement," and that they are the happiest times of the day, "it is such an honour to be permitted to love God," she adds.

At the same time the body was not altogether neglected for the soul, but cared for in a sort of rough, general way. Plenty of food, of a plain, homely kind, was provided for the children. When any one was ill, a feather-bed was brought down and laid on the floor of the sitting room for the comfort of the sufferer, outside appearances being wholly subordinated to immediate utility—a peculiarity which Mr. Hinton inherited, and which stuck to him to the last. But how deeply his mother's least injunction sunk into his heart was shown by one characteristic trifle. It was a rule that no child should be helped twice to apple-pie lest the supply should fall short. To the end of his life he said he had never been able to ask for a second help of apple-pie without a distinct feeling of discomfort, and almost of guilt.

When he was about twelve years old an event occurred which made a deep impression upon him. Scarlet fever had broken out among the children; but as they were recovering, little being then known or thought of infection, the eldest boy, Howard, was allowed to return into the infected atmosphere. He took the fever and died, without a cloud of regret or fear on his boyish face. James was enthusiastically attached to his brother, who was his hero and pattern in all things ; and his early death made a great and lasting impression upon him. Soon after, at his own wish, he was baptized, and made a public profession of religion in accordance with the usual practice among Baptists.

The tie between mother and son was thus made closer and dearer still by James, in consequence of his brother's death, becoming the eldest son. To him she chiefly poured forth her heart. She was a woman who, in addition to her exalted piety, took the highest views of womanhood. She emphatically held, in Père Hyacinthe's words, "that if the man is the head of the woman, the woman is the heart of the man." She, therefore, infused into her son an enthusiasm of womanhood, which is a young man's best safeguard against vice — a sacred passion which effectually casts out all lower passions, and made it impossible for him ever in word or act to do anything to the dishonour of womanhood.

Meantime, he was receiving a somewhat imperfect education—first at his grandfather's school, near Oxford, whence he was sent for a year or two, when he was about fifteen, to a well-known Nonconformist school at Harpenden, of which Mr. Leonard was then the head-master.

Mr. Hinton used to relate a curious physiological fact about himself. As a boy he was gifted with a memory which must have been almost as portentous as Lord Macaulay's. It was sufficient for him to read over a lesson once to know it by heart, and repeat it without missing a word. The spare time thus gained was spent in play, of which he was exceedingly fond, being an active, athletic lad, especially noted for his powers of running. But on one occasion, having rushed in from a game of cricket, as usual, at the last moment, to do his lessons, this remarkable memory suddenly left him, without his being able to assign any physical cause—any blow on the head, or any other method of accounting for it; he had only what an American writer calls a "sense of goneness," and that was all. His memory remained a good and serviceable faculty to the last, but its abnormal features never returned.

At school the boy seems to have been by no means remarkable, though his master must have had some sort of prescience of his abilities, since he wrote to his father: "I do not think your son has any particular bent, but he will succeed in whatever he undertakes." But as his acquirements in algebra did not extend beyond simple equations, at which point he resumed his mathematics only a few years before his death, and as his knowledge of Latin and Greek remained to the last of a rudimentary kind, his proficiency could not have been in any way marked. His remarkable intellect was late in its development.

He was now a pious, very orthodox boy, greatly mourning over the corruptions of his own heart, given to serious reflections, and occasionally writing religious verses, in which he expresses the usual melancholy sentiments of happy youth.

In 1838 a great change took place in the Hinton family. Mr. Howard Hinton left Reading and took the Devonshire Square Chapel in London, henceforth residing in town. Beginning to feel the pressure of his large family, he removed his eldest son from school, and placed him, at the age of sixteen, in the first situation which chanced to offer itself, and which happened to be that of cashier at a wholesale woollen-draper's shop in Whitechapel, kept by a respectable member of his own chapel.

He thus describes his new duties in writing to his sister Sarah: "The way I pass my time here is to rise at seven, and dust till eight. Then do nothing, or anything there is to be done in the morning, and ditto in the afternoon till nine"—including having occasionally to hand spirits across the counter to the best customers—"not forgetting to take my dinner at one, and my tea at five, after which I have my supper, and then have till 10.30 to write to you, &c., with little variation. I have no news, except that my clothes are getting too small—I'm growing so fast."

But hopelessly unfavourable as this first entrance into life appears on the surface, none who knew James Hinton well but can recognise in it "the divinity that shapes our ends." Whitechapel was the rough cradle in which his mind and spirit awoke to energetic life; and to the last he bore its impress on him. Brought up as he had been in a pure home in a quiet country town, and drinking in from his mother a reverence for women which in him was always akin to worship, he was suddenly thrust into rudest contact with our worst social evils.

> "The weary and the heavy weight
> Of all this unintelligible world"

came crushing down on his young heart with a most cruel force, and the degradation of women possessed him with a divine despair. Indeed, on that point, he was always, if I may use the expression, divinely mad, the true μάντις, according to Plato's derivation, with a prophetic insight on some points which the world's history may yet justify. On Saturday nights, in the back streets and crowded courts of Whitechapel, he used to hear women screaming under the blows of their drunken husbands; and come across others, wearing the same sacred womanhood as his own mother and sisters, with the same gracious dependence on man's strength and care, yet the victims of his passions, flushed with gin and trolling out obscenities. He got a sense of the cruelty of the world, and it got into him and possessed him, and never left him. It became the "unconscious constant" in all his thinking; he could think of nothing apart from this; and at last, as he once said, "it crushed and crushed me till it crushed 'The Mystery of Pain' out of me." He of all men learned to say—

" Blind me with seeing tears until I see !
Let not fair poesy, science, art, sweet tones,
Build up about my soothèd sense a world
That is not Thine, and wall me up in dreams.
So my sad heart may cease to beat with Thine,
The great World-Heart, whose blood for ever shed
Is human life, whose ache is man's dumb pain."

It was these early influences of his life that formed in him that thoroughgoing altruism which is so marked a characteristic of his thinking.

He retained his situation for about a year; and, on giving it up, went for a time among his relations in Bristol and Wales, partly in search of employment; his father endeavouring to get him into a bank or customhouse. He was ultimately placed in the City as a clerk in an insurance office.

It was here that that other great passion of his life showed itself—the passion to know. Occupied all day in mechanical duties, at which, so far as book-keeping was concerned, he never proved an adept, he would often sit up half the night studying. Dr. Johnson's remark on some one boasting to him that he was self-educated— "Then, sir, you had a very ignorant fellow for your tutor" —was at this time painfully applicable to James Hinton. He had no one near him to direct his studies, and had perforce to put up with the "ignorant fellow for his tutor ;" the result being a curiously miscellaneous course of study. History, Metaphysics, Russian, German, Italian, Arithmetic, Euclid, were each devoured in turn.

So consuming was his thirst of knowledge, and so great the practical difficulties in gratifying it, that at one time it was his habit to study all Saturday night and all Monday night, with the intermission only of a few snatches of sleep. But one night, having passed nearly forty-eight hours without sleep, he found he could not understand a simple proposition in Euclid. Retiring to rest in disgust, he found on waking that he could see it at a glance; and from that time took care to give his brain the needful amount of sleep.

At the age of nineteen he first became attached to the lady whom he afterwards married, after waiting for her many years. It was his first and only attachment. For some time his love met with no return; indeed he must have appeared rather a formidable suitor at this time to any young girl, having much the air of an abstract idea untidily expressed, very different from the singular charm he afterwards possessed in ripened manhood. Wholly indifferent to appearances, his clothes could never be made to fit him; while his mental absorption at this period made him guilty of frequent lapses of politeness, which are the source of endless expressions of contrition in his letters to his eldest sister, who evidently did her sisterly best to get him into shape. To the girl he loved he rarely spoke, only turning a little white in her presence. With all others he was intensely argumentative. It mattered not whether you were parted from him a week or a month, on meeting he would begin again exactly where the argument was broken off, giving the result of his further meditations on the subject in question, with a mental resoluteness that was never to be shaken off till he got to the bottom of it.

A few extracts from his letters to his sister Sarah, bearing about this date, will show his steady growth in thought and moral earnestness :—

" *London*, 1841.

" For my own part, I feel sometimes a deeper desire than I can express to be in some way or other the benefactor of my species, and yet I cannot help suspecting that pride and ambition have far more to do with that desire than philanthropy. I do not find in myself the same willingness to be useful in a way of unnoticed— perhaps despised—toil as I do in ones that should procure me respect and esteem, and be gratifying to vanity. Above all, it is difficult to give practically to God that pre-eminence which He so justly demands, and the withholding of which will render all we do worse than useless."

" London, 1841.

" I find that you are studying metaphysics; I make no question but that you are doing so with great success. Nevertheless I am rather sorry that Dugald Stewart was the first book on the subject you have met with, because (of course I speak with all humility and diffidence) whatever may be his merits in some respects, the view he gives of the subject is most partial and unsatisfactory. . . . Judge you yourself whether a scrupulous attention to *usefulness*—I mean an immediate beneficial influence on everyday affairs—must not exceedingly cripple and almost put an end to the progress of discovery in any science.

"Take chemistry, astronomy, geometry, or any other (and they are all, in their present state, of incalculable benefit to us), and consider whether, if they had been in their infancy prosecuted merely for their apparent usefulness, they ever could have made anything like the progress they have made. Is it not manifestly impossible ? How exceedingly useless must the speculations of the early mathematicians have appeared to a man of Stewart's way of thinking, and how strenuously would he not have urged them to give over drawing unmeaning lines; or, at any rate, to confine themselves to the more obvious facts which might be available—perhaps for the better construction of their clothes."

"*London,* 1841.

"I saw a short time ago an article in the last number of the 'Edinburgh Review' on 'Women's Rights and Duties,' with the other recent works on the same subject. . . . The principal object of the writer seems to be to prove the essential inferiority of woman to man *intellectually,* and to justify her exclusion from all political action. My perusal of it was necessarily very hasty, and I cannot now say with confidence what I think of it.

"My impression, however, is that he certainly did not prove the latter of his two positions, and not the whole of the former. His argument for the intellectual superiority of man was founded upon the fact that all great geniuses have been men, and that no woman has ever attained to the highest result in any department of science or literature. This must certainly be admitted as a fact; and I think I must admit the conclusion he draws from it—viz., that woman is not capable of doing so.* I am not quite certain of this, however; but even if it be granted, it does not prove his point. It proves merely that there have been since the creation of the world some dozen men of greater intellectual power than any woman has had. But the same thing can be said of all other men as well, and, therefore, it must not be made to bear exclusively on women; and cannot prove that the average amount of intellectual power (about which is the whole question) is in favour of man.

"For instance, Newton had greater strength of mind than any woman who has ever lived; but the same is the case with every man who has ever lived, except, say, ten. Take, then, these ten from the whole number of men, and we

---

* How precarious are all such asserted facts, and the inferences they are made to sustain, is proved by the subsequent rise of our great novelist, George Eliot, avowedly first in her own branch of English literature.

have two classes, women and men, all of whom are inferior in intellect to Newton. From whence does it follow
that the amount of intellect in one of these two inferior
classes is greater than that in the other ?

" All that is needed to be established is a general
equality, and not a capacity in woman for the attainment of the highest eminence, which, however, I feel
by no means inclined to deny to her. . . . Let there
be some boundary fixed to which women cannot attain;
let all the women and all the men who fall below that
boundary be taken, and I am persuaded there will be
found as much talent among the women as the men.

" With respect to the subject of education, the above-
mentioned writer maintains that, as a general rule, the
best education has of late years fallen to the lot of
girls, and that, while boys have been poring over useless Latin and Greek, the girls have been acquiring really
valuable information. But this view of the subject does
not fully meet the question.

" Education does not consist in the amount of information
imparted, but in the training given to the mind, and the
habits induced. Now, here lies the grand difference between
the education of boys and girls. Every well-educated boy
is taught to look to the cultivation of his mental powers
as of the highest importance, and as being his peculiar
duty. You know better than I do whether this is the
case with girls. My opinion is that it is far otherwise, and that they are taught to regard—I beg your
pardon for saying it—the being married, and the conduct of household affairs, as the chief end of their existence, while, if their attention is directed to reading (I
can scarcely call it to mental improvement) at all, it is
merely as an amusement and as something the control
of which belongs to men, and with which they have

no right to interfere. . . . How contemptuous is the phrase, 'literature for ladies;' with what different feelings one hears of a learned man and a learned woman!

"Besides, even if it were the case that the intellect of woman is inferior to that of man, it can only be true for a certain number. It is comparatively few men who can boast of powers of mind greater than have been possessed by many women; and yet every ignoramus thinks himself at liberty to look down upon them. I have heard puppies, with whom I should be ashamed almost to own a common nature, say, 'Anything will do for women.' Thus it is that they deceive themselves by an abuse of the general truth—if truth it be—that the male intellect is superior to the female, into the belief of a gross absurdity—viz., that *their* intellect must be superior to that of all women."

Meanwhile the double strain upon him of intense intellectual toil, and, what was far worse, the sense of the wrongs and degradation of women, was telling upon his health and spirits, and became so intolerable that he resolved to run away to sea, and fly from the thoughts he could no longer bear. His intention was, however, discovered, and increased illness made it doubly impossible to carry it out. His father, now seriously anxious about him, consulted the family doctor with regard to him. "The lad wants more mental occupation to keep his mind from feeding on itself," was the doctor's sensible verdict.

He accordingly advised his entering the medical profession, as giving the necessary scope to his mental activity. This advice, accompanied by some kind practical help, was at once acted on, and he was entered at St. Bartholomew's Hospital, having just reached his twentieth year.

Perhaps a vivid remembrance of his own entrance into life was in his mind when he wrote among his last words to his son, "And as to this, whenever any one comes in your way, especially a good and striving earnest man, think if you cannot help him, cannot, perchance, give him work in which you and he may mutually help each other. By this means you may perhaps entertain angels unawares."

No particular record survives of his student life. He himself always spoke with the greatest gratitude of his medical education, as having given him the intellectual training his mind stood in need of, as well as providing him with a knowledge of physical science, which so largely influenced his thinking, both as to method and material.

His remarkable powers and his mental assiduity enabling him to complete his course in a much shorter time than that assigned, and being anxious to gain some practical knowledge of the world, he devoted his spare time to performing a voyage to China and back as the surgeon of a passenger ship, "The City of Derry." His journal does not present any incidents of particular interest, and his stay in China being limited to two or three weeks, his remarks on that country are necessarily superficial, though showing the habits of a careful observer.

On his return to England with the ship, he took out his diploma (1847), passing his examinations with distinction, and having previously gained several medals. He then practised for a short time as assistant-surgeon at Newport in Essex.

By this time, he was aware that he had gained the affections of the young lady to whom for some years he had been devotedly attached; but having become unsettled in his religious opinions, a fresh bar was raised to their union. He thus writes to her sister :—

"It is agony to me to dwell upon the idea that I have gained your sister's love only to make it a source of misery to herself. I would to God that I had rather died. Do not suppose, my dear friend, that this letter is one of self-vindication. I cannot vindicate myself. I wish that I had some punishment to bear that might relieve me from that thought. To make her happier I would bear anything,—even that she should think, not only that I do not love her, but that I never did. . . .

"The *happiest* thing for me for time and eternity (for I always look upon marriage as a union for eternity), if I might choose, would be Margaret's love,—beyond comparison ; there is nothing that looks even tolerable beside it. But God has decided otherwise, therefore it is not *best*. I have, and will have, perfect confidence in God. Nay, more, I have thought sometimes, and have told Margaret that perhaps it is my first and chief duty at present to seek for truth, to devote all my energies and all my thoughts to the completing and the rectifying of my own religious opinions; and I hold that nothing can so well enable me to do that, can so well supply the kind of knowledge most useful, most requisite for me, as the seeing of mankind under all their various phases, the watching human nature and human passions as developed under various circumstances.

"I have strong hopes that by means of that knowledge, the acquisition of which is placed in my power, I might at last arrive at a well-grounded confidence, and put myself in a position in which I might labour with zeal and satisfaction for the good of my fellowmen. Do not misunderstand me ; I do not look for pleasure—for enjoyment—in any such course. I think that it may be the path of duty, though even of that I am not satisfied ; certainly, if the other were not closed, I should not dream of it.

"Of one thing I am quite certain, that I shall not settle down in England for a long while without the utmost repugnance and disgust; but that may be my duty notwithstanding. . . .

"To make my confession complete, I must tell you two reasons why, if your sister had not acted as she has done, her decision would have failed to give me perfect satisfaction :—

"1st. I think there can be no true union in marriage without *essential* agreement in religious matters. I think if Margaret and I had continued our communion I could not have helped disturbing her religious faith, and causing her at least the greatest distress, which Heaven forbid ; or if not, and we had been married, I think it most likely that I should feel it my duty to adopt steps in the course of my life in reference to religion which would occasion her, as my wife, the deepest anguish.

"2ndly. I should be afraid to have any woman for my wife who would deliberately sacrifice what she considered her duty to God for love to me. I should be afraid—for I wish to set my duty to God above all things, and I would wish my wife to help me and set me the example. Margaret has done so, and ·I knew she would, and therefore I have never hoped. . . .

"I have only one word of explanation to add. I never speak of any prospective alteration in my opinions, but that is only because I would not deceive myself, nor be unjust to Margaret. My belief is, that I shall never alter so far as the great question is concerned. Daily almost I seem to grow more satisfied, more at home in my convictions ; and I dare not breathe a whisper, nor

B

entertain a thought which rests upon the supposition of a change.

"Still I hope I am not resolutely prejudiced. It would be happy indeed for me if my eyes could be opened to see myself in error, doubly happy, as I might secure my own happiness, and try at least to secure another's. But these thoughts have had their influence, they have had too much, I dare not entertain them any more. Above all, I owe it as a duty to Margaret that they should not be breathed to her."

CHAPTER II.

SOME time previously a scheme had been set on foot by Government to supply the deficiency of the labour-market in Jamaica arising from the emancipation of the West Indian slaves, by importing free labourers from Sierra Leone. Many of these had been themselves captured and brought down to the coast to be sold as slaves, when the Liberation Act was passed; but having no means of returning to their own country, they were glad to embrace so good an opening as that offered by Government. A medical officer was advertised for to undertake the charge of the emigrants, and Mr. Hinton, actuated by the motives touched on in the preceding letter, applied for the position, being glad of the opportunity of studying savage life, and of forming some idea of man apart from civilisation and Christianity.

After a passage of five weeks in the "Simon Taylor," he arrived at Sierra Leone on Sunday, 15th October 1847. On going ashore, the captain and himself found as many as 1164 liberated Africans in the negro yards, or rough barracks provided for their accommodation. Out of these, 248 men, women, and children were chosen and embarked. A headman and headwoman were appointed, and the whole number divided into messes for the distribution of food and clothing; and on November 5th Mr. Hinton set sail for Jamaica with his novel charge. From the first he was exceedingly interested in them; he gained some knowledge of their language, the Yaroba tongue, and tried to get at their ideas and modes of life, forming on the whole a good opinion of them. The headwoman constituted herself a sort of queen on board, and proved his right hand in maintaining the obedience which is "the bond of rule."

The only thing which fairly baffled him were the feminine mysteries of dress. In his distribution of clothing he generally gave rise to a burning sense of injustice being at the heart of all things,—his choice of the neatest, and, as he thought, the prettiest prints for the best women, being often quite wrong, the appropriate reward of virtue being in their eyes a gaudy stripe or spot, only vice deserving the retribution of a neat sprig or check.

On reaching the port of St. Maria, Jamaica, after endless toil and difficulty he managed to get them into eligible situations. But wishing to satisfy himself with regard to their treatment and welfare, he resolved on remaining for a year or so in the island, and accordingly took the practice of a medical man who was out of health, making his house his home.

"During my residence at Roslyn," he writes home, "my time for the most part passed pleasantly enough. I lived well, saw a good deal of company, and had generally enough to do. The breakfast hour was at nine, the dinner hour four or five. The time between was devoted to practice. Every morning I had a treat—a cup of well-made, fresh Jamaica coffee, and six or eight newly-gathered oranges. You stayers-at-home don't know what an orange is, and Jamaica oranges I believe to be the finest in the world. They are prescribed medicinally before breakfast; and as soon as I got up out of my bed, I used to make some of the little African boys run and gather ten for me; and I always observed they would bring besides at least twenty for themselves. They were just in season when I arrived, and it is a pleasure even now to think of the enjoyment they afforded me.

" Very soon after my arrival I experienced the shock of an earthquake. It occurred in the middle of.the night, and was of considerable violence. I felt the bed rock under me once and again ; and a press, which was standing against the wall, seemed to lean forward as if about to fall, and suddenly start back with a spring. A kind of hollow, clapping sound, twice repeated, arose, as if from underground. I thought, as I found myself suddenly awakened from sleep, that it must have been an earthquake, but I could not be sure, and regarded the circumstance rather with curiosity and interest than alarm.

" I was struck the next morning by the seriousness with which it was adverted to, but I understand it now ; for though an earthquake may be experienced the first time with feelings of ignorant wonder, its recurrence cannot fail to excite the most solemn emotions. It brings a desolating sense of insecurity, and forces the idea of sudden destruction visibly upon the mind.

" At an earthquake all creatures seem oppressed with dread ; they suspend their feeding or their play, and look suddenly around them in terror. A horse, even if at full speed, suddenly halts, plants his feet firmly on the ground, trembles in every limb, and breaks out into a sweat. And I cannot, indeed, entirely divest my mind of the foreboding that these islands of the western seas are destined to changes in which agencies of this nature may play a fearful part."

As Dr. Cooke's representative, Mr. Hinton had the care of the Marine Hospital, the gaol, the poorhouse and out-door paupers, and all the emigrants he had brought over.

"In my capacity of doctor," he says in a letter to his sister, "I was frequently among them, witnessing the accommodation and food provided for them, and the work they were expected to do, and finding everything (I think I may say) as good as could be expected, and certainly better than they would have got at Sierra Leone.

"They suffer very greatly, at first coming to the island from chigoes (pronounced *jiggers*) in their feet, as they do not know how to treat them. The chigo is a minute insect that insinuates itself into the skin, especially between the toes, and there deposits its eggs in a small bag. This creates considerable irritation, and, if not removed in time, but allowed to propagate, is apt to cause ulceration, to which, without constant watching, the Africans are liable especially the men, who are too lazy or too clumsy to remove them. These 'jiggers' abound in dry and dusty places, and especially about the works of a sugar estate.

"One day when I was at Nonsuch, where there are thirty of my Africans, and among them my old headwoman, I asked them if they were comfortable and well-treated. She said 'Yes,' but the 'sugar' was very bad, rubbing her hands over her skin as she spoke. I was rather nonplussed by the expression, nor was it till after a good deal of dumb show that I arrived at a knowledge of the facts.

"All the Africans I brought out took well to work, and gave satisfaction, except a lot of seven women. It appears, from some unascertained cause, that they from the first refused to work; and the attorney, rather than resort to coercive means, sent them back to the agent. They were afterwards distributed on other estates, and I hear no more complaints. All of them are now, at the end of ten months, fat, hardy, and cheerful."

Some ill-feeling was felt against the new-comers by the Jamaica negroes, and much soreness of heart was caused by their being called "Bungoes"—a wholly unintelligible soubriquet bestowed on all emigrants. In vain Mr. Hinton assured them that he himself was a Bungo. Their philosophy was never proof against these two mystic syllables.

In one of his letters home he makes some curious observations on the position of women in uncivilised tribes.

"What I have seen this voyage convinces me that among some of the savage tribes of Africa at least the women have their own way, as of course they are entitled to have, pretty nearly as amongst the most civilised nations. Indeed, I rather opine that it is not the ordinance of man, but the laws of nature that determine that.

"If the women who were on board the 'Simon Taylor' had been brought up in servile subjection to the other sex, it would have been impossible for them to have assumed so immediately and completely the entire and unequivocal command, although hardly more than half the number of the men; and among these barbarians, even as among us, whose feelings are refined and softened, so that a woman's tear is more precious than a pearl in our sight, whenever a quarrel arose among the men, the women interposed to settle it; only not as among us, for they evidently acted by authority as well as persuasion.

"In truth, the women possessed in an incomparably superior degree the qualities of activity and intelligence, which always must bear sway in spite of strength; and no usages of savage life or barbarian life could abrogate that decree of God, any more than the force of public opinion and our own barbarous enactments can prevent a clever woman from governing a dolt of a husband. Only the other day I met some Africans of quite a different tribe. After talking a little in broken English, I asked one of the men a question; he began to give me a long rigmarole of an answer, but one of the women said a few words to him in African, and he never opened his mouth again. What was wrong I don't know, but she put him down completely.

" I don't want to write an essay on the sexes, but I'll just take the liberty of saying, that I imagine it possible that travellers may have been rather deceived sometimes by paying too much attention to customs and external forms, especially when they differ from what they have been used to see, and not sufficiently regarding less obvious but more important facts and feelings, which unite the whole human race, and underlie unchangeably all the varied forms and institutions of human life.

" For instance, all the world over, once let an occupation become assigned to women, the men—the best and kindest of them—will leave it to that sex. What man ever thinks of helping his wife to wash, much less doing the washing instead of her ? One example is as good as a hundred. Now, when an Englishman goes to a foreign country, and sees a man lying under a tree and smoking his pipe, and his wife standing in the river hammering at a parcel of dirty clothes, he doesn't consider it the man's duty to change places with his wife. But if this same person meets a man walking along a road, and his wife following with a load upon her head, he flies into a sudden passion, as I have done, against the stronger sex. But the two cases are exactly parallel.

" Carrying loads on the head in many countries is the woman's work, like washing and stitching and darning stockings in ours; and I am inclined to think it a good deal easier than the latter, at least when the stockings in question happen to belong to me. The men can't do it; they are not brought up to it, and it requires a good deal of practice; besides, the women wouldn't let them if they could. I've taken the trouble to find that out, and I don't believe a black man could make his wife (speaking as a rule) let him carry her load without taking it from her by force. . . . The power which practice gives of carrying weights on the head is extraordinary. I have known a girl not more than eighteen carry a box, which I couldn't lift without difficulty, no less than fourteen miles, over a steep hill, that I would hardly have undertaken to climb unburdened. She was sent by a missionary, too, and laughed when I lifted the box and wondered how she could carry it. A negro man couldn't have done it.

" I think, however, the relation between the sexes in Jamaica is anomalous, and not to be taken as a sample of that which exists either in civilised or in savage countries. It has been subject to many disturbing influences. . . . Slavery has left its stamp on the people—not yet éffaced, nor likely to be. It meets the eye everywhere, but nowhere, I think, more forcibly or more painfully than in their treatment of their children. The poor little wretches are habitually beaten most cruelly with sticks or whips upon the bare skin, often for the most trivial fault, or for none at all. They are made to work for their parents at the tenderest age, and almost as soon as they can walk are set to carry weights on their heads. . . .

" Even making all allowances, it is apt to disturb an Englishman's equanimity to see a great strapping negro walking or riding leisurely along, and his wife and one or more little children toiling after him with heavy baskets on their heads. This, however, is the custom of the country, and is seen continually. In short, it seems to be an universal principle among them that the strong should not use their strength to do work themselves, but to make the weaker work for them. It is the principle of slavery."

The following is the description he gives of a society just emerged from the practice of slavery:—

"Nearly all the upper and middle classes have been brought up in wealth, and are now feeling the pressure of comparative want; in fact, the same may be said of the labouring population, too, comparing their state now with what it was six or eight years back; and it seems to me to be the great key by which the anomalies of Jamaica society may be accounted for. For an anomalous state it is. A stranger feels it very soon; at least I did.

"I found myself surrounded by men of intelligence, courtesy, and good feeling; if not remarkable for their virtue, by no means pre-eminent in vice; with many faults indeed, but none from which I could hold my friends and acquaintances in England to be exempt; some faults which at home are concealed and kept in check, here open and undisguised; and other good qualities which in England are only to be seen with a microscope, here flourishing luxuriantly; perhaps a general principle of indolence pervading all.

"In short, I found myself among my fellows (not only my fellow-countrymen), only under altered circumstances. A few were bad, and deserved to be abhorred; a good many had a just right to be despised; the mass were passable (that is, I suppose, about as good as myself); and some were worthy of admiration and love. Now isn't this a pretty fair delineation of English society? And yet, notwithstanding the atoms were so decent, the aggregate was odious. All the social virtues seemed to be annihilated, save one, and that was hospitality; good faith not dreamt of, truth utterly disregarded, mutual esteem and regard unknown, no praise awarded to merit, no disapprobation fastened on vice, no conversation but complaint and scandal—the latter of gigantic growth—no amusement but dissipation, no desire even for improvement.

"It seemed a mystery. The people taken by themselves were good, that is, pretty good; they were not fools; they were not altogether selfish; they were not steeped in vice; they had hearts capable of generous emotions—feelings, if not the most refined, at least in a measure true to nature; put them together, and you made a foul, oppressive atmosphere, where little that was good could lift its head."

May we not see in these reflections on the problem presented by Jamaica society, as it then was, the first germ of the idea which afterwards became so strong a conviction with him—namely, that there is in man, as the result of the culture and effort of ages, enough goodness to regenerate society; but that society, as at present constituted, is built up on the wrong centre of self-interest and self-virtue, instead of on an altruistic basis, and cannot, therefore, form a well-ordered, organised whole; just as, to use his favourite illustration, astronomy, though right in many of its individual calculations, was hopelessly wrong as a system so long as the earth was taken as the centre of rest?

After a year or so of Jamaica life, Mr. Hinton began to get heartily tired of it, and his father having written him word that a London surgeon of the name of Fisher was anxious to secure him for his partner, and willing to wait for his return, he writes in 1849:—

"My mind becomes more and more decidedly fixed on a London practice as my ultimate destination. This is not a nice country to live in, after all; and, whatever people may say, the emancipated negroes do not possess many amiable or admirable qualities. The genuine African is a far superior being, as might have been expected."

Among these "genuine Africans" he left a lasting memory. Eleven years afterwards, he was much moved on being told that his name still lived in their hearts and on their lips, for all the kindly personal interest and devoted care for their welfare which he had evinced.

Having, therefore, resolved on returning to England, he took the opportunity of his homeward voyage to pay a visit to some American relations in New Orleans, where he was brought into contact with slavery in full work, and realised the progress that even the newly-emancipated negroes of Jamaica had made over their enslaved brethren. I remember his mentioning, that what first made him feel the evil in his own heart was his tracing a distinct feeling of satisfaction in himself that New Orleans was decidedly more wicked than London.

His stay in America was necessarily too brief for him to form much idea of the institutions and character of the people, but it was long enough to inspire him with a hearty liking for the Americans, and faith in their future, which never left him, and which made him set great value on the appreciation of his American readers.

It was just before starting homeward that he first revealed to his parents the great changes that he had been going through in his religious belief, and how he had been for some years past "sounding on a dim and perilous way," his motives for reticence having been the fear of their pain, and his reluctance hastily to sever the bond which had united him to those with whom he had worshipped from boyhood.

Brought up, as he had been, in a semi-Calvinistic theology, with its hard and fast dogmas—a theology that forces the conscience and moral emotions of man into its narrow logical mould, and views the atonement as a legal transaction—it was evident, as his own mind began to develop, that he must go through a great conflict before he could grasp his true relations to the Unseen, and lay firm hold on—

" Those mighty hopes that make us men."

Before intellectual difficulties his faith would never have succumbed; but coming to the Bible with the preconceived notions of a rigid theological school, he was led at first to reject it on moral grounds.

He writes thus to his parents :—" I sincerely trust that I have over-estimated the amount of distress which my avowal of the want of implicit belief in revelation will occasion you, and I am the more ready to believe that I have done so, inasmuch as you must yourselves know that the change in my opinions has not been the result of a course of thoughtlessness or vice, nor even the caprice of an undisciplined intellect. I appeal to you both, whether I have not applied myself with all diligence to the work of investigation.

" Whether I have done it with honesty, God knows; and from the judgment of men, I appeal to Him. In truth, I may say that the formation of my religious opinions has been (as it well deserves to be) the work of my life hitherto. To that all the knowledge and experience I have gained have been rendered subservient; and it is mainly for their rectification and completion that I desire more.

"Many years ago the work began. Looking back upon my mental progress, it seems to me almost like a providence. It began with an ardent, enthusiastic searching of the Scriptures. Doubts which arose, first stifled as impious, then submitted to a one-sided examination with a foregone conclusion and laid aside as settled, but returning, multiplying, harassing, and defying me, until my days and nights were one continued scene of misery, and I have wished myself dead many times, because I was determined to believe the Bible, but could not see that it was true.

"No one knows, my dear parents, nor except by experience ever can know, the agony it has cost me to renounce the Bible—an agony to which the preachers, the commentators, and the writers of addresses afford no alleviation. They do not understand and cannot meet the case—an honest soul striving to believe the Bible, and yet unable; and feeling as if he were clinging to a plank amid a waste of waters, and *that* was being plucked away from him; they seem as if they could not comprehend. But that was but for a time, and it was caused by a mistake, an error in which we are all brought up—that of confounding Christianity and religion. I thought that without the Bible I could have no confidence in God, no reverence, nor love towards Him. I have now found out my error—that is, I think so; yet my ardent desire and my belief is, that if I have been led astray, I may be brought back, and my eyes again opened.

"The true way to reach truth I take to be to pursue a steadfast, unshrinking course of thought, above all things and under all circumstances seeking to keep the heart right and the affections pure. I trust in God, that, as He knows I have sought to know His will, and (as I hope) will not refuse to obey it, so He will not leave me ultimately to believe a lie. . . .

" My wish is, if I honestly can, to commit myself to nothing at present, for I am not prepared to avow my opinions. I hold them lightly, and they may change. Indeed, I cannot bring myself to give up the hope that I may yet be able, ere long, to receive the Scriptures once more with implicit confidence; and though my judgment refuses its assent, my heart still clings to the doctrines of the gospel. I reverence their moral truth, I delight in their appeal to the imagination. I hold them fast as illusions (if such they be) too beautiful to be wholly false. . . . . Besides, I love Christians. I prefer them to all other people. They are lovely, because they love God, and therein I trust I can truly say I am one with them. It will be a severe trial to me to sever the bond, even though it be only an external one, that unites me and them. . . . I leave the matter entirely in your hands, trusting to your judgment rather than my own.

" This state of my opinion it was to which I alluded when I said there were 'other obstacles' to my partnership with Mr. Fisher. Please to make to him such communication as you think fit, or to let him read this letter, or part of it, that there may be no deception."

Elsewhere, speaking of moral doubt, he writes:—" Convinced, as I was, that the Bible was the Word of God, it appeared to me equally plain that some of its statements were opposed to the principles of justice and truth—so far as I could understand them. That was horrible. I own I can conceive no suffering more dreadful than what I then endured. I fear no suffering in comparison with it, and the like can never come to me again. Afterwards I came to doubt the existence of God, and that was wretched enough, but not so bad; for then I did believe in truth and justice, and their ultimate triumph. But an unjust God! Oh, I can conceive somewhat of what the universe would feel if *God* were *wicked.*"

It was on his homeward voyage that, depressed and alone, he gained that deeper knowledge of himself which gave him the key to the great spiritual records of our race. "It was not," he writes, looking back at the conflict he passed through at this time, "the prophecies that made me believe the Bible, nor the miracles, nor the impossibility of accounting for all sorts of things unless it were true, but it was simply that I felt myself to be unholy, and I did not think there was a power anywhere that could sanctify me unless it were in that book."

The following letter to his sister enables us to trace a few of the steps by which he was slowly regaining his faith in Christianity :—

"*Ship 'Arlington,' 22nd March* 1850.

"MY VERY DEAR SARAH,—As I suppose you will be at Oxford when I arrive at home, and that I shall not have the pleasure of seeing you immediately on my return, I wish to have a letter ready to send you directly. How eagerly desirous I am of regaining the family circle I cannot tell you, and I doubt even if you can imagine. How can I tell you how much I regret now that I suffered myself to be drawn into so prolonged an absence.

"During all this voyage I have been full of self-accusations; and one of the things that has grieved me most is the unkindness with which I have treated my friends, in not keeping up a full and regular correspondence with them. Indeed, it is by no means with satisfaction that I can look back upon the past twelve months, although I have seen and done in them many things—some of which might have been wise and interesting, if there had not been a prior claim upon me.

" However, it is not of these that I wish to speak to
you, but of matters more important, which deserve to have
a larger share of our thoughts. Do you know, it was
the hope that I might meet with some facts that might
throw light upon my religious views, and give definite-
ness and completeness to my sentiments and aims, that
chiefly determined me upon taking the voyage which I
have now completed, and urging it against the wishes
of my friends. Well, it seemed to me that all which
I saw went to confirm my previous opinions, and when
I embarked to come home, I felt more certain of them
than ever. Indeed, it was this conviction that I should
never change them, which, more than anything else,
I may say alone, has caused me to protract my absence so long; for it seemed to me that such a state
of mind would almost render impossible any satisfactory settlement at home. And I was very unwilling
to tell my father and mother my sentiments, not because I was ashamed to avow them, but because I
shrank from the apparent undutifulness of doing so,
and I thought it would give them pain and do no good.
I am wiser now, however, for I am sure that one of a
child's first duties, as it is one of his greatest privileges, is
to give his parents his confidence.

" However, though I had no misgivings about my
opinions, I felt much dissatisfaction with some parts of
my conduct, and especially that I turned so much time to
so little profit. About a month ago I resolved to read the
Bible regularly through, and went through the two first
books of Moses. Then a book on infidelity fell into my
hands, which interested me a good deal, for it was written
in a powerful style (it was Nelson, ' On the Cause and
Cure of Infidelity'). It didn't do much towards convincing me, but it made me resolve to examine the matter over

C

again, which I have been doing since that time with the
aid of several books—for the captain is a religious man,
who conducts worship daily with the crew, and has a small
religious library on board.

"It is wonderful what an effect this course has had
upon me, especially in the view I have been brought to
take of my own character and state before God. I used
to think that in my heart I loved God and holiness; but
when I looked at myself in the light of the Bible, I see so
plainly that I am altogether sinful. . . . Do you remember, my dear sister, the letter I wrote you a long time ago,
about the doctrine of the Atonement? Surely I must
have written rash words. 'I don't remember exactly what
they were; but now I would substitute these only for
them, 'Enter not into judgment with me, O Lord.' Did
I not say that the punishment of sin was its consequence in such a sense that it could be remitted only by a
miracle, and that no man ought to desire such remission?
I must have closed my eyes; for we see every day that
those physical evils, which are the punishment of sin, are
relieved and cured by means not miraculous; and the
nature of the Atonement, and the conditions on which it
is applied, take all force from the second objection.

"You will think that I am now a believer in the Bible,
but I cannot say that I am; though this, I think, I may
affirm, that I wish to be so. I cannot but be persuaded
that under the influence of the doctrine and precepts of
the Bible, I should attain to greater holiness than I can
without, that I should be more useful in this world and
better prepared to change it for another. I think this,
but this is not belief. For, to confess the truth, the subject is full of difficulties.

"I have read and pondered on what I have access to of
the evidences, but I am not entirely convinced, and the

reading of the Bible suggests incessant difficulties to my mind. I pray to God for His guidance, but I have not satisfaction yet.

"I am willing to give up any *à priori* arguments against revelation, at least, I think, I may say all, except my inability to receive that doctrine which condemns to eternal misery all who do not receive the Atonement ; because that class comprehends not a few of the very best people—to all appearance—in the world. My present difficulties relate far more to the credibility of the Scriptures."

A few joyful words from one of his sisters, enclosed with this letter, announce his safe arrival to an absent member of the family :—

" *London*, 9 A.M.

"Only think, dearest, that when your letter arrived our precious wanderer was *sleeping at home.* He came at half-past five this morning, and knocked papa up, and after speaking to mamma went to bed, where he is still. The little boys amused us at breakfast with their account of the intruder's manœuvres. John was startled into consciousness by the sudden elevation of the pillow with his head upon it, in James' endeavour to put his watch under it ; and Josiah said, with something between a smile and a pout, 'He turned me out of my warm place to get in himself.'"

CHAPTER III.

THE obstacle presented by his former religious views being now in great measure removed, he became engaged to Miss Margaret Haddon, to whom he had remained constant for ten years. He also entered into partnership with Mr. Fisher, taking a house in Bartholomew Close.

The following extracts are from letters to her :—

" Bartholomew Close, April 1850.

"I have had a conversation with my father, and we have decided upon my commencing practice in this house; with many misgivings and anxieties on my part, yet not without hope and thankfulness, — thankfulness for the many advantages God has bestowed upon me, hope in His blessing upon my exertions. I do believe He has good in store for me, and that He is making me fit to receive it, by causing me to feel not only how utterly unworthy *I* am of it, but also how incapable I am of attaining it by any efforts of my own. I have been very proud, very self-confident; I will try henceforth to cultivate a genuine humbleness of spirit, childlike and implicit in its reliance upon God, manful and untiring in activity and diligence.

"I wish I could lay the spectre that haunts me in the past. You, my love, who have so little to regret, who have acted so noble and upright a part, and fitted yourself so well for the duties that are before you, you cannot understand with what feelings I look back upon my misdirected energies, my misemployed time, the subjection of my whole being to false principles, its devotion to mistaken and unattainable ends. . . .

" My old feelings of despondency have come very near taking possession of me again ; but I won't let them. It would be both wrong and unreasonable, for it is certainly true that I have never yet set myself seriously to work at anything in which I did not succeed. For the most part, failure would have been no great misfortune, but the fact is the same.

" In my studentship I obtained every prize for which I tried, though that wasn't many. And there is another prize which, with God's blessing, I will yet obtain, and that is yourself. I have been so long accustomed to look upon it as utterly impossible that you could ever be mine, that it seems difficult for me even now to believe it true.

" Do you know, dearest, I have long been of the opinion that the love with which lovers love ought not to be regarded as anything peculiar and extraordinary ; but only as the nearest approach which we can make on earth to the true nature of that love with which we ought to comprehend all our fellow-creatures. In pity to our weakness, and in order that we might be able to comprehend something of what love truly is, God has made us capable of loving one person, that we might be able to form some faint idea of what that state must be where love is perfect and complete. For does not the true secret of loving, of yielding up ourselves to be another's, lie partly, at least, in this, that thus we can understand and appreciate most fully that other's character; the union of soul in love removes as it were a veil from our eyes. When in love, a partition is broken down, and we begin to understand another. *Humanity* is then re-

vealed to us—perhaps not as it is, alas ! for its glory casts
all its faults into the shade—but in some faint resem-
blance to what it was, what it might be, and what by
God's grace it shall be.

"My heart burns with indignation when I hear people
talk of the folly, and blindness, and exaggeration of love.
In truth, all, except those who are in love, are blind and
ignorant. It is a telescope given us (just for once) by
God, to reveal to us wonders and glories, hidden indeed
from the unaided eye, but none the less real and glorious
for that."

" May 1850.

"I have just received your long letter. I like to receive
such from you. They are a greater treat to me than you
can conceive; they come so from your heart, and they go
straight to mine. It gives you pleasure, too, to write
them, I know, as it should indeed, for they do me a world
of good. In religion you are my teacher—more than my
teacher, for you not only direct my thoughts, but also
persuade my heart.

"Do you say, dearest, that you also have known what
it is to doubt, and doubt so much that you could not pray?
I didn't know that of you. Tell me when it was and why ?
How you obtained peace and satisfaction ? I think I may
feel sure it was by the same path that promises it to me,
if I could only walk in it—the path of unreserved surrender to God, and of unwavering trust in Jesus as my
Saviour. You have rightly expressed what keeps me
back as yet from that state ; it is a feeling that may be
called 'conscientious.' It is the same feeling that operated
with me before ; the conviction that the course I take now
must be taken satisfactorily, permanently ; that I must
not lay aside, unsolved, perplexities that so treated may

arise again with a power fearfully increased, or compel to silence convictions which, if stifled now, will hereafter extort for themselves a hearing.

"Here is my difficulty, how can I pray to be enabled to do that which I think *I ought not to do*, or if I pray for *guidance* that I may know what is the truth, how can the answer to that prayer come, unless I am in the attitude of honest and resolute *inquiry?* . . . I *cannot* see my way, Meggie, at least, not yet.

"But it is not needful—it would not be wise or kind —that I should lay before you all my difficulties, or explain to you, even if I could, how my feet are entangled, how every path, by which I fain would come to a firm and peaceful repose in the Bible, appears blocked up— how every argument which I can frame to myself, or which I can find in others, seems to present some flaw—how I am driven back and repulsed whenever I stretch forth my hand to lay hold upon the consolation of the Gospel. I hardly like to write to you in this strain at all, and I would not, did I not know that you have a true and hearty confidence in God and His love, both to me and to yourself, which will keep you from being too much distressed. Indeed, it would not be reasonable or right that you should let my present feelings harass or distress you. They are needful for me, doubtless, and I cannot but think that the former change, or rather revulsion of my opinions, possessed an element of suddenness which needed rectification.

"I wish you were here with me, that I might talk to you, might read the Bible with you, and see in your experience a guide and pattern for my own. I am often disposed to murmur at the lot which separates us so much. It cannot be good. It is not good for me. I am always better when you are near me. . . . I have often thought

of the goodness of God in making men and women; each
perfect, and yet so incomplete—so beautiful, and yet so
deficient.   He seems to have designed in us a special
adaptation and necessity for love, by creating wants
which by love alone can be supplied.   That must be the
reason, I think, why men are so fond of insisting on the
weakness and dependence of women.   We are so conscious of our own dependence upon them, that we cannot
be content without claiming for ourselves a capacity for
blessing corresponding with our need of our being blessed.
I hope that in my future life, when you are my wife, I
shall be able to do something for you that can really
make you happier than you could be without it.

"Do you know, love, when once I get the idea of you
as my wife into my head, I cannot get rid of it, and two
lines of Coleridge are perpetually ringing in my ears—

> ' A pledge of more than passing life,
>   Yea, in that very name of wife.'

"Is it not true that a thorough union of heart and soul
implies a union for eternity?   Love would lose half its
blessedness if its province did not embrace our whole
existence, if its duration fell short of eternity."

"*June* 1850.

"We will look over Coleridge together.   'Aids to Reflection' is a book I admired beyond all things at one
time, but I have forgotten it so far that I hardly know
what I should think of it now.   It was written with
especial reference to the controversy with the Unitarians;
and, as you will see, begins from the very simplest ground
of morality, gradually advancing up to the most mysterious doctrines of Christianity.   No book ever had a greater
influence on the development of my mind."

"July 1850.

" I have hardly thought at all of those religious controversies since I last wrote to you ; and I am much better for it. The feeling that Christianity must be true, because it puts me in my right relation with God and with the world, then comes into play, and I am much happier. I cannot quell the doubts, but I can commit myself to God ; and being fully assured that when I am most a Christian I am the best man, I am content to adhere to that as my guide, in the absence of better light, and wait till God shall afford me more. Only sometimes the thought will come on me with overwhelming power that I am acting a lie, and doing violence to my convictions. These are sad times, but I trust they will not always last."

" August 1850.

" I may perhaps as well tell you a little more plainly, the nature of the objection entertained by the profession against Mr. ―――― (not Dr.) ; I do so not on his account at all, but because it may serve to render clear to you a principle of wide application, which the public seem to find it very hard to understand, but of which it is desirable that you, as a medical man's wife, should have a comprehension.

" In the first place, it is not an objection to the remedial moans he employs ; secondly, it is not that they deny the cures he has effected ; thirdly, it is not jealousy of his success, or a wish to underrate his merits ; the matter is simply this—it is a universally recognised law among the members of the profession that all improvements or inventions are the common property of the entire body, and are never to be held as secrets for the aggrandisement of one individual. Is not the reasonableness of this rule on the score of *humanity*, to say nothing of other reasons, manifest ?

"Again, it is a rule that the profession, and not the public, are the proper judges of the value of any remedy, whether new or old; and that the public opinion in favour of any is not to be sought except as the *results* of practice, and the testimony of the profession may silently and gradually ensure it. The reasonableness of this rule also, though perhaps not quite manifest to you, is evident enough to any person who knows the deceptiveness of limited experiments, and the deceivable-ness of mankind.

"Hence, you will perceive that any person who chooses to break these rules, voluntarily and deliberately, and for the sake of some gain, which is usually obtained, puts himself beyond the pale of the profession. The public think he is an extraordinary clever person, his brethren call him a quack. In this it is quite clear there is no hardship. A man has a choice of keeping his character, perhaps at the sacrifice of some possible pecuniary emolu-ment, or of sacrificing it for the sake of increased receipts. Tastes may differ as to the proper course to be pursued; but it is evident that a man cannot sell his character, and keep it too.

"You perceive, therefore, that for a man to take out a patent for any supposed improvement in medicine or surgery; or to advertise that he is able to cure any disease better than other medical men, is to make himself a quack. Mr. —— has done both, and in his case, as it almost invariably does in the present state of ignorance among the people, it has paid him well. No doubt he can afford to laugh at more scrupulous people, but for my own part I sincerely hope that if ever I do such a thing I may be made a beggar through it.

" After hearing such remarks as I have made above, people might say, That is all very well, but what is it to us ? If there is a man who can cure us, what difference does it make to us whether he advertises or not, or why should·we stop, before having recourse to him, to ascertain whether he complies with the regulations of the profession ? The reason for it is this, that every individual has a direct and immediate interest in the honour and integrity of the entire body of medical men. It should never be forgotten that when a sick person employs a doctor, he ·of necessity places his health, and perhaps his life, absolutely in his hands, and has no manner of security against their being tampered with except in the *character* of the individual. He cannot judge whether his modes of treatment are right or wrong, or at least only too late to be of any service to him, and the only precautions he can take are two—First, to be careful in the selection of his own adviser; and second, but not less important, to do all in his power to maintain a high moral tone throughout the body—or at any rate to let whatever influence he does exert be in that direction.

" Now I need not point out to you that any man who employs a ·quack exerts his influence in precisely the opposite direction. Every shilling which is so spent goes to swell the aggregate of a fund which is acting as a perpetual temptation to medical men to betray their consciences, viz., the income enjoyed by medical impostors. And this is so enormous, that it is not to be wondered at that men are continually to be found who accept the bribe; but the guilt, or at least the folly, lies almost as much with those who offer it.

" Now I have done. Don't think it tedious of me to write so; for, as my wife, I shall wish you to understand and uphold these principles, and to sympathise with me in any sacrifices (if so be there should be any) which I may be called upon to make for them. . . ."

"*August* 1850.

"I have had a great pleasure since I wrote to you. My mother's hearing has been entirely restored, of which I have been the humble instrument. I meant to say *happy*. The affair was simple enough—merely a syringing properly performed, which I should have done long ago, had it not been that I understood it had been done, and thoroughly done, repeatedly before. I had recourse to it myself, merely through accident, and as preparatory to some other steps which I meant to take; but to my equal surprise and gratification I found it attended with complete success, and my mother hears now as well as any of us.

"This little bit of good success has made me feel quite happy, for though it is rather more to my discredit, in not having tried so simple a means before, than otherwise (except inasmuch as it was modesty which prevented me), yet, according to all appearance, if it had not been for me my mother would have passed the rest of her life under circumstances of grievous deprivation. It is a great pleasure to us all to be able to talk to her so easily, and to find her once more a participator in all the enjoyments of our domestic intercourse. I remember it was one of the things which I especially looked forward to accomplishing when I came home, the restoration of mother's hearing. Last night also I performed the same kindness for an old man who has been long deaf, and with almost complete success.

"Another poor person in great distress applied to me this morning, for whom also I think I shall be able to accomplish a good deal; so that my sympathies are beginning to find a little occupation. And I realise a little of that on which I have set my heart as regards my profession,—the making it an instrument for doing good and diffusing happiness—not the mere alleviation of physical suffering (though that is a great privilege), but the prevention or alleviation of moral evil and degradation, and the ministering to a wounded spirit. It is wonderful how much my glorious profession enables a man to do, where no other person, hardly even a minister, could interfere without impertinence.

"I can hardly advise you, dearest, about the ragged school. I should be very sorry to counsel you to abandon any useful occupation in which you might properly engage yourself, because it is not only a pleasure to you, but also a delight to think of, and is laying up a store of happy recollections for the future. But, at the same time, if it is an engagement in which you cannot persevere without either over-exerting yourself or leaving other duties, I think you should give it up."

"September 1850.

" I have enjoyed exceedingly the various extracts which you have sent me lately. With that from Channing I sympathise entirely; and I trust that, to some extent, I acted upon it during my travels. It is most true that there is an inward power of good in men, not subdued or capable of subjection by the most adverse circumstances. I have seen it among the falsely refined Chinese, the untutored savages of Africa, and the degraded slaves. While humanity remains, it is never or almost never obliterated.

" God has not made any of His works in vain, nor allowed any of them to become wholly a prey to the destroyer. It is not adverse circumstances that can wholly debase the human soul—that can only be done by the deliberate choice and resolution of the individual himself; but I fear that it *can* be done. I fear that the men could be found who have given themselves up to evil until the empire of good within them is destroyed; who have refused to listen to the divinity that speaks within until its voice can be no longer heard. But that is not true of *mankind* anywhere. The most untoward outward influences cannot efface the Creator's stamp upon him, nor render inapplicable even now the original judgment He pronounced that all His works are 'very good.'

"But, dearest, it is not only in foreign lands and among barbarous tribes that we must look for an exemplification of this law, or be content to find it. Influences as adverse to all that is good, circumstances as unpropitious to the development of any kind of excellence as any that can be found in the arid deserts of Africa, or amid the crushing superstitions of Asia, exist here around us, and in our midst. And not less *here*, thank God, the evidences of man's indestructible goodness are to be found.

"Forget for a moment, dear, the untaught Chinaman, the degraded Hindoo, the savage negro, the worse than savage slave, and look into the byways and alleys of this city and of your town. Fancy that you see the hordes that throng the gin-shops, the multitudes that live by vice and crime, —it is a pitiable spectacle—you have seen none so badly trained, so deeply sunk; you might wish to turn away your eye as from an 'irremediable evil' (as Channing says), but you would be wrong. The divinity of human nature is not extinguished there, nor the innate goodness utterly destroyed. It is 'adverse circumstances' that have brought them so low, and against them the inmost soul of the victim revolts. The fact is one full of hope, and it has been established by abundant and indubitable testimony. I think, dearest, it is one that we should bear in mind.

" It is a more marvellous and more admirable illustration of the universal principle which Channing notes, than
any which the whole world besides can furnish, and to us
it is of infinitely more practical moment ; for it is connected
with our daily life, and intertwines itself among our daily
duties."

" *November* 1850.

" I want to add one little thing; it is this: When you
think it necessary to tell me of some comparatively
trifling failing, and I know you will find it necessary
very often,—try and treat it lightly and as a matter of
course ; tell me of it with a smile among other things,
and especially don't be afraid that I shall not take it
well. I'll tell you why: because the other plan de-
presses me too much,—almost, I might say, dispirits
me. I mayn't have a correct appreciation of my faults
in detail, but in truth I am not ignorant of them in
general. I look upon myself as a sort of conglomeration
of faults, a kind of aggregate of defects put into a
bodily shape; this is at all times my lamentation and
vexation, and I can see scarcely anything to counterbalance it.

" In fact, I do believe that I am habitually the worse
for that very reason. I am out of spirits with myself,
and have hardly trust and hope enough to set myself
resolutely to work to cure my defects. I need, I do believe,
rather to be encouraged to reform than urged to it ; and
when people gravely remonstrate with me about some
minor point, it is very apt to set me thinking that I am a
fool altogether.

" Don't think, dear, that I wish you not to point out
my faults. I hope you will always do so, when there is
occasion ; and the more, inasmuch as I have a habit of

abstraction which renders me very often insensible to
them, but try and do it in a cheerful way.   Haven't you
often heard people talk about 'going' to do a thing? That's
what I mean ; don't go to do it; don't let it seem as if you
thought it was something formidable or extraordinary.   It
ought to be treated quite like a matter of course and
spoken of as *freely* as anything else."

"*November* 1850.

"As regards my father, I myself see one or two things
in him (chiefly his manner) which are repugnant to me;
but if any one dislikes his nature, it can only be because
they don't know him.   I speak deliberately, and, I think,
impartially, when I say that I have never been intimately
acquainted with any man whose whole soul could bear as
searching and thorough an examination.   I don't know any
character for which I have so high a veneration.

"I don't speak of certain aspects only, but of the whole
of it.   It is alike great and good, with no more defects in
it than are necessary to make it human.   There are many
great qualities in him which are obvious to all, but I am
not referring to those.   I am thinking of his private virtues, which only those who live constantly with him can
appreciate or even know of.   I refer to his kindness, his
humility, his self-control, his willingness to acknowledge
himself in the wrong, and to make amends for any tran-
sient harshness of temper, his forbearance towards those
who are weaker than himself, his active and generous
benevolence, and the exemplary way in which he fulfils
his duties as a husband and father.   These qualities, I
know, do not appear, they are obscured to the public view,
but they are not the less real and genuine, and they exist
to an extent of which very few people have any conception.

"It is the rarest thing in the world, and you must not

expect it, to have opposite qualities combined in the same individual. Gentleness and charmingness are excellent things; and gentle and charming people could not be dispensed with; but neither could those men be who are by no means charming, and possess but little gentleness, but who nevertheless have large hearts as well as heads, and accomplish a great deal of very necessary work which gentle people would never undertake.

"And now, by speaking of my father, I have prepared the way for saying a few words about myself, and I must at once admit that I labour under many defects in regard to my manners and so on. I am very sorry for it, and yet I am not without my consolations; not that I undervalue good manners, but what consoles me is, that I can give a good reason for my want of manners, viz., that the time and thought which might have been spent in acquiring them, have been devoted to the pursuit of objects at least as worthy.

"Although not naturally gifted with gentlemanly manners, no doubt, I might have acquired them if I had given my mind to it. Politeness is like every other art, it may be learnt by time and study. But it wouldn't do for all to choose the same object, for then some important things would be neglected; and on that very account mutual allowances should be made. It would be unreasonable to find fault with a nice, well-informed, polite, agreeable young man, because he hadn't read Berkeley and Hume, and accurately adjusted the claims of Idealism and Materialism. . But it isn't much less absurd to call to account an unfortunate youth who has been simple enough to measure his strength against these and various other inscrutable mysteries, and has learnt thereby to know his own power and condition and duties, because he isn't equally useful at a party, and doesn't know so well how

D

to tie his cravat. Nor is it at all a just assumption that
the politest and most agreeable men are really the kindest
or most desirous to oblige. They are often utterly and
irredeemably selfish. I am very sure that many an awk-
ward, slovenly, young man, who never seemed to think of
any one around him, or to see what they wanted, has
thought and mourned for hours in secret over the evils
. which the vices of much more agreeable people than himself have inflicted on mankind, and has longed to make
himself a sacrifice to cancel them.

" I haven't in all this but a very remote and partial
allusion to myself; but the inference I want you to
draw is this, that you must be very patient with the
faults of manner you see in me. They are bad enough,
but they should have this to recommend them, they are
the price at which all you love and admire in me has
been bought.

" If I hadn't in my early youth shut myself up from all
companionship to pursue a course of solitary study; if I
hadn't pursued these studies with all my heart and all
my thoughts, even during the time that I mixed in society,
so that I lived as it were in a dream, and did not see or
know how the people around me behaved themselves,
and how it behoved me to behave; if I hadn't, looked
upon myself (with boyish vanity, perhaps, yet with a
man's intensity of purpose) as dedicated to some noble
object, in comparison with which all the pleasures and
amenities of life were as mere dust in the balance; if, in
my strivings after truth and uprightness and sincerity, I
hadn't been disgusted with the hollowness and rottenness
at heart of the social usages that surrounded me, and so
conceived a contempt for them, I should no doubt eat
more elegantly, speak more gently, dress more fashion-
ably, and do all things in better taste; but I shouldn't

have been as worthy a man even as I am now, and certainly not a man that you would love.

" Think for a moment, if in the course of duty, or even
in a conscientious, though mistaken effort to accomplish
some great good, I had become personally deformed, so
that no one could see me without pain. Would you let
that distress you and interfere with your love for me ?
And why should you not regard other blemishes, at least
as far as they have been incurred in that way, in the same
light and with the same composure ?

" Finally, for I think I have come to the end, don't
overlook an important element of the case, and that is
my *youth.* I dare say you have been thinking as you
read this letter that you know a good many men who,
with the utmost moral and religious eminence, have all
that is desirable in polish and refinement. That is true ;
but observe the point, they are *men.* If you could have
seen them in their youth, when the elements of their
characters were developing themselves, perhaps in strife
one with another, I doubt much whether you would have
seen what you see now. Instead of the composed, the
tranquil, the happy, and the lovely, you might have seen
undue eagerness and zeal, leading to some violence of expression, or severity of thought, producing ill-mannered
abstraction, and inward conflicts, imparting some asperity
to temper. Do you suppose that men don't improve and
soften as they grow older ; and when they feel more at
ease within themselves, don't become more naturally and
easily alive to the little wants of others ?

" Have patience, love. Consider it is but six months
since I was a wanderer over the face of the earth without
a home, or prospect of one, or care for one. Do you suppose that I am going to live as your husband in my own
home, and see young children growing up around me,

without feeling calmer, more contented, happier, in short, than I am now; and seeing more clearly what it behoves me to do in every position, and growing more sensitive to the claims which others have upon me? Let nature have its course and don't *fret*. I'm improving wonderfully, but a forced growth is no good, in morals, manners, or anything else."

"*November* 1850.

"Your letters fall upon my heart like rain upon a thirsty field. There is nothing to be complained of in my circumstances, and I do not make any complaint of them, except only that little point which I cannot give in, that I am too old to have my marriage deferred any more with advantage.

"The real cause of my discomfort is, I know, where you direct me to seek for it, in myself; and the cure is that which you point out, a closer union with Christ, and the cultivation of a more constant communion with God and devotion to His will. And this effort, dear, I am anxious and desirous to make; but I am hindered greatly by that latent scepticism which every effort at earnest thought has so great a tendency to call up into renewed activity, and so to recommence a conflict, the bare idea of which makes me shudder with dread.

"And yet against this also I have two resources—one is prayer, the other, activity. You teach me more about prayer than any one else I ever heard. I believe in the results of your prayers, and I endeavour to pray as you do, though, as yet, with little earnestness or faith. But this one great advantage I find even from the least attempt at prayer, viz., a new evidence of the fact of the atonement. It seems to me impossible to pray fervently, continually, and trustfully without feeling that we could not pray so unless we were first forgiven and accepted, without any reference whatever to our own deserts or deeds. The conscience would recoil from any such approach to God unless we could say at the same time, ' Not for my sake.'

" I see that I have only written what has been said a hundred times before, but I never felt its force so strongly; that is, I think, I never perceived before how natural and how necessary this intimate union between ourselves and God is; how irrepressible is the demand our nature makes for it."

Whatever conflicts James Hinton had yet to pass through, whatever marked modifications his religious belief afterwards underwent, from this time may be said to date the "low beginnings" of the great central truth of his philosophy, namely, that man's moral and spiritual emotions are in as true relations with the visible creation as his intellect, and their claims are destined to as rich a fulfilment; that his religious aspirations, his love, his worship, his loyal trust in the Unseen, all that lifts him above himself, are not a winding stair of a ruined tower leading nowhere, but are correlated to answering realities, so that truth will ever be found to be potential goodness, and goodness to be realised truth. As nature does not put the appeal of his intellect to confusion, but meets it with an intelligent order, with sequences invariable as the laws of thought, with marvels of construction and adaptation that appeal to interpreting mind, so she meets the appeal of his moral emotions, not with the moral negation of a mechanical necessity, not with the cold silence of a blank impenetrable mystery, but with a true response, a "glory that excelleth," the reality which underlies the phenomenon, and which we symbolise in our two highest words—love, rightness—a necessity which is perfect freedom, a law that is liberty.

CHAPTER IV.

IT was soon after Mr. Hinton's return to England that his attention was first turned to that branch of his profession in which he afterwards attained the first eminence. The cure of his mother's deafness, which has already been recounted, awakened in him an interest in aural surgery, which was kept alive by other patients who came to him on the strength of his first cure. Not long after he was introduced to Mr. Toynbee, whose successor he was afterwards to be, and devoted much of his spare time to attending St. Mary's Hospital with him. Their intercourse resulted in a close and lifelong friendship, founded on similarity of thought and aim, and general sympathy of character.

He also gave the most strenuous study to physiology, and to those curious and intricate problems of the influence of the mind on the body, which have since been so ably investigated by Dr. Carpenter. His remarks on homœopathy must be understood to apply to the old system of infinitesimal doses, which later homœopaths have so largely abandoned.

I continue to give extracts from his letters to Miss Margaret Haddon.

"December 1850.

"Indeed, dearest, your health is the great thing for you to attend to now, because that has already been much tried, and if you have to live in the heart of London all your days, you will want a stock of health to bear it. You know, I am naturally anxious about health, because I see so much sickness, and because I know how apt good people like yourself are to let themselves be over-excited until their strength is exhausted, and the occupations of life become a burden to them. It might do you good to know a little more of A——, for then you would see an illustration of the moral evils which come in the train of what seems like a venial (perhaps even praiseworthy) disregard of health.

" I have a right to speak on this subject. I am myself an instance of it. I labour now under, and shall always, I fear, retain, an irritability of temper caused absolutely and only by my foolish trifling with my health in bygone days, when I used to waste the time necessary for sleep in abortive efforts to study.

" So inconsistent are mankind (such good friends to doctors by the by), they ill-use their poor bodies most cruelly, most wickedly ; they treat them as a boy does a plaything; sacrifice their well-being to every idle whim of the mind, and every low caprice of the appetite. If they are remonstrated with they will pay no heed ; they say, ' Oh, I am very well,' or, 'I am never accustomed to think of my health,' or, 'I don't believe this will hurt me.' They will go yet further; they will shut their eyes to the plainest indications of suffering health ; they will not notice little ailments; they will think they are nothing and persist in all their evil practices, and all their friends encourage them; until at last the mischief gets a little worse, they become what they call ill, and all is terror and distress. A fuss is made, as unreasonable as the former neglect. Everything is sacrificed to this once-despised health, and yet when it is regained, it is only to be again trifled with in like

manner. Is it not a true picture, dear ? Mayn't a man
whose constant occupation is among such scenes be excused for feeling and speaking strongly about it ?

" Observe, dear, that I do not advocate people trying
to keep well, out of a cowardly fear of being ill, or suffering pain, or losing life, but as a religious duty, in order
that they may render to God the full service He demands
of them. A man was never made morbid by such a
feeling as that, I'll answer for it, nor never will be. This
is exactly the element that is wanting to rectify the two
errors, of negligence on the one hand, and over-anxiety
on the other."

" December 1850.

" I have no time for general literature, nor, indeed, do
I find any pursuit of that compatible with a proper dis-
charge of my professional duties. It is a sacrifice I am
obliged to make, and I do not grudge it much. But I
am obliged to make it entirely ; other reading has too
great charms to be ventured on. I am too fond of
certain branches of literature to allow my mind to be
open to them. It is a good thing that the science and
art of medicine furnishes of itself ample occupation to
the intellect and the heart. I must confine myself to
that for some years to come."

" March 1851.

" You haven't told me whether you have procured the
book you want about polarisation of light. I send you
some music to copy. It is a chant of my own composing.
I hope you will like it. When such ideas come into my
head I can't rest till I have written them down. Don't
criticise it too severely."

" March 1851.

" With regard to intoxicating drinks I am always

awake to the disastrous effects of their abuse, and endeavour, both by example and precept, when practicable, to
discourage their use. But as an honest man I cannot
deny their use, or set myself against their occasional employment, and, therefore, cannot work heartily with the
teetotallers; and, moreover, I incline to the belief that
drunkenness itself is but a symptom of a deeper seated
social disorder, and will be most wisely and effectively
combated, not by direct means, but by remedies which,
passing by itself, should aim a blow at its cause."

" March 1851.

"Ponder well my advice to leave off thinking about
yourself altogether. You have thought quite enough
about yourself to last till you are married, then you can
think about yourself in another way, viz., through the
medium of your husband, which is the same thing in one
sense, but in all respects much better. And those subjective novels too, they are all very well, and what you
say of them is quite true up to a certain point, but they
are susceptible of abuse, and you are not one of the
persons that stand most in need of them. Put all subjective things into subjection for the present, and be
content as God in His providence and His grace has made
you.

"Nature has wonderful remedial powers which can't
work while she is being interfered with; and you, in your
moral medication of yourself, have fallen into the error of
the old-fashioned allopaths in administering remedies too
constantly. Hold your hand a little. I have seen many
an obstinate case of disease improve wonderfully upon
being let alone. And the body is but a type of the soul.
Moral drugging, with self-examination and reflections and
resolutions, is every bit as bad as cramming with medi-

cines. For examinations are but cathartics, reflections
alteratives, and resolutions tonics. And, to make a
long matter short, I commend you to a spiritual homœopathy."

"I need something specially to do, something upon
which I can look as my work, as the thing which I have
accomplished, and which I can regard for ever as the
representative of my earthly life. Don't you understand
this want? Is it not one that it is right and proper to
feel until it is satisfied? I should not like to be without
it, and yet it seems to me at present only a source of
embarrassment and discomfort to me. I do not feel yet
what it is that I would do, what it is that I am fitted for.
Besides, dear, you also cannot devote yourself to me unless I be myself devoted to some good object. You can
dedicate yourself only to a dedicated man. I know that
is the case, and I am glad and proud of it; to say otherwise would be to belie your nature. I do not wish it to
be otherwise, and what my heart longs for is that we may
be fellow-workers, true helpmates, for there can be no
help where there is no labour in a good cause. Is not
that your wish too, dear?

"But I am embarrassed, therefore idle. Too many
things crowd upon me; none *commands* me. The thing
which shall fill my heart must be not for myself but
for others. To be contented I must toil not for comfort,
nor money, nor for fame, nor for love, but for truth and
righteousness. The habit has become a second nature to
me. I have been a dreamer so long (if it be dreaming)
that I must still live an ideal life. I must begin to do
something, the things that are nearest to me, heartily,
earnestly, perseveringly, and get light by working, which

is indeed the only genuine or safe illumination that can be got."

" 11th May 1851.

" What a world it is ! How wonderful that men should walk on it as if it were made of common earth, or go to California in search of gold. I never yet laid my hand with a resolute heart, upon any portion of God's universe that I could reach that did not turn to gold beneath my grasp. And I know it needs but work and a right spirit to draw, even from the commonest sources, an exhaustless treasure. . . .

" I have had to go and see a man in a fit; which, though an excellent performance, has somewhat changed the current of my thoughts; and, indeed, this last sentence, viewed in a common-sense light, has rather a ludicrous aspect even to myself. For this unfortunate gold which I find so plentiful, happens to be the very thing that I most need just now. What wonders even a little of it would perform for us. I must take care that I do not let the allegorical metal cause the real one also to continue a mere vision. That would never do. But a little patience and self-control and all will be accomplished."

" April 1851.

" I go now every morning to the Homœopathic Hospital at about seven o'clock, so that I am obliged to go early to bed as well. I find myself much better for the change in my habits, in body and spirits too. I am determined to investigate the matter to the bottom, for it cannot fail to repay me, and it would, besides, be such a grand thing if homœopathy were true. It would be a pity to lose a chance of finding it out. Only fancy what a splendid thing it is to feel that one has discovered the truth in medicine, that one may give over doubt, inquiry, and toil; that one always must be right, and never can have the responsibility of deciding between various modes of treatment, and choosing not only a good one, but the best; and after all, the consolatory reflection that whatsoever happens, there can be no fault on our part, that failure can be due only to inexorable fate."

"*May* 1851.

"But to come to my work. The last month has been an invaluable one to me. I have made a great step in knowledge, and have gained a great accession of humility. I have become wise and discovered that I was a fool. The two things must always go together, so I need not dwell on that. It has taken me weeks upon weeks to find out what I knew quite well before, what everybody has known from the remotest antiquity. A veritable idiot I have been. For my grand discovery is nothing but that simple fact I told you of before, which has been embodied in the common proverb that 'fancy kills or fancy cures.' But, then, before I only knew it, now I have *found it out.* Did you never discover the difference between those two things. I wish I could 'find out' afresh some few other of the things which I know too well. I wonder who invented that saying, 'Blessed are the ignorant.' He was a genius, and deserves well of mankind whoever he was. We know too much. It is our irreverent familiarity with things that blinds us, so that we cannot see that we walk in the midst of miracles, and draw in mysteries with every breath, and trample beneath our feet the sublimest principles of philosophy. I would that I understood the little things; our pride is our greatest enemy.

" Twenty years ago a doctor was walking through a field of peas. He took a few in his hand, and as he meditated he rolled them between his fingers. While thus engaged he passed by a house where lived a woman deranged in health. She thought if a doctor was rolling anything in his hand it must be a pill, and asked him to give her some, for she had taken much medicine and could get no better. He gave her two peas; she took them; the next day he called and found that they had cured her.

" And what did he do then ? He was amused and laughed. He told the story in joke to a friend. O vain and foolish man ! Did not God then take his hand and lay it on a precious fact, embodying a law precious beyond its worth of diamonds, and say to him, ' Discover me that law—collect more facts—investigate them patiently and it shall not be hid from you, and then proclaim it to your fellows ! Unfortunate wretch that he was ! He *knew too much.* He had heard of such things before, and he had a name for them, so he passed on in scorn to compound his drugs and theorise upon their action. And God and nature have avenged themselves.

" Now, if he had studied that fact, as God commanded him, what might he have done ? First, he might have spared the world a great part of the nonsense that has been talked about mesmerism, electro-biology, and homœopathy, and have saved from pollution the paper on which have been printed the cruel books with which mankind have been persecuted on these subjects. Secondly, he might have brought into practical use a mighty agent for the relief of our suffering fellow-creatures that God has entrusted to us. Thirdly, he might have put medical men in such a position, that they would have been able ere this to arrive at some satisfactory conclusions with

regard to the effects of medicines and the proper way of
using them.

"Now, that's enough.   It isn't nearly all he might
have done; but it's enough to satisfy the ambition of any
human being.   He did not do it; but be his faults forgiven him; we have all sinned like him."

"*May* 1851.

"I'll tell you why women were made to *blush*.   It is
that I might discover by means of it how it is that anything that acts on the emotions will cause and cure diseases.   I thought of that to-day in chapel.

"I think the matter is so plain that I can explain it
to you in a very few words.   It is as plain as the reason
why water rises in a pump, viz., that the air presses it;
but that was as mysterious while people didn't know that
the air had any weight, as it is now how an infinitesimal
dose should cure a disease, the mystery being simply
that people haven't yet discovered that the '*emotions*'
have weight.   I'll give you first the general principle,
and then an illustration, and so you shall have the essence
of the matter in a nut-shell.   The principle is this: All
the emotions produce a specific effect upon the small
vessels, capillaries as they are called, which is seen in the
face when people blush; the vessels become relaxed and
full of blood, and the face red.   All the exciting and most
pleasurable emotions relax the capillaries; all depressing
emotions, on the contrary, contract these vessels, which
also is seen in the face when a man turns pale with fear.
He is pale because the minute vessels don't contain so
much blood.

"Now the same effect that takes place on the surface of
the body takes place in the inside too; in fact, it may take
place in any and every part, and sometimes it does.

" This seems very little, but it is almost as vast as the whole range of human suffering ; for relaxation and contraction of the capillaries is the essence of disease. It is inflammation, it is morbid deposit, it is pain ; etc. Thus, you perceive, we see daily before our eyes emotion setting on foot those processes which constitute disease, and which also (for here is the point) constitute cure.

" Now, it has been from want of a due appreciation of this fact that the medical world has been at a loss, and several of them have come to believe that infinitesimal doses will cure the greatest diseases.

" Sir Astley Cooper published in his lectures (thirty years ago) that the only cause he could discover for cancer was mental distress ; and that, he was sure, would produce it. The whole medical world has read those lectures since. And yet, now, go to a medical man and tell him that a cancer has been *cured* by the production of emotions and he will laugh at you. Some few will invent a magnetic fluid and say that that has carried it away ; but as for admitting that a power which will cause a disease may be so applied as to cure it, that passes the bounds of their belief. You have the whole theory now before you. It is simply this : We see a power which continually produces effects which we admit, so far as we can discover, to lie at the bottom of almost all diseases. I affirm that that power does produce disease (which is daily seen, though not taken notice of), and that under certain conditions it will cure it.

" I will give you an instance, selected for simplicity. If a person loses too much blood he has a headache, which is due to there being too little blood in the brain, and the vessels, accordingly, too much contracted. Now we have seen that depressing emotions contract the blood-vessels, and as such an emotion produces a headache precisely the same as that which is caused by loss of blood, I presume that the same physical condition exists in both cases, viz., a contracted state of the blood-vessels in the brain.   Now, having got a headache arising from contraction of these vessels, what is the cure ?   Of course, to relax them.   And how shall we do that ? One way will immediately suggest itself to you, viz., to produce a cheerful emotion which, as you know, is seen to relax the vessels.   Suppose we excite *hope ;* is not the thing done ?—that is to say, give the patient a globule. I should think it would cure him.   If it won't, my theory is wrong—but I don't think it is, because a spoonful of water will cure, as in this case that Mr. F—— attended last week.

"A lady sent for him in a great hurry, late in the evening.   She was very ill, and her friends thought she was going to die.   She had intense headache, restlessness, vomiting upon the least movement, and so on.   In fact, the vessels in her brain were constricted by fear. Mr. F——, like a wise man (having profited by my experience), gave her a tablespoonful of water.   The first dose stopped the sickness, cured the headache, and sent her to sleep.   Is that a mystery ?   The interpretation of it is written easily on every woman's cheek.   The *hope* relaxed the vessels.   I haven't selected this case because the affection was nervous, but only because I could describe it easily in simple language.   I know of still more striking cases of real disease cured manifestly in the same way.

"But I will just mention one principle that I have established, and a very valuable one, as I think, viz., that if we wish to bring the emotions into play in the cure of disease we must *not give drugs.* They interfere with the process.   The globules will cure diseases that all the physic in the world wouldn't touch. I have had a lovely case that bids fair to withdraw from the ranks of the homœopathists the best and cleverest member of the body that I know. On Wednesday last one of the physicians of the Hahnemann Hospital wanted to go to the Derby. I was sitting by his side when the time arrived for him to go, and as there were a few more patients to be seen, it was agreed between us that I should attend to them and order them sugar-of-milk. This I did. On Saturday two of them came again. One was better, the other was *well*. And this had been a serious-looking case. If I hadn't known the power of bread-pills I shouldn't have dared to order him a globule. He gave an interesting account of himself. The day after he began the medicine (sugar, mind you, alone) he found the pains much worse, but they soon began to mend, and, in fact, had gone away altogether. As the doctor wrote down his words I saw his face grow red (you see the same thing occurred in him as had happened to the patient, emotion relaxed the vessels); and when he had done he rose and went to the other end of the room, and said, 'If this be so, all my labour has been in vain.' He knew before what my views were, and the fact flashed on him like lightning. Poor fellow! he has worked hard for Homœopathy, but, as I told him, that labour can never be in vain. The world owes much to the homœopathists; no one owes more than I do."

"*May* 1851.

"It is a whole week, nearly, since I wrote to you, but then you kept me so long without a letter, and I haven't had a moment of time that was not imperatively called for by the work I had in hand. It is perfectly marvellous what a light this new power of emotion throws on

E

all those mysterious phases of diseased and healthy action
that have puzzled us so long.

"I can tell you a pretty little thing I have discovered
among others not so elegant. It is the use of a tear.
When a person feels an emotion of grief the small cuta-
neous vessels which pour out the insensible perspiration
are contracted so that that secretion cannot go on. Instantly the eyes take on a compensating action, and the
tears gush forth, carrying away with them the matter,
which being repelled from the skin would otherwise become injurious to the system. And I can prove that the
forcible repression of tears materially damages the health;
it is counteracting a provision of nature. It is a violation
of the physical laws to order a child not to cry when
nature demands tears. It is inflicting an injury on the
material organisation. Of course, to control excessive
crying is another matter; but even the treatment of that
should rather be preventive than suppressive."

"June 1851.

"My most pleasing anticipation is, that I shall certainly reconcile the allopaths and homœopaths, if I can
prove to them (as I think I can by a chain of evidence
quite irresistible) that they have been both curing people
all the while by the very same power—which power is
precisely the same as that by which our much calumniated *u*
forefathers cured their patients, with charms and incanta-
tions, and that they have been quarrelling all the while
about a name, a whim, a mere fancy; then I think they
can never find it possible to go on quarrelling any more.
Especially when it must be evident that both are in fault,
that the allopath now and then prevents his patient from
recovering by an over-exhibition of physic; and the
homœopath consigns a victim to eternity occasionally by

withholding from him the means which God designed for his cure and for which our instincts irrepressibly long. Not that I flatter myself that this will take place yet. It will be many many long years before that can come to pass. Error gains too deep a hold of human nature, soon to be given up. Even my good friend, the homœopath, whose patient I cured with sugar-of-milk, and who admits the cure to be complete, seems quite unmoved by it. He goes on prescribing his globules as before, although, I think, I have opened his mind a little."

"*June* 1851.

" My imagination is a good deal sobered down since I last wrote, not that my speculations seem to have lost any of their theoretical or practical value, but I am beginning to look at them from another point of view, and see more of the difficulties of the case. What embarrasses me is want of time. Duly to investigate the subjects that have presented themselves to me would be a work of many years. I do think I can contribute something towards healing this ridiculous but scandalous feud that old Hahnemann had the infatuation to begin ; and can even give the Mormonites and Irvingites a lift towards the comprehension of their miracles, which puzzle them sadly at present; for a good many of them refuse to be referred, even on the showing of the parties who performed them, to any other agency than the evil one's.

" So that I have a blessing for all parties in my hands. But if I am to publish on this subject, I must work very hard for a long time. But that always does me good, because my way of working is not to sit down and fag, which always leads to all sorts of errors, but to walk about, and let all sorts of ideas come into my head, which generally turn out to be of value."

"If you talk about fear of sacrificing comforts or losing friends, it is because you do not know what feeling an enthusiasm for science is. To add one truth to our store of knowledge, I would sacrifice not only gain, but life. To-day I would be content to die, if so I might advance our knowledge but one stage towards perfection. Regard for self is a feeling that has and can have no place in any heart so occupied. It is doing God's work, and may God forbid that ever it should be done except with a single eye to Him. I care neither for fame nor profit, if only I can get a living and a wife, and do my work faithfully as between God and my own conscience. That surely is enough for any man, and that is certain for me.

"And now, Meggie dear, it is Sunday morning, and I will try and forget all those old week-day distractions, which are very hard to be kept in their place. It is well to do our work as to God, a blessed privilege to feel that whatever we do we may do it to Him; but it is blessed also to have a day for communion with Him in which we need not work. And it is no time lost either. There is a saying of Luther's which I have often thought of, 'To have prayed well, is to have studied well.' No man ever lost anything in this world by attending properly to the next. Indeed, it is only by that means that we can understand or use this world aright. How different it appears to us, according as we look on it, from amidst its toil, or above it and in the light of heaven. What a trifle is the approbation or praise of men compared with the love of God! What vanities are wealth or that enchantment of fame compared with the happiness He can pour into our hearts! I am glad that I know that happiness is only to be found in humble devo-

tion and consecration and obedience to God. For I am
ambitious by nature; even from boyhood my heart has
swelled with the idea that I might do some work which
men would not forget. And if it were not that I am
already contented, have found in God's love and acceptance' of me enough to satisfy my heart and make me
willing to forego all other blessings, these thoughts of
mine would have made me mad. Day and night I should
have dwelt upon them; I should have placed all my hopes
upon their success; I should have made my sole reward
to depend upon their acceptance by my fellow-men. And
succeeding or failing, I should have been alike miserable.

"Now with success or failure I must be alike happy. For
God looks at and accepts the heart, and does not estimate
the merit, or measure the reward, by the skill or talent
displayed, but by the motive. And it matters little
whether He have made me the instrument of advancing
knowledge—He has plenty of means of doing that when
He wills it should be done—if He has given me the privilege of working for Him with devoted heart, of conse-
crating to Him a small offering out of the abundance He
has given me, and will accept it at my unworthy hands;
then He has given me the richest of all blessings—a
blessing to which earthly honour can add nothing, from
which earthly loss cannot detract."

"*August* 1851.

"In spite of my grumbling nature, I must confess it
is sweet to sit down to write to you. I've adopted
your plan to-night, and have your likeness open before
me.

"I mean to begin with philosophy. In the first
place, I beg to thank your sister for her kind concern
lest I should spoil my book. I fear that her care and

my toil will alike, however, be thrown away. I have a sad conviction (to which I am almost resigned) that my book will certainly be spoilt, somehow or other, by metaphysics inopportunely introduced, or in some other mode not less disastrous. I have no idea that I can write a book on any subject without spoiling it. I shall be content if it isn't so bad that no spoiling can make it worse. But for the metaphysics, I beg her to understand that so far from exciting the wrath of godly people, that reverend divine, Mr. J. B., holds them to be especially admirable, not so much because, in his opinion, they clear up many things hitherto mysterious, as because they furnish a proof of the falsity of materialism, and such a clear evidence of the necessary existence of a spirit in man.

"And I must say that herein I agree with him. To a person holding my views, the idea of there being nothing bearing the relation which we suppose our spirits to bear to our bodies, must appear a palpable physiological absurdity.

"I confess, with feelings of the deepest mortification, that I hold myself to be a fool, with more blindness than can be attributed to any three beetles. I am ready every now and then to throw down my pen in sheer disgust at my own incapacity. It takes me weeks and months to find out the plainest, simplest things. It is only the last two days that I have opened my eyes to the most obvious deduction—namely, that we have a power of controlling our thoughts, and, therefore, if the brain thinks, it must be something else that controls its own action. That is too plain to need stating; it would be as reasonable to suppose that a muscle could regulate its own movements as to attribute that power to the brain. There is something in us, or connected with us, that makes use of our brain, supposing it to think; that's evident. Let any one say what that is, and he has given his definition of the spirit.

"I am a fool, as I said before. I have been diving into the abstrusest profundities of physiology, and mounting into the highest abstractions of morals, to find evidence of this fact, shutting my eyes to it all the while. Ten or twelve times during my recent investigations I have had the conviction brought painfully to my mind that I deserve a good whipping for my stupidity. I could wish there were some one here to give me one now. . . . But to return to the point. It is clear, as I said, that if the brain is the organ that thinks, there certainly exists something that makes use of it for thinking, just as it, in its turn, makes use of the muscles for moving. But then, you see, this logic is entirely overthrown unless it first be granted that the brain does think. If it does not think, we don't know what it does do, and perhaps it may be the organ that controls thought as well as motion. And if so, sure enough our evidence of a spirit rests on a rickety foundation.

"I thank God that, though I am stupid enough, there are other men who don't seem much wiser; at least they say things at which I should actually stand aghast. To this do-nothing, do-everything brain, the function of volition has actually been assigned. There is one excuse in men doing so. Divines and metaphysicians have forbidden them to assign to it its only possible function; and they could hardly, therefore, do otherwise than ascribe to it impossible ones.

"Yes, that is grand in its simplicity. The muscles work, but we know that there is a power in us greater than the muscles, because *we* control their movements. The brain thinks, but we know there is something in us greater than the brain, because *we* control its thoughts.

But muscle and brain act alike without our control sometimes.

"There I stand as firm as a rock. Whatever controls the brain's action is spirit. When I can discover that beasts control their thoughts, then I will grant that they must have spirits, but I do not see it at present. I think their brains act just according to the stimuli that are brought to bear upon them, and according to that action they produce actions in the body. I see no evidence that beasts ever divert their thoughts from one subject, and turn it spontaneously to another. . . .

"The brain is the organ of the spirit, the instrument by which the spirit carries out all its purposes, whether of thinking or acting. The spirit acts upon the brain, and thought results, just as the brain acts upon the muscles, and motion results. . . . No form of matter that we are acquainted with can originate action. Matter can only obey the forces that act upon it. The brain can do no otherwise; when put in action it will think, as a muscle will move when put in action; otherwise it will be as passive as a stone. . . . The capacity for thinking, the adaptation for producing thought, must reside in the brain itself, but thought can only be produced on the application of some 'force' to it, either from the body (through the nerves), or by some means we do not understand, from the spirit. The brain bears just the same relation to the spirit that your piano does to you. If you put it skilfully in action, you will produce sweet music (provided it is in tune); but if it be put in action by *any other cause*, it will produce sound more or less musical. Let the cat walk over the keys, and the piano will sound in spite of all you can do to keep it quiet. Let that same cat scratch your finger, and your brain will think in spite of you just the same. The brain is perfectly passive, just as passive as the piano. Get that thoroughly into your head, and you will see that both the spiritual theory of thought and the materialistic theory of man are equally untenable. Both imply one and the same false dogma—viz., that living matter can act of itself. That is a grand error. Living matter, like dead, can only act as it is acted upon.

"It is *physiology* that must clear up these metaphysical disputes; in fact, metaphysics must be merged in physiology, as astrology in astronomy. . . . Action once set up in the brain must produce an action in some other part of the body; it may be, therefore, and is sometimes, in other portions of the brain itself. Thus I account for the carrying on of involuntary trains of thought. . . . But the spirit can at any moment of its own will so act on the brain as to control and alter its action. . . .

"Don't you remember how Coleridge in ' Aids to Reflection' terms the understanding ' a sensuous faculty,' and exclaims, ' If there be a spiritual in man, the will is that spiritual'?

"It wasn't reason led Coleridge to say that. It was religion—it was inspiration. It was one of those outbursts of intuition by which great poets in all ages have anticipated the discoveries of science.

"It is clear whence has come the error that has led men so far astray. It is the confounding of thought and volition, two things as different as spirit is from matter. And who did it ? The metaphysicians—the divines. And how ? By confounding together the functions of the spirit and brain. The materialists have but paid them in their own coin, have used against them weapons forged by themselves. They said matter cannot think—the spirit thinks ; that implied that thinking and willing were actions of a similar kind—were actions of the same substance.

"That did for a time. Mankind thought the argument very clear, the conclusion very logical. There was only one hitch; if they could but find out what was the use of the brain. It was very odd that a spiritual being should want a material organ for performing an immaterial action. But the world is full of mysteries, they thought; it is not more mysterious than other things; and besides, the brain produces the nervous force, perhaps a nervous fluid; most likely it is a reservoir very similar to a Leyden jar.

"But men arose who had no fear of God or spirit before their eyes, and they used their scalpel diligently on the living and the dead, and they maintained, with arguments more wanting in religious feeling than in sound logic, that the brain did think and feel, and with the experiments and inductions of science they shielded themselves against all appeals either to their reason or their conscience. What then? The mischief the metaphysicians and divines had wrought began to work. They had attributed to spirit the functions of spirit and of brain; the others naturally transferred to brain the functions of brain and spirit. Hence the interminable squabble, both right and both wrong. 'Tis as bad to put together what God has sundered as to divide what He has put together. The dispute lies in a nut-shell. The divines say the spirit thinks and wills; the men of science respond, The brain thinks and wills. O never-to-be-settled controversy! What if the brain thinks and the spirit wills? . . .

"With regard to details, I think that M—— is rather confusing herself with words. I hold it fully as absurd to say that thought is material, as to say it is immaterial. Perhaps it is as bad to say that thought is physical, which expression I own to be mine. But I only use it for want of a better, meaning thereby that it belongs to the phenomena of the physical world, that it has, and can have, so far as we know, no existence except in connection with brains. To the expression that 'the phenomena of thought' are physical, I object, because it conveys no meaning to my mind. I don't know in what sense the phenomena of thought are physical; it is rather its mode of production that is physical. But to talk in this way is only to get confused; these general expressions are merely formulas devised of old, before men had discovered the way to search for truth. What I think is, that the brain thinks, in some sense, as muscle moves, *i.e.*, that the brain being put into its normal mode of acting, thought results. I decline to give any more explicit statements on the matter, partly because I don't know anything more about it, partly because I've got a few notions which might appear mystical and absurd, and in attempting to express which I should waste much time to little purpose.

"This is a horrid letter; you mustn't puzzle your brain about it. Don't you think the endeavour to understand ourselves should bring us into closer intimacy with our Maker? I feel it so. I cannot ponder on the wondrous mechanism of which I am composed, nor strive to penetrate into the depths of my being, without feeling afresh and more deeply the intimate relation in which I stand to God and His care for me, His love of me, the happiness it must be to do His will.

"I must go to bed; mother has come to remonstrate with me; but I want you to have this letter in the morning."

"*September* 1851.

"Have you read Shirley? It is a wonderful book, but what pleases me most is that the authoress says most distinctly and unqualifiedly that the brain thinks. In

fact, she is a wonderful observer. It is delightful to read
her descriptions of disease caused by mental affections.
Caroline Helstone's illness is a study for a physician.
There could not have been a better commentary written
on my doctrine of the emotions. She traces the entire
history of a fever caused by grief with inimitable fidelity.
Beginning with the right cause, the abnormal action of
the brain, she traces every effect as it arises, up to the
very verge of death, and then she shows the working of
an emotional cure.

"I am pleased that M—— approves my views of the
spirit. I dearly love to persuade people. There can
hardly be a greater pleasure (of a selfish kind) than to
feel you have brought another person round to your way
of thinking. One thing may be objected to my view,
viz., that it seems to separate our spirits from ourselves.
It produces rather a curious feeling to imagine that our
spirits do not think, and so on. But this I take to be, in
fact, an improvement, for in truth we have been all along
confounding our brains with ourselves, our thinking organ
with our essential being. It has been a great mistake.
Our brains are no more we than our muscles, our thoughts
than our movements. It is not our intellects that are the
essential parts of us, but our characters. We feel that,
although we have set ourselves against the theoretical
admission of it. But it is a thing that it is important to
recognise as well as to feel. For thus we can put into
words our instinctive perception of the fact that the man
who seeks to gratify his intellect at the expense of his
duty is, in fact, a sensualist. Many a man is spoilt and
ruined now through thinking that his intellect is himself,
and that his highest occupation is to cultivate it—his surest
path to obey it. It is not so. That is, to place the body
above the soul, to sacrifice the spirit to the brain. It is

the conscience he should, above all things, cultivate, and in all things obey: that is himself. When for the sake of intellectual pleasure, or in obedience to intellectual arguments, he does violence to it, or neglects it, he lets his brain enslave him, just in the same way as a man lets his stomach enslave him who indulges in gluttony or drunkenness.

" Another thought has occurred to me also, in regarding the spirit as the controller of the brain, viz., that we have a proof here of the intelligent nature of spirit. Not that I think that can be at all doubtful; but when we say that the spirit does not think, it suggests the idea of want of intelligence, very unfoundedly indeed, though not unnaturally. For a moment's reflection must convince us that intelligence must have many forms; it has indeed various forms even in ourselves. And thought, and instinct, and so on, all the modes of intelligence that are connected with brains, must be the very lowest of those forms. So we should never think of ascribing thought to God, except as a reverent adaptation of our mode of action to Him. And with a similar reverence we should think of our own spirit, which probably approaches somewhat to His nature, and has modes of intelligence, perception, and feeling which doubtless far surpass our utmost conceptions.

" But the proof of its intelligence that we get from this view of it is very simple ; it is just like the proof of God's ' intelligence ' derived from the works of nature. It is merely the fact that our spirits use our brains intelligently and for a purpose.

" But I must send this to the post. I think of you very very often, and never without a thrill of delight that I possess such a treasure."

" This reminds me that I did not notice what M. said about our instinctive consciousness, that it was *we* that thought, and not our brains. I must beg to be excused, for I feel particularly conscious that it is not *I* that think, but that I use my thinking faculty. I should be sorry to think that my intellect was myself. It is the most subservient faculty I have got, the logical department of it especially. I can turn my reasoning faculties about in any way I please; use arguments to support any side; create ideas in accordance with any hypothesis; in short, I use my thinking faculties just as I do my motor ones. They are both mere passive instruments for carrying out my purposes. Let them both be taken from me and *I* remain just what I was before."

" I'm glad you enjoyed my last long letters, and found something in them to interest you. At the same time, I had much rather that you should not devote any valuable portion of your time and thoughts to such subjects. Inherently they are questions of words alone. Even the principal terms of 'matter' and 'spirit' are themselves only words with no meaning, except such as is attached to them by arbitrary definitions. And the people who have thought most on the subject are undecided as to whether spirit be not matter after all, and matter spirit.

" For my own part, although I believe in a spirit, and think that I can demonstrate its existence by a process of my own, I nevertheless incline to the opinion that in truth the distinction between the two substances is only an imaginary one. If matter can 'think and feel,' as I have no doubt it can, what need to invent any other kind of 'substance' in order to satisfy our ideas of what a spirit must be? I don't doubt the same omnipotence that can give consciousness to brains, can give to other forms of matter a higher and more lasting form of intelli- gence; in fact, that if God can make a dog of matter, of matter He can make an angel.

"I have said these things not because I believe spirit is matter or the reverse—I don't mean to form any opinion whatever on the subject—but to show you how entirely all such questions are logomachy merely; to show you my justification for saying that metaphysics is like astrology; and that the entire science should be abandoned. My position is, that it is an abuse of the human intellect to employ it on such topics in such a way. That old query, 'How many angels can stand on the point of a needle?' is a fair sample of the lot.

"The real question at issue in all these discussions about matter and spirit is whether man is responsible; whether there is any virtue or vice, any higher power, to which we owe allegiance. What can be more puerile than to meet such inquiry with wordy disquisitions about the nature of thought? Suppose it can be shown that matter cannot think, and that, in order to account for it, we must suppose a 'spiritual substance,' what earthly help is that towards determining the only question that concerns us? It is quite as much beyond our conception *how* spirit thinks as it is how matter should think; and, indeed, how matter should *attract* is rather more mysterious still.

I think a correct application of material and physiological science to the facts of man's nature proves that there *is* some 'substance' or agent connected with him which is not appreciable by our senses after his death. I call that the spirit, but it really makes no difference what it is called. There is one great reason to suppose it not to be matter—viz., that it certainly has the power of originating its own actions (at least it seems so), which no other form of matter appears to have.

"But you see people have got the fancy that if particular metaphysical formulæ are interfered with, *religion* is in danger. They might just as well say that religion is endangered by the regatta to-morrow at the Isle of Wight. The two things have just as much connection. Why shouldn't men play with words as freely as they play with boats? Above all things, is science—the science of our own nature—to be impeded in its progress in deference to such an idle prejudice? I have a right to speak on this subject; for when I speak of my physiological views (to some first-rate men too), they say to me, 'I dare say you are right—it seems highly probable; but don't say it. Such views are not incompatible with religion in your own mind, but they would appear to be so to others.' I am not going to give way to such fears. . . . I am able, though not very willing to take the trouble, to show that not only are my (most materialistic) views not dangerous to religion, but that, if received, they would put religion on a better footing in respect to science and philosophy than she has occupied for many years.

"I always fill up my paper when I get on such topics. I am very much amused at myself. You see it is my brain that does it. My spirit I hope is wiser. But I make my brain work hard sometimes; and I consider it has a right to amuse itself now and then. So I haven't interfered with it, but have let one thought give rise to another just as it happened. But now consider this. At any time I could have left off. If therefore it was my brain that was thinking, what was the power that could have made it leave off? Not itself certainly. Can a muscle make itself leave off acting? I wonder the question has never been put in that light before. The more I look at it, the more satisfied I become with it, and I have found no one yet who sees a flaw in the argument."   .

I have purposely given copious extracts from Mr. Hinton's letters on the functions of the brain, because it is evident it was his physiological views on this point that started him on his most distinctive lines of thought. When once we have been led to accept the proposition, "The brain thinks,"—a proposition held by most of our foremost physiologists—it is evident we are on the eve of a fundamental modification of our ideas of the nature of matter.

"'Men,' says Herbert Spencer, 'who have not yet risen above that vulgar conception which unites with matter the contemptuous epithets of 'gross' and 'brute'"—and we may add "dead"—'may naturally feel dismayed at the proposal to reduce the phenomena of life and mind to a level with those which they think so degraded. But whoever remembers that the forms of existence which the uncultivated speak of with so much scorn, are shown by the man of science to be the more marvellous in their attributes the more they are investigated, and are also proved to be in their ultimate nature absolutely incom-prehensible—as absolutely incomprehensible as sensation or the conscious something which perceives it,—whoever clearly recognises this truth will see that the course pro-posed does not imply a degradation of the so-called higher, but an elevation of the so-called lower.' *

"'For after all,' to quote from another eminent physio-logist, 'what do we know of this terrible matter, except as a name for the unknown and hypothetical cause of states of our own consciousness; and what do we know of

* Herbert Spencer's *First Principles* (1870), p. 836.

F

that spirit over whose threatened extinction so great a
lamentation is arising, like that which arose at the death
of Pan, except that it also is a name for an unknown and
hypothetical cause of condition of states of consciousness ?
In other words, matter and spirit are but names for the
imaginary substrata of groups of consciousness.' " *

So far from leading to materialism, with Mr. Hinton
these convictions were the first step of the ladder which
led him up to the conclusion, to be worked out in " Man
and his Dwelling-Place," that the phenomenal or material
is the appearance, to us, of the spiritual world.   And with
regard to the proposition—" the brain thinks and feels "
—he afterwards held that matter and force, being mental
hypotheses, substrata supplied by the constitutive elements
of mind, it is impossible to derive thought from these
creations of its own.   Like most of the eminent thinkers
of the day, he passed through materialism and came out
at the other side.

* Huxley's " Lay Sermons," vii. 143.   Mr. Hinton, however, used to
comment on the curious tendency among those who recognise the unity
of matter and spirit to derive the better known, the conscious, from the
less known, matter.

CHAPTER V.

To Miss Margaret Haddon :—

"*August* 1851.

"So you are not satisfied with my letters, full of speculations, and want to know more about my own self. I
must confess it is natural, and I like it. But yet what
should be more myself than my thoughts, and how should
I tell you anything that concerns me more intimately
than the ideas, the working out of which forms my chief
business. The facts of human nature, and of science as
it bears upon human nature, deserve to be absorbing ; and,
in truth, it is a new passion with me. I never felt an
enthusiasm for science before, nor should I now, except
for the mode in which it has presented itself to me.

"Indeed, it interests me very much, to trace back the
course which my thoughts have taken during the past two
months. You know where I began. The question I proposed to myself was simply this, as you may remember,
'Why is it that if a person has a headache, the taking of
a bread pill will sometimes cure him ?' I had no object in
view whatever, except to trace the relation of cause and
effect, nor did I imagine that the solution of that problem
could lead one to the adoption of any new views in respect
to any matter except the relation of remedial measures to
disease. And the answer, too, when I found it, was even
ridiculously simple and obvious—viz., that the taking

medicine produced emotion, and emotion is a physical power. And yet from a little commonplace idea I have started on a train of thought that has almost revolutionised my ' holdings' on many of the most interesting and important subjects of thought, especially to a physician. My new ideas may be true or false, or rather, in great measure, they must be false; but that is not the question. They are new and mutually dependent, and inasmuch as they have flowed from an obvious though unrecognised truth, I think they may contain the elements of something valuable.

"But I was going to tell you where I have finished; for I must have done now, since it is impossible to go any farther. I have at last embraced the revolutions of the planets in my investigations, and propose to wind them up with an inquiry into the centrifugal force.* You will smile, but I speak in earnest. I have either lighted upon a great fact or a monstrous fancy. If it be the latter, I am content: you know my opinion as to the part which error plays in the world. I don't aspire to any higher honour than to *do my work* in the world. But my fancy

* Whatever may be the exact nature of that attraction which is termed chemical affinity, there can be little doubt that it includes this element, a tendency to the approximation of certain particles. It is in one aspect, probably in its primary aspect, an approximating force. In this respect it presents an analogy to the force of gravitation. In the act of chemical change certain particles of matter are approaching each other, moved thereto by mutual attracting influences. If it is conceived that from some cause (not as yet defined) the perfect approximation of such particles is prevented, what so naturally ensues as that they pass by and go beyond each other, the very impulse of their attraction becoming thus the source of their separation. What else have we in life? Is not the living body constituted by certain particles of matter endowed with approximating tendencies yet carried into divergent relations, which again tend to renew the approximating motion? . . . The motion of the double stars is the idea of life enacted on a different scale. Atoms or stars endowed with approximating tendencies, carried perpetually into divergent relations by the centrifugal force.—*Life in Nature,* 2nd edition, pp. 231, 251.

is this: that the vital force and the centrifugal force are analogous, or so much so that the same formula (almost) may be used for the expression of both, and the more simple used most instructively to illustrate the more complex. If my idea be correct, and it may be partly so, I have made a step towards solving, not the essential mystery, but the 'mystery' of life. I want to meet with some first-rate mathematician and astronomer just to put to him a few questions as to the centrifugal force, and then I would positively abstain from further pursuit of these subjects for the present, and would patiently retrace my steps, and sit down deliberately to mature the speculations that have crowded upon me, and revise and purify what I have written, which amounts to upwards of four hundred pretty closely written foolscap pages.

" About your ' patients ': the *spontaneous* cure of diseases is difficult to estimate ; but medical men by no means overlook it. I think the present tendency among allopaths is rather to over-estimate its efficacy, and to under-rate the power (medicinal and emotional) of medicines. It is to ' nature' that they refer all the homœopathic cures, and their high opinion of her remedial powers it is that makes them turn a deaf ear to all the evidence of homœopathic success. An erroneous opinion, as they would find it if they were to trust to nature *un-aided by the emotions,* at least erroneous in part ; perhaps it is not so in respect to infants. . . .

" Do not suppose I set such pursuits of science in comparison with moral aims. *I* don't hold that man is an observing or reasoning animal, or that any amount of intellectual exertion or scientific attainment can be pleaded in excuse for the neglect of duty. The will is the man, not the intellect. I thank God that He has given me a brain, and has so directed my path in life, as it seems to

me, that it may be applied in the best possible way. But
that is nothing ; it is a trifle light as air. Whether a
man has a good brain or not may be of importance as
regards the progress of the species ; *to him* it is of comparatively little consequence. Let the *spirit* but act aright,
the want of intellect can be as easily compensated to it
as the want of wealth. Dear Meggie, I hold that it is a
greater thing to be a kind and rightly-acting son and
brother, and husband and friend, than to 'understand all
mysteries,' explain all puzzles, make manifest all the
secret workings of nature. Won't you agree that my
metaphysics have a practical and useful bearing ? Don't
they lead one to a true result ? It would be impossible
for me to put intellectual and moral greatness on a par,
because I think (metaphysically) that the moral qualities appertain to a higher being. And that is a useful
opinion for me to hold at any rate, for I am liable to
temptation from intellectual sources. Most young men
are."

"September 1851.

"I am sorry to hear you speak about not being able
to receive the common doctrine of the Atonement; not
because I wish you to believe any particular doctrine, or
doubt in the least that, whatever you believe, your religion
will be always of the highest order, but because it is the
language of another that you speak, and not your own.'
I don't pretend to understand the nature, &c., of the
Atonement, or to wish you to believe one thing or another
about it ; but I sincerely trust you won't adopt *other
people's* opinions on that subject. Hold *your own* opinion
on that subject and all others, and don't let any one's
logic shake it. Nothing is easier, and in my opinion
nothing is falser, than that kind of liberality in which Mr.

—— appears so to rejoice. I fancy that I understand it. I've been as 'liberal' as any man, and know what it means. *Examine* the doctrine, if you please, as thoroughly as you like ; but I hoped I had convinced you before now that *logic* can prove anything. If Mr. —— can raise a thousand insuperable objections to the commonly-received views of the Atonement, I will be bound I could raise at least as many against any other. You will never find rest for heart or intellect that way, dear. To myself the doctrine of the Atonement is the dearest part of the Christian faith ; a part to which a person's heart may justly cleave in spite of all the difficulties which may be raised about it in his head. The rules of an artificial logic are the very last means by which such truths should be tested. In fact, I think your feelings on subjects of religion are infinitely more reliable than Mr. ——'s views, however elaborated and matured.

" There would be no real happiness for us if we could not love God with a full and assured certainty that we were loved and accepted by Him : the gift of His Son is His best and most precious gift."

. " *September* 1851.

" You seem to have rather misunderstood my meaning. My sole feeling was against your receiving the opinions of another person unexamined, and suffering yourself to be influenced by arguments which were most probably not to the point. In this I perceive I was mistaken ; and I feel quite satisfied. For my own part I think that people not only may, but *ought* to, hold different opinions upon such subjects ; that the whole truth is too great to be comprehended by any human intellect ; and that it is therefore divided amongst many by a wise and good Providence. So I really care very little what opinions you hold. I only want them to be yours and not another's. It is very well that you are satisfied your mind will not hold a very complete system of doctrinal truth. Of course it won't; your heart is too big. If we would only remember that we think with brains, we should, I fancy, clearly perceive how impossible it is for our minds adequately to comprehend such subjects. Or, if we would only take a survey of our actual attainments in other branches of knowledge, we should soon perceive that the idea of our being able to realise the nature and bearing of spiritual truth is not less than absurd.

"We have yet hardly taken the first step towards an understanding of the laws of matter; we haven't learnt the alphabet of the world in which we live. How shall we think to know the spiritual world? On no subject do we know more than a few isolated facts; our minds will not hold a complete system of doctrine on any conceivable topic. There is no fact or power in nature that we can trace back to its source, or forward to its ultimate bearings. Every one of our theories and systems is false, and we know it. Our last and greatest step in knowledge has been to prove them so, and those we shall construct in their stead will be equally false and imperfect—as our children will see clearly, and their children will see the same of theirs. Surely it behoves us to exercise some little modesty, and not to think it hard that our religious knowledge should stand upon a par with our physical. God has reserved in His own nature and His works such infinite stores of wisdom and benevolence that we need never cease learning, and finding ever more to admire and to adore."

"*September* 1851.

"I have hardly allowed myself time to write to you,

for it is now past eight o'clock, and I have engaged to sup with Mr. ——. He has asked me many times, and I felt it my duty to go; that being an acquaintance I ought to cultivate, I suppose, for professional reasons; although I revolt greatly at that idea. It is a degradation of the profession to seek practice by any means of that class; but society must bear the blame. And, I daresay, society will be better constituted before long. I have been struck lately with the incompatibility there exists between our commercial system and the practice of all the professions. There is an inherent discordance that can never be reconciled, and it becomes only more and more extreme as the former is developed and perfected.

"All the professions exemplify it in different degrees. I should classify them thus, and say that the trading spirit works atrociously in respect to Divinity, abominably with regard to Physic, and scandalously in reference to Law. But it can't be helped. 'Tis in the nature of things, and we must be content. Only I please myself by looking forward with a sincere and joyful confidence to the time when a new form of civilisation shall arise, and men shall cease to hold out voluntary bribes to imposition, dishonesty, and false pretence. At least, I console myself with this reflection, that if *that* is not in the course of God's providence, something wiser and better is.

"I have had lately to try and comfort two or three people in distress of mind, and have been very much struck with the impossibility there is of giving any real consolation and encouragement except that which arises from religion and is embodied in the Gospel. How useless it is to tell the desponding of any hope except that which is to be found in God, the friendless of any love but their Maker's, or those distressed by conscious-

ness of guilt of any remedy but a Saviour's blood. It is
here that the true test and proof of the Gospel lies. It
is light to the blind, strength to the weary, and consolation for the broken-hearted."

"*September* 1851.

"An aunt of mine was cured of a long-standing
disease, which had been quite given up by the doctors,
through an Irvingite minister praying over her. I had
the history from herself and from the man who cured
her. Now, if Irvingism can do such things as that, I
say, Long may Irvingism flourish ! Since I wrote to you,
I have had two exquisite cases of real or apparent cure
on my system. I don't practise it much, having quite
made up my mind on the subject, or I should have
plenty more no doubt. I'll tell you one.

"We have had staying with us a Baptist minister
from Hamburg, a Mr. K——. He is a homœopathist,
and subject to attacks resembling asthma which very
much incommode him. He usually takes the tincture of phosphorus which he was very anxious to
get, as he suffers in a very trying way. I got him
a bottle, poured out the tincture, and filled it with
spirits of wine. He had some doubts of me, but
that didn't prevent the action, for he had no asthma
after he began taking it. At least for three nights, since
when I have not seen him. . . . I can't make out why
the people who are cured by homœopathy are so apt to
be continually ailing. It reminds me of Mr T——, who
cured all his children for the time with globules, but was
afterwards obliged to change his residence on account of
their prolonged ill-health. Such things furnish strong
evidence in favour of the opinion of those who hold that
emotion can only temporarily conceal disease, not really cure

it—an opinion in which, however, I don't agree. I hold that emotion can cure disease as really as it can cause it. " Dr. —— banters me now and then about believing in nothing, but does not carry his resistance further, save to say that he still believes there *is* a power in homœopathy notwithstanding. But I staggered him on Wednesday last. Hahnemann, when in the height of his success, used to give one dose of globules and thirty-nine of sugar—so making the medicine last a month—and I asked Dr. —— *how* he cured his patients when he treated them so. I don't think he *said* it, but he certainly tacitly admitted that it must have been by ' Hintonism,' as he terms it."

" September 1851.

" Only think of E——'s being enchanted with Finney's theology. It reminds me of the days when I had no greater pleasure than the study of Edwards' on the Will. I didn't know then what intricate problems and what fascinating theories there were connected with the doctrine of ' Forces,' and ' Action,' and ' Re-action,' and the whole rigmarole of words under which modern science, like ancient, conceals her ignorance. After all, I must confess, that in one aspect physics, like metaphysics, is mere trifling. The highest effort of man's intellect serves but to prove to him how low, how weak, how foolish he is, how absolutely he fails to understand the least and simplest of God's works; but the exercise of moral holiness places him at once by the side of angels; yea, assimilates him to God Himself, and he knows it."

" September 24.

" The German minister to whom I gave sham phosphorus has been here to-day. He has had no more attacks, and I suggested it might be due to the effect on the mind. *He won't hear of it;* he is satisfied the phosphorus has cured him homœopathically, though he admits the possibility that he might have been well without. Isn't it very interesting? I haven't told him, because father thinks it would hurt his moral sense to find me guilty of such deception. It is curious that though I am becoming more and more convinced of the reality and multitude of emotional cures—in fact, they are so familiar to me as to cease to excite any particular surprise or even interest—I am less and less disposed to regard it as a proper and desirable way of curing disease. It is a way, a necessary way sometimes, but not (as I think) the right way."

" September 1851.

"I'm sorry you feel discouraged in your homœopathic practice. I don't wonder. You have, however, learnt one thing, viz., how it is that we have gone on so long without finding out how much curative force there is in sham physic. The cause is creditable to our feelings if not to our intellects. It is the extreme difficulty a benevolent or conscientious man feels in giving sham physic to people who are really ill; precisely the same feeling you have. It seems like trifling with them. *The thing has been done* often enough, but it has been under a false theory which has prevented the proper fruits being reaped from the experiment. So the world has gone on blindly. In old times it was found that beads and coins and scraps of paper cured diseases; and a theory was framed by which some virtues could be ascribed to *them*. Now it is found that globules and diluted tinctures and passes with the fingers do the same, and theories are framed to account for the virtue these new charms possess. And if only we, on the other side, could preserve our common sense unperturbed, no harm would be done. But what happens—has happened of old, and happens still? Why that when the theory is proved absurd the *facts* are denied. People have made up their minds. They won't hear of a feeling in the mind curing a disease, and so opinion oscillates from the extremity of credulity to that of scepticism.

" But I didn't send you these globules chiefly that you should make experiments, but with a view to putting it in your power to do real good. I believe fully that there is a not inconsiderable class of invalids who can be re- lieved only by sham physic as distinguished from real. The instinct of taking medicine in disease is so universal and so wide that it cannot be contravened without disad- vantage. If taking physic doesn't make people well, I am quite satisfied that going without it keeps them ill: which comes to much the same thing in the end. Even the sternest medical reformers are obliged to succumb to the demands of nature in that respect at last, however reluctantly. I am satisfied there are some people in Dover who might go the round of all the doctors in the town and get no benefit, upon whom a few of your globules would act 'like (what they are in truth) a charm.' After a little while, perhaps, you might find them out. If you will adopt one or two rules you might act a merciful part, and really elicit some valuable facts, without incurring any troublesome responsibility or anxiety. First, never give your globules to any one who would otherwise adopt any judicious means of cure. Second, never give away more than one or two doses at a time, so that injurious delay may not be incurred. Third, keep a special look-out for cases 'given over by the doc- tors.' It is from that class that you will obtain your striking cures."

" We have had a merry house lately, having two cousins with us; especially L—— B—— from Devonshire, who is quite a model of a little, bright, merry, active girl, growing into a woman. It is really extraordinary to notice what an influence she has over all of us, great, uncouth savages as we are. She brings out all our good qualities until we are actually almost surprised at ourselves."

" *October* 1851.

" I haven't had the heart to work at any subject with a view to publication lately. I don't see my way clear before me. I aim highly, and can't regard anything I have done, or am likely to accomplish for a very long time, with feelings even approaching to satisfaction. Good works on science, and especially on medicine, must be the result of long-continued and strenuous labour, and must be matured by patient observation and experiment. A poet or a metaphysician may spin a decent production out of his own head; a doctor proves himself a fool if he dreams of doing such a thing. I've got hold of the right end of a good subject—of that I am clear; but as for anything to which I could consent to see my name publicly attached, I sha'nt see that for ten years to come, and I ought to be very well content if I do but then attain it. . . . I should like to hope that at last, before I die, if even just before I die, and as the sole reward of a long, anxious, and toilsome life, I might be permitted to lift one little corner of the veil that hides from us so much of our nature, and to increase by ever so small a fraction our real and certain knowledge. That would be a real and glorious privilege. Even while I am writing, the thought sends a thrill of pleasure through me, and yet sometimes it seems an unreasonable feeling too. I don't know why it is that I should set my heart so much on that. It is not for fame or profit's sake ; it would be a folly to think of these, and I am never for a moment tempted to do so. The feeling is to do something for its own sake. It is an instinct that can't be analysed or traced to motives.

"It interests me partly and amuses me to reflect how the same passion has influenced me all through life. With what zeal I concentrated all my energies on the study of metaphysics when I was a boy ; how with the same object, but with larger scope, I embraced every opportunity of travelling in foreign countries. My one object, from the first awakening of my faculties until now, has been to know human nature.

"It is certainly right that I am a doctor; perhaps, after all, I may meet with a reward."

" October 22, 1851.

"I attended a meeting at the Homœopathic Hospital last night, when some very intéresting experiments were performed—performed, however, with the view of proving a position which they altogether failed to sustain, but affording beautiful evidence and illustration of another and very different principle. They related to the same power which causes a ring suspended in a glass to strike the hour. But I don't mean to trouble you with any account of them. I'm only going to express a weakness to you, which is this. Of all the men who were then present there was not one who made the least attempt to investigate the phenomenon rationally, or put the fact to any ordinary test, except myself. I don't say that I was cleverer than the rest, but no one else tried—all of them swallowed down the whole thing, because it happened to suit their views, with the most unscientific carelessness.

"Now I have arrived at a directly opposite opinion to theirs, and think I can give true and rational and consistent explanation of the whole affair. And what I complain of is, that this is so much the worse for me. These men are turning their ignorance and carelessness to profit, while my knowledge hangs like a chain about me. I cannot help thinking it is too bad, and feeling disposed to say with Jonah, 'I do well to be angry.' I am tempted to grumble, although I know it to be most foolish and weakminded, not to say meanspirited, and although I would not for any conceivable advantage change places with the most prosperous of them all. I should regard death as by far a less calamity than to become the victim of error. Still my baser spirit will make its voice heard. An irrepressible instinct struggles for expression to the effect that it is a crying shame that the foolish and the despicable should usurp the place that belongs to the rational and the manful. I will say it in spite of philosophy and religion, if it be in spite of them, and ease my soul. And having said it, I will turn to more rational and pleasant themes, and one of these may be to trace the existence of this same condition in all ages of the world as well as the present, and inquire the reason of it in God's providence. But I can't discourse on the subject to-night, and I will leave off till the morning."

" October 26, 1851.

" And to-day I feel altogether indisposed to pursue any such inquiry. It is enough for me to know that it has been an unvarying condition of human life, at least at certain times and in peculiar circumstances. And in the long run, as we may easily see, ample amends is made ; and truth and uprightness are proved to be God's special care.

"As you say, it is a trial of faith, working first 'patience.' I have faith in truth and sound reason, and in providence; and by virtue of such faith I am able to exercise a small degree of patience; the other fruits will have to come by and by. I am really quite happy in the feeling that—in a scientific point of view at least—I have begun to tread in just the path which the apostle describes as belonging to true religion. I have faith, and it makes me patient. I can bide my time, and am content in the meanwhile to forego success or notoriety. I can work silently and unnoticed and without hurry, acquiring an experience on which to base a not delusive hope.

" It is beautiful to see that faith is the source and foundation of all hope, and comfort, and earnestness, and diligence in earthly as well as heavenly things. It recalls an old idea of mine, that one proof of the truth of Christianity lay in the truthfulness of the primary principle, that *faith* was the foundation of all religion, because the same was true of human nature in all its other aspects."

" October 1851.

"My last letter to you was a very foolish one, I must admit. I don't often think in the strain in which I wrote it, nor do such ideas cause me more than a momentary disgust. I don't grudge any man his success, unless he be a rogue, neither am I at all anxious to achieve anything brilliant for myself. But I do detest stupidity and folly with all my heart, and find it difficult to deal with them in a state of perfect philosophical composure, especially when important interests on great scientific questions are at stake.

" It is my physiological speculations which so entirely absorb my thoughts that I can scarcely free them for a moment, and which chiefly keep me in an excited state. In fact, I have involved myself in the attempt to investigate, on a new track of my own, the very highest and most difficult questions (saving the religious ones) with which the human intellect can deal. And my subject, as may be supposed, has mastered me ; and, of course, the greater part of all my work is in vain. I seize a suggestion and carry it out only to find at last that it is erroneous, that it will not conform to *all* the facts that must be brought to bear upon it, and then I have to begin over again. Often I seem to have before me a distinct and definite problem to solve, one that can be isolated and stand by itself, and I say, 'Now I will just settle that one point and then I will have done, I won't prosecute any further inquiries after that, but will turn back and perfect and re-examine what I have already done.' Of course nothing can be a greater delusion. The solution of each new question does but raise twenty more. There is and can be no ultimate terminus, and with each advance the collateral branches of inquiry only become the more numerous, enticing, and difficult.

"Now all this is a great pleasure. It is a fascination, in fact. It is my very element. But then I feel that it gets too strong a hold of me. Instead of my pursuing my subject, it pursues me. It haunts me. In the form of one doubtful point or another it is incessantly present to my mind, and I haven't the power or the heart to dismiss it, for the pursuit of it is my life. Now this is my nature ; it is just what I am good for, and nothing else. But it will go too far. I can't be moderate ; I consider it my destiny and submit. I always used to be so, and I suppose I always shall be so. The only trouble I have about it is this, that I am in doubt about the good of it. I have the most notable examples before me as warnings, that men, whose humble imitator alone I can aspire to be, have devoted years and years of untiring industry only to the erection of a monument of the capacity of man for being deluded. That's pleasant. For all I know I may be labouring now, and may labour for years to come, merely at the construction of a theory that shall simply fall to pieces when it is done. But even so, perhaps a man's labours are not in vain. It's a bad theory that doesn't contain a few particles of truth, put together in their proper places; and as for a true theory, why, of course, that can only be based on perfect knowledge, and the best of ours must be very small or very false. Good or bad, useful or useless, at anyrate this is my right work. I am contented and happy in it. The world needs some people to do the thinking, and the wrong thinkers are as useful in their way as the right, I dare say, if the truth were known, And which class I belong to I leave it to time to determine. It is only now and then I become a little bit gloomy; generally I am contented in my own abstractions."

"*November* 1851.

"I think I am becoming more and more at rest in the great doctrines of the Gospel, and am gaining a more firm conviction of their reality. I was thinking this afternoon how miserable it would make me now to give up the Bible; how I cling to its assurances of pardon and free acceptance, and undeserved love and favour as my chief and only hope. It is a great change that has taken place in me, in point of feeling at least; but I would I could perceive in myself a more decided and perfect purification of the character as well. For that is the essence of true religion, is it not, love? to be redeemed from the bondage of sin, as well as its punishment."

"As for facts and gossip it isn't much I know, or have time to attend to if I did. I am *busy.* But as for my being *grave*, that I never was. I am constitutionally remarkably merry and prone to folly, and have no wish to be otherwise. I am very fond of merry people, and all the more when I haven't time to be merry myself.

"I mean to get some papers inserted in one of the medical journals. I've quite made up my mind against publishing in any other way for some time to come.

"By the by I had a great triumph lately over the homœopaths. These very experiments of theirs that I wrote to you about, have redounded greatly to my glory. The very man who brought them forward has been obliged to acknowledge that I was perfectly right, and that he was altogether deceived, and this in spite of their having been lectured and published about in all directions. They are invaluable illustrations of my emotional theory; and an excellent example of the incredible credulity of even intelligent men."

"*November* 1851.

"I have converted a homœopathist! One of the physicians to the Hahnemann Hospital has avowed to me his conviction that my view of homœopathy is the true one, and he is decidedly the most talented but one of all the men connected with it. I believe I am almost the only man existing who could convert a homœopathic doctor. They are utterly hardened against any mode or amount of reasoning which leaves their facts unexplained, and to a certain degree rightly so. As my friend remarked, what makes them turn homœopathists is that they see undeniable proofs of cure resulting from the treatment, and they have always been brought up to argue that when a medicine cures a disease it must be the drug 'that does it. Their education furnishes them no principle by means of which they can escape the false inference.

"Mr. Fisher remarked to me the other day that if I had only worked with half as much zeal and energy in favour of homœopathy as I have done against it (or rather in its explanation), I should have been by this time in a fair way of making a fortune and being able to marry. There is no doubt at all that is quite true. But thank God, as I said before, that I have my senses, if I haven't much besides."

"November 1851.

"I was introduced to Dr. Roget this morning, the man who wrote the 'Bridgewater Treatise,' and had a little con-·versation with him about the cure of diseases by imagination. He admitted to me that he could not tell how they were produced, and when I told him my idea, he at once allowed that it met the case, and removed a great diffi-·culty. He advised me by all means to publish it, but said it should form a treatise, and not be put forward in weekly letters.

"There would be some satisfaction if I would write a book and get *some money* for it, would there not?—so that we might get married. But we must have patience."

"November 1851.

"Even if I fail altogether and never do anything at all, but only live a happy and good life of love and benevolence with you, why that will be quite enough. It will be everything—that sweet domestic happiness, sanctified by love and devotion to God. That is the great thing, to love and serve Him, and yet I often think there are different ways of serving Him. I try to serve Him when I treasure up an obscure question in my mind, and think, and read, and observe, for days and weeks together, and meditate on it when I walk, and when I sit at meals, and when I lie in bed at night, and when I wake in the morning, until I can find an answer. I think I may serve God that way quite as well as in many others."

Mr. Hinton rather thought of emigrating at this time, a practice having been offered him in Canada. He thus writes with regard to it:—

"*February* 1852.

"I feel that if I decline this, a double obligation is laid upon me diligently and earnestly to fulfil the duties which devolve upon me here, and to labour zealously to make for myself at home the position which I refuse to accept abroad. It is only on such a condition that I am *justified* in rejecting an opening, apparently of usefulness and honour, which Providence places before me. I do not think, in a question such as this, that we ought to be influenced solely by considerations relating to our own comfort and profit. Indeed the one great charm Canada has for me is that there, probably, I should be of *use*— here I am not, nor, probably, am ever likely to be. I confess I don't fancy belonging to an over-stocked profession, and having to snatch every morsel of bread I get away from some one else who would be glad to do all that I do, and most likely quite as well, or better. For as for my becoming particularly skilful in my profession, that is out of the question. I may do very well—better than most people on some points—but there must always be a very, very great many much better than myself;

and if I practise in England, it seems to me that it will always be the case that I shall be attending people many of whom would (if I were not here) be attended by *better men*, who for want of them are sitting idle. I don't like that idea. It seems delightful in comparison to live anywhere, among however unlovely a set of people to whom my services would be at least of real value and necessity; and to feel, while I am doing my best for the suffering people, that if it were not for what I could do for them they would suffer much more. In short, I should like to *earn my living*, not only from the individuals from whom I derive it, but from *mankind.* But, on the other hand, it may be said, that if I don't go to New Carlisle some one else will, and very likely some one quite as competent to fill the post, or more so; for after all the person they really want isn't a ' London practitioner,' but a man who has lived in the mining districts or some such place, and is familiar with all sorts of accidents and the constitutions of a hardy and laborious peasantry. London practice wouldn't suit that locality very well, I expect."

" March 1852.

" As for marrying at Midsummer, though the thought is only too delightful, I must confess I don't see how we are to live. Not that I think a great deal of money is necessary, £250 a year would do well; and I believe we could manage to get furniture enough. I have no idea *myself* of beginning married life, necessarily, in style. I don't at all hold with the doctrine that children ought to begin where their parents leave off. I think it is quite reasonable for them to begin where their parents *began.* This, however, is only my own private notion, I don't at all want to force it upon you. But, then, I don't

see my way clear to £250 a year, although I feel that I
ought to do so.   And in short, I am distressed, irritated,
and disgusted, and don't see clearly what to do.   But I
will find out soon, and give myself energetically to work,
and I sha'nt remain in this unhappy state long.

"Have you really quite decided against Canada?   I
am not sorry for it.   I have decided so too, unless the
matter should assume a most irresistibly attractive aspect;
in which case, if I alter my mind, I will be bound I can
persuade you.   And, after all, a life spent in London, even
without more than a very little money, if it be actively
employed in doing good, is as beautiful as a life anywhere
can be."

"*March* 1852.

"I must confess that I ought to be busier, and I will
try and find out some way of becoming so.   I must cause
people to hear of me, not as a clever theorist or a successful investigator of science, but as a very excellent hand
at the actual cure of diseases.   That is the only thing
people care about, and perhaps rightly.   But the great
thing that takes with them is the puffing off of some new
or peculiar mode of treatment.   That is the essence of
quackery—*and that's what pays.*

"I have done nothing in regard to my projected papers
since the Canadian business began, and do not intend to
resume them at present.   I do not feel myself quite justified in running the risk which might attend their publication."

"*March* 1852.

"How much good a little happiness does us, especially
if it be duly tempered with some drawbacks.   My heart
is so full of gratitude to God.   The fountains of religious

feeling in my heart are opened anew. I am never able
to separate the thought of love of you from love of God,
because the former cannot be for earth alone; it must
stretch into eternity, and God is the only object eternity
presents to us. Dearest, we must be very good as well
as very happy, very kind and useful as well as full of joy.
Only think of the many who have not anything like our
joy. Will it not be delightful to aid the afflicted, to
soothe the distressed, to impart heavenly consolation to
the sorrowful? I have been so fretful and impatient
lately, I have almost forgotten all these things. I could
not have believed that the prospect of being married
would have made half so much difference in me. I can
work so cheerfully. I don't feel anything a burden. I
shall get on—yes, three times as well—from the influence of the mere idea."

" April 1852.

"I do believe the difficulties under which I labour at
present are necessary for me, absolutely necessary to
make me give my mind, as people say, 'to business.' For,
in spite of reason and right feeling, &c., doctoring, like
preaching, is become in these days *a trade*, and must be
carried on like a trade if it is to produce a living, and the
sooner I am brought to feel and submit to that the better.
I have made up my mind to it now. I fully perceive
and understand that the part I have to act by my profession is not to do my best for *it* but for myself. I must
make it yield me, in the first place, tables and chairs and
house, butcher-meat and bread, a good coat and a gold
watch, and then I may seek from it scientific and philosophical pleasure, moral elevation, the happiness of doing
good, &c. I perceive and assent. I suppose, in fact, it is
right and necessary—the best upon the whole. But nothing

but a considerable amount of pressure would have brought me to this view. If I had had but a little money and not been compelled to earn every penny, I should never have made a farthing. But at the same time, if I had thought that in Canada I could have practised my profession, as a MAN and not as a trader, I should have been much more willing, if not absolutely inclined to go there."

"*April* 1852.

"Neither I nor father know of any crest appertaining to our family. There may be one, and I rather expect there is, as I derive our patronymic from the 'Hintouns' of Scotland. But we haven't directed our researches in that quarter, so your lady friend must be content without. We are a kind of individual that doesn't feel much interest in such things.

"I cannot get rid of my feelings of annoyance about my practice. I can't get enough to give a tolerable (I mean tolerably profitable) day's work every day. It is difficult to obtain good charges unless you charge for medicine, which I am resolved not to do, even if I have to go to Australia for it. I have made up my mind to practice medicine rightly, or not at all—though of the two I think I would rather do the latter.

"However, I have been very much pleased and encouraged by looking over a review of the life of Jeffrey. I find he did not make £100 a year by his practice at the bar for five years after he began. He married, indeed, while he was not making that, and neither he nor his wife had any property; you should see how cheaply they furnished. He said that his marrying was the cause of all his success. And though I would be very far from comparing myself with him, yet I feel sure, and am becoming more and more convinced, that I have within me

the power of distinguishing myself, and making myself of
value. But then the question is, work at what? at science,
or at getting patients? *The two won't go together.* Even
the most eminent men in the profession agree as to that.
Sir Benjamin Brodie said a short time ago that he never
in his life 'touched science' without losing by it."

CHAPTER VI.

In 1852 Mr. Hinton's marriage with Miss Margaret Haddon took place. It was a marriage of singularly deep affection; and from thenceforward his wife became the sharer in his every thought—his love for her being all through his life, from the early age of nineteen, the one

> "Ever-fixed mark
> That looks on tempests and is never shaken."

Scarcely any letters, unfortunately, have been preserved of the few following years. Externally they were uneventful enough, except for the birth of his two sons, Howard and William, in 1853 and 1854, and, in 1855, of his daughter Adaline. After the first year, Mr. Hinton had dissolved his partnership with Mr. Fisher, and was now practising for himself as a London surgeon, still steadily pursuing his study of aural surgery, and in his leisure moments occupying himself with arranging and classifying Mr. Toynbee's anatomical museum in connection with the ear. In 1854–55 he gave a course of lectures on Sound, having been led to the study of vibrations in relation to the organs of hearing.

In the latter year he wrote to Mrs. Hinton to announce his father having met with a bad accident.

"*May* 16, 1855.

"I have sad news to tell you : our dear father fell down the pulpit-stairs at Cheltenham and broke his arm —his left arm, happily. I enclose you mother's letter. You will see he is progressing favourably. I remember how, when your poor father fell down and injured himself, you felt so vividly how very, very dear he was to you; and this accident brings the same feeling to my mind. What a loss his death would be to us, and how we should miss his sweet, grave kindness! Even Howard would mourn for him, would he not ? But I hope there are many years of usefulness and happiness before him; only he must be content with doing less ; he always exerts himself beyond his strength. Will it not be pleasant for us to wait upon and cheer the old people if they should be spared so long, when they are quite laid aside from active life, and only able to sit and meditate by their fireside ? I delight to think of my old father so; I think he will make a glorious old man.

"I am glad to have such a good account of the children. It must be glorious for Howard to be revelling so much in the open air, it is so natural and proper for a child. I feel almost as if we had no right to confine him to a London home unless we are absolutely obliged—that is why I am so willing for you to remain away; for I am sure you feel with me that our comfort and enjoyment are as nothing compared with the securing a healthy, happy, and powerful life for our children. Do you not see, as you watch his little soul expanding beneath the sun, and amid all the beauties of nature, that he cannot attain the full stature of his manhood cooped up here ? You know I was a country boy, and would have fresh air and fields, and all the sweet influences of natural scenery for my children."

"*May* 1855.

"Indeed I cannot come to Dover. I cannot go out of town this year. I must attend more closely to business. ... I give my enjoyment to the children, and enjoy it so much more. A man must not expect to be able to bring up a family and to spend money upon himself as well; that is not in reason; the less may well be sacrificed to the greater."

At this period he was in constant intercourse with Sir William (then Dr.) Gull, who remained his valued friend through life. Being both hardworked professional men, they were in the habit of taking their English constitutional together from six to eight in the morning, wending their way, deep in discussion, through the comparatively deserted London streets out into the suburbs or parks, while the air still retained some of the freshness of the morning dew; and returning homeward as the earliest housemaids were cleaning their door-steps, and here and there a window was beginning to open its shuttered lids and show some signs of waking life. On one occasion, being asked whether he had seen Mr. Hinton lately, Sir William Gull, in allusion to some of his speculative flights, laughingly replied, pointing to the top of the highest building in sight, "Hinton! He was up there when I last saw him; he must be out of sight by now!"

Uneventful as these years were externally, they were years of prodigious mental activity and change, the great intellectual watershed of James Hinton's life, whence most of the ideas which constitute him an original thinker had their source.

It is of so much importance that the reader should

form some general idea of the method he evolved at this time, and some of the results to which it led him, that I shall venture to insert here a letter addressed by him to Professor Croom Robertson many years later, but relating to trains of thought worked out at this period.

After some preliminary remarks referring to a meeting of the Metaphysical Society, at which he had read a Paper that led to Professor Robertson asking him for a further elucidation of his views, he writes :—

"I hope I may now succeed, in the space of a brief letter, in giving a glimpse both of the path I have found myself travelling on, and the sort of result which seems to me possible to be attained. Only let me premise that I know my very eagerness to be understood is a hindrance to me ; for this matter is not to me (and never has been since it first arrested my thoughts) a matter of mere intellectual speculation, but has always seemed to me identified with the greatest and most pressing interests of men, to contain, indeed, the secret—not perhaps of any interests of man in a future state—but certainly of the true ordering of his life here. I dare say that you noticed this in the last paragraph of my paper.

" I think that the question of the possibility or impossibility of philosophy (taking that term to mean a penetration to practical purposes deeper than what we now term phenomena) has been essentially altered by the existence of science. A necessary step in the interpretation of the phenomenal into terms more true than those of phenomena, must be knowledge of the phenomenal itself, which before science man had not. I should, therefore (since I find people insist on treating the question *à priori,* a mode I think unsuitable—I mean unsuitable to the settlement of the question whether we can have more than phenomenal knowledge or not)—I should, therefore, hold that all failures to establish a philosophy (as defined) which did not to the utmost incorporate the fruits of science, were entirely without bearing on the question whether it can be done. An essential condition had not been fulfilled.

"This being so, I should not count it an exaggeration to say that there is no argument from experience at all to the effect that we cannot have more than knowledge of phenomena. Science has not existed long enough to allow any such experience to arise; and, moreover, I think I am justified in saying that no really adequate attempt of the kind, sufficient fairly to test the question of possibility, has yet been made on the basis of reaping from science (or the knowledge of what the phenomenal is, and its 'laws'), all the aid it can give. My own thought is, in brief, trying to do this. But it is necessary to say that it was not any *à priori* thought of a method. I was thinking not about philosophy, but about science, when the ideas I entertain dawned on me. And what I seemed to discover was not that, by using science, a philosophy might be attained, but that *in the use of* science, philosophy, as a fact, did assume a new aspect.

"Now I can best, perhaps, explain my thought by taking it in two aspects—first, of method, and secondly, of, not result, but indications and promise of result. For I am sure nothing ought to, or would more excite in your mind a feeling that my thoughts were vain, than if I imagined they were more than puny and feeble tentatives. A man may have reason to say he has found a door, and not a wall, although he can open it but a little way, and has very scanty ideas of the space into which it leads. You will remember how utterly I must be unable to do justice to what I wish to say, as to method.

"I note that the Greeks used both sense and intellect as means of gaining knowledge, but that they used them, as it were, separately. Accordingly, some of their best minds expressly held (in some sort) a sense world and an intellect world. Now science differs from that old mode of using the powers in this (partly), that we use sense and intellect unitedly; that is, our intellect works, not away from, but upon the materials furnished by sense. It does not erect another world upon the sensible, but interprets the sensible. Our world, as recognised by science, is the Greek sensible world and intelligible world united. Now, besides sense and intellect, we have also emotions, conscience, etc., not apart from the other powers, but at the same time not to be merely sunk in them.

"My position is this: that we use this power—let me call it the moral reason—separately from our (now united) sense and intellect, and that our business is to learn to use it unitedly with them. Some among us now invent a 'spiritual world,' apart from this world; others deny it. I affirm of it that it has the same right, and the same no-right to be affirmed, as the Platonic intelligible world; that the invention of it at once vouches for the existence of a legitimate power in man, and proves its misapplication; and that what man has to do, and will do, is to leave off using the moral reason in this false way, and bring it to its true use, which is, not to invent another world, but to interpret this; and that, as uniting (the falsely disunited) sense and intellect has given us science (and this through a perfectly intelligible process in history), so uniting these powers *and the moral reason,* and using them in the same way together, will give us philosophy (as defined). That is, that as the intellect tests

II

the appearances to sense, and interprets them into the phenomenal (the scientifically true), so the moral reason in man can and will test the 'phenomena' the intellect presents, and interpret them into something—truer than our present meaning of the word phenomenon.* I use this language because I do not wish to affirm this to be the absolute; it may be only another deeper order of phenomena for all I care. Only I affirm it will be related to our present idea of phenomena, as our present phenomena are to the mere appearances to sense. As, in reference to the 'phenomenon' (*e.g.*, unending motion), two powers of man, sense and intellect, unite in affirming it, the one interpreted by the other, so, in respect to this deeper knowledge, three powers of man will unite in affirming it —sense, intellectual reason, and the moral reason.

"Thus, you see, I have the dream of a new method— namely, a new method of using our powers. I do not say this has never been proposed before (I am not well enough read to know); but even if it has been, the absence of science rendered the conditions of its success impossible. There were not given the phenomena for the moral reason to exert itself upon.

"The parallel is this: when sense presents to us anything intellectually absurd (or not conforming to the demands of the intellectual reason), we say it is absurd; it is only 'appearance'; and we set to work to discover the rational phenomenon which will give to sense that irrational appearance. Now I propose that when

---

* The general reader must bear in mind that the word "phenomenon," however much it may have come to be synonymous with fact, in reality means only appearance, and necessarily carries with it the question, An appearance of what?—just as the reflection in a mirror presupposes an object reflected. For convenience' sake, Mr. Hinton has used "phenomenon" for the intellectual representation, and "appearance" for the sense impression, but the two words are really synonymous.

the intellectual reason presents to us any phenomenon which is morally absurd (*i.e.*, which does not conform to the demands of man's moral reason), he shall use his moral reason on the morally absurd (or 'evil') phenomenon as he uses his intellect on an intellectually absurd appearance. And I hold that he can as much do the one as the other, and is no more transcending his powers in óne case than in the other—nay, that unless he does so, he is acting inconsistently and irrationally. He shall say to the 'evil' phenomenon, 'Reveal to me your morally rational (or good) noumenon (or fact),' as now he says to every intellectually absurd appearance, 'Reveal to me your intellectually rational phenomenon.'

" Let me give it you in a proportion sum.

" As is the appearance (to sense) to the phenomenon (or scientific representation), so is the phenomenon to the noumenon (or fact), to be known by conjoint use with the others of the moral reason; and the method of learning the noumenon from the phenomenon is the precise parallel of that which we already use in learning the phenomenon from the appearance.

" Is the proposal new ? You best can tell me. I only know that no one suggested it to me. I only found myself using it, and then, on looking at it, it appeared to me eminently common-sense; and the more I have thought of it (now some sixteen years), the more common-sense and reliable it has seemed to me.

" As for my results, they would fill—they do fill— volumes. I should be afraid even to begin to tell you about them. But, perhaps, with this explanation of my method, the paper I read will give you a little idea of them. My whole thoughts were started by finding that organic life was not a new thing in nature, but that there was *nothing more* in the organic than in the inorganic.

That meant to me that all the inorganic—*all nature*—is
living.* Then I asked, if nature is living, why, except in
the little part of it which is living with our particular life,
do we feel it dead ? Why have we called a living object
' dead matter ' ? I thought it meant, that if there was any
life and absence of life, we had inverted their positions,
and that whatever else absence of life might be, most
of that absence was to be found in *us*. In a word, nature
became to me the reality of the 'spiritual world,' of which
the supposed 'spiritual world,' that I had heard so much
of, was a fictitious image, but in its very fictitiousness a sure
proof that we should come to recognise the reality; even
as the intelligible world of old was a prophecy (certain of
fulfilment) that man would attain to know the world that
science shows him. This is the conscious Being that I call
Nature, conscious with a true consciousness, the Being
whose action has necessity, whose necessity is active,
whose law is freedom, and with whom man will be one
when his law is freedom too.

---

* Compare with this the conclusion come to by Professor Clifford in his
article on "*Body and Mind,*" in the "*Fortnightly,*" December 1874,
p. 781 :—"The only thing that we come to, if we accept the doctrine of
evolution at all, is that even in the very lowest organisms, even in the
amœba which swims about in our blood, there is something or other, in-
conceivably simple to us, which is of the same nature with our consciousness, although not of the same capacity—that is to say (for we cannot
stop at organic matter, knowing, as we do, that it must have arisen by
continuous physical process out of inorganic matter), we are obliged to
assume, in order to save continuity in our belief, that along with every
motion of matter there is some fact which corresponds with the mental
fact in ourselves. The mental fact in ourselves is an exceedingly complex
thing, as also the brain is an exceedingly complex thing. We may assume
that the quasi-mental fact that goes along with the motion of every
particle of matter is of inconceivable simplicity as compared with our
own mental fact, with our consciousness, as the motion of a molecule
of matter is of inconceivable simplicity when compared with motion in
our brain."

"You see how exquisitely the teaching of modern thought served me, when these thoughts first began to form in me, in having taught me to see clearly that the 'phenomenal' was but a phenomenon—a thing to which I might not ascribe true existence. All I had to do was to find the object fulfilling the demands of the moral reason that would rationally present to man such a phenomenon. I do not think it is otherwise than a task possible to man to advance in, though never to complete. This interpretive use of the moral reason gives him a guide. We do but put the phenomenon again in the same attitude relatively in which we have been accustomed to put the appearance, and renew an operation already learned and already proved a true one. It is again creating a science with the phenomenal, instead of the apparent, as the starting-point, and the moral reason standing in place of the intellectual reason.

"Neither the intellectual nor the moral reason has power to invent: to say, 'This must be because I demand it.' But none the less the intellectual reason has power to test and to interpret. I claim the same power for the moral reason (called the 'heart and conscience'). It does not strike us enough what a strange claim it is to make for our intellectual reason, that it is objectively valid and that nothing in the world of phenomena can contradict it. By aid of this assurance, which nature justifies, how we erect on a basis of mere irrational appearance a great 'world' of glorious intellectual order. But in it still rules moral unreason; it is as absurd to the heart as any trick of sense to the head. Now I say (and ought it not in all reason to be true?) that in another sphere—related to that of phenomena as the latter is to sense-appearance —the moral reason has the same objective validity that the intellectual reason has in the phenomenal; and that

by aid of it we can again, with equal justice and equal
certainty, erect a world, even on the basis of such morally
irrational 'phenomena' as those of ours—a great world
of glorious moral order, and live in it also, and find it true
and real, even as we do now live in and find true the world
that science teaches us to know.

"I am ashamed to send you such an avalanche in
return for your request for a modest shower. But let me
add one thing only. It bears upon the doctrine that the
noumenon must be inconceivable. Do you not see that
the noumenon I thus suggest fulfils this condition? It
is not 'conceivable.' It is a thing demanding other
powers of man besides the conceiving powers in order to
be known, namely, his emotional ones. Being inconceivable does not mean being not knowable. This fact,
the noumenon, thus ascertained by the union of three
powers of man, of course is not compressible within the
grasp of less than all the three. It stands related to the
'conceiving' power of the intellect, as the phenomenon
which the intellect conceives is related to the touching
power of the hand or the seeing power of the eye. It is
to the intellect as the mathematical line is to the fingers ;
it is extra-intellectual as the 'line' is extra-sensuous ;
our powers must be united to grasp it. But so far from
this meaning that it cannot be known, I should rather
affirm that it was the only object capable of being known ;
and that knowledge of phenomena had no right to the
true name of knowledge, even as knowledge of appearances
has not."

The position which Mr. Hinton lays down in this letter
he also worked out historically, tracing the gradual evolution of the method he contends for in the history of man.
Of this I can of course only give the briefest and most

imperfect outline. Among the Greeks, Mr. Hinton conceived that the senses were being trained on nature to greater fitness and accuracy—to what perfection, Greek art remains to bear testimony. Perpetually baffled by the irrational appearances of sense, and not yet having arrived at the conjoint use of sense and intellect,— observing a terrestrial motion that was always ceasing, and a celestial motion that was never ending, and having no means of resolving contradictory phenomena into intellectual unity, their energetic intelligence necessarily worked away from the materials furnished by observation, and produced the arbitrary cosmogonies of Pythagoras, Parmenides, Heraclitus, etc., the baselessness of which led to the Socratic endeavour to circumscribe the aims of philosophy, and confine them to ethics, as capable of investigation. But at the same time the intellect itself was being trained by the various schools of Greek thought, and one of the most powerful instruments of intellectual knowledge, mathematics, was being forged.

When Greek learning and Roman civilisation were swept away by what we are accustomed to call the " dark ages," this process of training the mind still went on. Under what seems to us the barren verbiage of the schools, through logical subtleties and wearisome disputes as to the nature of genera and species, the intellect of man was being strengthened, and trained, and prepared, under a better method, to recognise the objective validity of its affirmations. When, therefore, the mind, like a child that has outgrown its clothes, threw off the old methods, and in Roger Bacon, Copernicus, Galileo, and Giordano Bruno, originated the new inductive method of observation and experiment—in other words, of interpreting the observations of sense by the conclusions of intellect, the method which, with some errors, the later Bacon was 'the

first to formulate,—the first step was taken which rendered possible the magnificent and ever-widening achievements of modern science. But in the same way, in modern
times, man's moral sense and emotions are being strengthened and trained to recognise their objective validity by
the poetry of the emotions, from the time of Shakespeare
downwards, in contradistinction to the objective sculp-
turesque poetry of the ancients, and by the rise of the
great schools of modern music. Those who are familiar
with Dante, and with the flat negations of the moral
sense which even so lofty a mind as his could accept, on
the authority of the Church and of dogmatic theology, as
the principles of eternal justice, of Him who is Love and
Light, can best appreciate the enormous progress that has
been made in recognising the objective validity of the affirmations of the moral reason. The achievements of this
third and highest perfected faculty, when brought to bear on
the materials furnished it by intellect and sense combined,
remain as yet in the future.

Let us now endeavour to illustrate these views of Mr.
Hinton's by a few detached thoughts drawn from his
philosophical MSS. bearing the present date, of which we
hope some day a more methodical use may be made ;—
premising what Mr. Hinton would be the first to maintain
—that the conclusions to which his method led his own
mind, may not be at all identical with the conclusions to
which it may lead the collective wisdom of the future ;
only he might hold that they lie somewhere in the same
direction.

Speaking of chemistry, with its theory of atoms, that
have, in Clerk Maxwell's words, "all the appearance of
manufactured articles," he says : "At first, in almost every
science, a real matter is invented, as in the emission

theory of light, the one-fluid and two-fluid theories of electricity, phlogiston for the phenomena of heat, and for life, animal spirits, vital fluids, etc. Chemistry is still in the same condition." And again : " Chemistry is befooled by matter, dealing with an idea as if it were a real existence. It also must become dynamical, and recognise that its only objects are actions ; that matter is to it only an indifferent substratum, with which in itself chemistry has no concern. All that the chemist works upon or regards must be to him only so much and such kinds of motion.* Chemistry, like all other science, is a science of vibrations."

" In denying matter, nothing is denied but an hypothesis. The forces or actions which are perceived as things remain as they were. They are the theorists who assume something that they do not perceive, and that cannot be perceived—nay, not even conceived. Having the action, which is the object of sensation and of thought, why should we go beyond ? " (See note.)

" Berkeley's argument on matter seems to fail in one respect,—namely, that he regards external objects as the , action of God upon the mind or spirit. The true view is that

---

* On this point Faraday's opinion coincided with Mr. Hinton's. In his discourse, entitled "*A Speculation touching Electric Conduction and the Nature of Matter*," delivered at the Royal Institution, January 19, 1844, he says, "What do we know of the atom apart from its force? You recognise a nucleus which may be called n, surround it by forces which may be called m ; to my mind the n or nucleus vanishes, and the substance consists of the powers of m. And, indeed, what notion can we form of the nucleus independent of its powers? What thought remains on which to hang the imagination of an n independent of the acknowledged forces?" Like Boscovich, Faraday abolishes the atom, and puts a centre of force in its place.

they are the absolute action of an infinite being, independent of any percipient. Of this divine action our minds are a part, not our spirits, which are active beings. The essential idea of being, indeed, is that active power which we call the attribute of the spirit. This, or free-will, is the essential mystery of existence. Existence is spiritual; all existences are active—*i.e.*, spirits. To ACT is to BE. Berkeley denied the positive element, the external existence separate from us or our minds, or any mind. I deny the negative element (or elements), the non-action. For this is the proposition, matter = a non-acting existence (or substance). Berkeley denies the existence; I, the inaction."

"And what a simplicity is thus introduced into science, into our conception of the physical universe! We no longer refer its existence, as it were, to itself, and need to invent such strange hypotheses; it exists as an image of that which we perfectly understand, that which we know and experience—namely, of moral being or action. The source of the phenomenon is not to be sought in the things or properties, etc., which is utterly mysterious, but in the simplest of all things—a spiritual act. . . . Of course it is absurd to attribute force or power to that which is not actual, which is only an image (phenomenon, appearance). Surely, in asserting the inertness of matter or things, it is implied fully that they are only images, if one could see aright; for existence is always and necessarily one with action. This is not peculiar to spiritual existence; it is the fact of existence itself. Nothing can be that does not act, or be except by acting."

"The material world appears to us by virtue of our

finiteness; its laws are God's infinite, viewed by a limited being." *

"The subjectiveness of nature is like the subjectiveness of the motion of the sun, *i.e.*, it is not in ourselves, nor derived from ourselves, nor caused by ourselves—it is a thing which we *infer* from our consciousness of an effect produced upon ourselves by some action external to us, *i.e.*, of a being separate from us. In a word, it is a phenomenon to reveal a fact; which fact indeed it is, only perceived under a peculiar and inverted form, arising from its relation to ourselves. It is that which the fact 'becomes' by passing through us, as it were. The phenomenon is the polar opposite of the fact; we, as it were, being the limit, by which the fact *suppressed* exists as the phenomenon. This is the relation of cause and

* Compare with this the lines of one of our greatest poets :

"The sun, the moon, the stars, the sea, the hills, and the plains,—
Are not these, O soul, the vision of Him who reigns?
Is not the vision He, though He be not that which He seems?
Dreams are true while they last; and do we not live in dreams?
Earth, these solid stars, this weight of body and limb,—
Are they not sign and symbol of thy division from Him?
Dark is the world to thee,—thyself art the reason why;
For is He not all but thou, that hast power to feel 'I am I'?
Speak to Him thou, for He hears, and spirit with spirit can meet;
Closer is He than breathing, and nearer than hands and feet."

The limitation, which causes man to perceive a spiritual action as matter and force, is subsequently regarded by Mr. Hinton as an absence of life. This is one of the fundamental ideas of "*Man and his Dwelling-Place.*" This affirmation seems to be led up to by the tendency there is in modern science to substitute force relations for properties of matter, and to regard energy itself as not the ultimate fact. (See Professor Tait's address at Glasgow, 1876.) We are thus led to ask, What is behind these phenomena? and Mr. Hinton's answer is, That which the moral reason, working on the facts of intellectual apprehension, presents to us.

effect, the fact, the cause of the phenomenon, through us as the condition or limit."

"Do you ask how it is we perceive God's act as matter, *i.e.*, motion and force ?   I answer, I do not know, any more than I know why it is I perceive a rapid vibration as colour, or slower vibration as heat.   How can a vibration be coloured or hot ?   The same impassable chasm divides the world of the intellect from the world of the senses as divides the world of the moral reason from the world of both intellect and sense." *

"One step towards an appropriate conception of the universe I consider this idea to be—that it is a limit applied to infinitude by ourselves, originating so time and space, that causes the universe to be to us as matter and motion.   This is why each thing has so decided a two-fold character, one spiritual, the other material; speaking to us, on the one hand, by its beauty and moral meaning, and, on the other, being so much matter under such mechanical laws.   What is the link between these two aspects ?   How can one thing be at once a spiritual idea and an inert material mass ?   Is it not a contradiction ?   Yet the world would be no world for us if it were not so.   Take away the spiritual life from nature, and it is no longer a home for man, but a tomb, a loathsome charnel-house.   How, then, is the one thing two ?   Man has replied, and has replied truly and yet falsely; truly, for he has said, 'The world is what it is in itself, and also what we make it;' but also sadly wrong, for he has said, 'The world is in itself matter and mechanism, but we, from the riches of our spiritual being, cast over it an illusory glow of

---

* I have ventured to amplify Mr. Hinton's thought here, as in the MSS. it is in too condensed a form to be understood by the general reader.

loveliness and feeling.' Alas for us if this were so! Let
us thank God that it has not been left for us to impart
the spirit to His creation; that He has not mocked us
with a dead image to clasp to our warm embrace, and
vivify it, if we can, with our own life. Let us thank God
that the solemn friendship of seas and forests, the sym-
pathising looks of flowers and stars, the glad greeting or
sorrowful rebuke, alike full of love, wherewith the earth
and skies ever meet us, are not cold reflections of
ourselves. It is true, indeed, that nature is two things
—that which God makes it, and that which we make
it: it is true; but which nature does God make, and
which man? Question answered in the asking. The
love, the joy, the sympathy, the glad encouragement, the
sternly tender monition, the still small voice which the
soul hears through and above all other sounds—these, O
Father! are Thy nature; the dull material clod in which
they are enwrapt, too often crushed and stifled, this *we*
add."

"The laws are in us, not in the things; that is the law
of science. Nature truly obeys laws independently of us;
but they are not scientific, but spiritual laws. God's
action has its own harmony; it is truly wise and full of
love; but of that we cannot know, nor could words express
it. Dimly seen from a human point of view, in the simplicity and grandeur of material laws, in the repose,
dignity, and beauty of material things; but not being
these, our feeble thought cannot attain to it; to these
material things it is as God to man. These are Thy
works, O Father! as man's weak brain and narrow heart
can comprehend them. Thy real works infinitely more
glorious then; Thyself how glorious! This beauty and
simplicity that we see, this order amid unbounded variety,

this unrestrained variety of loveliness comprised in perfect order, the simple laws which regulate alike the vastest orbits of innumerable suns, and the delicate tints of the most fragile flower—all these arise from the limits which we impose upon Thy boundless work, and are but faint shadows of the grandeur in which Thou dwellest. Who by searching shall find out *Thee?*"

"That the mind also is a phenomenon, as the body is—mind a 'subjective passion,'* even as matter—gives the inductive proof of that which I have before seen as necessarily true; viz., that the mental and physical universe are God's act; that the only real being is spirit. It is not the spirit that thinks or lives the *mental* life. The spirit is greater than the mind, which is a phenomenon resulting from passion in it, even as the body is a phenomenon resulting from passion in the mind. How it exalts the spirit to understand that the mind itself *results from it*, as matter from mind! The personality which, by its subjective passion, has perceived an external mind—which is moral, holy or unholy —that is the reality of the man."

"God's action on our spirits is, then, phenomena of matter and of mind; then surely God's action on the spirit must ever be phenomena, and why not *such* phenomena? Is here the truth of the resurrection of the body? God's action on our spirits will surely ever surround us with a universe; it must be so. Heaven shall be so far like earth that we shall have *bodies*, God's action producing in us phenomena as now; but seeing God directly in all, it shall be truly heaven to us. Surely the whole difficulty

* Mr. Hinton here uses the word "passion" in its old sense of an affection.

found in the resurrection of the body lies in the figment of a real matter."

"The universe is necessarily as it is, because God is holy, and His act cannot be arbitrary. This physical and psychical necessity is, in reality, God's holiness. The necessity of the universe does not contravene, but reveals the holiness of God. Physical necessity is a phenomenon of which the interpretation is moral rectitude or love."

"To see that the evil (phenomenally) is not really evil, but only an effect produced on us by good, has this great advantage—that it enables us to face boldly the fact of that evil, and removes the disposition to regard the phenomenon as other than it is. Knowing that evil, too, as evil, is really good, we are no longer afraid to do justice to its proportions as evil, and to admit that, *as seen*, it is absolute evil, unredeemed by the least trace of good. With this faith in the absolute good (and it applies equally to beauty and ugliness), we can face the facts. It is just as in science; men could not really see nature so long as they thought she was partly false. The experimental inductive (phenomenal) science arose necessarily from the faith (for it was strictly 'faith'), from the conviction as a self-evident fact, that nature was absolutely and perfectly true. So will the same thing arise from the faith that she is really, absolutely, and entirely beautiful and good. A phenomenal art and philosophy will be the necessary fruits."

"Sin is not a fact or reality, but a negation, a refusal to share in life. So excellent is life, that not to live is that foul and fearful fact of sin. It is so simple, first, to see that nature is God's act; to see that all God's act is

absolutely good. To see what life is shows it all. It is
God's hand wiping away our tears. The universe is a
scene of absolute life and beauty and good; nothing is
there that is not so; only this sad fact, which yet stains
not its glory, that some spirits refuse to share in it, is the
great mystery of sin."

"We misinterpret what the Bible tells us of heaven.
It says, indeed, that God will wipe away all tears, that
sorrow and sighing shall flee away, and even that there
shall be no more death; but it does not tell us that there
shall be no phenomenal evil. That is quite another thing.
Still there shall be life, yea, more life, still *therefore* evil.*
But not sorrow and sighing, not tears; everlasting joy and
undiminished gladness—gladness for life, for evil seen to
be good. We fancy that if there be evil there must be
grief, sorrow and sighing and tears unwiped away. But
it is not so. To cure us of our grief it needs not to take
away the evil, but to show it us. Shall we grieve at
the evil when we see it as God does? Let me only
see the evil as it is, O God! and my eyes shall weep no
more, nor my heart know another pang.

"The motion of the sun was a source of error to the men
of former times. Now God has removed for us that error,
but He has not altered the phenomenon; still falsely—as
falsely as when first Adam witnessed the illusion—rolls the
sun around the earth. But God has shown it to us. The
illusion remains, but the error is gone; so shall evil remain,
but the grief shall be gone. The illusion shall not end, but

---

*I would venture to remind the reader who may be inclined to say,
"This is a hard saying; who can bear it?" that the ordinary conception,
of heaven, with its "sacred, high, eternal noon" and monotony of bliss,
exclude the highest joy of sacrifice, the very life of love, and therefore of
God.

sorrow and sighing shall flee away. Not the least jot will God alter His deed; it is eternal. But none shall gaze upon the life of heaven and say, 'I will not live.' So shall there be no sin there, no death."

"Stand up, O heart! and yield not one inch of thy rightful territory to the usurping intellect. Hold fast to God in spite of logic, and yet not quite blindly. Be not torn from thy grasp upon the skirts of His garments by any wrench of atheistic hypothesis that seeks only to hurl thee into utter darkness; but refuse not to let thy hands be gently unclasped by that loving and pious philosophy that seeks to draw thee from the feet of God only to place thee in His bosom. Trustfully, though tremblingly, let go the robe, and thou shalt rest upon the heart and clasp the very living soul of God."

CHAPTER VII.

THE following letters, extending over the next few years, are written to a friend in religious difficulties :—

"CHARTERHOUSE SQUARE, *September* 1857.

" I am sorry I can't see you again before you leave for Paris. I hope you will enjoy yourself and be much benefited. When you have opportunities, write a line and tell me of your well-being.

"There is no comfort, no satisfaction, no good in merely getting the intellect right. Only escape from death, cease to regard yourself. Make your own welfare and happiness no part of your regard in thinking—then all will be clear. In your thinking *give yourself* and don't ask to *get* —not even satisfaction or peace in the feeling that you are going right, that you may hope to attain something at last. Escape from that damnation. Thank God, the end of all thought, of all effort, of all labour is this—which lies here just as close to us at the beginning—that we should cease to regard ourselves; all is mystery to us and darkness, until then, though we had all knowledge and knew all mysteries, for that is itself darkness and ignorance.

"If we can make our thinking too a giving, a loving, an escape from the death of trying to get, then our eyes are opened—then we *know*. Think of that ever, to *know* is to *be*. Suppose you are bewildered and know not what is right nor what is true. Can you not cease to regard whether you know or not, whether you be bewildered, whether you be happy? Cannot you utterly and perfectly love, and rejoice to be in the dark and gloom-beset, because that very thing is the fact of God's Infinite Being as it is to you? Cannot you take this trial also into your own heart and be ignorant, not because you are obliged, but because that being God's will, it is yours also?

"Do not you see that a person who truly *loves* is one with the Infinite Being—IS—cannot be uncomfortable or unhappy? It is that which IS that he wills and desires and holds best of all to be. This is the love of God; it perceives this illusion of what is to us, and sees and joins itself to that which truly is, that is, to God, and being one so with God, to it also must be God's eternal blessedness. To know God is utterly to sacrifice self, to exclude the negation, to be one with Being, that is, to Be."

" September 1857.

"Most important I think it is to you to get out of that strange idea, that you ought to understand the meaning, or at least a consistent meaning, in every passage of the Bible. I can't conceive an odder mistake, especially in a person who believes it to be the Word of God, a book not for one man or age, but for all. You will certainly make a mess of the Bible till you can have patience with it. 'Tis as large as nature and as deep and as simple, and must be dealt with in the same way. If you don't understand a fact in nature, you don't fidget yourself till you can see how it agrees with what you think you do understand. You say, there's a fact I must study when I have time, and meanwhile you go on your way rejoicing—not least in this, that if your life is spared you will be wiser by

and by. Hold fast what you see, remembering that it
can't be the truth, *i.e.*, so far as it is intellectual or the
result of thought—and wait. Don't be in a hurry; above
all things, if you wish to think wisely, avoid forcing your
opinions, or forcing theories where you can't see, *i.e.*,
accept tentatively, in order to see how far you may be
able to get help so, what may seem the best present idea
of such and such a fact or passage, but knowing certainly
that if you 'put a construction' it will certainly be a
wrong one. . . .

"Do you not see that all this mystery and darkness, all
this horror and doubt, all these chimeras, spring from one
source, that putting the eternal into the future, denying,
that is, its eternity; which of course has this one root, that
we don't see that it is the present fact. 'Tis as Christ says,
'if your hand offend you, cut it off, and don't be cast
into hell;' don't be damned; as Paul says, don't sin.
If you will get this well into your heart, little that will
puzzle or try you much will remain; much unknown, but
not much dark.

"And now for the love of God and of our neighbour too.
The two commandments conjoined have struck me, I see
great beauty and wisdom in that. I find it thus. The
true love of God is, I conceive, love of the Infinite Being,
i.e., the universal fact. 'Tis the one great passion of man,
all passions mean this and no other—all love, all desire,
means, *is*, the love of God; our misery and sin is that
we don't know this, and seek to satisfy it with that which
is *not God*—not fact. Now this being so, you perceive
this love might tend to lead us away from thoughts of the
real or thing-al, it might be abused to a kind of abstract
love that should not comprehend much practical benevolence, so love to our neighbour is added to save us from
such an error, to show us that true love to God can only

be in love to man. In John, how the same thing is dwelt upon. But, as you say, all love is truly comprehended in the love of God—there is and can be no other love.

"*P.S.*—Try and remember in looking at nature, that it is the not-love, the inertness, the evil, that is added by our physicalness. It perverts the mind to allow it to think that this inert *selfish* world is God's work. It is not—it is our death; we ought not to be satisfied with it, 'tis the kingdom of the devil. I haven't said here nearly what I mean. The words won't come to me—perhaps words can't rightly say it. Give up wholly thinking of that which shall be to yourself. Let your thought be *love;* only ignore and abjure yourself wholly, loving Christ and Being. Then you KNOW more, infinitely more, than I do."

"*December* 1857.

"I think that almost all the counsel or instruction in respect to thinking that need be given to any one is comprised in this: to remember our ignorance determines our opinions, that while ignorant we must think erroneously if we think aright, and that the use of thinking erroneously is to show us our ignorance; *i.e.*, to remove it. So the thing to do is to think *logically*, regardless of the result to which we are led, and to change our opinion so soon as ever the best arguments are on the opposite side; remembering always that no opinion can be the right one in respect to any subject against which there is anything in our nature that protests. Only that can be the right opinion which is the union of opposites; which fulfils in itself the demands of those who have maintained opposite opinions, and is the reconcilement of disputes.

"I am glad you find some such excellent people among those who are so far removed from ourselves. It is a great joy to think of it. I daresay in many of these national communions there is a depth of piety in some aspects that we can little conceive.

"I hear you are likely to go to Russia. I hope you will; it would be interesting and instructive for you, and might be very useful. I am myself a believer in the destiny of the Sclavonic nations.

"Respecting the redemption of the world I am a believer, not a discoverer. I should never have known it, or thought of it, if I had not learnt it from the Bible, and though *once knowing it*, it may be seen clearly and demonstrably in nature, yet I find in nature no light as yet that takes me beyond what the Bible says. I rest on these words and such as these: 'All shall be made alive.' And there at present I stop. When I see . more I will say it.

"And in speaking of this matter it is the more necessary to be cautious, inasmuch as the actual, the fact, cannot be thought, we cannot form an intellectual conception of the spiritual. The heavenly state will not be conformed to any thought of ours. The thinking of necessity sets aside the fact. This, almost more than anything, is what we have to learn — that is, practically to learn. It has been the established doctrine of science and philosophy this long while, but has not affected practical life. One might almost say the error we have been under—the error from which all errors have been but offshoots and branches, has been the attempt to make the spiritual come within the domain of the intellectual. We have been resolved to *think* it, consequently we have set it wholly aside. This is the same old point—we are *dead* and don't know the fact. To know it is not to have any opinion, it is to have life. Don't try to *think* heaven; necessarily you make it but an unreal earth—if not so bad as earth, far, far more is it not so GOOD. Earth is infinitely better than any heaven we can *think*. Heaven is to be known as God is to be known. When you can conceive God, then you can conceive what man will be in heaven. God reveals these things to us by His Spirit.

"I think you are mistaken about Christ's teaching. Anyhow He, and the people who learnt from Him, have taught me all I know about religion. What makes you think He meant those who heard Him to think otherwise than the best you can think? I grant He meant better than we think, that we don't rightly understand Him; but if you will look into the grounds of that feeling you have, I believe you will find it an entire misconception. There are many parables which I don't understand, but in Christ's teaching, what I do understand I find to be wholly above me and not below. Is not the Sermon on the Mount the 'actual' ethics carried to their utmost perfection—that is, is not what I call 'ethics' a mere expansion and dilution of that teaching? I know what you are doing. You are carrying into Christ's words the construction that you have been taught to put upon them; you are not yet able to read them simply as they are. It was from those words about cutting off the hand, that I first received an insight into the knowledge that hell is self-indulgence. What perplexes you is that Christ is speaking rightly, and you are thinking wrongly. The very same thing that has put us all astray together about the Bible. Do you remember—

'Said a people to a poet, go out from among us straightway,
While we are thinking earthly things thou singest of Divine.'

That's the secret of it. We have supposed the men of the
New Testament were thinking, like we are, of what we
can get.

"I grant Christ threatens suffering and promises enjoyment—at least I think so—but I don't find that any
inconsistency. You entirely misapprehend 'actualism'*
if you think that it sets those aside. It is by no means
so. I affirm for all sin, suffering, those very sufferings
that men are afraid of, and for virtue, happiness. But, in
truth, you must rub your eyes and look at the Gospels
afresh."

"*June* 1858.

"Whenever I hear of troubles, I always think of the
wrongness that must be in us that we feel as evil that
which is good. Because we always say—all good people
do—that they know all must be good if they could see
it aright; and yet they so curiously take no notice of the
fact that their feeling is wrong, that they feel a good thing
as evil. This always strikes me so now. I can at present hardly think of anything else when I hear people
talk. It seems so odd to me, so very strange that people
don't notice it. They seem to pay all the attention
to the fact of their feeling itself, and the mere unplea-
santness of it, and none at all to the evident and admitted
wrongness of it. I seem as if I could meditate on this
for ever; it is wonderful. And, besides, people admit
that they would know the things they find so painful to
be good, if only they could see aright; they don't say that
anything would need to be altered to make it good—only
themselves—it *is* good. So it is evident if they could

---

* Mr. Hinton used the word "real," or "thing-al," for the material or
phenomenal world presented by the intellect; and "actual" for the
spiritual world of true existence.

see things aright they would see these things good now; but it would not avail much to *see* them good if we still *felt* them the same, the feeling them evil is the pain.

"Is it not evident that *we* want altering and nothing else? We can't say otherwise without denying the goodness of God; for the least devotion compels us to admit that the fact is perfectly good, however it may seem to us. Look as we may, we can't find any evil whatever beyond the feeling wrongly, feeling that as evil which is not evil, and which resolves itself into feeling forms as facts, things that are only phenomena as if really being. What we want, clearly, is to be made to feel right—not resignation, &c., but simply rightness, not to be deceived; not goodness evidently, but only not to be a fool. And this we can have. I know we can, for what do we want but to *know*—to know God and His work as Christ shows it to us, so that we do truly and absolutely rejoice and delight in it, and are content that things which are evil to us should be for the sake of it. Then we are different, then we don't indeed cease to feel as evil the things we do not like, but we do better, we rejoice even in feeling them so; we are no longer as we were before, the one self wanting what it likes, but a new and truer 'self' even, one may say, is given us. We are, as it were, two persons, the old man not liking the pain, the new man liking it and rejoicing in it, and the latter wholly ruling and triumphing over the former. So that we could almost be glad not to be without the pain, but rejoice that we dare suffer also for His work.

"What we want to make us right, is only faith—a true veritable actual belief that God does all things, and that *the* thing He does is that good thing. Then all is right. We have that foolish notion in our heads of little and great. We find it hard to believe that in our *little*

things the redemption of man is wrought. That's because
we are so little. And you see, I suppose it is only in
this way God could get that stupid pride which is one
aspect of littleness out of us.

"Since you have been away, I have written two papers,
one on a physiological subject, the Law of form or least
resistance, and the other a commencement of the more
interesting branch—the true *work*, viz., a short paper
on matter. I call it 'Common Sense about matter, by a
common sense mind,' with the motto from Shakspeare,
'But what's the *matter?*' It is very short and touches
the 'matter' very lightly, being meant to be entirely
popular, but it contains the most perfect conceptions (in
their rudiments, &c.) to which I have yet attained. I don't
think, however, I shall get either of them accepted by any
periodical, at least not without great difficulty ; and as for
the latter, it will want a great deal of polishing.

"I like the thought of acting on men not so much directly
as through others. I should be quite happy to say no more,
to have no part in the communication of that which I think
to the world, if that which is right and good of it could be
said, if the work that is to be done *were* done by others.
I think I would rather it were so. Meanwhile it is a
grand thing to be indifferent to success—to have our will
done in God's. It is indeed a strange miserable blindness
of man's, and insensibility to his true greatness and dignity,
that makes him insist so on having what *he* likes. I
wonder at it more and more. Only think what a gratification of ambition it is to have our will God's and so
certainly done. Why 'tis nothing more than knowing
and choosing rightly, nothing but escaping from miserable illusions and rising to the true right, man's rightful
kingship. Don't you see how Christ makes us kings to
God, and we reign with Him, how the saints shall judge

the world ? Of course, to be king and have his will absolutely done—that is man's destiny, when he only knows,
i.e., when he only IS man.

"Only get that negation out of us, which is the negation of humanity, and then we reign with Christ; we
must, because we are one with Him. The dominion can't
be given to us now, because it is man's, it waits for man
to Be, to attain to true existence. Those old mystical
doctrines about man ruling earth and stars, and all depending upon him, are not so much amiss. Only as Emer-
son says, 'There is no man; what is all this self-action
but so much death ?' Do you remember it ?

"It is delightful to have J—— home. I am sure he
will come to something grand in time, but nature won't
be hurried, and I think he does not know himself yet.
Faith he wants, and repose which is its child. Is not
that a marvellous passage : 'I will give you *rest*,' ceasing
from effort—the spontaneous, necessary, unfatiguing life.

"I'm glad you so enjoy yourself, and hope you will
travel to your heart's content. The world indeed is
wonderful ; it is divine, spiritual, eternal. This *is* heaven.
We do well to be intoxicated, ravished with its beauty
and wonder ; only evil when we say, 'All this is mere
dead matter and mechanism ; the beauty, the life, the
moral being is in me.'"*

"*August* 1858.

"I have an opportunity of writing to you, but my
brain is dry and I can't find your last letter. My news
is that I have nearly done my book, so that you shall

---

* Mr. Hinton once said to me in his emphatic way, "What is the world
that science reveals to us as the reality of the world we see ? A world
dark as the grave, silent as a stone, and shaking like a jelly. That the
ultimate fact of this glorious world ? Why, you might as well say that the
ultimate fact of one of Beethoven's violin quartettes is the scraping of the
tails of horses on the intestines of cats."

have by and by a standard to which I commit myself for the present. I hope I shall find that I have done a wise thing.

"I hope you feel yourself making progress. If you are stagnating in a quiet place, feeling very idle and given up to nature, and doing nothing but simply your day's work, I should say, judging by my own experience, that you are spending a very profitable time. I do believe I have thought of a great part of the things I have, because I was so mentally idle in Jamaica, I had such an entire break from all my previous habits and thoughts.

"Are not Faber's 'Oratory Hymns' beautiful, with Schulte's music? There must be in those universal communions something powerful and charming that the isolated Dissenters lose. I feel now that I foresee a time when men will be able to unite and have all these things in common, all the charms and aids of all systems. It only needs to put the intellect in its right place—it is a divider only while exercising a false dominion. . . ."

"October 1858.

"For my own part, I have not yet a sufficient comprehension of our relation to our body to form an opinion on the subject of asceticism. My opinion inclines against it, which is perhaps partly due to my having felt strongly the necessity of distinguishing between my own ethical principles, and the selfish asceticism which the world has rejected. But at the same time I decidedly think the ordinary Protestant objections against mortifications are not sufficient, nor going truly to the point, and think it quite possible that a true unselfish system of self-denial may be destined to arise. When one understands aright what this body is, this will become self-evident. I think my nature is such that I shall remain in the dark about it till then. I see practical questions, always through a theoretical light. But all people do not. I think it very likely that some practical geniuses may see, or perhaps do see, the right solution of that question without any ideas about the philosophy of the case at all. My impulse would be to submit myself to such a person, if I could meet with one, and be guided practically by him.

"But this is personal, I don't at all recommend it to others; with me it might be a voluntary obedience, with others it might be an enslavement. But I think it would be a pity if the 'Catholic' asceticism died out of the world before the question is settled and its substitute is ready. I have a fancy of this sort; that the true self-denial ought to be one in which all can participate, not confined to a class. I please my thought with the prospect of a time in which self-denial shall be the law of public and domestic life alike, and all orders of people be religious orders, in which society in fact shall be founded upon giving and not upon getting.

"Don't think you know, or have any means of knowing, what miracles are, or have any test for them, or that the idea of a 'suspension of the laws of nature' has anything in it. This matter also can wait very well. It is evident to me that the idea of a miracle to us must differ considerably from that which was entertained of it of old, merely by virtue of the great change in our ideas about all things. Few people have any notion how unlike our present entire conceptions of nature altogether are from those of the ancient nations, and those suspect it least who are least aware of the part which science has played in the last few centuries in moulding the entire thoughts of men, educated and uneducated alike. A great gap has to be filled up here, I fancy, before we can enter at all into the thought of the people who spoke about miracles of old. I have a notion that the miraculous power is the nature and natural power of man, and that the absence of it is a degradation, not the possession of it an exaltation. The miracle workers the world has seen I take to have been exhibitions of man's true relation to nature, viz., a command over the phenomenal—not according to its laws, but by means of the action related to the absolute; even as we, by acting on real things, can alter appearances at our pleasure, and in a way in which we could not by acting on the appearances themselves. A miracle worker may be conceived as working in that which causes us to perceive the phenomena. So he may *alter the phenomenon itself.* We, working on the phenomenon, can't do that, we can only alter its form. In the latter case, we work according to the laws of the phenomenon, in the former of course, we overrule them. Of course man's true and proper action can't be on the phenomenal merely, it must be on the absolute; that is, it is miraculous. Our defect of power is by our defect of being. So the old instinct is justified, that 'spirits' have the power of overcoming the natural laws (though it is rather topsy-turvy). I don't hold that man has now the dominion of nature."

"*January* 1859.

"It is a pleasant thing to write to you, and pleasant also to read your letters, and useful too. I think it was a letter of yours made me think of some things about prayer, which I never clearly recognised before, although they are very obvious when one sees them. There is a sort of feeling in our minds, as if there were no propriety in praying for a thing, if it is not *contingent*, as if a thing that was certain was excluded from its scope; and so to feel certain about things as being clearly promised or de-

clared by God, was apt to make us feel an embarrassment
in praying for them. I have felt this a good deal, but a
little while ago it flashed on me that there must be some
radical misapprehension about prayer in my mind, for it
is not at all that way that it is represented in Scripture.
There the representation of prayer is continually of it as
being for things which are certain, and which are known
and felt to be certain by those who pray. Just think of
a few cases—one or two will do—and you will find it runs
throughout the scriptural representation of prayer. Thus,
'My heart's desire and *prayer to God* for Israel is that
they might be saved,' and then he goes on, 'So all Israel
shall be saved.' And Paul, perpetually in his Epistles,
prays for things he is sure will be—for blessings on the
Churches, *e.g.*, which he knows God will certainly give.
So Solomon's prayer. He knew God had promised what
he prayed for. So the Lord's prayer. Is it not certain
God's kingdom shall come ? But I think the most
striking case is Christ's own prayers, which were for
things He certainly knew should certainly be. Think of
this a little.

"Well, then, you see our notion of prayer, if we have
such an one, as being inappropriate for that which is not
doubtful, is quite unscriptural ; and we must have a better
one. Prayer does not mean the asking God for things we
can't be sure about receiving if we don't pray. What it
is I don't pretend to say I see, but this is a relief and
blessing, surely, to know. It is something larger, higher,
better than that, better than what we are apt to think
of it. Surely this may do for us at the present, if it be all.
Can we not let our spirits expand and flow into an *unknown*
thought of prayer. When I try to think of it, as yet I
don't get much further than Paul's words, 'We know not
what to pray for as we ought, but the Spirit maketh inter-

cession for us.' Do you know, I incline to think that this presents the very truth of prayer for all times, and that we, and all who come after us in the flesh, will speak best of prayer, when they say, ' I know not what to pray for as I ought, but something within me, which is above myself, speaks for me to God,' and especially of those things which He has promised, and on the assured belief on which all my life is based."

" April 1859.

" I sympathise so heartily in the feeling of isolation and unlikeness to others. I have felt that very much, and still do a little. It is a great trial in one sense, but not altogether. God is always so near to us and so perfect in sympathy when once we can get the true feeling of His presence. And then our life develops perhaps the better; and I am sure that in power of usefulness and work, the sacrifice of present sympathy is well repaid. If God has a particular work He wishes us to do, how should we expect a fellow-feeling from those to whom He has given a different work ?

" We must not let ourselves be too much repelled by the expressions of other Christians. Every Christian man *means* love and self-consecration by the pleasures of heaven. It is notions about justice and so on which make them talk the other way. It is, indeed, the false thoughts which have been necessary to men—to all men —that make it impossible for Christian men to speak fully and truly. The representations most repugnant to us, almost all of them mean—at bottom *are*—assertions of some great principle which could not be given up without an utter loss of all.

" Think, for example, of the doctrine of the *everlastingness* of future misery. I find that most beautiful and essential. To give that up while men are thinking as they do of this life as probation, I think would be an irremediable loss. Do not you see now that means truly the ETERNALNESS of the punishment. Now when it is interpreted, and our thoughts have righted themselves, we see that it is but the necessary form in which the fact that *wickedness* is the true damnation expresses itself. Damnation IS *eternal*—*i.e.*, it is actual and spiritual, not sensational. While the general perversion of thought lasts, by which the eternal is made to mean a temporal continuance, it is right and necessary to hold the misery of the wicked, everlasting. That opinion is better than the ' destruction '—that is, especially in regard to the progress of our thinking—the one is bad enough in itself, but it is the road to a better, the other is a stagnation. So I think we should ever feel, recognising in every error the end of a truth, and that it could not be laid aside before it is *interpreted*, without irremediable loss. For you see, in the belief in the destruction of the sensational consciousness of the wicked, though it would be a loss to have it believed by all, yet is also a good. It is a protest against the other doctrine—a proof that that is not true and must be remodelled; it is a power in the progress of our thought."

" *September* 16, 1859.

" You write me funny letters. I always find them a study. You seem, indeed, to have quite a remarkable gift of creating puzzles and griefs for yourself. I never see you hardly, or hear from you, but you are unhappy or perplexed where no cause for either can be found. You are like those patients for whom one has always to prescribe a good dinner, a few glasses of wine, and a good walk. What is it that is amiss ? You don't understand about the Sacraments, or see all the meaning of the Bible;

K

and you find in yourself an irresistible impulse to be kind to everybody and do all the good you can. It is a sad catalogue. What is the prescription? But this, I think, I shall leave to you.

"Suppose you were to think of something really unfortunate, if you *must* be grieved, or, better still, were to leave off thinking of yourself altogether, your knowledge or your ignorance, your love or your want of it. It makes no matter, and if it were ever so important it can't be altered so. Think about the world, the things that are going on in Dresden, good and bad, great and small, and how God is redeeming man in them. And if a thought about your own ignorance and badness intrudes now and then, say—'Yes; I am ignorant and bad, but God will take care of that; and in the meantime He is saving the world, and *that* is *my* business, to take my part actively or passively in that; and for that my knowledge or goodness are no matter at all. GOD does that.'

"To speak quite plainly, I think you are *tired* and not well. Your letter, and all your trying thoughts, simply mean that your brain is fagged. You must leave off thinking for a time, and distract and amuse yourself in any way most accessible, especially out of doors. Everybody needs it. I can bear a good deal of thinking, but I get into just such a way if I go on too long, and I have been practising my own prescription; for since we moved I've hardly done anything in thinking—gardening and living most jollily all my leisure. And I'm vastly stronger and better.

"I needn't speak of any particular subject now. I'm happy to say I know no more of the Sacraments than you. But I'm very patient under it. Perhaps I shall some day, perhaps I shan't. Certainly I shan't by

boring myself about them. And if so be God should
choose to discipline me, by placing me in circumstances
where I acutely felt the want of knowledge which He
had withheld from me, why (unless I became poorly,
and so unable to act by the dictates of my wiser
thoughts), I should try to submit to, and profit by, that
discipline, and say to myself, ' Now God is benefiting me
and the world (never forget the world, nothing goes right
when that is left out!) by making me conscious of my
ignorance, and giving me experience of how to act when I
am ignorant.' And what patience and trust and self-control
and self-guard it wants—does it not?—TRUST, FAITH especially, which of all qualities is by far the most valuable
and necessary for us. And nothing strengthens it so much
as the feeling ourselves ignorant when we want knowledge,
and it seems as if it would be so useful for us.

"I should use such discipline (and who is without it?) to
strengthen my trust and my faith, and think nothing that
is good depends upon my knowing, but all upon God's
doing, and that is certain and unchangeable. If the cup
of painful ignorance may not pass from us, shall we not
drink it? and from what man has it ever passed, except
from the fool who is wise in his own conceit; and we see
very well what cup he has instead. And the more should
we say this, because that is the straight, direct, and unfailing path to knowledge. The road, and only road to knowledge, lies in the patient and humble acceptance of our
ignorance. You try this. Just once say manfully to
yourself about all these things that puzzle you, 'I don't
know, I don't know a bit about them, I haven't the least
idea,' and you will see what wonders it will work. You've
no idea of the efficacy of that charm; I try it continually
and so speak from experience. The darkness and heavi-
ness clear away from the eyes and heart, and a wonderful

lightness takes their place. For, after all, there is no reason we should know, nay, there is every reason against it; and besides, there is in prospect the fun or higher pleasure of finding out. And don't we know enough; don't we know God as the Redeemer, not of our wretched selves, but of the world? keep your eye fixed on that. We are glad, not because we are well off or good, but because the world is to be saved and all men are to be made good, and to acknowledge Christ. Our joy has the same ground and source as *His.* For is not that what He rejoiced in? What else, then, should we want?"

"April 19, 1860.

" . . . You, like myself, are puzzled with the practical questions of life. It is trying not to be able to see clearly what one's duty is, but, doubtless, it is a very good and useful trial. It certainly draws into exercise, or perhaps rather demands from us, the exercise of some qualities that might never be developed otherwise, and I suppose we must be content to have them exercised, though we might prefer many other things. Thus, I think, we may plainly see, to help our patience, that the practical problems of living ought to be the last to be solved; that nothing could be more fatal to our progress than to be able to arrange our outward life quite to our satisfaction, while other questions remain unsettled. The urgent need we feel of knowing what to *do* is the stimulus whereby we are made to strive to know and understand, which is not one whit less important, nay, perhaps, is more important. For there is real importance (that is, comparatively there is) in the development of our hearts and consciences, and inner being, by discovery of error and of truth, and knowing more, and so entering more into the work of God.

It is for this reason, therefore, I take it among others, that God has made it so difficult for us to know what we ought to do, not on what principles but in what details to direct our life. He wants us to feel this, in order that we may be made to apply ourselves diligently to things which otherwise we should leave quite undone.

"My own opinion is, that the truly wise and proper way for individuals or for societies to act is not likely to be clearly settled yet, perhaps not for a long time and until a great deal more is known. In the meantime, let us be conscientious ourselves and charitable towards others. Let each one do what he thinks right; most likely it is best there should be many ways of acting tried, such experiments may have much to do with proving what is best. It is by no means certain that what appears very clear to us is therefore true. A little more knowledge might make us turn quite round. In the early days of Christianity, they tried all Christians living in common, but it did not seem to be quite the thing, and I should doubt very much if that was right; even the Apostles don't seem, so far as I know, to have held any clear ideas on the point. Perhaps they were a good deal puzzled too, like us."

"_February_ 1861.

"I haven't written any letters for a long time. For one thing, I have much more writing upon me than I can do, and I cannot direct my energies. I like to write to you just to tell you how often I think of you, and wish you all good; but I know letters from me are not necessary to you, being quite sure you will work out your problems in the proper way at last. . . . You generally, when you do put a subject to me, take up just one on which I haven't any light, so that I know I can't help you much.

"In fact, your questions are very much my questions I expect, only I fancy I am much more *patient* than you are over them—less in a hurry to settle them—and if I have any advantage over you, I think it is very much that. You will say, that is partly because I am not situated like you with continual necessity for acting on those questions, and needing to have them settled for practical guidance. But this is not true, at least it is very subordinate. I am like you in that, in having to act on things in which I do not see my principles clear, and in feeling hourly the need of a better understanding for my practical guidance. But I am patient notwithstanding. If you ask why—partly it is because I know it is no good to be in a hurry, but partly, also, from constitution, and partly from habit. For no practical end could I hurry or 'scamp' an intellectual problem. It is not in me to do it, and if it were, I hold right thinking to be quite incalculably more practically important than any doing. The world is ruled by its thoughts, but no one knows what will come of doing. Moreover, I don't think the world is our business. If only we do our best (and, fortunately, also if we do not), God will take care of the world and of all things in the world. That last is much the more comfort, is it not?

"I'll just tell you what strikes me sometimes when I read your letters. Doubtless there is very much to admire in Russian society, especially that aspect of it which you see. I am very much interested in hearing about it, but I reflect, I don't know how justly, that Russian upper society has another side—it is based on slavery. Have you not been struck with the thought how easily a certain kind of goodness flourishes when there is plenty of money, and how vile the roots of the money often are?"

" *April* 25, 1861.

"So far as you fear being lulled into indolence I would just say two things; first, that I expect it really means that you are overdone and not well, and that repose is what you want. You must not reject this idea, as you will be disposed to do, at once, and the more, the more it is the truth. Every one feels just the same under those circumstances. I do myself. When I'm done up I'm haunted by the most painful conviction of my indolence, that I've never done anything, nor shall do, and that I don't half work. You have had like me a perpetual tax on your mind, an *unintermittent* one, that's what we can't stand. You must put it aside for a time, and then see. Not that I say you ought not, or need not, see that you really do what you can and should; but what we should do is really, very often, to be still. And if we want something to make us more active and energetic, watchful and holy, I know but one thought, that is *faith*—faith producing love. More trust and confidence and joy in God would be the secret—the only true or successful secret—of more goodness. And this should come quietly and calmly, not in great effort; this kingdom of God has come not with observation. I'm sure Christians as often and as keenly spend their strength in vain—trying to do, in respect to the active service of God, as unconverted people do in respect to getting justified and saved. It is not the doing—it is the believing, the trusting and the loving from it, is the thing. Rest and quiet growth, I expect, are what you want.

"And then there's another point, which should be both believed and remembered, though I grant 'tis difficult to apply—that is to one's self—namely, that feelings of inability and failure, and discontent with our exertions or our powers, are utterly irrational, and in point of fact *untrue*. They often co-exist, I believe they especially co-exist, with the best and most successful work, and this for two reasons (among others) which are very evident. First, That such work taxing our powers most, is most apt to induce a morbid reaction and give us feelings which are really due to fatigue and exhaustion; and, secondly, that inasmuch as the feelings themselves mean and express labour, and the striving with difficulty, since they can only arise from the exertion of the strength on obstacles which through that difficulty make their weight felt, therefore, of course, it is only natural that these feelings should be most felt when the exertion (and therefore the work done) has been greatest.

"So much am I convinced (by mere observation and experience) of this fact respecting myself, that I have adopted it as a practical rule to entirely ignore my own feelings in that line. I disregard and put them aside, knowing them to be no test at all, and take what they call in metaphysics a purely objective view, that is, I judge of my work by a critical survey at an after period, or get others to judge of it. And my experience is constantly what I tell you. I am beginning, indeed, to escape from a great hindrance by acting on this plan; for so continual and unvaried was my sense of utter failure and inability, that if I attached importance to it, it would have been a bar to my doing anything, and especially anything in those lines in which, as a matter of fact, I succeed about the best. It is very curious, and there is something I should like uncommonly to understand in this causing of untrue feeling through great exertion; but it is certainly a fact, and you should thoroughly recognise it, for both by your nature and your position you are likely to be a good deal tried by it. It affects reflective natures like yours and mine more than some others. It is, besides, especially prone to occur to those whose minds are subject to *constant* wear and effort—even though it may be but slight—where there is no chance, or but little, of obtaining, at short periods, complete repose and ease, but the thoughts must always be alert—or almost always—to something, even though it be to trifling things—there this sort of feeling is almost sure to arise."

" October 26, 1864.

"Let me advise just once. I don't like being an adviser much, but just this one thing, to be reverent where you are ignorant, and to attach no weight at all to your naturally *feeling sure.* We almost always *naturally feel sure wrong*—it is our fate—it is in our very being."

CHAPTER VIII.

In 1856 Mr. Hinton first began to publish, contributing a few papers on physiological and ethical subjects to the *Christian Spectator*.

In 1858 he published a paper in the *Medico-Chirurgical Review* "On Physical Morphology, or the Law of Organic Forms," suggesting that organic growth takes place in the direction of least resistance, a generalisation which Mr. Herbert Spencer has embodied in his *First Principles*.* "It is remarkable," Mr. Hinton writes, "that in the various hypotheses which have been framed to account for the forms of organic bodies, no attention has been paid to the fact that the process of expansion, in which growth consists, takes place under conditions which limit it in a definite way. It must surely have been from overlooking this circumstance that a mode of speaking has established itself among us, as if there were in organic tissue a power of forming itself into peculiar shapes, as if masses of cells, by some power of their own, could mould themselves into complicated structures. . . . So intent have we been in pursuing specific vital tendencies, or the final causes manifested in the uses of the parts [of an organic structure], that it would appear as if we had entirely forgotten that living matter is matter after all. Thus an eminent physiologist informs us, 'the tail of the

* *First Principles*, by Herbert Spencer, pp. 231–233.

cercaria, which was previously employed for locomotion, *is now useless and falls off!*'" *

Mr. Hinton proceeds to formulate his proposition thus:
" Organic form is the result of motion.
" Motion takes the direction of least resistance.
" Therefore, organic form is the result of motion in the direction of least resistance."

This position he illustrates and enforces by various phenomena of development, and especially from the prevalence of the spiral form in organic nature, motion under resistance taking a spiral direction, the explanation of this fact being very simple : a moving body encountering resistance is deflected, or turned at right angles, and a motion constantly turning at right angles and yet continuing is a spiral. " No theory has seemed capable of accounting for the fact [of organic forms] but that of a peculiar power inherent in each germ. . . . But what though the appearance to the eye, or even to the microscope, of all ova be the same, is it not certain that there is a difference of structure which escapes our observation ? Nay, does not the ascription to them of different powers involve that very difference of structure or composition which it is supposed to supersede ? And what can be simpler than that germs of different structure should undergo different

---

* Agassiz and Gould's *Comp. Physiology,* p. 343. Bacon's warning has not yet lost its bearing. "To say that the hairs of the eyelids are for a quickset and fence about the sight; or that the firmness of the skin and hides of living creatures is to defend them from the extremities of heat and cold; or that the bones are for the columns or beams whereupon the frame of the bodies of living creatures is built ; or that the leaves of trees are for the protecting of the fruit, and the like, is well inquired and collected in metaphysic ; but in physic they are impertinent. I say they are but indeed remoras and hindrances to stay and slug the ship from further sailing, and have brought this to pass, that the search of the physical causes hath been neglected and passed in silence."—*Advancement of Learning,* Book II.

changes. . . . Add to this that each change of structure in the process of development modifies all the succeeding ones, and it becomes no longer hard to understand how, from even imperceptible incipient diversities, the widest contrasts of form may accrue. Every divergence is continually multiplied.

"But how come the germs to differ? Clearly because formed under differing conditions. They are diverse, because their structure is the result of motion in the direction of least resistance. There is no *beginning* in a germ."

The paper concludes with a passage of deep general interest :—

"Here I should cease. But it would be affectation to ignore that the view I have taken will be felt by some as contravening the design that they delight to recognise in nature—as another step towards excluding God from His creation. I do not feel it so. I may not enlarge upon this aspect of the question, but the entire subject has been so mixed up with theological ideas that I may be permitted briefly to indicate my own view. I hold all vital forms to be what we call necessary, but it is the necessity of rightness that I recognise, and no other. God's act in Nature appears to us under the form of *physical* or merely passive necessity, but that is our infirmity and defect of vision. It is necessary truly, every least fact and part of it, but necessary by a truer, deeper necessity than we perceive, the necessity that Love should do infinitely well and wisely. Welcome to me are all proofs of necessity, all indications of law, all demonstrations that things could not be otherwise than they are.

Never does nature bring us nearer to God than when science excludes from it all arbitrariness, and teaches us to say, This must be as it is. For an intellectual we must learn to substitute a moral conception of creation;

we need to rise above contrivance; it is holiness that claims our reverence in nature. Well said Bacon, 'The three true stages of knowledge are as the three acclamations, *sancte, sancte, sancte;* holy in the description or dilatation of His works, holy in the connection or concatenation of them, and holy in the union of them in a perpetual and uniform law.' Was Newton ever held to be an irreligious philosopher ? Yet of him it is recorded that whilst contemplating the simplicity and harmony of the plan according to which the universe is governed, his thoughts glanced towards the organised creation, and he remarked, 'Idemque dici possit de UNIFORMITATE EA, quæ est in corporibus animalium.'"

The following letters are to Mrs. Hinton :—

"August 1857.

"DEAREST MEGGIE,—I went down to Wimbledon and saw Toynbee. He has had a severe attack, but is better, and is likely to be about again by Monday. However, when he found himself so ill, he says he began thinking again of what passed between us about my carrying on his practice; and he seems quite to have made up his mind to introduce me as his successor. In the meantime he wishes me to attend for him at Saville Row."

" 18 *Saville Row, August* 1857.

"I am doing duty here, as you perceive. I have not been very well. I think my visit to Manchester fatigued me ; but, at any rate, it was a change.

" Willie is a funny boy, very different from Howard—strikingly so, I think, for brothers ; but I can't describe him. I expect he will be much like me when he grows up, only a good deal better and greater."

He writes to a sister-in-law :—

" *March* 1858.

"I'm glad you've read 'Buckle.' It is a magnificent book—that is, in some aspects—but marred by mighty flaws, and disgraced, as it seems to me, by some amazing weaknesses. *E.g.*, the discussion on *the will* seems to me the most disgraceful, superficial, and pretentious thing I have ever seen upon the subject (almost, I should add, for I just remember something of Harriet Martineau's which equals it). Also, I believe his great learning is not sound. I have seen his 'facts' wofully called in question; and in respect to his physiology, it is certainly defective. Also, again, his thoughts are not to any considerable extent original, though striking, many of them, and all of them well put. I think, in a word, his great merit lies in his style, including in that term his total power of presentment. A great gift in this line always secures immense applause and immediate influence, sometimes long continued too. It is a fascinating book, one by all means to be read, by no means to be believed; though this, it seems to me, is to be said of all history. At least, you may know, I am a confirmed historical sceptic; *i.e.*, not as to well-confirmed events, but as to the true connection, dependence, and significance of them.

"Meggie, who has been quite ill, as you know, is better, indeed well, but nervous, being over-wrought as usual; and indeed I and the children are almost, but not quite, too much for her."

" *March* 1858.

"DEAREST MEGGIE,—Now, is not this good ? I was at De Beauvoir Square this afternoon, and Sarah said to me, 'Make haste and write your book; I will pay for the printing of it.' I went to Dr. Gull in the evening, having to speak to him, and mentioned it. 'Tell your sister I will divide it with her.'

" Being encouraged thus, I am setting to work in good earnest. Is it not striking how there seems to be a sort of success immediately attending me in writing, while in practice I have nothing but continual failing ? And my feeling respecting the two is so different. In philosophy I am in my element; I have such a glorious consciousness of power: I've no fear, and know what to do, and have an instinctive foresight of success. But in physic 'tis altogether different; I am a mere imitator and creeper—full of doubts and misgivings, dreading rather than desiring work. I think I cannot mistake the voice of God within me and without."

" *March* 1858.

" I feel sure the reason I am so slack is to make me write; for if only I were earning my living, I am sure I should not do it: I should leave off even now in spite of all resolutions. And this encourages me too ; for I do verily believe that when that object is accomplished—I mean the making me write—and I can safely be allowed enough to live on, I shall have it.

" For 'tis very curious, the most credulous superstition never equalled my belief in the intimate relation of all that happens to the Divine care for us. I can see nothing in all nature but the loving acts of spiritual beings, and know no reason for disbelieving anything that it should be conformable to love to do. It is a glorious world; I do delight in it. One can, and in a way that is almost worthy of it, when we no more care that it should be as we like, which of course we don't when we see 'tis right; and if we don't like it, we are wrong.

"I won't neglect anything in my practice, and will get on both with that and with the book as well.

"I didn't tell you how much interest Dr. Gull seemed to take in the publishing. He talked a long time about how it should be brought out in the best way, and by a good publisher; he thinks Murray. Of course, unless I can find some one to take it on its own account, I shall let him decide."

"March 29, 1858.

"I wish you were less subject to physical depression, that is, I should *like* it very much; but I blush when I find myself saying I wish things were otherwise than they are. I don't mean it. I can't mean it. I could not wish that, if I were to try ever so.

"People would think that strange, or difficult, or the result of some ridiculous philosophising. But they don't know the secret. They don't know how simple it is. They've no idea that it wants only FAITH (the most natural and easiest thing in the world when we can get rid of a few prepossessions of our own), and 'tis all done. I can't forget for one moment that man is being saved—the wonder and glory and joy of it fill and glorify all things. No one could forget it, or care in his secret heart about anything else, who once believed it. That's all. I do affirm nothing is wanted but faith. We are saved by faith, we are 'made right' by faith, that's being justified. Of course, it makes a man right to believe in Christ, in the redemption by His blood. He can't keep wrong. In spite of himself he is taken and turned right round, sees everything just the opposite to what he thought. He had no idea before the world was anything like that; all this evil was a mere mystery and perplexity to him, a thing he had to avoid as much as possible, to take as much care of himself and others as he could, and

—and—well, he didn't know; he could not understand, there were awful things, and very dark problems, we should not seek to penetrate so far, our duty was clearly to secure our own salvation and a happy eternity; and this world was clearly designed for happiness, man ought to enjoy himself, the creatures of God are good and to be received with thankfulness, it would be a beautiful world if there were not sin. And let us try to get such a position as will give us influence for good, for everlasting interests depend upon our exertions.

" Is it not so ?

" But if he believes! Behold old things have passed away, and all things have become new. There is not much to be said, indeed, words don't seem wanted. But, Meggie, the quiet bliss and wonder, and absolute surrender, the shame and self-abhorrence with which the heart shrinks back into itself, the new meaning there is put into that word ' God,' so that whereas before it came but feebly and with hesitation from our tongues, now it never will be absent—the fire that is in us to tell all men of this wonder, this God, whom it is eternal life to know— these things cannot be described. ' There is no more *want* ' —I think that comes nearest to it—we've got all. that we *want,* we wanted things before because we *didn't know* what the world was. Now hunger and thirst, and pain and nakedness, are welcome; they *are* what we want, for they are the salvation of the world. What we *like* is of no moment any more, to be crucified with Christ, that is our gladness ; our one desire, that our willing service should not be wanting in the work of God.

" Do not you see, darling, the brightness of that light, too bright for us to bear, and yet so mild and gentle ? we cannot gaze upon it, but we cast down our eyes and feel that it is there, and that contents us; that light which

L

swallows up all the darkness of the world, and the darkness of our hearts with it.

"Let us leave anxieties to God. Why need we bargain that our life should be a success, still less that it should not be a success purchased by sacrifices and sufferings? Let us leave things to God. If He starves us and our children, in so leaving them, we can BE STARVED. Believe me, there's nothing so very terrible in it; 'tis by no means the worst thing that can happen to a person, not so bad as constant anxiety, and doubt, and trembling, and questioning: 'Am I doing the right thing now?' 'will this answer, or won't that?' &c., &c. Look at the people who suffer hunger: are they so very unhappy? It does not strike me so.

"I know what incipient starvation is, having once upon a time gravely conceived the plan of shortening my life by that means, and abstained from food for a few days accordingly. It may be endured with a good conscience and a loving heart. Let us *believe in God* and rejoice in what *He* does, and if we don't like it, be ashamed of ourselves. That's what I am when I don't like the world. I think of old father Adam, and say, 'If it hadn't been for you, I shouldn't have been under this ridiculous illusion!'

"Don't you think with me, love, that the course for us is one of Faith, trusting in God, and leaving things we cannot see or know. Cast off these fears which may or may not be well founded. He's given you a work to do, viz., right or wrong, wise or foolish, mistaken or unmistaken, to support me in all things and fill me with confidence and joy and vigour; to make in truth the life of two persons flow through my single veins, that so my every word and action and endeavour should have a redoubled and glorified energy, should be felt by all as the work of two, and not of one, a more than twofold work, because instinct with love. That will SUCCEED. Meggie, I tell you, it will succeed, but whether it succeeds or not, is not the question; it is indeed no matter. It is God's will and work for us, it is the very type and image of Himself too.

"Only your own experience, and not even that, I think, can make you understand how I have missed you. I think of you all day, and I have come to the deliberate conclusion that being in love 'is a fool' to being married.

" This must be our motto, love, 'we accept evils ;' that's the hero's and the wise man's talisman. I must quote one thing from Jean Paul I read the other day. 'He who complains more of the wounds of poverty than a girl does of the wounds of her ears, is a poor coward, for they are alike designed to hang jewels in.' 'Twas in a review of Origen by young Vaughan ; a wonderful man he was, so good, so great, so poor. Dear, if some hope against hope, let us not despond against despondency. My 'philosophy' has been my good genius all my life, do you think it is going to fail me now ? "

"Man and his Dwelling-Place" was accepted by Parker at his own risk. Its favourable reception, and the consequent success of his first connected attempt to bring his philosophy before the public, seemed to justify Mr. Hinton in taking the step of giving up practice, and devoting his whole time to writing. Not only had he a dislike to the empiricism of the practice of medicine, which Voltaire has roughly defined as " putting medicines, of which we know little, into a body of which we know nothing," but he felt that the absorption of his mind in his thoughts unfitted him for discharging the responsibilities of a medical man. He therefore resolved on reducing his expenses to a minimum, and endeavouring to support his family with his pen.

He writes thus to his sister-in-law, Miss Caroline Haddon :—

" Charter House Square, August 1859.

"You are mistaken if you think there is in me any looking after mortifications for their own sake. I quite agree with you; they don't belong to my theory at all— are, indeed, wholly inconsistent with it. I feel my doctrine to be pre-eminently one of enjoyment, of rejoicing, and of doing what we like. You need not fancy any such inconsistency. But what there is in me, and I dare say what you noticed, is a doubt and uncertainty as to the right in practical life. I wholly doubt whether the plan on which the best of us base our lives—that of making ourselves comfortable primarily, and living better off than others because we have the means—is not radically unsound. I have not at present anything else to propose, but it goes against my feelings (I don't mean any ascetic love of self-mortification, I mean my true, natural feelings) to throw myself into that life.

"I know there is a better way. I know it must come; and though I don't want to hurry it, and have no confidence in my practical feelings, as I have in my intellectual ones, still at present it makes my life inharmonious. I am paying the penalty—the price, rather, perhaps—of future light. All my feelings on the point are vague and dim; but of this I think I am sure, that if the true human life were lived, the whole body of those who enjoy a 'comfortable living' in this country (and this includes us, Carrie, I am very sure) would rise up as one man and say, ' We will not live this way any more, while others are living as they do.' . . .

"With regard to myself, I want to take all care; but it is not much that is within my power. Can a plant not grow when the sun shines upon it? Is it not a condition of its being able to grow that it shall be under a necessity of growing? It is just so with me. I am under an inexorable fate to *think;* could not escape it if I tried or wished ever so much. And then, besides, I know also that deep at the bottom I do not wish, and never shall wish. It is not a passion—perhaps it used to be so; it is deeper than a passion. It is independent of pleasure and success. I could conceive it growing into a raging torture or a madness; but I think it will develop itself healthily and genially, especially if my external life succeeds, as I think it will. I know I am doing in the main the right thing. Crushed and fettered, my impulses might blast my life; but allowed to expand in natural activity, with varied and sufficient occupation, I think I may live a life most men might envy."

In relation to our accepted code of "the comfortable," to which he alludes in the earlier part of this letter, he used to say to his wife, "You must look at domestic comfort in its relations. You must take into view the want and distress of the other portion of the world; then that which appears bad is best. . . . We want to extend the sphere of morals; we must consider as coming within the sphere of morals our relations to other people. A beautiful house is not beautiful if other people are starving. Stealing does not seem wrong to some people; so, if we do not take into account our relations with others, it only shows what our moral status is."

It was, therefore, on principle as well as expediency that Mr. Hinton and his small family settled down in a tiny house in Tottenham, the dimensions of the sitting-room being such, that he used to boast that he could open the door with one hand, poke the fire with the other, and, had nature given him a third, could have opened the window, all without the trouble of rising from his seat. With only one servant, Mrs. Hinton had to lend a hand to most of the household avocations. None of Mr. Hinton's thoughts were perfect in his eyes till they had received her intelligent approval; and often he would plunge after her into the kitchen, where she was patiently endeavouring to master some culinary mystery, and keep up such a distracting blaze of metaphysics and physics, epicycles and parabolas, noumena and phenomena, as threatened to make the light pudding or pastry at dinner-time one of the heaviest problems to solve of even " this unintelligible world," and a painful proof of the reality of matter to the uninstructed digestive organs, its ingredients having undergone much transcendental confusion.

On one occasion, Mrs. Hinton, being anxious to entertain some of the poor mothers of the neighbourhood whom she had been in the habit of meeting, was betrayed by these influences into the untoward mistake of putting peppercorns instead of currants into a large cake she was making for their especial delectation, only discovering her mistake when her guests were assembling. But the blunder proved a happy one, for Mr. Hinton appeared among them, and made them a capital little speech, how a woman's words were meant to be as sweet as currants, and make life a perpetual plumcake to her husband, only somehow some of their tongues make a mistake, and put in biting pepper instead, and no wonder the poor fellow had to go and wash his mouth out at the ' George and Dragon.' Many a husband found his home the sweeter, at least for a time, for the " pepper-cake."

Household difficulties were further complicated by Mr. Hinton's peculiar views on education. He had a dislike of all punishments, as apt to base good conduct on selfish fears and make self-regard rather than regard for others the ruling motive; he considered that children could best learn from experience. But though Experience is a good teacher, her school-fees are proverbially high, particularly in a small house, where strict order is especially necessary. So that "plain living and high thinking" were carried on under some drawbacks.

At first the experiment seemed to answer fairly well, Mr. Hinton earning with his pen considerably more than the £200 a year to which Mrs. Hinton's care and economy had reduced their expenditure. Thackeray, the then editor of the "Cornhill," accepted for that periodical a series of papers called "Physiological Riddles," exclaiming, "Whatever else this fellow can do, he can write!" These papers, endeavouring to prove the unity of the organic and inorganic from the scientific side, were afterwards published, with a few additions, under the title of "Life in Nature." Most of the papers afterwards published as "Thoughts on Health" also came out in the "Cornhill" at this time.

It was in his narrow little Tottenham house that the "Mystery of Pain," to the genesis of which allusion has already been made, was written, though not published till some years later. It was in his small suburban patch of a garden that the gathering of a few green peas gave rise to that train of thought which loosened the burthen of years from his own heart, and, when afterwards given to the world, proved a "door into heaven" to so many a troubled soul—a book of which even so profound a thinker on moral subjects as Dr. J. H. Newman said that "it contained things both new and true."

The following extracts from letters to two of his friends contain the first germ ideas of the book:—

" *Tottenham, January* 1862.

"Don't you think I might hope for acceptance for a
little book under the title of 'The Mystery of Pain: a
Book for the Sorrowful'? For the motto I should take,
'I cried unto God, What profit is there in my blood?' I
seem to feel the volume in my heart; and when I have
done with 'Life in Nature' (the 'Riddles'), which ought to
be soon, I think I shall begin it; perhaps, at the same
time, by way of balance and completeness, as well as ease
to myself, making a commencement of—what I think I
ought to do—a thorough statement of my metaphysical
position, to be called, perhaps, 'Outlines of a New System of Metaphysics.' I should like to do these two
together; and for my own sake I ought. I hardly could
be content to do either alone; so I could perhaps
better keep the metaphysics out of the first, and the
questionable rhetoric out of the latter."

" *Tottenham, July* 1862.

"Whatever the world is (morally), it is certainly something very different from that of which it gives us the
impression; whatever the fact is, it is surely something
unlike the seeming. Don't you see, even without special
scientific training, how clear *Science* has made this? In
the end of my little paper, 'Seeing with the Eyes Shut,' I
just referred to this. . . . The fact in contrast to the
phenomenon must be unseeable. If we could 'see' it,
it would be an invention. I think, indeed, that my utter
unimpressibility to the fact of our not seeing—my perfect
and inevitable assurance that the truth must be one invisible to us—does as much as anything here and elsewhere to make my arguments seem insufficient. I can
hardly help taking it for granted that every one 'sees'
this. I believe my scientific training helps me here. All

science is a recognising the invisible; and, indeed, that general attitude of mind, that conviction that our seeing is not seeing—is nothing at all in respect to true or false —I think ought to be acquired on scientific ground; that is, on other than religious ground. A man should come to theology with this conviction grown into him, not having to acquire it there.

"Don't you see, indeed, that 'walk by faith, not by sight,' is really 'walk scientifically,' knowledge-wise, according to the truth; and, indeed, that the sum of all that man has learned is the conforming of his thought to that precept?

"And here is the whole point between us. Are not you, in your questionings and doubts, really demanding that you should walk by sight? It cannot be given you. The salvation of man—I mean the fact and doing of it— is to the human eye (I should say the self-eye) invisible; and must be invisible, because it is so large and good. I feel I am simply transferring to modern terms the words 'walk by faith' when I say 'regard in all things the (necessarily unseen) fact of man's redemption.' I don't demand an intellectual vision—only a heart-vision—only the indispensable demands of religion."

" Tottenham, July 1862.

"Now there's another idea has just occurred to me— one of a sort of which I have had many, and which please me as being a kind of union between that which refers to thought and to life. For there is a thing that I clearly see, that the laws of the mental, the physical, and the ethical (or practical) are one; each may be expressed in terms of the other. Now, here is a rule in science, a rule of thinking — viz., that effects have not always single causes, but continually depend on compositions of causes, of which two may neutralise each other, and not be apparent in the effect; so that causes are not to be learned only by a study of effects. Very different effects may be while causes are largely the same.

"Now this struck me as having a practical bearing, and a really very pretty and useful one. In our efforts to remove effects (say grief or sorrow), we continually try to do it by removing the causes. Would it not be wiser to try 'composing' them? Given a cause of grief, how is the effect to be averted? Causes can't be got rid of, nothing can—*i.e.*, at bottom and ultimately; and practically, even, this is often, very often, the case also. But something can always be added to the cause—something which will neutralise, or better, alter, even invert the effect, make joy instead of sorrow. You see the bearings of this, don't you? so that I need not apply it.*

"In fact, is it not exactly my practical idea, almost the whole of it? I would seek to get different results, not by removing or setting aside, but by adding; and the beauty is, that this is simply better science. Men's ways of acting have represented an imperfect, mistaken, necessarily failing scientific method. It isn't according to nature that they should have succeeded.

---

* To those who are not familiar with Mr. Hinton's thoughts, this may want an application to make it clear. Take the instance of the offices of a mother to her babe. Abstract the love, and what have you? Pain, weariness, wakefulness, anxiety, toil. But add to the causes of pain a mother's love, and you have the unspeakable joy of a mother over her first-born. The pain, the weariness and wakefulness, the anxiety and toil are all there; but they have become the glowing heart of a great joy—the very conditions of self-giving which make the joy deepest. So the presence of pain in the world proves nothing against the possible blessedness of man, points rather to the world "having been adapted, altogether made. to be the scene of an overpowering, an absorbing love." We cannot get rid of the pain or its cause, but we may bring in other causes which, here or hereafter, will turn it into the very heart of joy, the blessedness of love made perfect in sacrifice.

" There are no thoughts that give me more pleasure than such as these—those that show reason and necessity in things that have seemed evil and unaccountably depressing—and the more so because all such perceptions are the fullest things possible of hope. If men have tried wrongly, then the failure is no sign that they shall not succeed. As certain as possible it is that men shall be happy, shall find in all things cause for joy. They shall certainly succeed when they know how to try, when they have learned to use those causes rightly, to make them elements in a larger and more adequate system of causes. . . . Isn't there a light on the whole of human life in seeing this ? Take all its activities together except a few, and are they not all included in the vain effort to get happy by putting away instead of using causes of sorrow ? 'Tis just like a foolish bad science ; they haven't found the law of things, and for the remedy there is needed—what ? Evidently knowledge."

" Tottenham, July 1862.

"Do you know—to show you how simple it is—all my philosophy about pain is contained in this little incident. It happened at the time I was thinking about it, and was one of the things that gave my ideas more thoroughness. You must remember that all nature exists in the least—*tota in minimis.* It was an Italian said that—I forget his name, but I hold him among the greatest of geniuses ; that one sentence is enough. He was a physiologist.

"My incident was this: riding home one evening, I found myself, about half a mile from the end of the journey, alone in the omnibus. So I said to the conductor, 'Don't go on for me if you are not going otherwise;' and accordingly he let me out and turned back. Now, as I walked along the road, I was, of course, distinctly glad, not only that the men could go home to their families the sooner, but that it was my walking (and wearing out my shoes) that enabled them. Don't you see I must have felt this? that man is made to feel so; that in this (at least) his nature is shown; that if he had a larger life, it would be so with greater pains; that—here's the point—the true bigness of his life *is measured by his pains?*

"Let me tell you how I came to that last idea. It is another case of a 'least.' I was gathering peas in my garden, and, of course, in doing that one gets one's face scratched a little, and sundry small inconveniences, which, in fact, make the fun of doing it. Now, while thus employed, I thought—how could I help thinking of this very thing?—it is our nature that the enjoyment of our life demands little inconveniences, exertions, small pains; these are the only things in which we rightly feel our life at all. If these be not there, existence becomes worthless or worse; success in putting them all away is fatal. So it is men engage in athletic sports, spend their holidays in climbing up mountains, find nothing so enjoyable as that which taxes their endurance and their energy.

"This is the way we are made, I say. It may or may not be a mystery or a paradox; it is a fact. Now this enjoyment in endurance is just according to the intensity of the life; the more physical vigour and balance, the more endurance can be made an element of satisfaction. A sick man can't stand it. The line of enjoyable suffering is not a fixed one; it fluctuates with the perfectness of the life. Now, don't you see the step I took? Is it not a perfect revelation? That our pains are, as they are, unen-

durable, awful, overwhelming, crushing, not to be borne
save in mere misery and dumb impatience, which utter
exhaustion alone makes patient,—that our pains are thus
unendurable, means not that they are too great, but that
we are sick. We haven't got our proper life. Only think
of this being our heritage, our proven nature and destiny,
a life so intense and so large that it shall make all
human pains the conditions of its exuberance! I see this
in my heart so plainly, I long with quite a painful intensity to be able to make others see it with me. Do not
you see it is the moral side of my idea of our being altruistic,—having a consciousness co-extensive with humanity ? . . . So you perceive pain is no more necessarily
an evil, but an essential element of the highest good, *felt*
as evil by want in us—partly want of knowledge, partly
want of love. . . . Christ's life and death, which seems
so separate from ours, so contrasted with it, is, in truth,
the type and pattern of our own, is the revelation of it,—
of our life as well as of God's."

Speaking of our involuntary sacrifices, our unaccepted
pains, Mr. Hinton once put it thus : Suppose, instead of
Curtius, a slave, hating Rome, and cursing her with his
last breath, had been bound hand and foot and thrown
into the gulf to save the city. Yet suppose, in some
future state of existence, that slave had come to see the
part Rome was to play in the civilisation of the world,
and was to say from his heart, "I am glad I was sacrificed for Rome," at once the involuntary sacrifice would
be made his own, filling him with an infinite joy and
satisfaction. So Mr. Hinton held that our most blank-
seeming woes, the pains and privations we have the most
grudged as barren of all good, may have forward ends—
be, in fact, so much stored-up force—and become the
very material of the noblest joy when "the more life and

fuller" shall have revealed the true uses they serve in the redemption of the world.

But in tracing out what gave rise to Mr. Hinton's thoughts on pain, it must ever be borne in mind that the real source of inspiration, with regard not only to the "Mystery of Pain," but to so much of his highest and most helpful thinking, lay not in the secluded study or in quiet contact with nature, but in the back streets and slums of London. He was a man who emphatically dared to look upon the awful face of life, believing that it was the marred and thorn-crowned face of Love; believing that the evil phenomenon is ever to reveal a good reality behind it, which alone has actual existence; that, however black and meaningless it may look, it is the stained glass window seen from without, radiant with martyr and saint and divinest meaning when seen from within.

"I thank God," he exclaims in his MS. notes, "there is so much ugliness and evil, so many illusions, because each one of them is the voucher for a beautiful and good reality, as each illusion of the sense in science is evidence and voucher for some true scientific fact. I clasp evil and wrongness to my heart; they are life, they are God's tenderest love. He says to me in them, 'Look, my child, and tell me what I am doing; 'tis painful to you at first, but you will love it when you see it.' By faith, I see it even now, O my Father! and love it, though unseen, because thou doest it. . . . Blessed love of God! that by the evil of a phenomenon expels the deadly real evil that affects the spirit; loving ministers that come around with sharp swords to slay, not us, but the death that is within us."

CHAPTER IX.

The following letters are to his friend Mr. Henry King, on a recent bereavement :—

" Tottenham, July 30, 1860.

" I have just received your letter, for which I very heartily thank you. If I had reflected I should perhaps have hesitated before touching so lightly a chord which vibrates in your heart so deeply, yet I can hardly regret doing that which has gained for me your letter and its profound expression of feelings which are common to all hearts, though perhaps experienced in all their intensity only by a few. I feel that an experience such as yours almost demands rather a reverent silence than an attempt to urge thoughts, which may be felt to be full of consolation by those whom Providence spares from the deepest affliction, and yet may be found to be quite powerless over the heart when really lacerated. I know how different a quiet contemplation, at our ease, of that which ought to comfort us in sorrow is from the feverish and unavailing effort to calm a present grief.

"And yet I cannot renounce the pleasure of trying to impart to you some thoughts which I have had bearing on the subject to which you refer, which I think are really adapted to soothe some causeless grief and remove forebodings which do injustice to God's bountiful goodness. I shall try to avoid, in expressing to you my thoughts, what might seem like abstract speculation remote from human sympathies, and yet, if my language should seem to be of this kind, I know you will be able to understand that in my feeling, those speculative truths are the form under which the dearest and most human joys and sorrows, hopes and fears, and aspirations clothe themselves.

"I have thought on meditating on the future state, and the change which we cannot doubt will take place in our feelings and our very being even, in that higher state, that almost all which is capable of paining the heart or of seeming repulsive to that emotional nature which is the best and highest part of us, arises from a view which may be shown, even on admitted principles, to be a mistaken one. And that is, that conception that the difference between the heavenly state and ours depends, even in any part at all, upon the loss and *taking away* of anything we now possess. I think the difference consists wholly in an addition to our present faculties, leaving us therefore all that we now possess, all that we now feel,—all relations except sinful and evil ones that we have ever borne,—all being as much as ever they were, only altered and placed in a different relation by added faculties and perceptions, to reduce them to the true position, cause them to be felt, not as realities, which they are not, but truly, as they are, phenomenal—the signs and evidences, nay, the very fact (as it is capable of being presented to certain faculties of ours), of a truer, higher, reality.

"May I use my own illustration to make clear my meaning ? A being with sight only would feel mere appearances as realities; but when there was bestowed upon him the fulness of his faculties (as related to the physical), and he becomes able to use the power of the touch, then the appearances would not be realities to him any more; they would be only appearances; but they would be to him all that they were before, nay, they would be unspeakably more. He could understand them, use them, value them aright, and in every sense find them more and more worthy of regard than when, by his deficiency, they were felt as realities. And so it is with us; feeling and thinking of phenomena as realities, they mock and deceive us; but feeling and knowing them but as phenomena, surely they would be full of unutterable worth, signi-ficance, and glory. I cannot think (I speak not of my feelings, but of the hardest and severest thought) that spirits in heaven are lost to earthly things, or feel or think them less. Rather it must be that they then truly grasp and possess them, and learn to estimate their worth. In the utmost earnestness of belief, I hold that this world is the eternal world,—as much so to spirits in heaven as men upon earth; and that while we can rise to the true level of the grandeur and glory of this poor seeming life only by hard striving with sense and passion and unbelief, and never can worthily attain to it at all, those that have been clothed upon with the house that is from heaven see it with unimpaired vision, know it, live in it, rejoice in it with an intenser life and a more vivid apprehension, as well as with a calmer and more unruffled joy than ours.

"Indeed these words of St. Paul express my entire thought, 'Not that we would be unclothed, but clothed upon.' To pass into the spiritual is not to be 'unclothed;' it is to be added to, to be made more complete, and that is all. It is by want and loss that we are not in the spiritual. The flesh is not something added; it is something wanting only; the false substantiality of the physical

M

phenomena to us is the seeming only arising from the defective power within.

"But I know this only meets half your case, and that the doubt whether the moral change which accompanies entrance into the spiritual world, the perfected holiness, may not break the bonds of mortal sympathy, weighs not less heavily than the other. On this ground, too, it seems to me that a true conception of the facts must remove all question, and give us a joyful assurance. It must be that the sympathy is intensified, not diminished—made perfect, and not chilled. It becomes like that of our Maker, who knows our frame, though He does not share its weakness, and remembers that we are dust; sympathy like that of a parent for a child, which is surely the deeper and the tenderer for being above the sphere of its little passions and mistakes. Whose sympathy with a child is best and truest—that of another child who has all the same follies and errors, and petty interests and cares, or that of a mother who knows them all, but does not on her own behalf share in them; who lives in them and feels for them only through her love? The deliverance from our needs and weaknesses and passions, from our errors and delusions, even from our sins, cannot quench sympathy, but rather first enables it to burn with a pure and deathless flame. We must remember that we are under illusion—they have escaped from it; we are diseased—they have been restored to health. Can this diminish love or dry up the fountains of pity? or, if it did, how could that be heaven?

"I think of the case thus:—Which sympathises best with a poor delirious patient—another sick man who is delirious with him, and shares his illusions, or the friend who tenderly sits by his bedside, watching for and cherishing each gleam of returning reason, but whose heart throbs none the less with deep emotion over his visionary joys and sorrows?* . . . For a true sympathy with our weakness, our folly, our uttermost unworthiness, we want one who is delivered from their power, one who has no more the struggle to maintain, who can come down and enter into the lowest depths within us, because he can no more fear a fall, can touch and heal the darkest stain, because incapable of soil. . . .

"Such as this, I think, must be the change from earth to heaven, except that any image is infinitely too feeble to express the bestowment of a deeper and truer life, that giving us a perfect consciousness of the eternal reality which shall redeem us for ever from the dream-consciousness of a life lived in shows. For this radical conception it is which seems to me to give the true clue to all these questions, that our present consciousness is strictly like that of a dream, in that it is a feeling of things as existing which do not exist. We are still condemned to feel the dream as if truly existing; even though we may *know* otherwise, we still *feel* so. Our friends in heaven have awaked, and know it is a dream. But how should that break the bonds of love?

"You will excuse my writing so long a letter to you, but I feel as if in such thoughts as these there were sources of legitimate consolation and strength, and I believe you will at any rate accept them as a token of sincere sympathy."

" Tottenham, August 17, 1860.

"I am sorry so much time has passed before I have had an opportunity of taking up again the subject of your

---

* So Dante of Beatrice :—
  " Ond' ella, appresso d' uno pio sospiro,
    Gli occhi drizzò vêr me con quel sembiante
    Che madre fa sopra figliuol deliro."—PARA., Canto i. 100-103.

letter. I have indeed, I must confess, somewhat shrunk
from doing so, partly, that I have feared lest I should do
too great an injustice to the subject, partly, because a
personal grief like yours seems to me a sacred thing, to
be treated rather with mute reverence than with words,
especially by one who has not been called upon to undergo
the same, and who therefore cannot tell how vain those
words might easily be made to seem, even to himself. I
do not think I could attempt to meet the questions you
propose, except from my confidence that you so desire to
know my thoughts upon them, that you will be sure to
overlook all faults in their expression.

"Do not suppose that I have a perfect or consistent
theory or scheme upon the subject of our intercourse [with
the dead], that I can apply to the solution of all difficulties, and that there is nothing which remains to me still
dark and doubtful. Until the receipt of your first letter,
I had not given particular thought to the questions it
suggested, as, indeed, in God's kind providence there had
arisen no event particularly to press it on my mind. What
I wrote you was simply what occurred to me as the obvious
bearing of views which seemed true to me in other respects, upon the questions which weigh on your mind. It
is a great happiness to me that you have found them at
all suitable or helpful, and I rejoice also in the belief that
you will find them capable of meeting further questions.
But, I still feel that for full justice to them, there ought
to be a personal feeling of their overwhelming urgency,
the thoughts should be deepened by profound emotion.
I know that in this respect I am on quite a different
standing ground from you, and so I cannot escape the
consciousness that words which may seem to me to go to the
heart of the subject, may be felt by you to play merely on
the surface. You will pardon me, therefore, if it be so.

"I will begin with the latter of your two questions, that of recognition. I understand you to feel thus: if in this state our feeling has not been true, if the events over which we have rejoiced or grieved have been not real events, but only things which seemed to happen; nay, if we ourselves are not what we are conscious of being, but something, although even more glorious, yet different, how shall we, when our feeling is made true, and our consciousness is of that now unknown reality, REGAIN our friends? Even supposing the friend restored, will not that restoration be of something not to be recognised as the *same* friendship that was enjoyed of old?

"If I have stated your thoughts rightly, it seems to me susceptible of an answer entirely satisfactory—of many answers indeed, or rather, it suggests many topics. But, the direct reply, I think, is, that it assumes a loss of remembrance, hereafter, which is not, even in the remotest degree, connected with my view of the present state. Do you see this? It seems to me as if the entire force of the feeling rested on the idea, that if this state be one of a false (or *inadequate*, for that is rather the fact, it is false only by defect) feeling on our part, therefore, what we now feel cannot, or will not, be remembered perfectly hereafter. But, is there any real connection here? Why should not all we have felt, thought, performed, in any way experienced here, be as much an element of our conscious remembrance in the future upon the one view of its nature, as upon the other? Am I right in thinking that this needs only to be pointed out to be recognised, and that it removes part of the feeling you express?

"But, besides this, in respect to recognition, I think the view I entertain of the relation of the physical to the spiritual, so far from being at a disadvantage in compárison with any other, has especial advantage. Let me repeat, that I hold the change from this earthly to the heavenly state to be by *no loss at all*, but only *by an adding*. All, therefore, that belongs to the one state remains in the other, it is altered only in its relation to us. Our feeling in respect to it is altered, by the giving of new life, a more perfect being, and more adequate powers to us. Think of the case abstractly: going to heaven, is, on this view, simply, the *perfecting of our nature and being*. Might we not then put aside any particular difficulties which might occur to us about details, as it were, and be fully assured that this could not possibly involve us in any loss, or inflict on us the sacrifice, especially of that which God has made dearest to all that, in our present state, is highest and holiest within us. Surely that which can make us fear that we shall lose by being made perfect, must be an error. I think I see clearly that it *is* an error, but even if I could not do so, and could not logically extricate myself from such a conclusion, I think I should have none the less confidence.

"But I may perhaps make my view clearer to you by coming to a lower ground altogether. I think you will allow fully that if we retained in heaven recognition and enjoyment of the inferior pleasures and occupations of this earthly life, it is certain the higher ones would not be absent. Now this is what I do think—that is, I think it negatively so to speak,—it would agree perfectly with my general view, there is no logical reason why I should not entertain that idea. For it is evidently not forbidden to us, if we think of this physical as a mode in which the spiritual, the eternal is perceived; which is, in one point of view, the very basis and corner-stone of all my thought: It is this I am seeking—very imperfectly and inarticulately I know—to say. We *are* in the spiritual and eternal world—there is no other in which we can be—for there *is* no other. These physical existences, as we call them, are the spiritual and eternal existence *as it is perceived by us*, related to the true existence as the 'appearance' perceived by the eye is related to the physical object of which it is the appearance, that is—they are the phenomena of it; or to speak in recognised metaphysical terms, 'the unknown ground of the known phenomena is that spiritual and eternal, which we recognise by the religious faculties.'

"These phenomena of course do not answer to the truth of that of which they are the phenomena. They cannot because of the littleness of our faculties—but they are rightly perceived *as phenomena*, even as the eye rightly sees 'appearances' which by no means answer to the truth of the object so perceived. If, therefore, we had our perfect being, the physical would still be perceived, just as it is now perceived (probably), but—and here is the essential point, *it would be perceived as only a phenomenon*—that is, it would be perceived truly, as it *is*. *Now*, by our defect, by absence of the faculties which would give us a conscious perception of the reality as it is, *i.e.*, of the spiritual and the eternal—and here I only repeat the accepted dictum of both science and philosophy by their best exponents—that essential existence is not *consciously* perceived by us, but only phenomena. I say by this defect in us, the phenomenal is *felt* to be—not as it is, only phenomenal—but as absolute and real. This is the wrongness, the illusion of our state—that that which is only phenomenal (and is indeed therefore rightly 'perceived') is not felt as it is, as only phenomenal, or apparent by virtue of our faculties, but *as actually the existence.*

"Now, it is evident what, holding this view, my con-

ception must be of the heavenly state, when the wanting
faculties, by which we may consciously perceive and feel
the absolute being, are added to us; I must conceive, not
that we shall cease to perceive the phenomenal, but that
we shall perceive it in its true relations,—perceive it
rightly—FEEL it rightly, and therefore not as now (which
is our error and evil) as really existing, but as the mode
in which to certain faculties of ours—faculties which perceive things not as they are, but only 'inadequate' appearances of them—the spiritual and eternal reality (the sole
reality) appears.

"I think you will see the parallel at once between
this view and the relation of our physical sight and touch;
and that 'going to heaven' may be compared to adding
touch to one who had previously possessed only sight,
and by whom, therefore, 'appearances' had been *felt* as
(physical) realities, and who, accordingly, would have
been deceived, been under illusion, and would, in a word,
have felt and believed himself to have had to do with
one thing, while he truly (speaking of the physical) would
have had to do with another; and would, of course, have
failed and blundered and been disappointed, and have
found his life a mystery (physically). Need I say, just as
we find our life a mystery, *spiritually?* or point out how we
do so for the very same reason; viz., that we have thought
we have had truly to do with things which are only
phenomena, while in very truth we have had to do with
the eternal spiritual realities which we have ignored. I
trust I have made this intelligible, but I know I am very
apt to fail. I will, however, assume that (by means of
omitting the parentheses, and with the help of the patience
which I believe you will not grudge) it is clear to you.
And then I will trust to you to refer to this, as to a
standard, your remembrances of any other expressions I

have used bearing on the same point; they have all been attempts to say *this.*

"Now, taking this view, must not my '*à fortiori*' argument be granted me? The spirits of the just made perfect have all the part in the phenomenal that we have—that they ever had—that *can be had.* It *is* only phenomenal; and he who perceives and feels and knows it *as* only phenomenal, knows it not least but MOST, perceives most in it, possesses it most truly. This applies to all phenomenal things, even the least and lowest, as I have said, and if to them, then surely to the highest.

"I trust this does go—I confess it seems to me to go—to the very root and heart of your question about recognition. There must be recognition, because all that was, still is—only more is added. Nay, indeed, only for us who are left behind can it be a *re*-cognition at all, for to them it is a continued undisturbed *cognition.* They cannot recover knowledge, because they have never ceased to know; we shall know again when raised up to their level, and not only the old sympathy is restored, but a new sympathy infinitely outweighing all. We shall know again, we may well say, for then we shall see this dark, toilsome, disappointing life must be known again to be known at all. I thank you for this thought, which your letter has thus suggested to me, of knowing our earthly life again. My heart rests in it, and cannot you partake with me in the feeling? It seems an epitome of all my thoughts. We are to know, we must know, our life again. It seems one thing to us; it *is* another. It is for that I thank God. It seems, alas! how dark, how sad a scene; it *is* the redemption of the world. Is it not a joy to think that when we clasp our friends again in heaven, and look back with them upon the past, it will be to see it, not as we have felt it, but as it is; to take not man's view, but

God's; to know, and know together, that the dark scenes were dark with light too bright for mortal eye, the sorrow turning into dearest joys when seen to be the filling up of Christ's, who withholds not from us His own crown, bidding us drink of His cup, and be baptized with His baptism, and saying to our reluctant hearts, 'What I do thou knowest not now, but thou shalt know hereafter.'

"It is not loss that we shall then know and feel our life to have been a different thing from that which we feel it now—shall so feel its spiritual and eternal bearing that all else shall evidently be to us only the phenomena, the appearances, the forms of that. There is no other loss but the filling of these forms until they are known and felt to be but forms.

"I am writing too much to you, but I like to dwell upon these thoughts. I do not see how any one could grow weary of them. The conviction that God's work of saving man is really, truly, done in this petty, wearisome, false life of ours, that will not be got right (because it IS right) fills me with joy. It satisfies. It is a boundless gratification to the heart, a boundless interest and stimulus to the intellect. I verily believe if this gospel were preached we should hear no more of the difficulty of making daily life religious, or of fixing the thoughts upon eternal things. *There are no others.* I love this revelation, because it makes religion everything, by making everything religious.

"I think a very few words will suffice for the first of your questions. What proof have we, so that we may feel sure, that physical things are not true existences, but are falsely felt so by us? My answer is—The qualities of them are incompatible with the idea of existence. Sense gives us the impression of their existence; reason, which has authority in respect to what ought to be thought, denies it. We are bound to believe some other reason for our feeling their existence (which feeling, no one more strenuously affirms than I; the doctrine of man's defectiveness rests on his feeling that to exist which does not exist), some other reason, I say, must be given (and must be discovered if it be not known) for our feeling the existence of physical things. Their existence is disproved. If I entered on the question *how* it is disproved, I should not be able to do it any justice. May I mention, that in 'Man and his Dwelling-Place,' Book ii., Chap. 2 (I think), I have stated, and tried to answer, the very argument you use about the order, &c., of physical events? I need only suggest one thing in which you will, I think, agree with me, that a definite and rational order in events has no necessary bearing on their being actual or phenomenal. In fact, phenomena, must, by the nature of the case, be orderly and have a rational nexus. I use passive, necessary (*i.e.*, rational) sequence as an argument of phenomenalness.

"I think you will now perceive in what sense I say our present consciousness is a *dream* consciousness. It is so only in one respect, viz., the feeling and assurance of existence in respect to that which does not exist, of doing that which is not done, but only to man's feeling is, or is done. (This also I have tried to make clear in Dialogue 3.) Of course it is not a dream of the *individual man*, but in relation to the whole humanity.

"I seem to have done very poor justice to the questions you proposed, and I trust that you will be so kind as to let me know what points remain to your mind unanswered, and what need fuller explanation. With you I feel that I am like 'a child crying in the night,' and yet I seem to feel, also, that a revelation has been made to us, and means given us by which we may rise, and are designed to rise, to a state of knowledge and satisfaction much higher than we occupy at present; that it is in ourselves, and not in God, that we are straitened. Yours most sincerely,

"JAMES HINTON.

"*P.S.*—Although I have written so much, I cannot refrain from adding one thought.   In respect to our recognising the love and tenderness and self-sacrifice which have glorified this life, I think we may draw great assurance from a fact which seems evident to me, viz., that these feelings and the other deep emotions which seem to be excited by physical things, really have relation to the eternal, and not to the phenomenal; that we feel them because it is our nature and our destiny to have a conscious relation with the eternal which we have not now, so that the future change is but the fulfilling, setting free, and perfecting of this part of our nature.   I conceive that the emotions raised in us by physical beauty or grandeur, for instance, are of this kind, hence the 'mystery' of the power of 'matter' so to move us.   *It* has not that power. These things move us as pictures or images.   The emotion truly applies to the reality."

Elsewhere he writes, "What trifling nonsense to be amazed and awed at mere mechanical necessity, just what is in lifting and dropping a piece of paper, only very large and very small.   Good God! it can't be this in nature that fills our souls to overflowing with awe and wonder and delight, that speaks to us of God, and patience, and love, and peace, rebukes us for sin, comforts us in sorrow, gives us assurance of infinite tenderness and wisdom— there must be more in it than we can see that way. Think of the sublimity, the beauty, the grace, the rightness, the life, that lifts us above ourselves, and fills us not only with an unutterable joy, but with longings unutterable too, that says to us, Be more, be better, come and join heart and hand with us. Can this be merely that which science shows us? so much matter, so many properties, motions so numerous and rapid, mere mechanical necessity. Let us bethink ourselves a moment, if there must not be more in nature than we can see with such glasses."

"July 8, 1861.

"DEAREST MEGGIE,—Where do you think I am now? I am at Dr. Gull's. I have taken up my abode here for a week or so, to do a paper with the Doctor, the one we were talking about before. I want to be engaged on matters of this sort, and not to be compelled to bring forward my own ideas too soon. I want time for the thoughts to mature, and so that they may present themselves in fit shape to me, and not need to be worked up.

"YOUR LOVING HUSBAND."

The next letter in relation to "Man and his Dwelling-Place" is addressed to one of his Australian friends.

" Tottenham, July 1861.

"DEAR MR. BLAIR,—I shall address you in the style and with the freedom of an old friend. For, to say the truth, though I think I never had the pleasure of seeing you, yet having so frequently heard of you from my brother-in-law, James Haddon, I had something of that feeling towards you before I read your review of my book, for which I now thank you very sincerely. I am much obliged to you for it, and appreciate the sympathy and kindly feeling it displays, as well as the pains you have taken to make your way through its ' confusion.' I don't mean this by way of remonstrance. I am quite aware—was long ago indeed—of the justice of your remarks on that point. The book is the very soul of disorder, but then, I was, metaphorically, all of a heap when I wrote it; and I was harassed beyond measure with the idea that people would not get my idea, so that I kept on giving it them all in a lump, over and over again. I'm aware of that; but then it is my first book, and considering it has been ascribed over here in turns to Whewell, Vaughan, Kingsley, and one or two others (even Whately!), I hope it may pass in a crowd.

"By the by, I'll mention it before I forget it, what makes you say it has excited a sensation in America? Let me know all you know on this point, for though I know it was reprinted there, I have never heard a syllable about it thence from that day to this. Your review is the first intimation I have seen on this point. I am naturally, therefore, curious.

"But now I am going to call you to account, or perhaps rather to confess to a great failure of expository capacity in myself. For I must tell you that you do not quite rightly represent what I meant to express. I know I have not properly guarded against the misapprehension, and I wish I had received your review only a few weeks earlier, I would have touched on the matter in a short preface I have written to the book. My real statement I think just meets the objections you very justly urge against the view as you put it. Do not you represent me as saying that our defectiveness makes us *think of*, or *conceive*, nature as dead (inert)? What I mean to say is, that it makes us FEEL it so, makes us *experience* it so; I think you see the difference. It is a question of *being*, and not of thinking. That there is a real difference between what I meant, and what you gathered from my book, is proved by your criticisms, which are applicable to the latter, not to the former. I entirely agree with you that the change which can make us feel nature truly must go deeper than the reception of Christianity, it must go deeper than any *individual* change; I think, deeper even than bodily death itself—it must affect our very being, and our *physical* as well as our moral state. What part 'death,' commonly so called, has, I leave unsettled, but in principle I entirely agree with you. What affects us, I take it, is a deadness affecting MAN (not the individual primarily). What can deliver us, therefore, must be something also affecting man. I have spoken of this (too briefly) in Chapter ii. Book iii., ' Of Life.'

" I am glad you feel my little work to be of a practical and transforming nature. It was this kind of influence I hoped it might exert in some small degree; I thought it must if I could succeed in uttering what I had seen and felt, because I found its transforming power on myself. I am little anxious that it should turn out that my particular ideas are the right ones; but I long to see a purer and worthier life of piety among those who possess it, and what must, I think, come with that—a wide and ruling influence of it over the world. I think the time is near when both must be.

" With sincere regards and hearty thanks, I am, yours very truly,

" JAMES HINTON."

The following letters—to two of his friends—amongst other topics, refer to himself as a thinker :—

" *Tottenham*, 1862.

" Schlegel is not a great scholar; it would be easy to turn his work into ridicule. That's exactly what I feel of myself—I'm not a scholar, nor is there the making of a scholar in me. ' But,' Müller adds, ' when a new

science is to be created, the imagination of the poet is
wanted even more than the accuracy of the scholar.'
That I feel, too, that though I am by no means a poet
in any technical sense, yet my affinities are all with
them, and I have for 'some time been well aware that
my faculty is imagination.   I made this discovery,
and felt rather interested.   I think I recognise in this
one reason of my difficulty in literature.   I have not
my imagination at command for *artistic* purposes, because
it is. engaged, absorbed in *work;* it is not available for
the form of my thoughts, because it is built into their
substance."

In other words, his imagination was like the actinic
rays which are only partially available for the photo-
grapher of foliage, being already taken up in performing
work in the substance of the leaf, leaving but a black and
imperfect impression on the sensitive plate.

                            " *Tottenham, September* 1862.
    "Thank you very much for your correspondent's criti-
cisms.   These things are very useful to me.   I should
never find out myself how to meet the thoughts in other
people's minds.   Altogether I should be vastly better for
more of the dramatic element, the power of putting myself
into other people's minds.   In writing especially it would
help me immensely, would it not?   I'm not without
hopes that it will grow up in me when I get rest—which
I earnestly anticipate—from thinking.   I almost expect
that quite new faculties will spring up within me, which
now the other keeps latent.   Now I have confessed to
you one of my weaknesses, and having got so far, shall I
indulge myself with going on and confiding to you my two
great ambitions ?   One is to make some useful mechanical

invention; the other, to write a tale! Don't you pity me?"

" Tottenham, September 1862.

" I taught myself German, in a fit of enthusiasm, at about seventeen, procuring a grammar and dictionary, and, of all books in the world,' Faust.' With these I sat down, and read ' Faust,' with a few exceptions here and there which beat me, and I remember it to this day. I wish I read German with facility, but I seem never to have time to sit down and master it, or even to read books in it, though lately I have compared the greater part of Kant's ' Critique,' sentence by sentence, with an English version; so I shall be obliged to you for any scraps of German you may think pleasing or useful to me. . . .

" Thank you for reminding me of Grindon. Do you feel, as you read him and the like, that certain conditions want fulfilling for what they say to be true? It seems so to me, and that what is peculiar in my own ideas is just the fulfilling of these conditions. I have the same feeling with regard to Maurice. To these thoughts and thinkers I am the humble servant. I can do for them what the mouse did for the lion. Indeed, this is what I feel of myself altogether. The heart of man is now bound down by a net. I can gnaw the threads; and I know, with a most perfect assurance, that what I am privileged to see is the setting free of the human soul into a new liberty. I know it, and I know it will be found so, whether people see it while I live or not. I don't really care about the latter, except as it seems a test by which I may tell whether I do my work aright or not. But I rejoice in the liberty I foresee. . . . It isn't needful for me to pursue the practical applications, or to point out the glorious light that falls on theology, or to try and raise

N

men's thoughts up from self to altruistic views of religion.
All this is sure to be done, and much better than I can
do it.   What is wanted of me is to untie the knots of
false thinking which prevent it all.   I seem as if I must
keep at that.

"I perceive the resemblances to my views in the books
you mention, but, as far as I am aware, it is not they that
stimulate or guide me; but it is from books that give
opposite views that I get my illumination.   My obliga-
tions are absolute to the Positive school.   I am, indeed,
the most advanced Positivist I know.

"As a matter of fact, my thought was not suggested to
me from the spiritual side—and I am sure it never would
have been—but from the scientific.   Such writings as Mr.
Grindon's used to repel much rather than attract me,
until I got the key to them.   Indeed, to speak the truth,
they rather repel me now.   I am more affected by the untruthful than the truthful side of them. . . . I fancy logic
is an insuperable bar to me; and I feel that deep revolutions in the foundations of our thoughts are necessary
before the beautiful things that are said can be said
honestly; for bad logic always presents itself to me as
intellectual *stealing.*

"My thought, I say, came through science, through
seeing that an absolute inertness perceived without, meant
a negative within, and so on; and thus I came to my 'Life
in Nature.'   You will see—for I avail myself of your kindness, and post you the MS.—that I try therein to show
how my philosophical and religious views grew out of my
science. . . . .

"The word 'altruistic' I borrow from Comte.   Is it
not a capital word?   I am resolved to naturalise it.   We
want it.   It is the antithesis to 'self;' self-being=dead-
ness; altruistic being=life; and so on."

" *Tottenham, September* 1862.

" I can't tell you how much obliged I am by your so very kindly looking at my MS. . . . You can hardly understand how intensely I suffer practically from the feeling that what I write is bad and won't do. This is quite unconnected with any misgivings about my thoughts. In them I have an absolute assurance. . . .

" If you can't conveniently read now the last two chapters, send them back unread. I should indeed be glad to have them pretty soon, as a friend has kindly taken the rest to look at. I should like him to see the whole without too long a pause. . . .

" I think I might avail myself of the opportunity, and add a concluding chapter, with a view of saying some things that might put the reader's mind as far as possible in a receptive attitude towards me in the future; might try and point out what lines of thought open out, and what prospects there are, leaving him, if I can, with his head screwed round my way (as my friend Dr. Gull says). I know I am unimaginably remote from present ways of thinking. I feel it flash over me now and then with a kind of hopeless despair; but not so often now as it used. Nor do I expect acceptance except from a certain class of minds; but there are altogether a good many of that class. . . . It is just like every doctrine that denies what we feel conscious of. It is only a few that can pass to it from former thoughts, but all can drink it in with their mother's milk. Only think how few *could* believe we were whirling round, if it was new? Not so many by far as can believe we feel nature dead through wanting life. You must remember that I find some people,—and some of these are among the strongest-headed, most practically-minded men,—who see it as clearly as I do myself,—to whom it comes just as the very thing they have been wanting."

" *Tottenham,* 1862.

" As for 'Society,' excuse my plainness of speech, you really ought to see better. To the self-life, the self-regard must be primary. ˜ That's *deadness.* Don't you see ? How can you imagine difficulty to me here ? 'Tis what I say. 'Tis a different mode, radical basis, and plan of being, man wants for true life.

"Have I given you an illustration of mine about the self. Look at a shadow. It is 'to us' (*i.e.*, to our perception and impression) a *thing,* a *non-luminous existence.* It is truly not this, but exactly an 'absence of luminous existence.' Do you not see? Carry on the idea, then. We feel the self. It is 'to us' a thing, an existence *not altruistic.* It is truly not so, but only absence of altruistic existence.

" Try this, in head and heart, and see if you can't get to feel it and think it,—to think of getting free from self, positively, not negatively. We want self ever, doubtless, but for its true use, as the condition of giving, *i.e.*, of sacrifice."

" *Tottenham,* 1862.

" That point about the individual and the race, I thank you for telling me, wants more clearing up. It seems quite plain and simple to me ; but I dare say I should not see enough in what I have written if I did not know it before. I think I shall refer to Paul's words. Does he not describe himself as ' made alive,' and yet exclaim against the body of this death? And do we not all apprehend perfectly that we both *are* and *are to be* saved ? Don't we, in a word, beside being sanctified as we can be

upon earth, desire to go to heaven? Do we not look on
that as a needful deliverance? To my mind there is all
here. The individual change we can individually have,—
that is life, that is salvation,—but we still 'groan, being
burdened,' until *man's life* is perfect. Then we are
free."

After the first year, Mr. Hinton's new mode of life,
which had at first seemed to answer so well, proved a
failure. The remorseless activity of his intellect seemed
to leave him no leisure for composition. Money ceased
to come in; another little girl was born; anxieties
thickened.

He thus writes to his wife :—

" Tottenham, July 1862.

" I am glad to be put into possession of your real feelings on the state of our affairs. I sympathise with them
very heartily. I know they are natural, especially in
your circumstances, and at a distance. But though I
sympathise, I do not share in the least the feeling of
being disheartened and cast down. . . . It is not things
of this sort that depress me, or ever will. The contrary
things, praise, openings, the feeling of the greatness of
my work, and my inability in relation to it, these things
oppress and cast me down; but little hindrances, and
closing up of accustomed or expected avenues, and the
presence of difficulties to be overcome,—I'm not going to
be cast down by trifles such as these. They stimulate
me, and deliver me from that timidity which is my great
hindrance, and which it is not failure, but success, that
exaggerates in my case. . . . In fact, I know something
of myself, and I believe that exactly what I want is being
driven to desperation. That self-mistrust that is in me
wants just that to counterbalance it. It is apt to amount

almost to a kind of moral paralysis, and the life we have been leading is calculated to encourage it.

"Don't you know how I shrink from doing anything, and feel that I can't? And does it not stand to reason that the only remedy to the 'I can't' must be the 'I must'?"

Affairs getting worse and worse, and he himself more nervous and irritable in consequence, it became evident that, in justice to his wife and family, he would have to return to his profession, from which he had, however, never wholly severed himself, as he had continued to see a few aural patients twice a week at his father's house.

The following characteristic letter to his wife was written in this crisis of his affairs :—

" Tottenham, 1863.

"Thank you for your sweet note from Maidstone. . . . I wish, while you are away, you would think over again your feeling that you could not have Mrs. A. in the house for the reason you said.* I have thought of it, and I can't feel any way but one. Nor can I believe you would, if you gave yourself a fair chance, and would look beyond what is to be seen in the case. It seems to me exactly like being willing to give a person who had fallen down a civil helping hand, provided it was merely a matter of form ; but if it should turn out he had broken his leg, saying, 'Oh no ; I should have to bear his whole weight.' I can't get over it. . . . I don't think, nay, I won't believe, that you have any idea how much these kind of things are to me. I am sure you don't see. Personally, and so

---

* Mrs. A. was a very poor and not very cleanly person, to whom Mr. Hinton thought it might be a service to take up her abode in their house during their absence. Fortunately she preferred in the end not to have the trouble of moving from her own quarters.

far as I am concerned, I had rather far the house and all
the things in it were burnt, and I were thrown houseless
on the world, than that it should stand empty while we
are away, and so many who might be, *not be* the better for
it. It seems dreadful to me, and the reason more dreadful
still. No, Meggie dear, it is of no use; you do not see.
That sensitiveness of your senses to dirt makes you blind.
If you could see my heart as well, and what you do for
the sake of a clean house, you'd make it a pig-stye first.

"But to come to less important matters,—though I
hope you won't pass too quickly,—this Guy's matter
seems to be really prospering well. I send you a letter
from Dr. Wilks, which explains itself. He's the man who
is chiefly acting in it. I expect this to be, and perhaps
it may be, all you desire. When 'tis settled, we must
think what to do. I think I shall try and see what can
be done in medicine. I do believe I am in a condition to
make some real progress there, and nothing perhaps could
be better worth doing. I am disgusted with those evening
meetings; perhaps I should rather say I have been in-
structed by them. I see 'tis no use to attempt to hurry
people about my philosophy; I must speak to those who
are prepared, and leave the rest alone. It must have its
time, so I ought to turn to something else, and let that
take its course. I told King so to-day, and he said he
was delighted that I had come to that opinion, and hoped
I should stay there."

The "less important matter" referred to was his approaching appointment as aural surgeon to Guy's Hospital—an office which was created for him with the purpose
of securing him on the medical staff. He accordingly
resolved on accepting so flattering an appointment, and
setting up a West-End practice as an aural surgeon,

taking a house in George Street, Hanover Square, for that purpose. But experience had already taught him that he could not carry on practice and attend to philosophy at the same time; indeed, his strong sense of professional responsibility made him shrink from making the care of human life and well-being a mere subordinate work. He knew he must give his whole soul to it. But believing, as he naturally did, in his own powers, and believing that he possessed the key to some of our modern problems, to give it all up for the sake of making money for his family was to him a literal laying down of his life at the call of duty. But, with the determined thoroughness that belonged to him, the sacrifice was accomplished. His MSS. were all locked up out of his sight, and for some years he restricted himself to a sedulous attention to his aural practice.

What it cost him is best shown in his own words to his wife :—

" George Street, 20th September 1863.

"Let me know at once if you really come home on Tuesday, that I may meet you. If you come I shall be glad enough. It will be happy to be together again. I haven't had a good week, and have been very miserable on Sunday; but also sometimes I have been able to be not only unconcerned, but glad. Surely, I have thought, I do not want to have a grief which would not be a grief. I feel that I shall be able to take up my cross in a religious spirit soon, and then it will be all right. And do you know I have been feeling so much the beauty of the Lord's Prayer too. It has come quite newly to me that prayer for the daily bread. I have felt the kind sympathy and humanness of it so much more. And then the closing words, 'Thine is the kingdom and the power.' I felt as if

I had never realised that God did rule on the earth before. You see I have felt things far abroad, but it is now necessary for me to feel them close at hand too. It was not fitting, perhaps, that I should hold the world at arm's length as a mere matter for study any more. I think,— indeed, I know,—that I must learn very much from this trial, which really, however, is very hard; it breaks down all my resolutions sometimes."

" George Street, Hanover Square, 1863.

" I've been thinking how I can manage to get reconciled to practice. I ought to be, and really it is too ridiculous to grumble when one thinks of what so many others have to grumble at. Yet I have been feeling horribly to-day. I do believe—indeed, I am sure,—that it is in part my having had my thoughts turned to philosophy that has made me so. It is most odd how the effect follows; and still, though not so easily provoked as it was, I felt something of it when first I returned,—a kind of deadly chill over me on entering the consulting rooms ; but it has been worse to-day, partly from Mr. W.'s visit on Thursday, but mostly from the effects of last night.

" You must know your mother had a little company last night. We did not have much deep talk ; mostly, if not external, a kind of serious joking, almost wild sometimes, but it brought with it thought, and talk about the world; and somehow this morning found me intolerable, especially—and this is the worst of it—as there came a great number of gratis patients. When I'm out of sorts many of these without any others make me savage ; and yet it ought not to be so, for in fact there's no doubt I would much rather practise for nothing than be paid for it, if that were practicable. But somehow you see it is so plainly an accepted fact with me that I took to physic

again *for money*, and only for that, that I don't get right
to it. I don't say I can't, for I've been thinking only to-
day that really I can,. if I just go the right way about it.
You can, and do indeed understand how I have, as it were,
been put wrong to the profession in respect to the idea of
doing good, *i.e.*, unremunerated good, which is and ought
to be one of its most attractive aspects, and is one indeed
which for the most part is very considerably felt. But I
came to it in exactly the opposite way; to give up attempting or hoping to do good was exactly the condition
of my taking to it. That was and is the bitterest part of
it; there is so much that I might do, that seems to me to
want doing, so much so important to be done—and I must
give it up. That has been the sole idea with which it
was possible I could enter physic. It must remain till the
end of things the paramount idea; but perhaps it need
not be so exclusive. Hitherto, I confess the free service
I could render in physic hasn't (practically) weighed with
me one bit; and, placed beside my other work, I confess it
sinks to me into total insignificance. Yet I think it must
be in my power now (I daresay it was not before, and
that trying would only have made things worse) to recognise and take up into my happiness the pleasure of rendering medical services—questionable as they are, my
inveterate medical cynicism compels me to add. You
see, so long as any consideration of that kind only brought
back into my consciousness how much of service I was
foregoing, how much more and greater than any other I
could hope to render, it would have been futile to try and
do this. But I think my bonds are sufficiently loosed to
enable me to take this pleasure. There is no reason that
I should not feel the greatest satisfaction in my gratuitous
work. It would be most natural for me to do so, if I
could once get free from the feeling that in practising, I

am giving up doing good for the sake of money (which, nevertheless, you must not forget *is the truth*). If you forget or ignore this, you won't be doing justice to the problem, and therefore won't do or speak wisely. The thing is, I don't see that I may not practically forget it, now that the objects foregone have less overpowering influence on me. If I can thus feel the happiness of gratuitous work (the altruistic pleasure of it), I shall be comparatively, at any rate, all right."

" Sunday Evening.

" Don't you think, love, if there were any celestial creature watching me, he would be infinitely amused at my schemes for altering my nature? I need not tell you, of course, that my last plan for escaping from myself has utterly and totally broken down. Though I did fairly try it, of course it couldn't stand. It only brought into my head the cases in which I hadn't done good, and had taken fees, any one of which, I confess, to me in point of *feeling* outweighs all there are or will be for some years on the other side. I have had no fee-patients but one all the week, and have been as wretched as ever."

" Sunday Evening.

" Perhaps this sort of dislocation and upsetting of my mind will appear all orderly and right from a distant point of view, or indeed from one not very distant ; but in the meantime it *is* a dislocation and upset, and takes me at every disadvantage. My hands seem so tied, I am turned from every good work. It is this having to earn money and not by mere labour, but by skill, which seems to make it my duty to husband, as it were, every minute for that kind of useful labour; it makes one's own conscience, as it were, turn against one, and shut one up.

"I turn over sometimes my own peculiarities in my mind. I don't know there's much good in it, though perhaps there might be if I could get a clear understanding of the case. It seems to me as if the very intensity of my mind continually defeated itself in everything except the one thing—*thinking*. I fancy it is so, that that intensity, which is the secret there, is a sort of hindrance elsewhere; or rather, perhaps, as if that mingled intensity and indolence, as it were, capability of not doing, or learning, which is the exact requisite for thinking, was not the requisite for other things. Often when I read, I feel as if I wanted to engraft another intellectual nature upon my own, as if that keenness of my intellect wanted to be laid aside, was a hindrance to other gifts which I should intensely like to enjoy. I wish such a change would come over me, I would willingly endure even working at physic, if that were a means of bringing it about, and I fancy sometimes it may be so. I say I wish such a change might come over me, a blunting the edge of my thought-power so that it would no longer cut so sharply. I fancy then other powers might grow up in me, other possibilities open to me. I think of it in relation to myself as beating the sword into a ploughshare, and the spear into a pruning-hook; that is what I want. I don't despair of its coming, perhaps through this dreadful tedium. I'm sure I feel dull enough already, so far as that goes. I think how nice it would be to have, as it were, another kind of mind, the thought-work being done, that terrible edge not being wanted any more, to have the instrument changed into some kindly implement of social or domestic life. It quite delights me to feel that some change of that sort is what I feel in this cramping; perhaps 'tis as a caterpillar is cramped into a chrysalis, and can't *do anything.*

"I've had a nice day at Guy's; a good many new patients came."

"Never be afraid," he would say, "of giving up your best, and God will give you His better." In 1871 he thus writes to his wife of the very sacrifice which at the time seemed so hard: "Is it not wonderful, beautiful, the contradiction here of the seeming to the truth? You knew reasons, and you felt more than you knew, that made it your duty to accept that sacrifice from me, though I rendered it with so many agonies and with such despair, though it seemed to me the utter loss of all the best things, of the holiest duty God had given me. And here is the beauty, that though I could not see it, could not even have imagined it, that giving up was but the condition of my having a better thing—a better thing even of the very kind that I gave up—my having that insight into the practical life, which is more even than all I had before."

He learned at last to see that his practice had given him that real contact with life, with individual men and women, which was absolutely necessary for the development of the practical and ethical side of his thinking, It is a question whether to the last he "knew the world," whether he so far escaped from his own dominating individuality as to realise that all men were not as pure and disinterested at heart as himself, and whether, therefore, with all his keen insight into the principles of ethics, his applications were not apt to be visionary and erroneous. His brain was always throwing out such a white blaze of thought, that all other individualities were blurred and lost in it. But so far as he did gain a knowledge of human nature, and the practical bearing of his ethics on life and conduct, he owed it to his profession.

"Never fear to let go," he says in his philosophical notes; "it is the only means of getting better things,—self-sacrifice. Let go ; let go ; we are sure to get back again. How science teaches the lesson of morals, which is ever, Give up, give up; deny yourself,—not this everlasting getting ; deny yourself, and give, and infinitely more shall be yours; but *give*—not bargaining ; give from love, because you must. And if the question will intrude, 'What shall I have if I give up this?' relegate that question to faith, and answer, 'I shall have God. In my giving, in my love, God, who is Love, gives Himself to me.' "

CHAPTER X.

On Mr. Hinton's return to practice, his consulting rooms in George Street not being adapted for a family residence, he took a house near Regent's Park, just vacated by George Macdonald. But owing to his eldest boy showing some symptoms of delicacy, the London house was given up after a year or two, and 1865-66 was spent at Barnet and Brighton; Mr. Hinton joining his family every Saturday. He often spoke of this period as one of great enjoyment, his mind and body being refreshed by the invigorating country walks he took during the spring and summer, and his depression gradually passing away.

He writes to a friend :—

"George Street, Hanover Square, 1864.

" I have arrived at that stage in which ·I can thoroughly enter into the feeling—almost it is my own for the time —that my notions, though really rather clever, are the merest moonshine, no more likely to be true than that cats should walk on their tails; and that to trouble ourselves about anything of the sort is pure absurdity. Why should a man go into fits about the world ? or what good is likely to come of it if he does ?

" But between this frame of mind and that which was mine lie dreadful torments."

The following letter is addressed to an intimate friend

Mr. Berry, a medical man like himself, on the loss of his father :—

" *George Street, Hanover Square,* 12*th September* 1864.

"I do indeed sympathise with you in the loss you have sustained, and with the more appreciation of your loss, from having had so frequently of late before my own mind the feeling that the time cannot be far distant when I shall have to part with one or both of my dear parents. I cannot bear to think of it, but seem to have a terror about it, which enables me perhaps to know a little what your feelings are. You do not need, however, to be consoled, knowing, as you do, how great his gain is,—how far indeed, what we call death must be from being any true separation of our friends from us. Though we seem parted from them, I often think, and I do believe, that it is for them a much truer and closer approximation to us,—a deeper and more intimate knowledge. For them veils and hindrances are taken away, all that relates them to what is individual rather than human in us,—veils and imperfections which are necessary for us because our light is darkness, but, thank God! are no more necessary for them.

" Is it not a beautiful thought that they may know and feel their nearness with us, though we cannot feel it with them ? that they are hidden only because they have come nearer, and need to be known by powers more intimate, more penetrating, more true,—which give us true *know-ledge*, without that distance and separation which here must baffle us when most we feel our nearness—powers, for the true use of which we must wait, as they have waited, and not in vain. Even of our friends, as well as of our God, we may truly say, 'Now we see through a glass darkly,'—through sensuous images, through feeble words, through shrinking sensibilities, that dare not let the true soul appear; but then we shall know them even as God knows us, living in them, our natures rich with their life, their joys our own. We may be rid of this self-limitation some day. Their deliverance is the pledge of ours, for in actual verity we are not many but one.

"Try to come and see me soon; I should so much enjoy it. Your quickened sensibilities from your recent illness and your present loss would make your conversation and sympathy still more valuable and delightful to me than they always are. And I need some one to do me a little good. I have been dreadfully crushed down and cramped and deadened lately, and don't know how to raise myself up. Come and give me a lift. I am very glad I have you for a friend."

"George Street, Hanover Square, Nov. 1865.

"DEAREST MEGGIE,—I enjoyed Brighton very much, and had a delightful and thorough change; I was all day out and saw a magnificent sea on Monday. King and I had some talk, but I was already feeling free from my depression so that I did not care so much about my own affairs . . . I saw two people who knew 'Man and his Dwelling-place,' Stopford Brooke, Editor of 'Robertson's Life,' a famous jolly fellow with lots of power, and Mr. Ross, expelled from the Presbyterian body, and now just entering the Church, feeling the recent decision of the Privy Council gives him freedom. He preached through the West of Scotland at the time of the Free Church movement with great effect. Toynbee invites me to dinner on the 23rd at Wimbledon.

"Your loving Husband."

"Mr. W. has given us some beautiful thoughts lately. His soul has grown with his afflictions, but he told me the other morning—I mention it because it seemed such a reward for me—that no one had given him so much light on pain as myself; that I had greatly influenced his whole thought in that region. Coming from such a man, and from such an affliction, was not that a satisfaction? He said no one could understand what I said until they had had to suffer—but that it bore the test. This rejoiced me, because it is hardly possible for any one to feel his life more wasted, or himself more helpless in face of the waste, than myself."

"*June* 1865.

"I never liked or admired Toynbee as much I think as I did on this last visit. He is a powerful working man, and has wise and wide sympathies. He is full now of his local museums, for which he actually fills one with an enthusiasm. They would give a bond between rich and poor, as he says; and I feel too that my views of nature would have a much better chance among people who really know something of how wonderful it is."

"*January* 1866.

"I am charmed to have so good an account of the boys. It seems to me it is really a good plan we have lighted upon. I think Mr. D. will make them study, and teach them to like it too. I know, darling, God will be with you, and I hope you will feel Him as enabling you to give the best and highest training to these dear boys, and to lift them truly out of self into life. They will gradually grow into your spirit and get deeper and truer appreciations of things under your influence. It must be nice to you to have them so much and so fully under your own heart. I like the thought of it very much, and that I can come in and out now and then,—just enough of me, I expect."

"I dine to-night with the Guy's men; Gull in the chair. I shall go down with him and get a little talk. Certainly there seems a great want in my days and a restlessness which is your absence. I don't exactly seem to live them, only to pass them."

"To-morrow night I am going to take Maurice's place at Marshall's, he being unable to come; and I am going to present my position, that the moral faculty in us is the true knowing faculty, that as in science we find the world rational, so in a true knowledge we shall find it right and good. You must think of me about eight o'clock."

To one of his sons he writes :—

"*George Street, Hanover Square, Dec.* 1865.

"DARLING BOY,—I was very glad to have your letter, as I always am, and it interested me very much, because it showed that you were thinking in earnest about God, and loving and serving Him, which is the true business of our lives. I know I shall have the joy, darling, of seeing you an earnest-hearted, loving boy, and, if I live, a true and good man.

"I do not wonder, dear, that you say you cannot feel as if God were your father. We do not see Him as we do our friends whom we love and trust, and we cannot love

Him until we know Him and feel Him closer to us than any other friend. Then we love Him most of all. But this takes some time, and it grows with our experience until it seems like our very life. The way to think of God so as to know Him, is to think of Christ. Then we see Him, and can understand how tender and merciful and good He is. Then we can see that even while He condemns our evil, and hates all that is mean and selfish and unkind and untruthful in us, yet still He is full of love and gentleness towards us, and seeks to take away our evils, all of them, bearing them for us Himself that we may be free. And then, too, we see that if He sends us sorrows and difficulties, He only sends them because they are the true blessings, the things that are truly good; what He Himself took when He too was a man among us. He would have us like Himself, with a happiness like His own, and nothing below it; and so as His own happiness is in taking sorrow and infirmity, and ever assisting, and giving and sacrificing Himself, He gives us sorrows too, and weaknesses, which are not the evils that we think them, but are what we should be most happy in, if we were perfect and had knowledge like Him.

"So there is a use and a service in all we bear, in all we do, which we do not know, but which He knows, and which in Christ He shows to us. It is a use *for others*, a hidden use, but one which makes all our life rich, and that richest which is most like Christ's. Good-bye, dear, dear boy, I shall be so glad to see you at home. Write to me as often as ever you like and can.—Your loving father,

" JAMES HINTON."

The next letters are to his sister-in-law, Miss Caroline Haddon :—

" George Street, Hanover Square, November 1865.

"You say, 'It is such a hard thing to believe in God, in Christ, as well as such a terrible thing not to believe.' Of course it may be by and by that I shall find myself in a different state of mind—more than one cause might produce it—but I want to tell you again how at present it is not hard to me, and seems as if it never could be hard, so to believe. If all my thoughts had been expressly devised to render it impossible for me not to believe, they could not have been more exact. *Everything* compels me to believe in God, in Christ. I see nothing else anywhere. All things in the world, bad and good, physical, intellectual, moral, everything which my thought touches or can touch, speak to me in the same language. Man is altruistic as God is, and Christ reveals Him. . . .

"We want a revelation, precisely because of our defective relation to the actual, to tell us of it. 'I declare unto you that actual life,' of course because we don't rightly perceive it of ourselves. It is just as a man living in a sight-world that gave him only images, would want some one outside to tell him of the real, or touch world. Don't you see the real (*i.e.*, physical substance) would be to that man just as the eternal (*i.e.*, the actual) is to us? And we must have a revelation, just as he must. . . :

"How beautiful, how exquisitely lovely and enrapturing, the thought-relations of things are. What sacred and delicate, and what multitudinous yet most exact links bind all things together, showing the most unlike continually to be the very same, and the same in such glorious and exquisite ways—nay, ways so full of fun, and of humorous, as well as profound suggestiveness. Ah, me! I do love thinking. It is the most beautiful and enchanting of all the arts, except—except the poetry of the future, which will rise to the true dignity of art, by accepting the serious work of interpreting for us the phenomenal into the actual. Only think what our lives will be then, when our most serious, fixed, and deliberate, nay, most natural and inevitable thought of every object and every event is poetry—rather is what poetry now but faintly guesses at and suggests. I half fancy it won't be so hard then to live a Christian life. It will be full of unsought aids and promptings."

" November 12th.

"The other thing I wanted to say to you was in reference to your expression, 'It is such a terrible thing not to believe.' I don't think this. To my feeling it is not true—as you mean it. It is often not terrible, but most right and good, not to believe. . . . Nothing is 'terrible' that is the true and legitimate result of our best trying, and that truly expresses our nature. It may be painful, it may involve evils, but it is good. You feel this, I am sure, and perhaps meant nothing else; but I hope it may become a calm and cheerful faith with you. . . . Don't you think that you need a little course of disbelieving? Don't you think it might do you good? namely, in making you feel again that you were not believing, or trying to believe, more than you really could feel sure of. You think of this, whether you have not gone a little too fast. Much as I shall regret to part company even for a time, I would be willing, because I have no doubt at all as to the course you would steer; and the first necessity for a perfect fellowship is that there should be no latent doubts."

Elsewhere he says, " I find the Bible the secret of all truth ; all I truly know I derive from it; and yet I would

say to every man, 'Don't believe the Bible if you cannot
see clearly that it is true. Deal freely, boldly by it.
Don't be afraid. 'Tis a friend, not an enemy; if you
don't treat it straightforwardly it cannot do its service to
you.

"Don't be afraid. God won't damn you for not believing the Bible. God won't damn you, indeed, for anything; 'tis not a future affair at all. To be damned is
not to have eternal life—'tis to be dead; not to have love
is the only damnation, and that is a matter for present
consideration; the future is as the present—it can't be
worse, save as more wicked."

Here are two pretty little letters to his youngest
boy :—

"*October* 1866.

"DEAR WILLY,—I am glad to have your letter, though
I must say the spelling was not all quite right. Still
I managed to make out that you had tried to show
love to Mamma, and that makes me happy. I hope,
and quite believe, that you have had another good day
to-day; and if you haven't been perfect, you must not be
discouraged, but must only try again and the more. And
remember the art is to *do at once;* delay is the great
enemy. If you do at once what you are told, you
can hardly imagine how beautifully everything will
go, and how sweetly happy Mamma will look. Only
think of your ship; you see as soon as ever the wind says
to it *go,* it *goes at once.* It doesn't wait a moment; and if
it did, would it get on well, do you think? You know it
wouldn't. Why, it would topple over, and its friend, the
wind, in its very help, would only hurt. Now we ought
to be like ships before the wind, and the wind should
be love, moving us *at once.* Do you know, the Spirit,

God's own Spirit, is called by the same word that means the wind? And I daresay one reason is that He fills the sails, and that they yield freely and happily to Him, like ships before a favouring breeze. Kiss Howard and Mamma for me, and learn well.—Your loving

" PAPA."

He would often paraphrase our Lord's words on the new birth thus: "Be a child of the water, that you may be a child of the wind; be such a one that you may be able to obey your impulses."

"DEAR WILLY,—I was very glad to have your little note. It shows me you have tried, and that makes me sure you will succeed. Did you hear a nice account of the review from Philip G.? I hope you will be a volunteer by and by; but I hope you will never have to fight. Some day all the nations will resolve never to fight any more, but to deal with each other in love only. That will be a good day, will it not? And every one who lives resolved to suffer evil patiently rather than revenge himself, helps to make it come soon.

"I shall not forget to look out for a steam-engine book for you; but I am not sure whether I shall find one this week.

"Look well after dear Mamma, and make her rest."

On the death of his dear and valued friend, Mr. Toynbee, in 1866, Mr. Hinton succeeded to his practice, removing to his house in Savile Row, and henceforth taking the first rank in the branch of the profession which he had adopted.

The few following years were outwardly perhaps the happiest in Mr. Hinton's life. Realising a large in-

come, which not only set him free from harassing pecuniary cares, but—what was far more to him—gave him a
definite prospect of release at the end of a few years, and
freedom to devote himself to those larger questions which,
in one form and another, were always haunting him;
with unbroken health, and possessed of the greatest
domestic happiness, his whole nature seemed to expand.
His own wish seemed realised for a time, the terrible
keenness of the thinking faculty in him was blunted
down into a kindly implement of healing; and his mind
was set free to develop itself in other directions without
incurring that "Nemesis of disproportion" which is so apt
to follow any exclusive devotion to one pursuit.

Though not a very early riser, it was his habit to come
down about eight o'clock, begin the day with drinking a
glass of cold water, and then go for a rapid walk round
Berkeley Square, often with a book in his hand, unless
his little girl Daisy was trotting by his side, returning to
greet his family at breakfast with a fresh joyous smile,
and such a look of exquisite happiness at the sight of
them, as made the very existence more precious that
could bring such joy to another. The house at this time
was rarely without guests, who came in for their share of
joyous greeting; and the breakfast table soon became the
scene of some animating discussion, often on some of the
abstrusest questions of philosophy, lit up from within
and made luminous to the simplest comprehension present
by his wonderful powers of illustration, and only reluctantly brought to a close by the arrival of the first patient.

It is difficult to give any adequate idea of the charms
of Mr. Hinton's conversation to a mind at all in harmony
with his own. His most marked peculiarity was the intensely emotional character of his intellect. Nature, to
him, was no cold abstraction, no cunningly contrived

machine made up of matter and force, but a mighty spiritual presence, a living Being, tenderly and passionately beloved. The laws of nature were to him the habits of a dear and intimate friend. It was not the artist's delight in nature, nor even the poet's, but a combination of the poet's and the scientist's which was quite unique. He would apply to some of the delicate mental operations by which her secret processes are traced out, the kind of epithets that are more commonly used for objects of natural beauty—pretty, elegant, delicious — while his action was often as if he were tenderly handling some exquisite living thing that he held in his grasp, and on which his gaze was intently fixed.

But keen as was his delight in purely intellectual operations, he valued everything chiefly, if not only, in its relation to the moral. How often and how urgently would he insist upon this in talking to the educators of the young : " Your business is," he would say, " to teach in all things the art of living." And he held that all things properly understood will teach it, for one principle of life pervades all. The law by which man lives is the law of stars and crystals, of flowers, of music, of painting, of mathematics. How often, from some comparatively remote region of thought, or of art, would he flash down a light upon some practical matter, showing perhaps a neglected duty in its vital relations, or revealing an order in what looked like moral waste and confusion.

Owing to this strong recognition of the spiritual unity of all life, never was there a man in whom the barrier between the religious and the secular was more completely effaced. Most people seem to require to be screwed up periodically to give a more elevated tone to their thoughts, and at certain stated times, they feel it right to exercise a deliberate selection of topics for their thinking

and reading; but for him this would have been an absurdity. Man's growing life, his redemption from death,
that was the object of James Hinton's constant passion of
desire; all things in art, science, sociology, were beautiful and interesting to him as they exhibited that process; and often when he spoke of the world to come—
that is, to come here and now—as he gazed upon it
in thought, a strange unearthly light would come into
his face, a look that those who have once seen could
never forget.

Mr. Hinton from a boy had always been passionately
fond of music—Mozart and Beethoven being his favourite
masters. One of the few relaxations he allowed himself
was the Monday Popular Concerts. "I go," he would say,
"to see how the world is made." The only poem he ever
wrote was written during the performance of one of these
concerts. It was his wife's birthday, and on his return
he brought it to her, saying, "Here, Meggie, love,
this is my birthday present to you." It illustrates so
well the interpretative uses of music to him that I
give it here.

> " Oh passionate wail ! that is not sound alone,
> Nor only man's, O nature, but thy breast,
> Unveiling, doth proclaim the deep unrest,
> Thy dole and ours, that maketh us as one ;
> One in our smitten heart and end unknown,
> In baffled hope and longing unconfessed ;
> One, tho' in darkness we, and Thou in glory dressed.
> Let it sound on, and on, for ever on,
> It maketh joy of anguish, it filleth even
> The void it witnesseth with light of heaven.
> Nay, doth it end in triumph and delight?
> Is sorrow rapture, and doth agony
> Reveal itself as bliss ?

So listenest Thou, O Christ, with heart intent,
But knowing all the chords ; the passionate cry
Of hearts grown sick with hoping, tears unspent,
Weakness, oppression, ruin, purpose high
Frustrate and vain : all, all Thou knowest, Lord,
Thou hearest—we the music—one accord."

"Now, also," he says in his MSS. notes, "I perceive how music represents the universe. It is an ideal, and it is emphatically a representative of the universe because it especially embraces discords, things evil in themselves, yet making an essential part of the perfection of the whole. From music best we may learn how nature may contain so many evils and yet be a true ideal; perfect music is the highest mode of the soul's affirmation that the universe as a whole is absolutely beautiful. Perhaps it is in the emotional world that we best perceive how partial evils contribute to a perfect result. In the intellectual world next : we better see the use and good of an error than of an ugly thing. Our view expands as we rise from the merely perceptive through the intellectual to the emotional."

Mr. Hinton's love and study of art had a much later date. For many years his wife could never get him to share her artistic tastes; it was not exactly apathy, but an inability to enter partially into any pursuit, which prevented him from even visiting the Academy. Shortly before Mr. Toynbee's death, however, the two friends used to visit the Water-Colour Exhibition together, Mr. Hinton being the learner, and profiting from Mr. Toynbee's more cultivated taste. Some pictures that were not worth claiming having been left in the house in Savile Row after Mr. Toynbee's death, out of regard to the patients that crowded his consulting rooms, and had often to wait many hours before their turn came, he began to replace them by better ones; and in doing so, was led to enter deeply into the study not only of pictures themselves, but of the principles of art, which, with that singular habit of seeing one thing in and by another that characterised his mind, he afterwards found threw such light on morals, and led to some important modifications of his ethical views.

About this time he established his evening meetings for philosophical discussion, either at his own house or at one of his friends, in the place of the earlier classes he was in the habit of holding for any who liked to attend them, the formal lecture giving place to a more conversational tone. Many date the beginning of a higher life from these meetings, that conscious reconciliation of their moral and intellectual faculties which constitutes the deepest want of the present day.

Over young men, in particular, his influence was especially happy. One whose whole life will bear its impress, writes, " My thoughts about him are so many that I am afraid I could not say what I wished in a few lines, nor could pages and pages express the feelings that well up from my heart. Yet if you think it desirable I will send this message to young men, Read his books, follow his teachings and study his thoughts, and you will find a sure guide through this world of ours, a guide who will ever urge you onwards and upwards without a chance of slipping back, and whose watchword is ' Others' needs.' "

Nor were the needs of others a mere watchword on the lips, they were an ever-present reality in James Hinton's life. No man's heart was more open to any in need, no hand more quick to help. Dr. Cassells, of Glasgow, relates how, when comparatively a young and unknown man, on the mere strength of his admiration

for Mr. Hinton's writings, and without any previous introduction, he wrote to him, asking him for instruction in
aural surgery; and receiving a prompt and hearty response
to his appeal, he went up to town, and describes his first
interview, at Savile Row, with the eminent aurist.　After
waiting a few moments in some trepidation at the step he
had taken, the door burst open, and with that impetuous-
ness which characterised all his movements, Mr. Hinton
advanced rapidly towards him, grasped his proffered hand
in both of his, gave him a hearty welcome that set him
at once at his ease, and oblivious of the numerous patients
waiting for him, oblivious too of Dr. Cassells' travel-stained
appearance, dragged him off at once to his consulting
room, where he introduced him then and there to work,
placing his whole professional skill and knowledge at his
immediate disposal.

It was this magical sympathy, so prompt in action, that
endowed him with an insight into the hearts of men and
women which seemed to them little less than miraculous.
The young, the sorrowful, the tempted, the fallen, were
drawn to him by an instinctive conviction that he at least
could understand and feel for them; and often has a perplexing knot in practical life been loosened by his wise and
kindly counsel.　This may seem strange in one who in
many ways was so unpractical, and who, with a consciousness of this defect, generally left the practical application
of his principles to be worked out by others; nevertheless, it
is true.　Of the practical in general he had no knowledge;
but give him an individual case, the conditions of which
he could understand, and the keenness of his moral vision
revealed to him at once what was the right and straightforward thing to do.

The following letter, which bears the date of his new

residence, is addressed to the wife of an intimate friend, who, having no children of her own, he hoped might be persuaded to adopt some poor little orphan child. The rarity of such adoption in English life, especially of orphan little girls, who might thus be saved from the lovelessness and contamination of the workhouse, and know the good influences of a pure home, was a ceaseless surprise and regret to Mr. Hinton.

"18 *Savile Row, November* 1866.

"Does it not make our hearts bleed when we think of those poor infants who are born not so much into any decent earth, but into a hell worse than the blackest theological imagination ever painted;* when we think of the poor little girl with capacities for heaven destined to become a thing below humanity? Mothers are happy, but they know not the happiness, in being mothers, of preventing that. Do you never think of the tiny fingers which might press your bosom? Think of the little fingers which are being stretched out in vain for bosoms that the cold earth covers, or that shame has turned to stone. Oh, amid the merry laughter that rings like a mockery in your ears, does not there mingle sometimes the long wail of a starving babe? It isn't yet out of *my* ears, I know; and I do not wish it should. The things that are done here are too dreadful to be thought of; much more are too dreadful to be forgotten.

"Does there not every now and then intrude between you and that baby face which haunts your eyes, a long procession of baby faces, streaming—the happiest only of them—to the grave?"

* "Children not so much born as damned into the world."—SOUTH.

In reference to a little paper on the divinity of Christ, which he wrote after hearing a sermon on the subject by his friend Mr. Stopford Brooke, he writes:—

" Savile Row, August 1867.

"I feel that, although a bungle, it is yet the right thing in the main. . . . Perhaps it is less as bringing God near to us, than as showing how near He is to us, that Christ is most to me. I do not know, I do not say it ought to be so to others. But think of those words, 'He that hath seen Me hath seen the Father.' What do they mean but that our experience is God's experience, only divinely known, divinely borne ?

"I am quite strange to myself, Carrie. These things fill me with a passion when I think of them. They thrill me like music, and bow me into nothingness like love ; and yet I have put them so away that I live quietly, and hardly know that I am not content without them. I live apart. I wish I could, but I cannot mix the two."

" Savile Row, September 1867.

"You see, dear Carrie, that I have got home again. I came this morning by mail from Scarboro'. Meggie and the boys are coming round by sea, and I expect them to-morrow morning to breakfast. We have had a glorious time.

"Your letter contains so much, I seem as if I should never have done answering it. For instance, when I reflect on your remark that martyrs were not metaphysicians and philosophers, I begin to think it probable that a considerable proportion of them were. It never struck me before, but it is really interesting to think how akin the martyr and the metaphysical character are in some aspects. The martyr must have been eminently idea-led, placing his conviction infinitely above results, accustomed to look at things not visible. . . . . . I feel this the more from my own understanding and sympathy with the Pietists (I mean like Mad. Guyon), and their over-whelming feeling of the love and loveliness of God. That is my feeling now. The infinite beauty of God devours me with a feeling to which no words could be extrava-gant. I recognise their feeling as my feeling. But mine came to me through what people would call my meta-physics. It is my vision of God, my seeing of the world, that ravishes me so. I cannot but believe that their feel-ing must have arisen in a way essentially the same, how-ever seemingly diverse.

"Have I made you see, or rather feel, what I mean by altruistic being? how love is the expression of the fact of God's existence? how all goodness is *embodied* in His nature? Do not you feel this, at least, that, taking the world and nature as it is, at the worst, though we cannot perhaps explain fully any one thing, yet altogether it does consent to be *the phenomenon of a life that is in sacrifice?* However darkly we may grope about the wards of the lock, yet do we not feel that we have grasped the key? I do.

"I had this thought as I rode yesterday through that wonderfully beautiful Yorkshire. Surely nature is worthy that it should require some profoundness, some delicacy of thought, some linking together in one of things that seem opposed, something that is a tax upon our powers of thinking, to understand her. Ought it not to be so?"*

---

* Canon Mozley has pointed out how the same age that has developed the scientific analysis of nature has also developed a new sense of natural beauty :—"The tendency of the analysis of nature is to reduce the idea of the Deity in men's minds to a negation, and to convert the First Great

P

"Savile Row, February 1868.

"MY DARLING MEGGIE,—I have enjoyed thinking of you to-day, knowing you would have many pleasures. Nor have I been dull. Offord and I heard Lynch this morning. He gave us a nice sermon of his sort. The prettiest thing he said, speaking of the 'weightier matters of the law,' was this: There are different kinds of weight. Sometimes a father has himself to make a coffin, and put his own child in it, and carry it along the dreary road to the grave: how much heavier is the child then than when he is carried, laughing, on his shoulder! So it is with the weight Christ takes off from the heart, and the weight of willing service He lays upon our shoulder.

"I have finished H. W. Beecher's 'Norwood.' The last volume is quite worth reading. It should do us good to be made to feel as deeply and really as we may, what a deep and terrible discipline of heart and soul that nation has gone through,—at least many of them. There must come good fruits from that. I like to try to enter into their enthusiasms and sorrows, and feel knit to them in my soul."

"February 1868.

"Last night Savory came in after the Medico-Chirurgical. He's a great lover of feminine women; says, although he doesn't see why a woman should be the

Cause into a mere physical force. But the admiration of nature as a creation of beauty, on the other hand, tends to support the moral idea of the Deity. . . . The impression of the visible world as a chain of material causation has been more or less counteracted and counterbalanced by the visible world as a spiritual sight. And so we generally find that no one set of ideas is allowed to domineer and monopolise ground in any age, but, when one rises to power, another is provided to meet and check it."—*University Sermons,* "*Nature,*" p. 159.

worse for knowing Euclid, yet he prefers them if they don't. This came up from my saying I thought the medical bodies ought not to refuse to examine women. He thinks they ought."

" August 1868.

"It is wonderful how quietly my life goes on. Nothing happens but the little regular flow of patients, now not too excessive. It seems to me a very quiet life; and I have very little impulse to try and make it otherwise. To all intents and purposes, I seem to myself as quiet, as retired, and remote from real contact with the world, as if I were already at Queensferry.* Indeed, I should then be much more in contact with it. I suppose it shows how this medical work remains, as it were, outside of me, and cannot penetrate into me. If I did ten times the work, my soul would be a hermit still. Most likely, however, it is your absence that I feel, and that makes everything else seem unreal to me. I half meant to-day to have seen if I could have written something of my Nottingham lecture; but the day is all gone without. I feel I could not satisfy myself.

"But all this does not matter. You and the children are having a nice time, and getting health and refreshment, and living in the beauty of the earth and sea, and that thought enlivens me enough. When people come to our age, it is in one another and in our children that we live. One's interests and hopes begin to transfer themselves, and to take a new root. Is it not strange that four children should seem too few to carry one's hopes ? I wonder whether forty would suffice?—not better, I expect. But this is a great joy, that whatever I may teach or fail to

---

* In Scotland, where his wife and children then were.

teach them, from you they cannot fail to learn goodness."

He writes to an intimate friend, who, on meeting
him after a long interval, was struck by his apparent
indifference to his old subjects :—

" 18 Savile Row, August 1868.

" I am just the same, as you know; but I am compelled
to put on an external covering, or I could not get on at
all, and it fits too close to be thrown off at any moment—
not to say that there is danger of wounds which a spontaneous instinct makes me avoid. I simply cannot at
any moment, and in haste, let my nature really respond
to the appeals which things necessarily make to it ; indeed
I cannot do it at all without a great expense, for which,
in general, I see no adequate return. My self-control has
been acquired too painfully, and only by the aid of fostering
circumstances which I fold about me as a shield. I am
in a perfect maze of pleasant conditions, and I will be
glad in them (since I can). Why should I not ? when not
to be so would serve but to put farther away all that I
most desire.

"You have been deceived here, I think, and have
attached too much importance to that which is for you
quite unimportant. You should not see my external
ways. That is only my method of holding at arm's
length things which, if they came too near, would stab me ;
but it is my own heart which I hold at arm's length too.
And I have gained a victory, such as it is ; but I loathe to
think of it. I don't wonder that to other eyes it seems
more like a defeat. Ah me! and it is a defeat too. I have
not risen to an appreciative renunciation; I have only
flattened myself down (there is no other word for it) into

a mock indifference, and it makes me worse, I know it
does, truly, in some respects. But I do not care—I cannot
afford to care. I do not seem to want to be good; I only
want to be absorbed in the passion of the altruistic life,
which isn't good, but only a necessity, and merits no reward. And for myself, I only want to do my work. But
this it is my daily task, my duty, *not to want.* But how
can I cease to want my breath?—how but by dying? Yes!
there is one way, *I hybernate.* By the by, there's quite
a new light on physiology here. I am a hybernating
animal. A wintry torpor has fallen upon me; that is all;
a kind of living freezing, wherein there exists just vitality
enough to keep one going till the spring. I feel a new
sympathy with dormice and hedgehogs, and every kind of
hybernating animal. I know their sensations, especially
how disgusted they feel with themselves.

"Still there *is* the promise of a spring, perhaps even for
me; and God made me, I suppose, with the capacity of
cherishing deep inside a life debarred from outer manifestation. Has he not made others so—nay, all? But
don't you know that if you rashly touch a hybernating
animal, it falls into a fever and may die? Beware,
therefore, how you touch me."

In the spring of this year, Mr. Hinton having delivered
a lecture at Nottingham "On What we can Know," he
writes to one of his auditors:—

"Savile Row, April 1868.

"Thank you for your abstract of my lecture, which is
of interest and of use to me.

"I will tell you what I think on the question you ask.

"First about the falsity of our sense-perceptions being
to our advantage, I note two points: (1) How much more
valuable, so to speak, the perceptions are in themselves.

Suppose we perceived all light and heat and sound as only so many varieties of *motion*, what would the world be worth? (2) We can get more knowledge by modified impressions, by having *limited* senses, than we can conceive ourselves getting if we could only have exact ones. Perspective is a case in point. If distant objects did not look small, how could we see an extensive surface at all? 'Tis contradictory. How have got any idea of the heavens, if the stars had looked even a mile across? Again, light gives us at once perceptions of form, of distinctness, of objects, &c.; but how could vibrations, perceived as vibrations, help us to such conceptions?

"So with touch, again. If we had no impressions from touch but accurate ones, we could learn from it about no object that extended beyond the reach of our fingers. And if things did not to our touch begin and cease, how many objects could we possibly take cognisance of? Just so many, evidently, as could be crowded at one moment into our sensuous apprehension; an infinitesimal portion of the things our senses have taught us about, from the very fact that things do have the goodness to take themselves out of the way, although this is making our senses report distinctly false. Is it not clear that the false perceiving of our senses is altogether the only conceivable condition of their becoming the means of large and varied knowledge? Not to say that this sense-lie of beginning and ceasing is the precise basis of our knowledge of succession, of order—in a word, of science. Put the problem, How will you give a being of limited perceptive sphere the power to comprehend? The answer surely must be, Give him modified, especially negatively modified, apprehensions, with power to *use* them. Surely it shows in the strongest light the unreason of the present Positivist leap, 'Our perceptions, in this aspect, are modified, *therefore* we cannot know.'

"Then for your second question: the proofs that the scientific result is but phenomenal are very many; but many of them abstruse, and incapable of being popularised. I confess the one I prefer and think the plainest is the inertia. I cannot conceive anything more axiomatic than that; only, like other axioms, it needs to be clearly understood. Our perceiving an objective inaction, and not as an absence of existence, but as the very character of existence itself, carries its own interpretation to my mind so plainly, that I cannot conceive anything making it plainer. Especially when we look at it from the other end, as it were, and see that, of course, when we examine a phenomenon, we find it hasn't action.* It cannot; not to exist and not to act at least are one.

" But still the other arguments are very numerous. The conceptions of matter and force involve contradictions which Herbert Spencer has argued out at great length, and shown that no statement of them will bear examination. (See his 'First Principles.') There is another argument, too, which this lecture has suggested to me, namely, that in the conception of the world as matter and force (which is the scientific phenomenon), the intellect does not really rise above the senses at all, but simply endorses and universalises the presentation of nature by touch, the most palpably subjective of all our senses. It is still a sen-

---

* See Essay, "The Fairy Land of Science." "Whatever is that secret activity in nature, of which all the forces are exhibitions to our sense, we know one thing respecting it, viz., that it is not force. . . . Force is a sensation of our own, and is no more to be attributed to the object in connection with which we feel it than is the brightness of a colour or the sweetness of a taste. When we take upon ourselves to alter the arrangements of the universe, we feel pressure, push, or pull; accordingly we attribute to insentient matter our sensations, and we speak of an arch pressing on its abutments, of particles of matter attracting or drawing one another, and so on."—" *Thoughts on Health,*" p .274.

suous apprehension. . . . It is very odd how that mechanical sense-apprehension is used to banish all the
other lovelier ones, all that makes nature dear and delightful and awful. . . . The present demand, it strikes me,
is precisely for us to emancipate our thought of nature
from the effects of *touch*, from the subjective elements
which it introduces.   And this has two bearings of
interest.   In the first place, it gives a more definite character to the problem,—as the Positivists put it, it is so
vague, 'we cannot transcend our consciousness,' 'we have
no faculties,' &c., &c.   These are exactly the modes of
expression under which all sorts of fallacies impose themselves upon us.   No problem ever was or will be clearly
seen through so.   But, Can we, or can we not, transcend
the conceptions imposed by this particular sense of touch ?
is a rational and practical question, to which we may
reasonably hope to obtain a clear and demonstrable reply.
And then, secondly, it makes the question so clear, and
parallel to the case of sight.   We *have* transcended
thoughts imposed by *its* subjective elements, and chiefly
by the mere force of reason operating on the facts of our
experience.   I can't for the life of me see why the force
of reason should fail in this other case.

"Then the question resolves itself into two points : 1st,
Negatively, Can we affirm of the data of touch that they
must be subjective, whether we can go beyond them or
not ? and, 2nd, Can we refer those impressions given by
touch to any other elements wholly or partly given us in
experience, as by experience of motion we refer light to
motion ?   Of course you see at once how I answer both
these questions affirmatively.   I say that if we knew, and
could know, nothing but matter and motion, we still could
negatively lay our finger with demonstration on certain elements given in touch, and say, These are not objective ; and

again I say that there are other facts in our experience by which our touch experience may be interpreted and explained.*

"Now you see this brings me to another of your questions, which shows that perhaps even you have not quite fully perceived my statements. It is my exerting effort makes me perceive nature as containing force and resistance (which is the same); it is this effort of mine makes nature mechanical to me. It is our self-action introduces the non-action into nature. From this came my thought of the arbitrary action (self-action) and necessary passiveness (mechanical necessity), the two halves phenomenally apprehended of the one actual necessary action—love, holiness, the reality underlying the phenomenon.

"Then as to your next question, I should say two things. First, I don't deal with words, nor care about them. If any one found any difficulty as to man's deadness, as to whether 'deadness' was the best word to use to express man's defective apprehension, I should say, Drop the word altogether. The thing I point out remains just the same. To me they cluster most perfectly around the central thought of a lack of life in man. But in the meantime I won't embarrass myself and raise up artificial obstacles by a word. If any one feels that, for man's moral emotions to be available for interpreting nature, there can't be a deadness in him, by all means let him not think of it so. Provided that he agree with me in

---

* See Essay, "The Fairy Land of Science." "The feeling from which we derive the idea of force"—conveyed to us by our touch impressions—"rests upon a consciousness of difficulty, of resistance, of imperfect ability. It arises from resisted efforts. In fact, it is our own imperfection we ascribe to nature when we imagine that our feeling of force truly represents its working. In it there is neither exertion nor resistance, but a perfect order—an order to explain which we must look deeper than to our sensuous experience."—" *Thoughts on Health,*" p. 275.

thinking that nature is truly active, and a want in man makes him feel inert, &c., we agree quite enough. . . .

"I demur to your statements. I think that man's natural thought of right and good is diametrically opposed to God's good and right; and, indeed, as idealised in his invented 'heaven,' comes very near to the true being damned, viz., in utterly excluding possibility of sacrifice. So you see I do think man's deadness shows itself in his moral emotions, there eminently. If spiritual life has any meaning at all, is it not death that is expressed in the thought—it cannot be denied to be man's natural thought, his 'hell' will stand fixed for ever to attest it—that suffering is worse than sinning?

"Then I say, as for the objective validity of the moral emotions, where, I should like to know, was the objective validity of the intellect till it was made valid by interpreting appearances? What were its inventors worth? Were its arbitrary cosmogonies or its 'intelligible world' more rational than our heaven is *good?* The parallel here is perfect, it seems to me. Both faculties are alike perfect for their true work, impotent for that which they assume; their true work being to judge the representations of the subordinate faculties, and to be themselves regenerated in the doing of it. In spite of the radical unsoundness of man's moral sense, putting the self-good as the good (the intellect also radically unsound, putting self-being, self-action, for *the* being, *the* action), it has—nay, in some respects, not in spite so much as in virtue of this belief in self-good as good—it has an adaptation to begin the work of interpreting, *i.e.*, now that the way has been prepared, and, observe further, now that the revelation has been made to it from without. I have never said that man could interpret the phenomenal if Christ had not lived and died. Full life-possessing creatures with altruistic consciousness may have (surely do have ?) the same task of interpreting phenomena by the moral sense. I suppose it is the normal condition of the creature; but their moral nature is different, and the task is clear and straight. But of this one might think.

"Then, finally, as you know, by saying there is a deadness in man, I do not mean to imply there is no life. Certainly there is life now. 'He who hath the Son hath life,' and this doubtless was also in the earliest ages. This human experience is the raising up of man to life; this you know was always my proposition. When I say broadly, 'Man is dead,' I still feel I speak rightly, though I know I may mislead. I mean death gives the whole character to the scene, lies at the root of it, is the foundation of the whole mode of experience which we call human life, determines the nature of our perceptions, of our inevitable feelings; and our natural thoughts express it—to understand it we must think of it as death. But I do not exclude thereby the growing life. I make even that intelligible, for that is to be rightly understood only as a light shining in a darkness that comprehends it not. Man's full *life* is heaven, as far as the heaven is above the earth from this.

"Now, as to your last question, whether what we shall know by interpreting the phenomenal will be *the* being, real existence. I say it will and must be; but I will put the case before you.

"1. Supposing it were not, still my argument is good. It would be something beyond phenomena; it would no more be phenomena than phenomena are sense-appearances. And we should have got a victory over another stratum, so to speak, of subjective elements.

"2. As you say, if it were not so, it would not matter, because the object known answering to all our faculties would truly suffice for us. It would also truly suffice for the regulation of life. The moral unreason of the world is unquestionably the true impulse to a desire for knowledge beyond the phenomenal. And here comes a suggestion respecting the moral status of Positivism. As a system, I should say it was certainly defective, because it leaves the moral nature without objective support. It leaves it to invent its own idea of good, exactly where the intellect was left of old. This is not only a defect, it is an inconsistency ; it is against its whole spirit and all its principles. But, then, see the fatal dilemma which besets it. To have an objective basis for the moral nature, it must find the world good, and a good world means a God. Positivism in this aspect, again, proclaims its own shortcoming, and of course, leaving the moral sense thus on a mere subjective basis, its claim to regulate life must be rejected on its own grounds.

"This is curious, too, the affirmation of a revelation is the affirming an objective basis to the moral sense ; and it is really very striking how early and how widely the affirmation was made, as if an objective basis for the moral nature was felt as a want sooner and more deeply than the need of one for the intellectual nature. So Plato, though quite content to *speculate*, makes Socrates say that we want a revelation above all things,—I believe on moral grounds. It is curious to note the inversion here, how the Positivist, binding intellect down to the objective, don't object to let the moral sense float free.

"I think even if there were a moral subjective element, we should never ask with any sincerity of questioning whether we could not go beyond the appearance to the moral nature, at least not until some other and further faculty in our nature revealed itself; then we should try, but also we should succeed. And on this point I used often to think whether the emotional nature

as a whole did not really contain distinct faculties destined to be used in succession—viz., the conscience and
emotions, the sense of right and the affections. But I
don't think it is so. They are a true unit, I believe; very
likely there is a parallel to this twofoldness in the subordinate faculties.

" 3. But, in fact, the moral sense used objectively *must*
show us the actual being (*i.e.*, if it is capable of this
use.) This is why the existence which alone the moral
sense can recognise, inasmuch as it must be good and
holy (you see this, I think ?), must *be*, because it must *act*.
Only that which *is* can truly act, and only that which
acts can be the existence the moral nature can recognise ;
or, to speak metaphysically, do you not see that to exclude inertia is to exclude phenomenalness, even in the
utmost extension of the word ? That which is phenomenal, inasmuch as it is not (and it makes no difference
to what faculty it is phenomenal), must have the quality
of not acting.

"And so you see, knowing the actual is knowing God;
it is eternal life. It is a thing different in kind from the
knowing of a phenomena. It is a process of being. In it
is a true identification of object and subject. And so, in
one sense, a most true one, here, while death reigns in our
members, at the best we see but in a glass darkly; but
then when our perfect nature is given us, we shall know
even as we are known."

The next letter is an answer to a question as to how his
doctrine of the objective validity of the affirmations of the
moral sense was related to certain doctrines of Kant and
Fichte.

" *Savile Row, May* 1868.

" My recollections of Fichte are a little bit misty;

and in what sense the doctrine that by the moral sense
we know the absolute is his, I can't say. I recognise it,
however, as in a certain sense Kant's; it is his doctrine
of the practical reason; and in some sense surely it is now
everybody's (except the Positivists). In fact, it is very
old, as old as anything to be called religion. I don't
claim any novelty in that. What I say is, that it is the
work of the moral faculties to *interpret nature.* I daresay there are previous forms of this affirmation. I
should be sorry to think there were not; but I should
doubt if they were in the form of clear and tenable pro-
positions. You see that the idea requires that the
conception of the physical as the phenomenon of an
actual should be clearly before the mind. I don't think
this was Fichte's thought. If my infirm remembrance
holds, he said of nature that it was a limit of man's personality, a self-imposed limit apparently,—not at all a
bad idea; indeed, very splendid taken in its order, involv-
ing, for example, a magnificent feeling of the negativeness
about it; but quite incompatible with any idea of seeking
the absolute in it. In fact, Fichte, like the later Germans
in general (though I fancy by no means the latest),
taught the absolute in *man.* The substratum of the
phenomenal in Kant's thought was still a *thing.* He calls
it the '*Ding an Sich,*' you remember.* In fact, with all his

---

* Kant held that though we can have no direct knowledge of noumena
(*Ding an Sich*), their existence is a necessary postulate. Although we can
only know the appearances of things, we are forced to conclude that the
things exist. Thus, in the case of a rainbow, we discover that it is only
the appearance of certain drops of water. These drops of water, although
owing their shape, colour, &c., to our sensibility, nevertheless exist. They
do not exist *as* drops of water, because drops of water are but phenomena;
but there is an unknown something which, when affecting our sensibility,
appears to us as drops of water. Of this unknown something we can
affirm nothing, except that it necessarily exists, because it affects us. We
are conscious also, that that which affects us must be something different

acuteness, it never occurred to him that inertness meant
phenomenalness—a thing whereat I cannot cease to
wonder, and shall not until I have had time (in my next
life) fully to study his mental history and see the necessities of its course.

"Plato, who must always be thought of in this connection,
to whose general thought and aim I in my ignorance fancy
my own are nearest of all akin, I think laid hold of the
unfixed and floating Greek term αἰώνιος exactly under the
same impulse and with the same object as I take the
"actual." Plato clearly thought that the actual of the
phenomenal was to be discovered by the intellect. His proceeding was the false image of science. In short, you will
find, I think, that all through the idea has been that the
moral faculties deal with another world, with other existence
than this physical one.* That is the point to which my
proposition refers. Their work is in this world, and there is
no other: they must be used together with, not apart from,
the intellect. It is just as, in using intellect with sense,
we have not two worlds, of sense and of idea, but *one* of

from ourselves. This the law of causation necessitates. A phenomenon,
inasmuch as it is an appearance, presupposes a noumenon—a thing which
appears; but this noumenon can never be positively known; it can
only be known under the conditions of sense and understanding, ergo, as a
phenomenon; Kant's "*Ding an Sich*" is therefore wholly indeterminate
in its nature. But Kant also maintained that there exist elements in
consciousness not derived from experience, but which are necessarily true,
namely, the *à priori* truths of mathematics, the ideas of God, virtue, and
immortality—truths practical, not theoretical, founded on certainty, not on
demonstration—ultimate facts from which there is no escape, not conclusions deduced by reason. Hence his "Critique of the Practical Reason."
to which Mr. Hinton alludes.—See *Lewes's* "*History of Philosophy*," II.
516, 517.

* The dove cleaving the thin air, and feeling its resistance, might suppose that in airless space her movements would be more rapid. Precisely
in this way Plato thought that by abandoning the sensuous world, because
of the limits it placed to his understanding, he might more successfully
venture into the void space of pure intellect. —*Kant's* "*Kritik*," *Einleitung.*

science; so, if I am right, we shall have one world only, neither of sense nor of science, but of philosophy, or, as I think it will be best to call it, of *knowledge*. When we really *know* we shall perhaps see no reason against saying so in Saxon. . . .

"You see how the feeling of the phenomenal as that which really exists, was necessarily in the highest degree misleading to the intellect. Though itself an error, not of the intellect but of feeling,—of experience, one might say,—yet it imposes inevitable errors upon the intellect, the greater, in some respects, the more true its operations. It altogether vitiates its starting-point. It gives a wrong standard for existence, and involves it in a labyrinth of perplexity: this can easily be seen. But some time ago I saw, alike in history and in necessity, that this is the course through which thought goes, must go, starting with the phenomenal as existing, and yet being as it must be, really related to, and springing from, the actual. The first thought ascribes to the phenomenal (imperfectly) actual qualities (*e.g.*, the mythological age, when each natural phenomenon of nature is the action of a particular divinity). The next, based on examination of the phenomenal, or the scientific method of observation, resulting in more or less complete discovery of its qualities, assigns to existence phenomenal qualities—inert matter and force, taken as the existence of the world. These two stages must precede the discovery of the nature of our experience as feeling the *existence* of phenomena. But it is not only in this respect, as referring to the interpretation of nature as a whole, that the order applies. I think I saw it in many others. In fact, it is my law of anticipation, theory, and interpretation. Do not you recognise it?" *

* This was a favourite thought of Mr. Hinton's. He once illustrated

"I am glad you like my idea about the art of the Greeks. I want to know something about the true significance of those stages of human history, and these various elements of human nature.

"You see art bribed men to train the senses, as utility in our day bribes them to train the intellect. By training, I mean making them work on nature, and learn to conform to her demands. One can, I think, go on a little further thus: (Greek, and say Italian) art, or the training of the senses—science, or the training of the intellect,—to be succeeded by philosophy, or the training (in the same sense) of the moral faculties.

"Well, but then science had a precedent stage, the mediæval or dark age, in which the intellect was very active, emphatically so, but was not being trained on nature. I think I see the significance and necessity of this period of

the three stages of human progress to me in a child's learning to walk. The mother holds out her arms to the child, the child makes a bound forward to reach her and falls; its idea is right, but wrongly expressed. Then comes the stage of learning to walk, when the child's mind stops short at the process, and each step becomes an end in itself, instead of a means. The idea is wrong; that which is only a means has become a laborious end; but it is a wrongness that is leading it to the right. Lastly, the final stage, when the child takes back the old suppressed idea, having learnt the right movement in which to interpret it, and the process is again merged in the end, but with a truer and larger result. In other words, human progress is not in a straight line, but in a spiral, which Mr. Hinton would say "is the direction of least resistance," as is shown by the rise of a bubble in water. Any one can trace out these spirals or triplets for themselves: 1. The tribe. 2. Mechanical government, exacting no blood relation between the government and the governed, peoples being united or disunited on the "theory" of hereditary succession, &c. 3. Modern nationality, the old tribal feeling enlarged. 1. The patriarchal age. 2. The Mosaic law. 3. Christianity. Or, to take the one to which the present letter alludes. 1. Fetichism (divinity in nature, but arbitrary). 2. Physical science (hypotheses of matter and force). 3. Divine action, apprehended as phenomena, and whose necessity is active or moral.

Q

preparation. Then was not there a similar period before
and preparatory to the training of the senses, a time when
they were active, eminently active, but not being trained
on nature? Is this a clue to the pre-artistic epoch of
humanity? It was the dark age relatively to the senses,
as I affirm this is the 'dark age' relatively to the moral
sense, the time when the faculty is sharpened, prepared,
but scarcely used.

"Now this strikes me as pretty. You know what I say
of mathematics and poetry. The Greeks made mathematics, but did not use it; they made it for the pleasure of
it. (I've just been going over the 47th Proposition with
Willy, and really it is beautiful.) But modern science
puts it to use by making it interpret nature; and you
see how she develops it. Is it not created in the
work? Surely the old 'mathesis' was but a 'power to
become.'

"And then of poetry I say the same. We make it for
pleasure, and think it beautiful; but that is the idea of a
child; its destiny is to be *trained* to be *created* in its right
use of interpreting nature. That is its fruition, its destiny. Our past and present verse is but a prophecy
that poetry is to be a true interpretation of the phenomenal into the actual. Is not that a delicious thought?
And is it not wonderful how all these things come and
make themselves one? And there is this immense advantage in these various forms of the same fact, viz., that
we can study all the others in any one and each. I verily
believe that this is a fact. Each one makes visible, reveals some character and some relation which is hidden in
the rest; so that we can discern what was in those we
cannot directly learn about, by seeing what is in those we
know. The physical organs, the progress of the human
faculties, the history of mathematics, &c., all will be in-

terpreted by each other, and so things quite undiscoverable will be discovered, being seen in something 'other.' For knowledge, as I have often said, like love and being, is altruistic.* And this is how I find out many of the things I am gladdest to know : I perceive what is in something which seems quite different, and yet which I have seen to be a parallel, and then I can see it in the other also. That is about as near as I can express my art of thinking. . . .

" My thoughts always come with the ends cut sheer off (unless, as often, they grow into a complete something that was incomplete before), and there they remain till they grow again, I being perfectly patient meanwhile, because I know that if I went on, the end would be a cutting off just the same, and probably at quite as tantalising a place. . . .

" As for your remarks about theology, you know I reverence all that expresses man's aspirations, and sense of holiness and sin, and desire for good. Though I may speak strongly almost in an opposite sense, that is really only because I venerate these things so much, and see in them a significance so much beyond themselves. Even the weak and evil side of them has its glory, and bears ·· :tness to Divinity. Do not I say in 'Man and his Dwelling-place,' ' Let death have reverence ' ? It is what I feel ; we must recognise the death, or the glory too is wanting. Man's history is sublime and glorious as is the cross of Christ, and only so. Read otherwise, it is as black as hell. And yet men are good, wonderfully good, and God loves them. He loves them—this I am sure of— with a passion of delight, to shadow which forth He made the love of man to woman, and with a tender joy of sym-

---

* For instance, the falling of a stone must be seen in the rising of a fountain, or of light bodies, before the law of gravity can be educed.

pathy which restrains its impatience to deliver, only lest it should mar the blessedness and crush the tenderest flower of paradise ere its brief day be done. For I think man, of all God's creatures, the most blest, dowered with the deepest sacrifice, with the highest life. He has been privileged to die; there is an awful glory about this thought. This word death, which seemed to man the sum of all horror, has become the sacredest and holiest of all."

Mr. Hinton once said, talking to his friend Mr. Berry, "Not so long ago all people believed in the sense world; and, on investigation, it was found to be irrational and unintelligible. So the best informed men thought the 'rational world' was far away, and they would only be able to get there after death. The belief held sway for many centuries; now, by patient searching, what is the result? Why, this curious fact, that the rational world (now called the scientific) was the world which people had always been in, though it appeared to mankind, for so many ages, to be contrary to reason, because they only used the sense faculty to understand it. But see, the world is now to the best people, in relation to the heart and soul, exactly as it was to the head and the reason; as the rational world was thought to be far away till they rightly understood it, so we think heaven, or a world conforming to the moral sense, and answerable to the needs of the heart's satisfaction, is 'far away' too, and where we hope to be on the death of the body. But when the world is rightly understood and interpreted by the aid of the joint powers of the sense, intellect, and heart of men, they will find there is only one world where God is; and that fallen human nature is in the process of its destined restoration, mankind first beginning with the sense impression, and for centuries believing in that; then for ages believing in the scientific or sense-intellect world, and at last finding that this is the world of love and goodness, where God dwells and has always dwelt. But they did not know it because they were dead and thought themselves alive."

CHAPTER XI.

In the autumn of 1868 he accompanied his friend, Dr. M'All Anderson of Glasgow, to Germany, with a view to studying the aural practice of that country, and also of visiting the different mineral springs which had acquired so much celebrity, ending his tour with a brief visit to the North of Italy. He writes home to his wife :—

"Breslau, September 1868.

"I find my journey even more valuable than I expected not that I have gained finished convictions on many subjects, but I have so greatly increased my grounds of judging. I have quite avoided thinking, and only tried to receive impressions. If I had thought as well, I should have been utterly worn out. And there is another principle I always act upon (almost without expressly meaning it), and that is to let my special views be swept out of my mind if they possibly can be. I wish to give every possible chance against them. If a larger observation of men and things leads in that direction, let it have its full effect; I do not wish to interpose any obstacle. I don't wish to believe my own opinions if they are not true, and will not of their own power withstand all opposing influences. . . .

"I will scarcely tell you anything about Dresden. Of course there is vastly too much to endeavour to report in a letter, but we had, on the whole, a capital week, seeing lots of doctors, and learning not very much, but a little. There were some aural surgeons there, and they and we formed a conference and described a good many points of treatment. It did not come to much; but still it was interesting. . . .

"I saw, with the greatest interest, a little of the higher schools at Dresden and Breslau—very little, I must confess, but still enough to give me some understanding of them, especially of the manner science is taught. It struck me very much, however, that in Dresden the master of one of the largest 'Real-Schulen,' where the apparatus for teaching science was truly enormous, thought that an education chiefly classical was for all purposes the best. . . . It is very striking to see how the Swiss and German boys are taught business as well as other things, and the value of the money of different countries, and so on, from whence comes great practical advantages. But I think there are drawbacks, and the result of my observation altogether, is that, while I admire some things very much, I do not wish to see England germanised. We must do better, especially we must avoid the deliberate absorption in material things. . . ."

"*Vienna, Sunday, 27th.*

"I am glad I have seen something of these Catholic countries, and have joined in what seems to be, and I am sure often is, the sincere worship of multitudes. I have a much larger and better knowledge through it ; and of this I am sure that in the Roman Church is still one great hope of the world. That which is impossible and rotten in it is familiar enough to us; but its persistent hold upon, and guidance of, the religious emotions of so many persons, is a thing never to be despised. The Protestant Church seeks to gain a hold upon men now by becoming less and less religious; the Roman Church, at least, holds those whom it does hold with no such sacrifice."

" Milan, October 1868.

"I have had quite a new experience. I have seen, though it was but at a distance, perhaps better so, a mountain in its glory. That is a solemn thing; one hushes one's breath when one speaks of it. It was at the latter part of the journey to Trieste; its name is the Gonberg—part of the Italian Alps. I did not know what it was before, nor can I tell what it is that overwhelms one; but it is so. Other things are grand and sublime and lovely; but this smites you with awe. . . .

"Till I left Vienna, I had really worked very hard; but this is my holiday, and I make it so. Good-bye, love. It is just twelve, and I am to be called at five to go to the Cathedral and see the sunrise from the Tower. . : ."

On his return home he writes to his mother, then in infirm health, on her birthday :—

" Savile Row, December 1868.

"To us, dearest mother, who are in health and vigour, you are scarcely less useful now in your example of cheerfulness and patience, and thoughtfulness for every one else, showing us how infirmity should be borne, than you were in the old days when we were the feeble ones. It would be a pity if the relation of parent to child were not so far inverted before it ceased; it would lose almost half its use, and a great part of its delight."

In the course of a conversation in 1869, an eminent

London surgeon suggested that, as Mr. Hinton had now attained to the highest skill in his profession, he would be perfectly justified in following the bent of his mind after the business of the day, and turning again to philosophy. So for the first time for six years he unlocked his MSS., and devoted the evenings to writing down his thoughts. Only those who knew Mr. Hinton intimately, could realise the intellectual passion that thinking was to him, how certainly, once indulged in, it would resume its sway over him, and how impossible it was to carry it on safely in addition to the immense strain of a London practice. From this time his brain was in a state of tension, which could not but prove fatally injurious in the end.

Mr. Hinton had always been in the habit of writing down his thoughts till he laid aside philosophy—a habit which he now resumed. Wherever he was, at a friend's house, in the street, at church, at a concert, he jotted down his notes on scraps of paper, backs of envelopes, bills, and programmes, writing them out in full in the evening. It was a sort of mental photography, his MSS. being an accurate photograph of the processes of thought rather than a record of finished results. Mind being, in Mr. Hinton's view, a part of nature, the phenomena of thought were to him at least as much worth recording and studying as any others. He accordingly put down his thoughts as they came, altering nothing, forcing no conviction into accordance with another, ever regarding a paradox as the promise of a larger truth, in which the opposites would be reconciled in a higher unity. Indeed, the process of his thought was eminently Hegelian; first, each idea, as he himself says, " by its dialectic force limiting itself, and suggesting or becoming its opposite ; then that again becoming a third, which is the union of the two, a judgment being—idea, its opposite, and a polar union making opposites one."

A mass of MSS. having thus accumulated, he procured the assistance of a literary friend in revising and striking out repetitions; and ultimately devoted a large sum to having them printed, that so they might be more available for use, either by himself or by others who should enter into his labours. They were never intended for publication, but those who have had access to them are unanimous in their judgment that they far surpass Mr. Hinton's published works in profound and suggestive thought, and place him in a far higher rank as an original thinker.

He writes to his wife :—

"*June* 1869.

"I am going to set to work and print my early MSS. These papers of mine will give me a sort of stimulus to work I have not had for years; and if I do them, I can easily imagine that I should also do more in aural surgery, being more girt up to work. The more I think over the papers, the more disposed I am to carry them out, though the task is enormous."

"*August* 29, 1869.

"You are very good to let me stick to my work; at the same time, I confess that, feeling so little tired as I do, I don't see that there is any reason, except custom (which is ever worse than none, when it stands alone), for taking a holiday. But still this isn't the question. The thing is, that I love you very much for giving the chief precedence to my work. That is like a wife. I never heard anything more characteristic of a good wife than what was said of Mrs. Gladstone when she thought her husband was being killed; her first feeling was, 'What will become of the Irish Church Bill?' That is the wife for a man to have. But I am sure you would feel the same for me, so that I am as happy as Gladstone, anyhow."

To his eldest son while at school at Rugby :—

"18 _Savile Row, June_ 29, 1869.

"MY DEAR BOY,—Thank you for your letters. It interests me to read them. I like to think of you as turning your mind to such subjects. Still, as you know, I think the knowledge of the phenomena, that is, of what the senses can perceive, is the best basis you can lay, and that the superstructure is of secondary importance till a good basis is laid,—though the exercise of the reason, especially with good strong criticism afterwards, is a very useful thing.

"I am glad you like the idea of studying geometry as an exercise of direct perception. I think it must be specially valuable so; and I am very pleased that you think it practicable and useful. The habit of looking thoroughly and minutely into things, alike with the eyes and with the reason, so as to cultivate the power of _seeing_ their qualities and relations, and not merely trying to infer them, must be a most excellent one. It will be very valuable to you.

"I do not, at present, see very much in the formula you quote from Professor Boole, but perhaps you will be able to make me when you show me the book. It is true the advance of thought has consisted in simplification, and must do so still; but then, before this can come, there must be a perception of the apparent complications; so that there are two processes, a recognition of apparent variety, multiplicity, disharmony, and a resolving it into unity and order. We must have both, and if the first is not *ample* and *exact*, the last is petty and fictitious. Write to me and tell me about the school and your companions; what boys you know, and what they are like. I am glad you are an early riser. I used to be one also; there is no plan so good.

"JAMES HINTON."

To his eldest daughter:—

" 18 *Savile Row, September* 9, 1869.

"MY DARLING ADA,—Though we shall meet so soon, I was very glad to have your little letter. The sight of your handwriting always makes me feel glad, and especially when I open it and find you have been so happy, and that your chief disappointment has been in other people's bonnets. It must be difficult to paint from nature, but mamma is very clever; with her help you will get to do it quite well. You and Howard will be the drawing ones; Willy and Daisy the musical ones; only, you make such progress with your music that you will belong to both divisions. Willy really gets to manage the harmonium quite nicely. I expect some day he will take to playing and succeed well. Then what concerts and singing we shall have with him and Daisy. They will be getting up musical parties, at which *you* will have to preside, and to arrange for everything; that will be nice. You will find that you will be looked up to for everything by those careless little creatures. And you will have to keep mamma from doing too much, too; as for me, I shall be quite forgotten. But then I shall also forget myself in my enjoyment of you all, so it won't matter."

To his eldest son :—

"18 *Savile Row, March* 24, 1870.

"MY DEAR BOY,—How long I have been wanting to write a letter to you; but I have let other things, which always seemed to want doing, make me defer it. It was too bad, but I suppose I knew in my heart that letters between us were not very much needed. Each knew so well what was in the other's heart.

"I am glad you decided for yourself about the confirmation, and also I am glad you decided not to be confirmed. It might have been in many respects good, but I think you did right not to consider the advantages it offered equivalent to its being connected with a mode of religious thought and action with which you had not perfect sympathy, so that you could not throw yourself into it without reserve. I think, and I believe you will think with me in this always, that in all that we call religion, the very first and chief condition is, that we should be utterly and absolutely sincere, open, straightforward, and free from pretence, and should consider nothing an advantage that has to be purchased at the least shade of falsity. In other regions, as of material advantage, though falsehood must always be a crime and a mistake, yet at least some visible results may be for a time secured by it, it has some *excuses* if no reasons; but in religion the whole meaning and worth of which lies in honesty, purity, holiness, and devotion of the heart, the least shade of insincerity, or of endeavouring to secure *results*, is as absurd as it is hateful. If religion means anything, it must mean absolute truthfulness. We may dream we can serve our fellow-men by pretences, but to think of serving God by make-believes, is to insult

Him.　But, indeed, I know you feel this as much as I do, and I am sure that you will try as much as ever I could wish you to make all your life transparent, and to banish all the false pretences which fill our present life with evil.

"If you wish to spend another term at Rugby, I think we must spare you; you will make a good use of it.　We want you to come soon and live at home; because the opportunity won't last so very long, and it is time now you began to share our life.　We want you to do so very much; but still distance does not prevent this, and that is the best sharing which best enables you to take up what we leave unfinished, and perfect what we do incompletely.　I am sure it is a great age of the world for which you are preparing—an age in which the great question of the true significance of human life will, at least, begin to decide itself.　I like to think of my sons and daughters having a part in that.　It need not be great (as men call greatness), but it cannot be *little* if it is honest and faithful.　This is one question men will have to answer, Is it our nature to take the best care of ourselves or to live in giving up?　I know how your heart would answer this, and I think the time is coming when all men will give the same.—Your loving father,

"JAMES HINTON."

With regard to the Established Church, reference to which is made in this letter, Mr. Hinton had been much prejudiced by an incident which occurred to him in his profession.　He was once called into the country to a clergyman whose life was despaired of unless an exceedingly delicate and difficult operation could be performed through the ear.　On the strength of the report that he had been given over by his own medical man, the living was sold at £500 additional value. The notion of two men daring to gamble over his patient's life, and that an established ecclesiastical system should render such a transaction possible, made Mr. Hinton justly indignant, more especially as he held that, had it come to his patient's knowledge that £500 had been staked on the certainty of his death, it would have inflicted a nervous shock that must, in his critical state, have proved fatal. As it was, he had the satisfaction of saving his life, and cheating one of the parties to this ecclesiastical bargain. But for some years he maintained a resolute protest by refusing to enter a church.

In 1869 he published a pamphlet on "Nursing as a Profession." Mr. Hinton was in favour of every girl being brought up, like boys, to a profession, so that every woman, whether she needed to earn her bread or not, should have her own distinct line of service—proficiency in any one thing being generally an added capability in all, and therefore likely to make her a better wife and mother in case of marriage. But of all the avocations open to women, he gave the foremost rank to nursing, and was anxious it should be raised to the dignity of a profession. He reversed the usual estimate of the relative importance of doctor and nurse, believing that the real curative power lay with the latter. An expression of surprise was once quoted in his presence "how any woman could condescend to be a doctor who had the chance of being a nurse." "Exactly so," he replied. "When a commonplace young man says, 'I want to be a doctor,' I say, 'Very well,' because I daresay he will do well enough. And if a commonplace girl wants to be a doctor, I take it for granted she will do well enough too. But if a girl says, 'I want to be a nurse,' I begin to consider whether she has the requisite qualifications. For the nurse's profession embraces all that is good in both the medical and clerical professions; the positive elements of each without the negative elements of either. She has the doctor's science without his drugs, and the parson's religion without his dogmas."

At the close of this year he joined the Metaphysical Society on its inauguration, at the wish of the Poet Laureate, who had been much struck by some of Mr. Hinton's writings, and henceforth he regularly attended its meetings.

In the year 1870, the year of the Franco-German war, an old acquaintance persuaded him to relieve him of a property in St. Michael's, one of the islands of the Azores, which had become burdensome to its possessor, but which he represented to Mr. Hinton as likely to prove valuable. In order to see the place, he resolved in the autumn to make a tour through France and Spain, touching at the Azores on his way home.

In summer he always wore a white or buff silk coat, which, together with his peculiarly earnest look, made him the observed of all observers. Reaching Orleans in the middle of the night, Mr. and Mrs. Hinton found all the hotels crowded with panic-stricken fugitives from Paris, and had to put up at a little wine-shop. The next day they walked through the city; recruits were everywhere being drilled, drums beating, soldiers tramping in every direction. As they sat taking their chocolate in the square, Mrs. Hinton took out her pencil to get an outline of the cathedral. They noticed several of the soldiers looking at them and whispering, and presently they were politely ushered to the mayor's abode, after having had to stand in a small office for some time in close proximity to persons of obviously not very good character. Followed by a throng of people, they appeared before the mayor, and he inquired their business and examined their passports. Having satisfied himself that they were not spies, only that unaccountable breed of the human species, "Les Anglais," he let them go; and on Mrs. Hinton inquiring whether there was any danger in going about freely, contented himself with saying, "No, madame; but you must not sketch."

Mr. Hinton was again arrested at San Sebastian; but so far from being deterred, he was greatly amused at his adventures, and resolved on going, contrary to his banker's advice, into the mountains to see the monastery and birth-place of Loyola, a proceeding attended by some risk, as the Carlists were scouring the country.

Though the whole bearing of Mr. Hinton's thoughts was opposed to asceticism, there was in his nature a strong element of sympathy with it; he used to say he was never comfortable but when he was a little bit uncomfortable. It was therefore with the profoundest interest and emotion that he studied the old monuments of asceticism, the convents and monasteries which met him at every turn in Spain. Mrs. Hinton well remembers how one day, at the convent near Cintra, as she was exploring the lovely alleys of cork and peach trees, their great branches fringed with the hare's foot fern, and thinking to herself in that paradise of verdure, that the old monks at least knew how to fix upon the loveliest and most fertile spots, she heard her husband's voice calling to her; and with intense emotion, almost awe, he led her silently to a cell in the rock where a great man, once the governor of the Portuguese settlements in India, lived for many years, and where he died—the cell being a mere hole, and so small that there was no room to lie down in it.

R

During this year Mr. Hinton's thoughts turned especially to ethics. He writes :—

"I gave up my work to take to practical life, and as my reward, is not the vision of the practical life given to me ? I was given a seed, and when most I loved it, I was bidden to bury it in the ground; and I buried it, not knowing I was sowing. Now, I see quite a new thing in the Gospel. Christ redeemed the world not by teaching, but by dying; and with what a wonder it strikes me—His agony, His shrinking, His prayer. It was a thing He did not like. He could not see and feel it to be good. Do we not lose by separating Him too much from ourselves ?

"I enter also more into martyrdom; we don't think of that, that men gave up the being useful, the doing work for God.

"And Abraham's sacrifice, too, I see. He gave up the son, *the world's hope*, not his own love alone, but him in whom all the nations were to be blessed; he *trusted* God. All these things have a new meaning for me. Full of infinite beauty is that sacrifice of Isaac. The men who cannot tolerate it have not *felt*, they do not know. To me in the end of the world, that speaks; and the beautiful reward ' Now know I that thou lovest Me.' "

In Spain, as we have said, he was brought face to face with asceticism, and was led to study man's endeavour to attain to goodness on the basis of the self—of the individual soul—and its inevitable result, the putting away of pleasure and the infliction of austerities, in order to possess merit in the eye of Heaven—a tendency which he recognised as certain to crop up under all sorts of disguises as long as

man is thinking about himself, even about his own goodness. "Let the world come to an end, but let this self
be killed," the ascetics cried. "They sought to kill the
pleasure for the self's sake; what they did was to kill the
pleasure but not the self." True goodness, man's redemption from self, like health, like happiness, can only be
attained altruistically.

But it was not till the end of this year and the beginning of 1871 that he passed through what he always
spoke of as a moral revolution; and that he finally
worked out what he sometimes called a new idea of
right, but in reality held to have been taught by Christ,
though since obscured and almost lost.

From the first, Mr. Hinton had learned altruism from
modern science. In nature, nothing exists in and for
itself. Each force, to live as power, must merge itself in
some other force.

> "Alles sich zum Ganze webt,
> Ein in dem andern wirkt und lebt."

Nothing stops short at itself. All nature's ends are
larger means. "I don't know whether it is fanciful, a
sort of sublime punning," he once said, "but what I see
in nature is the power of an *end*-less life." And man,
by erecting himself as an end, dislocates this order, and
can only be made one with nature by living in others, and
subordinating himself to a whole.

So much misunderstanding exists as to what is meant
by altruism, that it is necessary to define the meaning
which Mr. Hinton attached to the word. The common
sense of all practical thinkers tells them that egoism is a
necessary factor in life; the only mistake is in thinking
that altruism, at least as held by Mr. Hinton, denies it.
'If,' says Mr. Herbert Spencer in his well-known papers

on Sociology, 'the dictate "live for self" is wrong one way, the opposite dictate "live for others," is wrong in another way. The rational dictate is "live for self and others."'* In other words—the words in which Mr. Hinton would sum up his altruism—Have a true response to every claim whether of self or others.

But the practical question still remains, how are you to obtain this—directly or indirectly? For, as Mr. Hinton often pointed out, if you teach a child to divide its duties into duties to self, and duties to others, the question will be perpetually forced upon him when it comes to practice, "How much for self, and how much for others?" Not only will some of his energy be used up in the work of deciding, but, in his endeavour to serve two masters, he will practically fail to strike the balance, and will tend, as all history shows, either to do things because they are hard to the self—in which case his very thought of right will be perverted and his virtues mischievous, as in the ascetic ages—or he will tend to sink into a more or less self-centred life, regardless of the true claims of human good. The only way, Mr. Hinton would urge, to get a true response to *every* claim, is to look upon ourselves as means to an end, and the means to be cared for because of the end; not the dual principle, "Myself and others," but the moral unity, "Myself in and for others," which can alone set us free to take whatever is needful for ourselves, with the same healthy impulse as we take food, not as an end, with the glutton, but as a means for service, with the man. "The curve described by a planet cannot be understood by thinking at one moment of the centripetal force, and at another of the tangential force; but the

* Herbert Spencer's "*Study of Sociology*" (*International Series*), viii. 201.

two must be kept before consciousness as acting simultaneously." * And the only way, Mr. Hinton held, practically to achieve this, is by what, from want of a better word, he called altruism.

To take one of Mr. Herbert Spencer's own illustrations, " Every one must admit that the relation of parent and child is one in which altruism is pushed as far as is practicable. But even here it needs a predominant egoism. The mother can only suckle her infant on condition that she has habitually gratified her appetite in due degree. And there is a point beyond which sacrifice of herself is fatal to her infant; and therefore a point beyond which, if she is thinking of her child, she will not go." † Surely it is an obvious fact that hundreds of over-tired or anxious mothers are only induced to take regular and necessary food, not from " a predominant egoism," but from the very thought Mr. Spencer himself suggests, that otherwise they will not be able to nourish their infant? Are there not thousands of men and women who only care for life enough to go on living, from the thought of the helpless women and children dependent upon them? and is there not, therefore, in altruism a more powerful principle of self-preservation, a more robust egoism, than in egoism itself—a principle that never gives way to suicide or recklessness? The general who has the sense of other lives depending upon him is surely less likely to expose himself than the foot-soldier who has only himself to take care of. Indeed, with a large class of minds the only idea of altruism seems to be the short-sighted folly—too common, alas!—that defeats its own end.

How little altruism in some must lead to the develop-

* " *Study of Sociology*," viii. 203.
† *Ibid.*, viii. 201.

ment of selfishness in others, as has been sometimes urged, is best shown by some thoughts of Mr. Hinton's bearing the present date.

"Is there not," he says, "a real light in the command to love God with all our heart, and our neighbour as ourselves? There is a real strangeness in this command in respect to our neighbour. It has even been quoted as a reason for not making great sacrifices for him, on the ground that we should not like any one to do so much for us; and were not this right, indeed, if there were not with it that which is the condition of this loving our neighbour as ourself, viz., the absolute, all-absorbing love to God? If we have thought of what loving God is, then is not the place of the neighbour plain? Does it not mean that individuals are not to be to us as man, as the world, that that is to be the first, and all men thought of and served for it?

"For what is loving God? Is it the love one gives one's lapdog? Is not the only true love sympathy in God's work, devotion to that which the loved One loves, in which He lives? Is any other love worthy of the name, least of all any other love to God? Is not this the only true thought of love to God, devotion to His work, absolute desire and care for that, a passion, ruling and absorbing all, for man's life, for the world and its redemption? and all else that assumes its name, all devotion that is not devotion to some good, some work that is His work, is it not mere superstition? Man, man's life, the growing into life of the world, all passion for serving—that is the love of God, all else is mockery.

"Then see this in the command, Love God with all your soul, be devoted with all your passion, with every

power, so that there is nothing in you that is not absolutely absorbed in it, to man's life. And then love your
neighbour too, man being men. But them love not so ;
love them as yourself—as yourself, which you subordinate utterly, and devote to man, so love them, so devote
them.

"Is not this the true meaning, and do we not see
how true it is, how right, how needed ? Do we not
see what fatal evils the false place the individual holds
with us, inflicts on us, and how vainly we strive to
rectify them by some imaginary loving of a God whom
we invent ? How futile that love is to enable us to
love our neighbour—the nearest as the farthest off—
truly with a true and worthy and human love ! For in
truth is this not a command to love them thus : wholly in
subordination to man and his life, to God ? Is it not a
revelation to us of the way to love them ? For them,
also, how can we love otherwise than in so using them,
even as ourselves, for God, in man ? Thus loving them is
loving them most, most honouring them, giving them
most. To be loved more than God is to be unloved ; to
be set above humanity is to be cast below the beasts ; the
other love is the true love, which must give the best, which
must accept, that the beloved may give. This command
how beautiful it is ! It is God fulfilling for us the condition of our being able to accept sacrifice from our friend,
our child, our nearest and dearest, and so to give them
the best, enabling us to love them with a worthy love,
and accept from them, because accepting from them, not
for ourselves, but for Him. For truly without that great
and absolute love to God which leaves no other love
besides, but must include all loving in itself or exclude
it wholly, there were possible no love to man that were
not mockery, and did not mean pampering, which is scorn.

To be able to love, we must be able to accept, and that must be for another.

"That love must be this, and demands that absolute devotion to a work, the love for God and His work, how well we see in what that which we call love is sunk to. See what love has become in absence of that loving God. Love? it is another word for greed; it does not know how to accept. It murders whom it would sustain, degrades whom it would raise. When with absolute passion God again is loved—that is, when again His work is seen, and rouses a passion, as it must, that consumes all others—then again human love shall find its place on earth, and we shall know again what loving one another means.

"And this accepting from the loved, what is it but exactly the giving being made implicit, made perfect? How shall we have even our love truly great, truly a blessing? We are so unwise, it hurts its objects; we cannot even love aright. And is not this God's answer, 'Love Me with all your heart; let man's life rule your passion, so that all else whatever, whomsoever it may be, must be absolutely used for that, because you cannot help so using them, then you know how to love them. You have fulfilled the condition of all perfect doing; in that not loving, you have truly loved.

"How exactly it is one with that doing which is not doing that is in all true art! That is how nature teaches the painter to paint. He says, like man of loving, 'How shall I truly paint this? my very care and pains, so ignorant and unperceptive am I, hurt it; how can I be true to it as I would?' Nature comes with her reply, God's very word to man, 'Love Me with all your heart and soul and strength; be true to me, and you have learnt to be true to that object too; see, in that not loving it you have loved it perfectly, in that not giving to it, you have made it wholly rich.' This it is which, from a mere draughts-man, makes him a painter, and gives him the gift of truth to nature,*—a change which images the love with all the soul to God, that is, to man, to a whole, to which all the individuals do serve."

A few more thoughts, partly drawn from his letters, partly from his MSS., will further illustrate his position in morals. For their full understanding, it is necessary to bear in mind that Mr. Hinton considered that the moral faculties in man had lagged far behind the intellectual faculties, and are still in that earlier deductive stage, when the intellect, perpetually baffled by the contradictoriness of the sense appearances, worked away from the materials furnished by sense, and busied itself with abstract ideas, or submitted itself to the authoritative dicta of theology. In the same way the moral sense is at present trained, not on facts, but on intuitional principles, on the dictates of the Church, or the written precepts of the Bible, a rational response of the moral emotions to the facts of the world we live in being scarcely so much as taught. And Mr. Hinton held that our moral disorders must go on, like the earlier intellectual disorder, till we learn to introduce the intellectual methods into the moral life, and get rid of the

---

* Mr. Hinton often alluded to the three stages of painting, in their deep moral significance. 1. Rude and inaccurate drawing, whose freedom is the freedom of a scrawl. 2. Where the whole is sacrificed to a pains-taking accuracy of details, the "picture being all to pieces." 3. Where the details are seen with reference to a larger whole and a deeper fact, so that not they, but only the effect and spirit of them, is in the work; first license, then restraint, then liberty, illustrating the progress of man from the selfish freedom of the lowest savage to the true freedom of service, *through* rigid, fixed laws and self-virtue; in other words, the three stages of breaking, obeying, and fulfilling law.

non-regard to facts out of our moral, life, as we have already got rid of the non-regard out of our intellectual life, which existed before the rise of inductive science. To have a due regard not to some but to all the facts, to see everything not isolated but in its relations, to bring every conclusion again to the test of facts, in one word, accuracy of regard, this is the fundamental principle of modern science; this it is which has enabled it to evolve a great world of glorious intellectual order out of previous chaos, and made possible its ever-widening achievements. The scientist would be disgraced who held himself under some supposed necessity of attending to one class of phenomena that told for him more than to any other. But this which is held as a shame and disgrace in the intellectual world, and as a certain road to error and disaster, is still formulated by many of our moralists, if not as a duty, yet as a necessity in the moral world. Man labours under some supposed necessity of attending only, or chiefly, to his self-interest; to the one class of facts which tell sensibly upon him, just as it was once taken for granted he was under a necessity of stopping short at the sense-impression. But in both cases nature pursues him, as once with intellectual disorder, so now with the intolerable moral disorders of our present life.

In both cases, Mr. Hinton maintained, compromise is useless. It was of no use to say, "Base your life on the impression of your senses, only restrain your intellectual passion for truth when it leads to wrong results." No restraint would obviate the consequence of the error at the foundation. In the same way, it is of no use to say, "You may base your life on self-interest, only restrain your passions that you may do no wrong." The task is as impossible in the one case as in the other. In both there is a falsity at the foundation which must vitiate the results.

Our moral disorder cannot cease till we recognise this, till we learn to use the self-impressions—self-regard, self-love, self-interest—as we have learnt to use the sense-impression, as that, namely, which brings us into sensible relation with a larger whole, recognising that both present but partial facts, and in both cases bringing in the elements left out; regarding not only the little class of facts that belong to our own life, but the facts of the lives of others, and interpreting our self-interest as we interpret our sense, in subordination to the larger whole.

"You know," he writes, "how it seems to me that it would be of great advantage to us to use a negative term to express the negative in respect to our emotions, and to call absence of response to facts not selfishness, but non-regard. Now, it seems to me, that not only our thoughts but our efforts are often twisted awry by this treating an absence as if it was something. So, *e.g.*, how people strive against selfishness, but in truth there is no selfishness to be striven against, and it is futile to strive against it. The only remedy for not regarding facts is to regard them.

"There is another point similar to this. The true state of the emotions, duly responsive to every fact which has a natural relation to them, what I call a true regard, you observe is *true;* its character is that it is *accurate,* accordant with facts; its absence is falsity, inaccuracy, distortion from the fact. You see this. Now would there not be an immense advantage in our keeping this simple fact in mind, and thinking of it, and speaking of it so, as *true,* and the question of it as a question of truth and falsity? You see what we do instead, we call it by quite a different name; we call a true regard not simply 'true,' but benevolent, generous, kind, or some term of that sort

which conceals from us the simple fact that it is a matter
of truth or error. And from this is it not obvious how
there flows one great practical evil ? we hide from ourselves
so the real nature of the practical problem, and come to
act upon a notion obviously absurd, as soon as ever we
recognise that it is a question of truth we are concerned
with. This error, namely, that calling a true regard by
other terms than *true*, we come to feel as if it might be
done without, as if other things might be substituted for
it.

"This you see is the very mess we are in ; we are trying to make some other thing or things 'do instead' of
love, but if we called it 'instead of truth' we should see
at once that it was nonsense. No one would seriously
suggest to do without accuracy or truth, and try to do
with something *instead*. There is no substitute for truth,
we must have *that*, and its absence means disaster. And
it is just as much so in the moral as in the intellectual
world, of course. But you see, how, by calling what is
really a matter of simple truth by the name, *e.g.*, of benevolence, we come to lie down under the feeling that it is a
nice thing to have, yet if we have not got it we must do
without it; and that there are some contrivances or other
—just laws, a good police, prudence, balance of interests,
punishments, &c., &c.,—which may do instead. But call
it *truth* and the absurdity is manifest at once ; it becomes
as manifest then in words as it is in facts. Would
it not be worth while to make this correction in our
thoughts ? "

"Most curious is the feeling that we do not see why
our emotions should respond to the facts, why we should
'care.' It is the same as not seeing why our intellect
should respond to facts, why we should think according

to them, why is a thing being the fact any reason for our thought being according to it? Probably men did not always see this; may we find traces, perhaps, of men not having perceived why the existence of a fact was any reason for their intellectual consciousness corresponding?

"Most curious, for instance, is the question raised as against utilitarianism, why is it 'right,' a 'duty,' to prefer the greater pleasure of others? curious, for one thing, because it shows the eye so intensely fixed upon ourselves. Is it not simply thus: the needs, or wants, or capabilities for happiness of others are facts in nature, as facts they must be regarded, or we are untrue to nature; it is the same with the emotions as with the intellect, the regard must be true to nature. If it is not, of course there must come the fruits of untruth; and especially this in each case, that the true, natural, fit operation of our powers will lead to false results, that is, in the practical life, where these results of our faculties are rights or laws, it makes false rights or laws."

"The true right at bottom, is it not simply truth to the fact, *i.e.*, the correspondence of our emotional consciousness, as of our intellectual, to the facts around us? *e.g.*, if two persons are hungry, another and I, and my feeling only responds to the hunger of one, it may, or may not be wrong, but assuredly it is untrue, as untrue as there being four of anything and my thinking there are but three, and though '*I*' may go on so all my life, man will assuredly correct it.

"Does not the thought of morals become simple thus: the non-regard is not wrong: we see it is not, it becomes the basis and ground of the most intense and most painful right—it is not wrong, but it is untrue to fact; and so, as in the intellectual life, it necessarily works itself right, producing effects which compel a rectification. Now, is not all that we call 'moral' simply the experience of this process? The untruth to fact in feeling will have the very same effect as a corresponding untruth in thought, namely, it will start man on a process which is a *reductio ad absurdum*, and end in a correction of the feeling. An individual may live all rightly and contentedly enough with any falsity of thought or feeling, but man corrects it, is compelled to correct it, and then the individuals find it their nature, their only true nature; they receive it from 'man.'"

"The present relaxation of our hold on pain (ascetism, self-discipline) is certainly due, really, to the greater regard to others, but then, with this greater regard seems to come the recognition of our non-regard. Man's thought that he does, must, may, base his life on non-regard (*i.e.*, self first) has come with the very elimination of the non-regard. But is not this necessary? Does he not now, at least, so much regard others, that he does perceive that in the basis there is a non-regard of them. So naturally he is puzzled and comes for the time, as the best he can do, to take it for granted it must be so."

"God," says Bastiat, "has confided the realisation of His providential designs (true community) to the most active, most personal, most permanent of all our energies, self-interest, a principle embedded in our inmost nature, which never flags, never takes rest." Is it not strange that Bastiat does not see how exactly this might answer to a setting forth of sense as the basis and rule of the mental life? Why, it is not so long since true intellectual scientific activity was as rare and feeble as the altruistic element in us. Yet, did that rare and feeble element reveal the true ruler. Sense needed to be what it was, only as a basis and means for that.

"And in respect to practical life it is as it is in respect to thought. All men can receive science; society can be organised according to it on the basis of the intellectual powers and not of sense merely, although intellect is predominant only in a few, and the mass would be altogether incompetent to emancipate themselves from sense. The few can do it for all.

"So they can in the other respect. The mass, feeble as are the altruistic elements in them comparatively, are quite good enough to be organised of free consent into an altruistically based society. It only needs those faculties to do their part in the few who are so made as to be fit to lead; the rest are sure to follow.

"Having self first, and believing the sense-impressions are evidently the same, both merely a leaving out. And so the one is as certain to be cured as the other. The attitude of science is simply that of taking in the things at first left out,—having present to our regard the universal."

"Acting for self is not *wrong*, it is inevitable, a matter of course as much as any other false premiss into which man is born, as much as his beginning by believing the sense-impression, the earth being the immovable centre of the universe, &c. But in both cases, by refusing the things it makes right, nature brings the power of the right against it. It is the same as all correcting the premiss; the false premiss is not illogical, not foolish, it is simply where we find ourselves; but because it makes logic come to certain results, nature by refusing those results, brings the whole power of logic to bear against the premiss; the whole power of logic against a thing not illogical, of reason against a thing not foolish. For a false premiss is not foolish; we see as wise and clever men have believed them, as will ever believe the true. As good men have taken acting for self as the basis of their life, as will ever refuse it. It is no question of goodness, any more than true knowledge of nature beneath appearances is of cleverness, only of man's having, or not yet having, worked out problems intellectual and moral respectively."

"Will it not be a beautiful clear moral vision when we look back and around on all the deeds and forms of human life with one standard, judging them by one test; when the badness in all bad things is looked at simply according to one law, the truth or falsity of the regard to facts, to things in their relations. When we look at slavery with its lists of ruined captives, and depressed industry on the one hand, and competition with its war of classes, its ruined weakest, and scamped work on the other, and see them not as one bad thing and one good, but as one evil operating, one falsity spoiling two things (which can be had only by being so spoiled). And so, again, the enslavement of women under the name of wives on the one hand, and on the other the falsity of the home, its selfish withholding, its deliberate acceptance of its support on prostitution. When we look at things not merely from the outside, and pride ourselves in them, but judge with one judgment all around and see how falsity spoils all things."

"This is our state; it is like a bar pressed on at both ends; because out of its natural position at one end, encountering force at the other also, the distortion at one end causing a distortion—that is, a tension—to be also at the other, so that the two forces co-operate. There are two things awry; on the one hand, the acting for self (a distinct tension and *wrungness*); and, on the other, the relations of life are distorted, and made to be against the natural demands; the one distortion brings the other, that is, brings it with man's growing life, because it brings with it a feeling that 'right' means that which it is right to do for self, an isolated right, a thing seen apart from its relations, and therefore not truly seen. There are two twists or strains, and they balance, as it were, so that both get right together. First, there is the one distortion, the self-life, and there is nothing to put *it* right, no power present to free the bond that holds it wrung; but by degrees there arises this other force, the distortion of the relations of humanity that come by the nature of the virtuousness this self-life imposes. And the very fact of this distortion is a force making against that other distortion; its coming is the arising of a force, the bearing of which is against the bond that holds the other. For a time it is resisted, but it grows. The two distortions are put against each other, as the assuming sense-impressions to be true, and the distortion of reason that resulted, and the one puts right the other; they become right together, for the force of each is united."

"A good woman said of another, 'How splendidly she dresses, but then there is no reason she should not, she has plenty of income and has a right to dress so.' The question of how others are dressed is 'no reason' for her dressing otherwise, and so the rights accordingly follow. But how simple it is; a person who is moved by all the facts, on whom everything has its power, wants no other right, there is no place for right or law, no emptiness for

S

them to come into. A person not moved by all the facts, of course, must be looking about for a right, and make laws for himself. Not being guided by a true response to the ever-varying claims of human good, he must find his right in certain rigid things which he may or may not do. And then, how plain, that a being with his regard too much on himself, when he comes to 'good' will infect that also with that condition of his own, he will make his good or right also a thing too much about himself.

"That acting for self necessitates right in rigid things, is so simple, so obvious, that we are apt to get confused if we try to think it out. We look for something abstruse instead of common, something unknown instead of known quite well; we look *beyond* the object and so cannot see it. It is involved in the fact that the things which can be rightly done for self, are not the same that may rightly be done if the regard is on others. A child may not neglect to learn its lesson for its own pleasure, but it may neglect to learn it to nurse a sick relation. You remember what Mr. W. said of the Sunday, 'If you are wishing to serve God you may read the newspaper;' that is, if you are acting for self your Sunday must be a rigid thing; there are certain things you must not do; but if you are not, it is an action, and the thing may vary. Look at the Commandments: is there a law 'you may not kill'? Certainly not, the law is 'you may not kill for yourself— if acting for self, you may not kill.' The executioner or the soldier in defence of his country does not break the law—not acting for self, for them the right thing varies. That which is wrong when done for one's self, may become right when the claims of human good demand it. And this is my complaint against our life, that the right recognised and insisted on in it is one that implies acting for self at the root."

"A thing being always right or wrong means that it shall not vary with its relations. This is why our moral life is such a confusion, that we have made our morals consist in shutting our eyes to the relations of things and refusing to let them ·have weight. The tendency not to see things in their relations is man's chief tendency to error intellectually, and we have made morals formulate this into a duty."

"Acting for self makes right a rigid thing, and a rigid thing in man's life is precisely as a dead thing in the living body. It cannot partake in the life and so is disease. It is as a foreign body, a thing unmoving in the midst of a moving whole. And just as nature, as soon as ever a dead thing is in the living body, begins instantly to turn it out, so does man's life begin instantly to turn out a dead or rigid right, a right that is a thing and not an act. And by the very same processes that are disease; she makes an abscess round the foreign body, she surrounds the dead right with crime—we call it dis‧soluteness, the abscess state. Crime and vice are the means by which nature casts out rigid or dead rights, that is, puts away acting for self. Give her time—indeed that we must give her, for she takes it. Our attempts to put these down or away are simply the attempts to cure an abscess without the casting out of the irritating body. In presence of the dead thing, spiritual and physical alike, nature's forces take that form, the form of disease. These are her best forces, that is their action; all the goodness in her life goes into it. It is vain to try to make it better while the irritant remains, the abscess is the goodness, the form which life so must take."

"To make life better, what is proposed is more and

more regard to others or facts; in order to make a life based on non-regard, on self, go well, more regard to others is proposed by all as the means for a better, no one proposes to do without it; but should it not be used, not to patch a life based on non-regard, but to change its basis? May not our efforts now be almost summed up as efforts to make a life based on non-regard go on with sensuous and moral satisfaction. So it is a restraint there, and a restraint here, restrictions everywhere and ever increasing; and for every new evil, some new special remedy just put on, leaving all the rest the same as it was before, not seeing that every change must run through the whole as in a living frame."

"It is necessary to see the change in man's regard— the new aim, and life—as a thing that is to be, or at least to keep our thought on it as a conceivable issue, in order to make it possible to see the world as good. For its evils are good if we see them as powers, the powers by which man's life is brought; but we cannot see this unless we see a 'life' that may be brought, a change in his soul which they may effect. Unless we can recognise this, we cannot recognise them as powers, for there is nothing for them to do."

"Here is the difference of nature's law to the self's. Nature's is: indulge pleasures, instincts, impulses, as service leads, and do not desire against it. The self's is: abstain, restrain passion; it changes the law into this, its eye too blind, too bounded, its thought too shut up to itself, even to see if it be service."

"Let man back himself by the powers of his passion for service, and then see if he is weak. Does he not succumb so to things because he refuses the power by which he could stand against them? Observe, while he refuses this, his weakness and failing are proofs rather of his power—they are proofs of the mightiness of the power he might use. Does not service stand, as the other powers of nature, as fire, steam, electricity, &c., stand, waiting for man to use them, hurting him till he does?"

"Understand, I don't say an existing generation can be changed. Such a thing is never in my thoughts, as I believe it has never been in history. What I think of is a truer thought of right being taught to children, and it wants three generations. I propose that all children shall be taught a new thought of right—I mean a new thought from now, not new in the world, only Christ's—this, namely, that God's command to all is, that the desire of the heart, the true preferring and wish and choice of the soul, should be for good; that a care or wish for anything about ourselves, *as against that*, is sin —the one sin, the breach of the one command, to love; that whenever their desires so swerve, they have sinned, and must repent and amend; that nothing less than this is God's command; that nothing less than this can possibly avail.

"And for proof *we* shall stand. If any child should ask, 'Why should we insist on this? why would it not do to think first of ourselves, and then have laws according to keep?' men shall point back to history and say, 'Our fathers tried that, and it brought them to the nineteenth century. Shall we go back to it? You can if you like; only let your regard be first to yourself, and it will come.'

"Now if this were taught to children, would it not be a new teaching? And if it were taught effectually, and became as well obeyed as are now the other rights that are taught them, would not the world be a new place? If men obeyed this law on the desires *as they do obey the other laws* which we have now, would not the change be enormous? If one could go to every man and say, 'You are bound to be desiring good and serving it absolutely in every act,' as we can now go to him and say, 'You are bound to be honest,' would it not be different?"

"If true goodness be in that which expresses and comes with acting not for self, is not the training we try to give as means of moral uprightness, the training in the being able to resist pleasure, to overcome the passions, so as to resist them when coming as temptations—is not the power very much wasted? Ought not this to be the thing cultivated, the inability to desire against service; to strengthen that positive feeling of this power of service to rule the desire absolutely, and in a way not capable by any pleasure (while the mind remained sane) to be over-balanced? So having no need to think about being able to refuse pleasure, the whole feeling being that, to *be* pleasure, the thing must be service; strengthening, not the power to refuse pleasure, but the inability to find pleasure except in service. It is not that there should be none of the other, but which should be the aim? Then having the true as the object, the other would take its place naturally; and even be strengthened by this very perception that it was but a means to another and truer thing."

"You *may* have your thoughts wholly on others; you need not put even your virtue first. It is a liberty to enthrone others absolutely that I have discovered, and which, when I tell it to other men, they say often is a new life to them. I don't mean to say a man has not to attend to his own moral state *in order for service*, even as he has to attend to his own physical state; that is so clear, I've very likely often omitted to say it. You don't contradict me in saying that. Don't think you do."

"Is not the secret of true doing simply the finding what wants doing, the reason for doing, the regarding that, and that merely? If this be true in all cases, then of course it will be true of pleasurable things as well; and the good is that so virtue will never mean doing mischief; for the other way, not only our self-seeking but our self-virtue will be mischievous. The real hindrance is people thinking not simply what wants doing, but of what is expected of them—that is, of themselves. That makes them go also into silly luxuries; it is this one thing holds them to their bondage, to pleasures that are not pleasures, and to their virtues that are cruelties; they cannot do simply what wants doing, they must think of what is expected of *them*. And it may be said, 'This is easy enough if you are not caring about people; be indifferent to others around you, and you can easily not mind what is expected of you. But is that truly caring for those others? is it not a mockery, really caring for ourselves under the form of it? How much of what is called regard for others is really regard for self, a thinking what is expected of *me*?"

"That question, 'How shall I be a good person?' gets into man's thoughts; substitute for it 'What will really help and be for good,' and is not all done? Here we have the law again; we must do, in doing something else, lose our life in order to save it. It is true, as J. S. Mill states in his Autobiography, that happiness, to be truly attained, must not be directly sought. It is true also of being good. Direct 'being good' is thinking of self. Is it not the universal difference between the seeming and the fact ? To be truly attained, must not everything be not directly sought—that is, is not all true attaining altruistic ? and is not the problem in every case to find the other thing by which any (given) thing may be done ?"

"Was there ever anything so curiously twisted as utilitarianism ? Thus, *e.g.*, 'it has been found that the best for all comes from each one's attending mainly to his own interests;' therefore what? that men must put themselves first! How curious! Why not attend mainly to their own interests, because that is the thing that is best for all? Even human good must not be too directly sought.

"Of course, altruism is felt to be absurd, by being made to mean sacrifice altogether. Insisting that it be sacrifice is making one's self, and not the good of others, determine it."

"The altruistic plan of life wants a guide; and political economy furnishes it. Its principles, and self-interest, furnish the guide to that which is useful, needed, should be done. It must be embodied—most perfectly fulfilled too—in the life based on the opposite principles. Only by knowing what political economy teaches, by acting on what it proves, can an altruistic life be lived without intolerable failure, just as the laws of science must be based on a careful study of the phenomena. And it is beautiful to see how this conscious apprehension of true 'economy' is wanted for an altruistic life, and for what reason, therefore, it exists ; not for the supposed end of getting rich as fast as possible, of material prosperity, but to prepare for, to allow, an altruistic society—a better good than that aimed at.

"For thus the practical rules for life are plain—the things to be done, the modes and directions of activity, are those which political economy points out; the principles on which these things are to be done, the aims sought, the voluntary activity, should be those of an altruistic life. Here again we see very prettily how political economy is perfected in altruism, while altruism is not, and cannot be, taken up into it (as guiding life on self principles); it must be crushed then ; demonstrating *which* is to be subordinated."

"Here is our debt to political economy—it has taught us the relation of all our deeds to the necessities of others. All our action *is* in relation with things on which the very 'soul's' life of others turns. If we only recognise, see simply as a fact, as political economy shows it to us, what our choice is, how simple it becomes, scarcely a choice, rather a necessity laid upon us."

"How distinctly there has grown in recent times the twofold feeling, on the one hand, of thinking of, seeking the visible and traceable good of others ; and, on the other, of not seeing any reason for refusing pleasure. These two are essentially connected together, although the false premiss of self-interest still retained, distorts our life, and turns it to evil. These two feelings it is that should be cultivated, perfectly carried out, and to their full meaning. That is the true advance ; till it comes to perfect regard for others' good, and no refusing pleasure—the perfect rule of service."

"It may well be, however truly the law of service may be the true law, that it shall not, even for generations, be possible to all till the thought of men is better trained. So that it might be more true to say, there must be made free the *choice* between these two laws : the law of service, and the law of restraint of passion, truly, between having a self-passion and a nature-passion, for a nature-passion is a passion that is already restrained, even as, long ago, I saw nature is passion restrained; the choice is of a restrained passion, or a passion needing restraint. A man may choose whether he will have his own interest first, and accept the limits within which he will pursue it; or whether he will have the law of service, and will consent to *its* condition, that his thought, his desire is on good."

"Is it not the sign of the despair that has settled down on us, this conviction that has so fallen on us that our lives must be centred round self, that it is not even suspected any longer that this is what is the matter with them, and what keeps them full of evil? Is it not plain here is a good life, truly good, and full of every kind of enjoyment; that might be for all, for all children that might be born, too, just by their accepting that one thought, our right shall be putting good first, and not our own advancement? No; instead of this there is to be fewer lives. Not the 'comfort' or 'advancement,' but the existence of the children is to be forgone; they are not to be at all.*

* Mr. Greg has pointed out in his "*Enigmas of Life*" how Malthusianism stands in direct conflict with the law of heredity ; for, if recognised, it would lead to the highest and most self-controlled individuals of the species either refraining from marriage or marrying late, leaving the world to be populated mostly by the improvident and the reckless—the worst instead of the best of the breed. The ultimate population of the

The child is to be denied, not a great place in the world, and the means of scraping a great deal of its pleasant things around himself, but Being altogether, all things. It is life we are to refuse our possible children, and this all the while when putting others first would do not only as well, but so infinitely better; instead of a good life for all, it is proposed to have fewer lives—fewer lives, that the lives that are may continue self-centred, and yet be comfortable."

"You see what I aim at and am working for is that human good shall be the thought and aim even in the relations of men and women, and shall give them their right and wrong — human good, not man's pleasure. . . . I want one law for men and women, but a law of the spirit—one law, the absolute desire for good in both. Aim at this, and we can get the unity. What has prevented has been that we left this, and went down to laws of *things.* Carry the law up to the spirit, and we can and shall have it one.

" I am looking for women to initiate a power that shall go to the root of man's confirmed habit of putting questions about himself before questions about others, and pluck it up. What really bothers women so about us (one chief thing) is exactly this, that we are busy about a goodness for ourselves which is its own end, and is not as means for service. Men are taught to think about their own virtue, not about the good of women. Virtuous young men say, as you know by experience, 'I know how to take care of myself,' not 'I know how to take care of

world, Mr. Hinton considered, was a question which might be relegated to the future to be dealt with, and the consideration of which as immediately pressing tended to paralyse our efforts in dealing with more urgent problems.

the weakest woman that comes in my path.' Give men something better than mere self-restraint to overcome by. Let women say and mothers teach, 'The needs of others must be absolutely enthroned.'"

"My thoughts don't go much to questions of outward order. These settle themselves. Granted that monogamy is the law of service, as you hold; then if we can get the law of service recognised, we should so gain a true monogamy. Do you call English life monogamous? explain to me—I don't understand. Are we speaking of names and pretences or of realities? The problem is not how to keep, but how to attain to monogamy. Is the second wife better because a woman is basely forsaken for her sake? or is it better that twenty should have preceded and been totally disregarded, that one, the twenty-first, may be held in apparent honour?

"What is the meaning of 'maintaining monogamy'? Is there any chance of *getting* it, I want to know.

"Our daughters cannot have a human life while womanhood is where it is. It would be better for them to die than to grow up, and live in such nice homes, with those their sisters round them."

"O my God! can it be true that the end is not come? Didst Thou bring me hither only to torture and delude me? Yet, as Thou knowest, the torture is welcome, and I am willing even to be deluded; for if I see not then Thy will is better than my vision. But let my strained eyes close, and be at rest. They cannot look longer if hope is to vanish. Let the world's evil run its course uncheered by one gleam of hope, but let me cease to witness it. Even so. It is good, but I have borne enough."

"If I am to be remembered at all," Mr. Hinton once said to a married friend of his, "This is what I would be remembered by, that I was the man who said, 'Man is so made that he *can* rise above the sexual passion, and subordinate it to use.' There even if that is false, and all else I ever said was true, I would rather be remembered as having said that one falsehood than by all the truths."

CHAPTER XII.

He writes to a friend :—

"18 *Savile Row, 7th September* 1870.

"You know that is the terrible work I have had to do this year; to see afresh the whole thought of right and wrong, to see that not restraint, but the condition in which restraint is no more called for, is the only true good. I call it a terrible task, and indeed the word is far too light to express it; and I look back upon it as something too painful to be remembered.

"Don't you see that genius gives up its best? Think, is it not plain, that the power to do this is exactly what makes it genius? that is, its power to do this, holding on to it at the same time. For all true giving up has holding on in it. Do you not see what genius does is exactly to attain a better than any best before it, its own of course included? How can a better be attained but by and in giving up every other? All men do and must do this, but the difference is that other men only can or do give up their best for a better which they see before them. Genius gives up its best for a better, yet unknown, unseen, unproved better; it has to give up, making no conditions, to go out from its father's house with no assurance of a better land, unstipulating it shall not be an outcast for ever; having only the assurance that what Nature says *is* better, must be, than any conviction, any devotion of its own, and willing, if it be not, to take what she has to give. It takes Nature for better or for worse, and makes no bargain it shall not be for worse. That, I suppose, is why Nature never deceives it—but, indeed, she cannot, for that would be to betray herself. . . .

"Now I know that with a little time you would see how Philip II. taught me this, but it isn't worth puzzling over. You are right about him, I dare say, but can't one see a thing by its contrary? Philip II. couldn't give up his best, the catholic unity of the world—a 'best,' in my opinion, as worthy of being held fast as any that more than a very few men indeed have ever seen. Conceive it. Was it not a grand vision? Nay, too grand to be a vision merely. I think we shall see the truth of it yet. He couldn't give up his best. When one sees the Escurial one sees the man. Protestantism loathes his name— and justly, on one side. But which of us can give up our best? Which of us isn't sorry for the evils that seem inseparable from it—and resolved to hold to it still? . . .

"Do you not see how different the giving up the best is in the world of thought and in that of morals? The one is a trembling, astonished delight, with such glad news to tell ; the other leaves you crushed and wounded, glad with a joy that hardly knows itself from grief—which cannot spare the grief that justifies it to itself, and with a burden on the tongue that it can hardly either utter or conceal."

" 18 *Savile Row, August* 1870.

"You have sent me two good little letters, and if I had not been very much occupied I would have answered them at once. If it seems to you that there is a contradiction between two things which both seem to be true as facts or to have fair evidence, that is exactly the universal

problem, that is the condition for seeing. I should be disposed to say—though this would want more considering—
that true knowledge always comes in that way, and must.
Till there is the contradiction—as I should have the impression—there are not the elements for completing the
incompleteness of the perception. I should say it was
there that the whole art of the process lay. Whether or
not, there may be some rule found for the process, I
would not be sure, but I much incline to think there will
be, and that given two contradictions, a distinct method
for excluding the negation from each will some day be
formulated. One may say 'Note such and such signs and
proceed in such a way;' not that this could ever limit
thinking and reduce it to a routine, the recognition of
order, unity, and necessity always gives liberty instead of
restrains it.

"But at present I do not see this general process, 1
only feel it must pretty certainly exist. In the absence
of it, I have chiefly to say that the art of letting the
two unite is to abstain from force, not to make them
one but to let them become so. It is a seeing, not an
adjusting. Here you see we come to what I saw about
Genius, that it is willing to feel it does not know; that
which is not Genius insisting that one or other of the
not known things is knowledge. Genius accepts the
contradictions, feels, 'I don't know that.' You see it
means dissatisfaction, unrest, where others are satisfied.
It means doing the best it can, very likely one thing at
one time, and at another time the opposite; alike with a
sense that neither is the truly right thing to be done. In
a word, it is consciousness of *not-seeing*; but a consciousness
of not-seeing in an active, stimulating, not in a paralysing
form, a consciousness of not seeing that is neither content not to see nor capable of saying 'I see,' when it does

not, nor of putting things together for its own convenience and saying they are so.

" Now if you are in this unhappy happy frame of mind about those points you indicate, I congratulate you; that is seeing in its becoming. You see the state has two characters ; on the one hand, you are compelled to seek with the extremest energy, for perhaps this conscious not seeing is the unease which the human mind bears of all most unwillingly; and on the other, you are forbidden to invent, to dream, to affirm false seeing. To that frame of mind, the fact, if the conditions of its being seen exist, is sure to reveal itself—the fact which gives both the contradictories as demands. Take Copernicus, for instance : he felt that simplicity and unity were demanded in our thought of the unknown; he felt that complexity and disorder were forced upon him by observation. He would not deny either, that was all, his whole soul being intent upon the problem. Then he saw what satisfied both the demands at once, and that proved itself, that is always what does prove itself. It brings with it an absolute conviction, which he, I think, who has once truly experienced, never can be mistaken in again. He who has once felt this has an unfailing instinct. He demands it always again, and the least glance is sufficient to show him where *it is not*. He has felt the touch of nature on his soul. But, also, as I have often said, a man who has genius may fall, is fallen, as soon as he consents to accept evidence, any evidence but that. He has no gift of knowing that can supply its place; his only faculty is that of knowing that he does not know. Yes! it is that throws down the barrier we raise between ourselves and nature, and renders it possible for her to make herself known to us."

In 1870 we find the following entry in his journal :—

T

" In case I should never be able to carry it out, I should like to put on record what my wish for my life would be, namely, to live among, and, as nearly as compatible with health, in the same atmosphere, and on the same food, as the lowest class in the East End of London, and as near as might be to the scene of my beginning of life in Whitechapel. Living there and thus, to mix intimately with and become the friend of the lowest and poorest class, and do all that was natural and straightforward to raise them and convey to them truer thoughts of their own life and of the world; and especially to have a place in which I could put at their command all my books and pictures, &c. With this to combine a school, not carried on by myself, but, as far as was necessary, at my own expense, to which I could get people familiar with science to come frequently and interest the children, and I might, as far as I could, do the same. I would also organise visits to places of instruction and pleasure, and especially to art collections. Then, in conformity to a thought suggested by M., I think that to take some existing gin-shop, and, without repelling its frequenters by attempt-ing any control, to seek gradually to substitute wholesome drinks, and bring natural moral influences to bear upon them, would be the mode I should think best to carry out this plan.

" The other objects—some with ease, the others with more or less difficulty—can be united with it. For this life I would cut off to any extent that might be necessary my intellectual work; and I long for it as a man longs for his wedding-day. . . . And, as far as I can see into myself, this necessity is a part rather of my in-tellectual than of my moral constitution. It is a result of that demand for unity that goes all through my thoughts. The discordant lives of the differently placed

individuals affect me with an intolerable sense of disorder."

With the ordinary philanthropic schemes, conducted
by committees, public dinners, and subscription lists, Mr.
Hinton felt himself out of sympathy. " I am not pleased
with the feelings which are excited in me by the hearing
of benevolent schemes, plans for ameliorating the condition of the poor, &c. I do not like the unsympathetic
state of mind they seem to arouse in me; I have even
suspected myself of jealousy, absurd as it seems. But I
think the truth is this, that it is another form of that
repulsion I have from intellectual statements which are
like my own but yet are not like—which differ essentially, and yet might seem the same. And is it not that
I miss in both alike sacrifice taken as the foundation,
the recognition of that as *the* good, as the end for which
all exists? All helping without taking the burden, all
serving that is not heroism, all giving that has not
absolute losing in it, I cannot but have a revulsion from,
a feeling almost as if I feared its success. Seeing the
hope of so much more, I cannot but be discontented with
the thought of less."

He thus describes his habitual attitude of mind:—" I
am like a man climbing a mountain, every limb strained
to the utmost, every nerve tense; and he or she who
would be with me must accept life so, must climb the
mountain or be content to keep upon the plain. They
must accept the strain, the effort; they must face—
closing their eyes, even, that they may not see—the
precipices with sheer death at the bottom of them, the
pathless rocks that mock all thought of progress; they
must breathe that thin keen air, and be content to walk
on ice where each footstep is a slip, and would be a fall,
but that it enables us to take the next."

No wonder that he goes on to add—"The key to my treatment of people, especially of those I love, I know, is, that I cannot feel any other way than that every one . wishes most, and is perfectly willing, to be utterly sacrificed for the good of the world. I cannot really believe, nor by any means get to believe, that it is not so. It seems as if Christ had so revealed man to me, that I cannot see any man except through Him. And in spite of all evidence, the feeling, the conviction clings to me, and I cannot escape it, could not, I believe, even if I tried. Surely this must go deeply into my nature. Why cannot such plain proof and demonstration drive that conviction out of me, that that, and not all that one sees, is the true nature of man? What makes me cling to that conviction is that which makes me altogether. I see that must be the truth, and the senses cannot avail to contradict it to me. It is as if I had seen the true fact somewhere, and persist that all else is but its phenomenon.

"And, indeed, this is the secret of what some call my tact. I treat men as if no self were in them; and this is true, after all, though not true. Especially it is what makes women feel I understand them. I take it for granted there is no self in them, and they know it is true. It is the *fact* of them. A woman will always love the man who says to her 'Lay down your life' better than the man who says 'Take up your rights.'" "That's true in the abstract, in theory," one of Mr. Hinton's most intimate friends once answered, "Half my life I feel that I want no consideration, only to be made use of; that I have enough, and care only for being of use. But the other half of one's time one yearns for sympathy and kindness, and to be cared for." He smiled, and said, "Don't you see, women were made that way, in order that real sacrifice might be possible to them? There is no sacrifice in giving what one does not care for. That is just the little 'minus' which was necessary to make the 'plus' possible, and people have thought that little minus, which was meant to be sacrificed, was the whole of women, and have treated them by yielding to that, and 'considering them,' and giving them 'nice things,' instead of making them of use as they long to be."

"It is in those we love," he says, "sacrificing themselves, and our accepting it; it is in *that* we shall truly learn sacrifice. Do we not here see in light the dark riddle of God's cruelty? What does He do but take? So He gives us sacrifice. How could He keep the best thing for Himself? how not give it to us? Did I not say long ago it was *in us* God sacrifices Himself?"

If it be urged that these are very uncomfortable views of life, I might suggest that Christianity itself, with its fundamental axiom, "He that loveth his life shall lose it," cannot strictly be defined as a comfortable religion. I would ask whether our modern worship of "the comfortable" has given us a life that really satisfies even the most worldly amongst us; whether, on the contrary, it has not bound down the free play and joyous movement of life under a "weight of custom, heavy as frost, deep almost as life," debarring us from the healthy joys of "high thinking and plain living," from the lofty enterprise and joyous heroism that "feeds the high tradition of the world," and from the deeper blessedness of sacrifice,

"That makes us large with utter loss
To hold divinity"?

Whether in one word, our modern "enlightened self-interest" enables its disciples to write of the world as this man wrote in 1871?—

"Will my friends try after I am dead—for I cannot do it myself, I cannot say it as I mean and wish to tell the world—how beautiful and rich, and absolutely good, full of joy and gladness beyond all that heart can wish or imagination paint, I feel that the world is, this human life. I know it by my own, which is no exception, but only life made smaller, that it may be seen; made smaller—for the ends served, achieved by every human life, the most lost and wasted, are wider than the ends visibly served by mine, as the heavens are wider than the earth. Nor, indeed, is this little visible use of mine more than a mere fraction of my use; it is as nothing to that which God has given me, though I know it not. He does not give me less ·because He gives me this little; He does but lift a little corner of the veil and say, 'This is what all human life is, all like this little bit of yours; *be glad.*' I have heard such wise men speak of our thoughts, and the ideas we can form of things and of our life, as being so impossible to be true, as being like the notions an insect might have of a Madonna of Raffaelle's. And that is what I mean; so much does this life surpass what we thought of it, so overwhelmed, and merged, and lost, and sunk in gladness. That is what life is; and to say this properly for me is what I wish my friends to do.

"And in the joy and delight and feeling of new life given them, which people do find in seeing what I see (some few people, I mean, those who do truly see it), what a testimony there is to the tension, the crushing that is put upon the soul by the modern life, and that it is ready for a sudden spring to a different order—a sudden spring in which the forms will rearrange themselves in a new order, free from effort."

On one occasion he had been reading a literary man's

account, of how he walks in his garden among the
beauties of nature, and yet is sad. "Sad? of course
he is sad. How can a man be happy living a life which
is not his own life? If R—— had to plan a life for
himself, would he ever build a big house and *shut up*
works of art in it, and put a wall round his garden to
shut in the flowers? It is the old baron's castle a little
modified; it expresses not R——'s life, but the life of
some remote ancestor of his, who was probably a robber
by profession. Only he has eliminated out of the old
baron's life its one human element—the relation of loy-
alty between him and his dependents. The baron would
have risked all he had to avenge any retainer of his who
was injured. After some fashion he loved his men. But
R—— pays the police to protect him; he contracts for his
men, and knows nothing about them."

If, instead of our self-centred lives, and their right and
wrong in outside *things*, and self-restraint as the principle
of observance, we were to recognise God's command to
love, the claim of humanity on the heart and desire for
absolute service, which abolishes all law in fulfilling it,
and sets us free to take as much pleasure as we feel
needed to give us healthy elasticity for our work, might
we not know a little more of the joy and a little less of
the sadness Mr. Hinton speaks of? "Do you mean to
say I may live as I like?" was once indignantly asked of
a great preacher who had learnt this lesson. "Would to
God," he replied, "I could live as I like, for then would I
live holily."

In this year Mr. Hinton sent his most valuable
pictures to be exhibited in the East End of London.
Had he lived, he would have used his whole influence to
make his gift the nucleus of a larger collection, to be the
especial property of the very poor. "To make White-

chapel a little better," was ever the thought engraven
on his heart. "At fifteen I walked about the streets and
cried about these poor people, and now I am fifty I do
just the same. How little I could have thought then of
what I should be—that that fifteen would have come to
this fifty!"

"Late one evening," Mr. Berry writes, "James Hinton
took me for a walk in the Strand. He led me into the
Alhambra; we were very soon surrounded by women of
loose character. He took no notice of them, but held me
by the coat with both hands and looked me in the face,
and began quietly talking about 'unconscious sacrifice.'
Soon his gentle speech attracted the notice of the women,
who grouped themselves round him, with the policemen
who attend to keep order (the acting was all the time
going on on the stage), and all were spellbound while he
sweetly discoursed on Christ's hatred of sin and pity for
the sinner; and finished a most touching address of some
ten minutes by saying, 'If our Saviour were on earth,
where would he be? Why here?' And then we left, and
my dear friend wiped tears from his eyes."

The following letter is in acknowledgment of Mrs.
Hamilton King's beautiful poem, "Aspromonté":—

"June 1871.

"I must do myself the pleasure of writing you a line
to tell you how much I have enjoyed your little volume.
I fear I should not have read any of it yet, if it had not
been for the lucky accident of my having to read my
wife to sleep the other night. I took up your book,
which I had kept near at hand, and began 'Aspromonté,'
nor could I lay it down till I had finished 'Orsini.' I

hardly know when I have had more pleasure; for it was not only my delight in the feelings and their expression—which I should have had at any time—but they came both to my wife and myself as a special message of encouragement and comfort. If they had been written for us they could not have been more exactly suited to do us good, and relieve the feelings of pain and depression under which we were together suffering. Indeed, you have given us a great boon, and I have to thank you for her as well as myself.

"Your little preface, too, awoke such a chord in my heart. Perhaps Mr. King may have told you (if he has ever had time to talk of unimportant things with you) that I had to leave off work in which my whole heart was engaged with no seeming prospect of ever returning to it; so that when I read your words I knew how much they meant. And I don't know if it was presumptuous in me to·feel that perhaps, as your words had brought help to me, so if you knew my experience it might not be without encouragement to you. I think no bitterness of regret or hopeless longing could have been greater than mine; but I have been taught to see that that utter forcing from my hands of work that seemed to lie open before me, and that had engrossed all my passions and desires, was the very condition of my doing it in any worthy sense; that if I had not been called on to give it up, I could not have achieved it. What I have found in my own case has made me feel sure that it is impossible for anything to be taken away from us, except because it is to be more completely given us, and in a more perfect way. I could not have known what I think I know, except through having had to lay down all that I valued most. And then all the rich experience, that the other work we are called to, gives us, is added on to our former one besides.   I often think how God gives us seeds, and we should never *plant* them if He did not *compel* us."

"The seed gives up, surrenders itself," he says elsewhere in his MS. notes; "it yields before the forces of nature; they enter into it, and take possession of it, and seem to put it altogether aside; but the end is that they reappear *as it*.   The seed 'comes again in glory' in the harvest.   It comes altruistically—made one with nature, embracing her.   Truly *it* comes because no more itself, but more."

To his Wife :—
" 18 Savile Row, September 1871.

"Isn't it odd, Love, I have had to-night another application from an American publisher to reprint ' Thoughts on Health.'   It seems to suit the American taste.   That is the third application.   He suggests I should reprint ' The Brain,' ' Thinking with the eyes shut,' ' Fairy-land of Science,' ' Skeleton and Force,' with selections from other volumes to make a volume.   I shan't do anything till I have seen King, but it will be nice to be read in America; I like the thought."

" September 1871.

" War, speaking generally, is the very strongest instance that could be imagined, that right is in the act and not in the thing.   The soldier's duty is to murder and to steal, that is, to deprive people of their property, but he has to do it not for himself.   This should be noticed too, if a soldier meets in battle a personal enemy and kills him, not because it is his duty to fight, but because he hates him, he commits murder, and is as wicked as if he murdered him in peace.   Don't you see this ?   On the other hand, if a soldier, for his own comfort or for a bribe, refuse to kill

an enemy when he ought to kill, he is a traitor, and if
evil come to his army the blood is on his own head. Is it
not wonderful how right is in the action, not in the thing;
the thing will twist about any way without the least
confusion, or distortion, or difficulty in keeping the moral
question right."

"18 *Savile Row, September* 10, 1871.

"This is a pretty satisfactory letter from Mr. B———,
is it not ?   Mr. C——— also called; he is the person who
said I had given too much for Grena.*   He reckons the
place worth £4000 ; but I do not consider that I should
be justified in attaching too much consequence to this one
opinion. Mr. B——— will give me some day a true estimate.
As it is, I do not mind ; it would not be worth £4000 if it
would not yield £200 a year clear, and this is more than
the funds would give me on the price, and I would much
rather have it than funds.   No one knows what the undisguised and bitterer growing war between rich and poor
will end in ; the natural end is ruin.   It may be averted,
but only by a moral revolution, and no one knows
whether that will come in time.   Therefore, though perhaps Mr. V——— may have cheated me somewhat, I am
content with Grena.

"Mr. C——— said the trade of the island is certainly
improving.   St. Michael's oranges are still the best; he
himself is introducing steamers, and is going this year to
send a steamer to America.   That trade is only just beginning. . . .

"I have had so many thoughts since I came home,
and they fill my soul so.   Love, do not you forget them
whatever you do ; make them your life ; yield to them
wholly ; no other thing matters.   It is my one care, my

* The property Mr. Hinton had purchased in the Azores.

one anxiety, that your soul should go with mine, should
let itself be carried away wholly by the same passions.
You know what they are. I wish you could perceive
with the same intellectual conviction as I do, how a basis
is possible, is laid now, for our life in everything; what
an enormous· change even science alone has made, and
how wide it reaches. But this does not matter if only
your heart responds fully; that is all, but also that is
everything. That is everything to me; it is the question
of whether, so far as my own individual life is concerned,
it is worth my having or not."

The next letters are to his sister-in-law.

"*18 Savile Row, September* 1871.

"Many thanks for your kind care of our dear little girl.
I am glad she is good to you. I know she will get good
from you.

"But there is one thing I wanted to say to you:
whatever of good or bad there may be in her, I want
there not to be this, the shame and deception of our
modern life, the feeling that first satisfying our own
pleasures, and then putting out our hands to help others,
is good.* She must not have that which I find everywhere—the grafting of devotion to God and man on first

---

* How little helping others is put first in our modern Christianity is
perhaps best shown in the choice of a house. Next to the question of
health comes a pleasant neighbourhood, fashion, agreeableness, &c.;
service, except in the case of a professional man, never once enters. Who
thinks of taking a house in a healthy but low neighbourhood, because
there the people most want raising, holding our social advantages as *what
they are,* a trust for the good of the many? If it be urged that the
thought of our families must come first, Mr. Hinton would say, "Yes,
the devil always comes to an Englishman in the shape of his wife and
family." Not "l'egoïsme à un," but "l'egoïsme à deux, à trois, à quatre,"
is the great stronghold of self in England. But would it not be worth

surrounding ourselves with every comfort and pleasure; recognising what we do of our duty to God and man, and then first surrounding ourselves with houses and lands as nice as we can get them for our own pleasure, and on that, grafting the doing something, be it little or much, for our fellows. Let her feel at least that she has to choose between God and Mammon. I really don't care much which she chooses in face of this fatal uniting both. Don't get that into her, nor aid in its being in her. I don't say it isn't already; for indeed how is any one to grow up in these days and not be poisoned with it before he is aware. Nothing but my having lived in White-chapel (I thank God every day for that) saved, or could have saved me. It is ingrained, absorbed, ground into natures infinitely better and fuller of natural kindliness than mine. Let her devote nine-tenths of her energies, or nine hundred and ninety-nine thousandths if she likes, to serving herself, provided she does not think it good. That's our wretchedness; self has taken possession of our goodness. We don't find him so dreadfully raging and fighting perhaps as he was; but does an enemy rage and fight when he has taken the stronghold and bound the garrison? Surely we might at least *see*, whatever we do; unseeing, all our actions turn to ill."

" September 1871.

"I do not admit that regard for others is in any relative deficiency in the world now (*i.e.*, in England, which is all the world we know about), but hold that

considering whether, in the evils around us, we have not, as it were, the weights, the pulling down of which would do our work of raising and elevating in our families, as well as outside them, far more effectually than our too often futile endeavours to raise and elevate our children by our own efforts? Might we not use the evils without to cure the evils within?

there is every reason to believe that there is as much as is for the present wanted. I for my aims do not want more in men or women; more will be wanted, I fully believe, and will come when it is wanted. I don't believe it is wanted now, but only a different *use* of what we have— a different position of it or order. We put it last, whereas it ought to come first—that is all. The consequence of course is, that being out of its place, it itself comes to evil, and we dare not indulge ourselves in it. Till we can use what we have how can we tell if we want more?

"This is what your letter is like: Suppose there is a great reservoir of water up in the hills, and it keeps on overflowing every now and then, and doing a lot of mischief. I propose to put a pipe in and supply a starving town below: you come to me and say, 'But what is the good? it is water that we want; how will you secure water?' The heavens secure water. At least let us use what we have. If regard to others, rested on our urging, there would be a drought indeed; nor would I waste my labour in making pipes; I would be jolly. Those words of Paul's keep ringing in my ears: 'If the dead rise not, let us eat and drink.' I say with him, If man can't be man, let us be jolly. I know what I would do—I am all prepared.

"Think of all the people you know; if they had the making of the world, would they make it as it is, even if making it otherwise detracted ever so much from their own pleasures? Would any one of them? Not one of the people I know would. Then there is a certain amount of regard for others which is not used, which cannot find its vent. I seek to use this. No one can affirm its quantity; to me, studying it, it does not seem at all too small. When I find the want of more, perhaps I shall try to increase it. Perhaps, I say; for it hardly seems likely to me that I should judge it worth while. I have scruples about filling up the world with print, and can hardly conceive myself adding any more to the multitude of appeals on every hand full of all sorts of motives and urgings to regard others, and deny self, and be willing for sacrifice. There is distinctly too much talk on that subject; I believe there is less action for the multiplicity of it. How could I possibly add to that? Are there not deaf people to cure?

" But what I notice is, that with all the talk about it, and things not at all likely to get put right by means of it, there is a distinct mistake as to what it means, and what the real effect of regarding others' needs is. To put this straight seems to me to want trying, and to be likely to come to something; but why it should be mixed up with a talk about the motives I cannot understand. Let those who want to be urged by motives go to church, take up a volume of sermons, or a good person's novel, or a child's story-book, or go to any of the hundred of stores where that article is sold. . . .

" Your letter gives me the key to another thing: you do not make adjustment for difference of sex. Of course regard to others has two sides or forms—caring about the world and caring about persons. Now these two sides are given to men and women. The true regard for others is the man's and the woman's together. Now young girls —among whom you live—don't care, and find it hard to care, for the world: nay, you yourself do not truly care for it—your words betray that you *don't*. You do not see it; your 'humanity in the concrete,' which is 'so apt to be disagreeable,' means that you do not see it. You are a person who cannot see the wood for the trees, and may revenge yourself by saying that we men cannot see the trees for the wood. Now boys care for the world. I believe that almost every boy who has

had a chance—that is, who has ever heard about the
world, has had any knowledge by which his true feeling could be drawn out—cares distinctly more about
the world being as it ought to be than about how he
can make it best for himself. I say that is the natural
reaction of the boy's mind, and that if he grew up into a
human life, he would require to be taught that men ever
did anything else. The whole lot of us are forced into
self-regard—that is, *such* self-regard as ours. Because men
tend to begin that way, does it follow that they like what
comes of it? Why did they not then persist in liking
what came of believing their sense-impressions?

"But there is immense hope in this division of regard
for persons and for the world between women and men.
As in all such cases, there is a negation in each half, and
an infinite multiplication effected by their union. But
have you not been confusing acting for service with regarding the world, perhaps even more than ever I meant?
The people we have to regard are those who stand visible,
though beyond our own circle; going beyond the family
does not mean putting the world first.

"But there is another point still in which we may see
together, and that is where you lay such stress on the need
at present for willingness to do all most painful things for
others' sakes. You know I don't deny; I take it for granted.
Perhaps I say so little about it because I am conscious that
I have been thinking of it too much rather than too little,
or at least relatively too much. But there is another
reason for which I say little of it, and that is because I am
so sure there are plenty of people ready. That willingness
does not need creating, only opening a channel for. Any
one who thinks that if a clear call came for martyrdom,
be it what it might, there would not be the people ready,
thinks of this age not only positively in itself, but, as

compared with all other ages, infinitely worse than I do. I say that in its actions it is worse, as a chrysalis is worse than a grub, but in its soul it is at least as ready, I say that the people who will do all painful things that service shall want ,doing, are ready and waiting."

" January 1872.

" I don't wonder that the fear of society is so strong on you, or indeed on any woman. I doubt, indeed, if it is really stronger on any one than myself. My shrinking from the putting myself into antagonism with those I most love and respect is extreme and absolute. I cannot imagine it and simply shut my eyes when it suggests itself in detail. I know the persons, whose thoughts and ways and doings I repudiate, are beyond all comparing better than myself. But then how can it be helped ? What is the good of thinking of it ? One might as well keep moaning that the sea is deep. How one will do it, one does not know ; but it simply has to be done. . . .

" But of hypocrites I take no note. What people ' might say,' who are not really trying to find the true thing to say, is to me like what wind might blow."

" February 1872.

" You know I have no objection to be one of the dreamers ; what does it matter ? I am just as content to be that as anything else. But one thing I am sure of, that I do not want any one to yield one iota to my personal rule, or to believe anything I say, except because, and just so far as, he sees it true. And another thing I know too, and that is, that I do not want to make any select or separate

U

society,* or people with any different right or law from the rest of men and women. So many seem to have come to shipwreck on that; but here I have no temptation. There is a true law, indeed, and a false, but the true law is the law for all, the false law for none. The one duty is to come from under the false to under the true, which is, not do this or do that, but be such that you can do whatever is wanted to be done; not a fleshly commandment, but the power of life for all, and here."

"*February* 1872.

"You say you don't see how being guided by pleasure is to be distinguished from acting for it. I rather wonder, because that is so completely settled by our eating. Which of us does not eat for service, absolutely? Yet for that very reason do we not let pleasure entirely guide us? If we do not, we are diseased, either in body or mind. There is no eating perfectly for service but by letting pleasure guide the eating. Without professing perfectly to see this, my strong feeling is that this gives a key to all, to what all man's life will be; and that when he has come to understand it fully, it will be found that pleasure will be in all things as much a guide as it is in this. But apart from this illustration, if the desire is for service—and that is the only right, the desire being for service—then the doing what is for service will be the pleasure. We think very falsely of pleasure, confounding it so much with pleasant sensations; pleasure is the play of passion, and varies constantly. Let the passion

---

* This was Mr. Hinton's *bête noire*. He once said to me, when we were out walking together, "If I thought the man would arise who would use my name to denominate a sect, I declare I would knock him down by proxy in the first man we meet."

be for service, and it is plain being guided by pleasure will be following service. So God does according to His pleasure. Man will be man only then, when the same is true of him.

"But besides this, as the facts of nature in man's life appear to me at present, it seems to me that when once he has made service his end and desire, what he will be called to will be absolutely the most pleasurable life in every way, with only such exceptions as will be needed to prevent a monotony of pleasure.

"But on these points I fancy my thoughts are a little influenced by my own particular experience. I have ever since I lived in Whitechapel—for it was that that did it—desired service, and acted for it—desired with a desire that has no second, no second even in the *sum* of all other desires I have ever had, that the world should be better. Now what has it meant? That I have acted according to my pleasure. I expect that among men not grossly vicious, and even perhaps including some of them, there has hardly been a man whose doings have been so much pleasure-guided as mine. I am conscious that it is so; aware that I must seem a most self-indulgent man in many ways to very many people; aware that good, even decent people, do restrain themselves from pleasure in very many ways that I do not. And I feel a distinct connection between the two things. Not only does my doing what I seek to do constantly lie in my doing the most pleasurable things— studying what I like best, going to see pictures, going to concerts, &c., but besides this, and more strikingly still, my desire being for service, makes pleasure my guide. It sets me free so to follow my instincts. Of course I do not think of it—that would spoil and contradict it—but I *act* it. I cannot really like anything I do not feel to be for my work; all most pleasant things are irksome, nay, intolerable to me, if they seem to me to be hindrances to that. Then what follows? Why, that every impulse that can attract me I *feel* to be for my work, whether I know how it can be or not. I do according to my pleasure, for if I were not persuaded somehow that the thing is for my work, it would not be my pleasure; it would be my hatred.

"So it is from a kind of private experience I speak here when I *feel* so sure that desiring service will mean being guided by pleasure. This is, of course, the 'instinct' or apparent 'self-indulgence' of genius. It is pleasure-led, and safely. Pleasure which leads all others wrong, or seems to do so, leads it right. I am speaking of it in its working, not as a person, taking, perhaps, to drinking. Why does pleasure lead it right? Because it cannot have pleasure save in that which seems its work's truth. That and pleasure are identified with it; so the law not to be guided by pleasure is abrogated for it. Its work is the law, 'Love and do what you like,' written in terms of fact. But this being guided by pleasure has in it an immense amount of what is not pleasure, what one least likes to do."

Mr. Hinton wrote much on the phenomenon of genius; it was indeed his autobiography; its mysterious joys and sorrows he felt in some measure to be his own. The man of genius, he was wont to say, is simply one who perfectly yields himself to the control of nature, who cannot resist her, but is strong with her might against all opposing forces. To talent may belong power, wisdom, elevated beauty, laborious research, clever adaptation; genius may lack any or all of these qualities; its gift is a special organisation that fits it for its one function of seeing and uttering the truth, which at that particular time is the outcome of the progress of humanity. He saw how the man of genius is often led to commit apparently wilful and wanton breaches of social rules, to inexplicable and motiveless actions that cause trouble and perplexity to those nearest and dearest to him; but he contended that this is the price the possessor, or rather the victim, of the heavenly gift must pay for his power. If he is to see that hidden thing which he has to reveal to all men, he must often be blind to that which all men see. Flexible as a reed to every breath of nature's inspiration, but often utterly impervious to good advice. Seeing what excellent reasons can be urged for a different line of conduct, but constrained to assert that the instincts that guide him have nothing to do with good logic—this contradictory being, at once so weak and so strong, the despair of prudent friends and advisers, Mr. Hinton strove to interpret and to commend to those sympathies of which he of all men stands most in need.

To his Wife :—

" Savile Row, 24th August 1872.

"I have seen a vision of my little book on the Ear. I shall enjoy doing it, and it will be as much like me as anything I shall have done at all. I have seen what made it unattractive to me: two things—one, the saying over again so much, things that have been written dozens of times before; and the other—putting down things as if you knew all about them, when you know quite well that they are as doubtful as possible. Now I shall escape both these abominations, and do just what I like to do. How do you think ?

"I shall write—not a treatise, manual, text-book, guide,

in short, an oracle, but—guess—'The Questions of Aural Surgery.'

"Of course I am speaking of the little book that is to go with the Atlas, not of that, which must be separate. Is it not jolly? So I shall lay the whole stress of the book on the points which want clearing up; and what is known, or what I personally advise, will come in, not as an essential part of the book, but as a kind of ground-work, mentioned incidentally, as it were, but for that very reason more impressive and better to be remembered. There will be, as it were—in the fresh point of interest raised—something besides itself to remember it by.

"The idea running through the book will be:—These few things we know; this plan I follow as the best I have tried; these others are advised by other men; but the points we want to know are *these*.

"Now I shall get on with that. My heart quite failed me in the thought of writing an ordinary book, saying, this is that way—do this, &c.

"I think it will be more interesting to the reader, and distinctly help the study of the subject ever so much more."

"*September 2, 1872.*

"Do not you see, Love, the thought by which life might be made new? It is natural enough, it is not wrong to put our own advantage or pleasure first, but if we do— if we do one single thing not because it is good for that to be done, but because it is for our pleasure—then there comes on us a whole law, perverted and made false by this same consideration of our pleasure. We have made false the law under which we live, and can no more say, simply and humanly, What is for good? that is my right to do, but must bring in the alien question of our pleasure, and say, 'What things can I do for myself?' Men have not thought of the effect of acting for self on *right*. They have taken passively the right which acting for self imposes, as the true right. No one proposes to them a new right and its condition. Is it not plain the problem has changed, that past experience, however full of failure, is no ground for expecting failure in the future? Failure thus is the assurance of success, its condition, the means by which it is brought. That goodness of limited desires and restraints, based on an accepted putting self first, shall pass away; and a new thought of goodness, good put first, and all things free, shall come in its stead."

"18 *Savile Row, December* 3, 1872.

"My Dear How,—I am very proud of your Balliol exhibition, for I know you have worked very hard for it; although it is not worth so much as the other one, I would rather you stopped at Balliol. Do not do yourself harm; you will be tempted; but it is unwise. It is contrary also to good for others. Willy comes out like a real student."

"*December* 6, 1872.

"I am very glad you have done so well, and particularly glad that your old friends at Rugby find pleasure in your success. To me it is more still. As a reduction in the expenses of your education, it is a distinct facility for doing things which else I might not have been able to do; and I thank you much for helping me. Of course, also, it will render you more able to be free to do the work that your heart may be set upon, by rendering it possible for you to be more free from the need of earning money. It may not, however, be particularly advantageous for you to be able to do this, because I have found having to devote myself to earning money, the very greatest help and advantage in my best work, and this most when it looked least like it. One of the chief lessons of my life has been that what seems most hindering is most helpful."

The next letter is to a friend on the pain and sacrifice involved in carrying out some conscientious convictions.

" Savile Row, 29th February 1872.

"If you felt how I feel about this, how absolutely and wholly I prefer to have the thing to do shown me, brought me to do without any choice of my own, or even against my choice, you would feel, too, that this being talked about and misrepresented, as you say, must be exactly as welcome as anything else. It simply marks out what to do. I wonder whether it could possibly be the same to you? Probably not quite, and it must be much more painful besides.

"I do not see what there is to be said for you and others situated as you, except that taking that position means making all pain whatever welcome, and that when it comes there is nothing to be said but that it has been most welcome long ago. To refuse to take any part in the matter, to say it is not true, or that, though it is true, you cannot have anything to do with it, is open to any one; to say the contrary and take any note of pain, is not. There is only one thing—pain must be to you as if it were not. It is *one* effort, or rather it is one consenting, one great, huge, passionate regret; but it exhausts all power of regretting; it is over—done for ever. There is then no more pain, that is, no more pain in the same sense that there was before, no pain that you wish not to be. Of all pain, past, present, and to come, you have asked one question, Do you mean this being done? and it has answered 'Yes,' and then your soul has answered, 'Then I count you joy; pass on.' Pain is not pain if you love it; only the pains you cannot love, the pains you give. You will find it true and false, false and yet true. You will say the pain is welcome, and your own tears will contradict you; and you will not know whether it is welcome or not, only that you have no choice but to choose it.

"Am I sorry for you or not? I do not know. I cannot write without tears, yet what would I have altered? Why must Life come in pain, and joy be forbidden even to be desired? There it stands; and we are content. It is best to turn away. There is the torn heart; was it unjust, cruel? nay, it did not wish not to be. All is said; may one not *choose* sorrow? But there is a groan, too, beneath the contentment, and it is right; and no ear shall be deaf to it—not God's ear, nor man's; it is right, only there is the contentment, too, above the groan.

"But then, when the pain is welcome, I do think it is often very much less than we should have feared, very much less even in its external causes. We often think more pain will be given than is, more difficulty encountered than ever arises. Simplicity and truth find paths when all things else fail; and often, indeed, things that seem most unlikely are the very things most prepared for."

The two following letters are to a disciple of Jacob Böhme, who had sent him a criticism on a little tract Mr. Hinton had published anonymously, called " Others' Needs."

" 18 *Savile Row, January* 1873.

"Thank you for reading my paper, and for expressing

your criticisms, which of course, are valuable. I should have been disposed to think with you that the ideas were too complex for ordinary folk, but I don't find them so; and I think you will be pleased, as I was, to hear that a minister to whom I had sent it, told me the other day that, having to give an address to some quite poor people at a Welsh chapel, he introduced the idea of the paper, and found that it was quite understood and best received of all. That I was glad to hear, for I want to speak to the simple; and I think there would be so much good in the thought of that paper being clearly seen and borne in mind.

" I am very interested about Böhme. But you high-and-lifted-up people, who see all through the world, ought to understand that you are very tantalising to us poor folks (and also that we envy you less than we otherwise should), because you are so unable to share your treasures. Will you not try to tell me what this truth is (I say this truth, not these truths), by which all is made so plain, so that we can understand? I agree to be judged by my own standard. I also think I see a truth that makes a great many things plain; but I hold it is not the true truth unless it can be made available for all.

"Do tell me one thing that Böhme has taught you. Observe, I do not speak doubtfully: I believe, entirely, he saw wonderful things; but I think less of his seeing because he has not made more people see. . . .

" It is real genuine interest makes me want to know. If ever I am tempted to pride, it is when I feel in myself (which I do) that I belong, however low down, to the same class and order as he. And so I can better explain to you why, what you said some time ago, that your belief in Böhme made it impossible for you to go along with me—gave me the slightest feeling that might almost be called pain. It is not at all that you hold 'to other opinions than mine; that I like quite as well as if you did not. But—there is vanity in the feeling, perhaps, but it is sincere—it makes a feeling come over me as if some years hence some one might use, *misuse* me as you do him, and say he cannot listen to those other things because I said so-and-so, and he must believe as I said. That would grieve my very soul in heaven, and I am sure Böhme is grieved by you. He would not be so abused by any one if he could help it."

"*January* 1874.

"Thank you very much for your kind letter. Our father's death was most happy—no pain, and perfect peace. Many thanks for the violets; Margaret and Ada delighted in them, and little Daisy too. They are appropriate as well as beautiful.

"By and by, I shall have more time for reading and study, and then I hope to know more of Böhme. But in the meantime I am of opinion, as I have said before, that those who are so aided by him are, to outside observers, much to blame for not endeavouring more to bring before others that which is so valuable to themselves. You will agree with me that to tell any considerable number of persons to read the existing translations of Böhme, even if they were to be obtained, would be quite unreasonable. They are not translated into intelligible language to *us*. And if they require, as well as deserve, a real task of study to be able to understand them, then people ought to have something to put before them which should make them feel that it was worth their while. In a word, I do not think the Theosophists of the present age do their duty, and that if the world suffers, as is very probable, from a lack of knowledge that they possess, they will be called to account hereafter for having lived in selfish isolation of privilege.

" And now, having vented my spleen, which is partly a personal feeling (for why does not some one, enlightened by Böhme, give us a new translation of one of his works, with a general account of them, so that we might know ?), let me say to you also, that I feel you misunderstand my relation to the Theosophists, or, as I am in the habit of calling them, the mystics. I feel myself to be one with them, and always have felt so, ever since my first acquaintance with them. The few things I have made out of Böhme's charmed me; and I am quite sure that under the veil of his (translator's) words there is some great 'method' hidden, some method of finding the spiritual in the physical, which, I agree with you in thinking, is the chief want of this age.

" Surely no real spirit-led Theosophist ever wished to make the world stand still just at *his* point of view, and never to advance or change? If Theosophy means *that*, I trust I shall never be one, never be willing to have the spirit killed for the sake of a letter whose whole value is that, at one particular time and state of human vision, it best expressed the spirit. I think the spirit of Theosophy will find itself other expressions still, as every living spirit ever does, and that it is quite possible to be blind to the very power of the same spirit now that was in it of old, by insisting upon seeing it only as it appeared, and hearing it only as it spoke, then. This may indeed be part of the cause of the seeming selfish indolence and neglect of the Theosophists with regard to the present time. Their souls may be barren because they do not open their eyes to the present as well as the past. Is the earth forsaken of God? Has the work of man in the last two centuries not also been a work He has ruled? is it to

have no part in his vision of spiritual things? I am sure
that lack of sympathy will never be a true help to
spiritual seeing; nor would one of the men of the past,
whose words seem so wonderful now, have had his inspira-
tions from above if his soul had not throbbed in profound
sympathy with the strivings and the achievings of the
men around him, and the age that wrought within him.
The next voice of God to men (and it is a voice to us we
want), I venture to believe, will have in it a revealing of
the meaning of all this great and earnest toil, especially
in science, of the last few centuries.

"With best and kindest regards and sympathy, though
my letter may read harshly,—Yours most truly,

"J. H."

CHAPTER XIII.

THE following letter is to his sister, Sarah :—

"18 *Savile Row, November* 1873.

"MY DEAR SARAH,—Thank you very much for reporting the conversation. It is very interesting, also very good sense, as far as it goes.

"What I observe about it is, that there is a very sound argument, and what comes of it is a very intolerable condition; and I infer that there is something more to be thought of. I am not sure how far you know my opinions about society. Don't imagine them, nor receive them from any one but myself. Perhaps they are peculiar. I hold the present state of things horrid; but as for the reason it is horrid, and the way of mending, it may be that my views are my own. . . .

"I don't object to rich men. I have tried to become one myself. I would try more, except that other things draw me more powerfully. Also, I own land, and, for that matter, have a large house upon it (though I don't live in it), but I try to get rent for it, and have been recently raising my prices; and I make a profit, too, out of the wages of more than one other person, and should be glad to do so out of more. Moreover, I speculate now and then (in pictures), and turn an honest penny that way. So you see I have no objection to rich men, or to the means of getting rich. I distinctly wish I were richer.

Moreover, I do not believe much in co-operation; that is, I think individual masters and workmen, and so on, are the natural order, and will not be superseded to any great extent. Getting profit, and collecting it into masses as capital, is a thing essential to the well-being of society; and, like most other things, is best done by people with natural gifts for it, and unfettered. All these things I don't remember ever doubting. The question it seems to me men overlook, is one which has no special relation to riches, nor indeed to anything but man's soul. Is it truly human that a man should employ his powers for himself? What does 'for himself' mean? Yours, ever,

"J. HINTON."

The next letter is to his wife, on being called away to see a patient.

"18 *Savile Row, Tuesday Evening.*

"*I.e.*, Abingdon. I am here all right, dearest, and hope I shall do the little girl some good. It is nothing very serious, but needs attention. She is a nice little creature, with such pretty little hands.

"I hope, darling, you have found papa and mamma very well for them, and happy, and that you feel happy too, and will enjoy yourself and rest. Was it not a nice walk we had last night? You must think of it often, as I am sure to do, and especially when you are disposed to become unhappy and desponding. . . .

"But, speaking of the difficulty of seeing what truly is in me in spite of what seems, Mrs. Boole came in the morning to see you, thinking you had not gone so soon, and we had a little talk. Among other things, she said any one would naturally feel sure, from my ways, that I never thought of anything seriously at all, but did everything in the most rash and offhand way, that it looked as if I acted utterly without consideration. Now, I can quite understand that it should *look* so. One reason is that there is ever so much latent in my mind. This, you will easily see, must go with the constitution that makes one feel *that he does not know.* This feeling cannot do other-wise than lead to the collection, as it were, unexpressed in the mind, of a whole accumulation of observations and thoughts, just adapted to give the appearance of utter inconsideration. This, of course, must be the secret in part at least of the sudden promptings of genius, that suppressed accumulation in the mind. No doubt it is true to a great extent of women, is the key to part of their quickness of insight and rapid convictions; and I fancy it is very much indeed true of you, mixed with other things. But I only referred to this because it joined itself so curiously with what I had been thinking of—the difficulty it must have been to see me truly against the seeming of me."

The following letter explains itself :—

"*Savile Row, August* 1872.

"But now, love, I am filled with such a solemn joy. I hardly know how to bear it. Think, darling, it is truly, absolutely possible that in one year and a little more I might be wholly free. It seems my God gave me all things. I have a feeling it might kill me when it comes, with the ceasing of the tension on the soul, which may have been so much more than I know. But don't let this frighten you; besides, it is not really likely, and certainly the longer it is deferred the more likely it is to be. Oh, it would make me so quiet, and I see I shall not be violent and angry any more. I want only to beseech. It is only my being so tied makes me so full of rage. But this is the question, love; I want you to think of it, and tell me shall I fix it now or not?"

The rest of the letter is occupied with careful calculations of whether it could be done without too much sacrifice to his wife and children.

The absolute necessity of his retiring from practice was becoming evident to Mrs. Hinton from his increasing mental excitement. The rage he speaks of was in part due to the state of nervous tension he was in, so little realised by those who took offence at some of the excited things it led him to say and do. But in part it was natural to him, the intensity his nature being nowhere more strongly displayed than in the force of his indignation. His face would blanch and every ·fibre of his frame quiver with a passion which, when over, left him utterly spent and exhausted. But it never vented itself on individuals; only on false principles, and on the goodness that is so busy taking care of itself that it has no time to think of others. On one occasion, some intimate friends of his told him of an acquaintance of theirs who, because he was too virtuous to revenge himself on a man who had injured him, allowed him to retain a post for which he was unfit, and in which he was doing great mischief. His rage on hearing it knew no bounds, not against the individual so much as against the state of social feeling of which it was an instance. When he had quieted down a little, he said, "It's just as bad to sacrifice other people to your virtue as to sacrifice them to your pleasure. Indeed, I think it's worse." "But," said his friend, "self-virtue is one of the stages that man has got to go through sooner or later, and therefore it is better to

X

be in that stage than the preceding one." "Yes, you're right. It's further advanced. It's like having to go through a slough. When you have got to the middle, you're *fur- ther advanced* than when you were close to the edge, but you're deeper in. Self-virtue is the middle, and it's worse, it's deeper in, than sacrificing other people to your pleasure, although it's further advanced."

But most often this passion of anger would come upon him while reading in the police reports of the crime and punishment of some poor outcast of society, abandoned by the selfish rights of our so-called Christian civilization to every evil influence, born and bred in circumstances which make virtue a name, and vice a necessity, and then, when degradation has borne its legitimate fruit of crime, ruthlessly punished and crushed by the society that has denied him the social conditions for better things. It was the "right" that makes virtue so much a luxury of the respectable classes which was the object of his most un- sparing wrath.

But towards the person, the individual who erred or did amiss, Mr. Hinton was ever tolerant. Even those who knew him most intimately can never remember hear- ing him say an ill-natured thing. This was the more marked because he was a man who, partly from his erratic, unconventional ways, and in part from the strange originality and eccentricity of his mind, inspired the strongest dislikes as well as the most devoted attach- ments. He was perfectly conscious of the former, and felt them keenly; but perhaps only his wife knew that he felt them at all. He habitually treated those whose dislikes he was aware of with a frankness of manner in society, and an untiring kindness on all occasions, that often puzzled its recipients. Never was there any one so difficult to quarrel with, or who took so graciously and magnanimously all that people said of him or to him; never one who had more of the Greek ἐπιέικεια, the "sweet reasonableness," which was ever ready to listen and to weigh, with none of the "pugnacious dogmatism of partial reflection."

The preoccupation of his mind in his thoughts, and especially in social questions, about this time, occasionally led to very funny mistakes, though his strong sense of professional responsibility kept it from really injuring his practice. On one occasion he gravely handed a patient a prescription with the following remarkable direction:— "The ointment to be rubbed round the world night and morning;" only just perceiving his error in time to snatch it back and rewrite it, "to be rubbed round the ear." This slip of the pen has its quaint significance to those who had experience of his enthusiastic nature, the despair of less sanguine temperaments, and how often he seemed to them to think that some great moral remedy could be "rubbed round the world" as a sure and certain cure to all the ills which flesh is heir to.

To one of his friends he writes:—

"Savile Row, 1873.

"By inventing our God, I was not speaking of the historical origin of the idea of God. I spoke of *our* idea of a God, which is a very striking phenomenon— the God that our race and generation have affirmed. I do not want to insist on the darker side of the thought, but the God who sent little children to hell, and values Sabbath-days and other physical doings more than human lives, how came man to invent that God, I mean? Did not the conjoined and yet incompatible wishes not to think of himself, and yet to feel himself good, contrive that fiction as a means of their co-existing? It does look like it to me; and if you look simply at human life, a desire for restraining his passion, *i.e.*, for feeling himself good, looks as if it were wonderfully near being a primary passion of man's. Why should it not be, *i.e.*, if there are any primary passions at all? Why should he not as much 'like' the feeling of being good, as the taste of sugar? the feeling of being good which he cannot have except in restraining his passion—be his passion what it may, casting himself into the fire to save his enemy, even, he cannot feel himself good if he is indulging it. No man can feel himself good in any self-sacrifice if he likes it. How feel good (which is feel self-good) if we are doing what we like? Has not that phrase come to be used as the very contrary to being good?

"Look over the world—where is not man engaged in thwarting his desires for the sake of something he calls *God?* but how does he get at the God who wants him to thwart his desires? Is not a passion for thwarting his desires likely to have had part in making the God, as well as *vice versa?* I only say that this is a very curious subject for study. Cruel idols seem to me very like 'projected reasons' for something man found himself doing, and had to make a reason for. The God who wanted men not to be healed on the Sabbath-day was, I should say, demonstrably a projected reason. The Jews had made him up, because they had forgotten what the Sabbath was for. But if this be one case, it is certainly a type of many. Don't shut the question up.

"But as for man having a primary desire for feeling himself good, see what that wonderful writer of Genesis says. The command on man was, not to avoid evil—not to avoid even knowing evil—but not to know *good* and evil. As if one might say the primary passion of man—

the source of his mischief—was his wishing to be (self)
good. Do not let us shut questions like this up. If
men had really answered them anything like they feel
they have, they would not be making such a frightful
mull of their life now. . . .

"I know I am always most obscure through taking for
granted that which I mean the most, as if all must know
it—the point from which I start, and on which I build.
And I learned from Mr. B. to recognise what a latent
thought of God there was in my thought of the law of
the service of man, and indeed must be. It is not possible to say, ' The traceable needs of men and women are
the rule of our life,' without meaning they are the law of
God. The two cannot be separated. We see it in Christ;
the most intense in His thought of God, the most absolute
in His insistance on the law of the traceable needs of
man. They are one. People say ' human good is the
law,' and invent their own God, or leave him out, if they
make up their own idea of human good; for they put
into it just as much self-goodness as they choose, and
that contents them. But they *cannot* say the traceable
needs of men are the law of right, and leave out God. It
must be seen as His command before it can be felt as our
right. Let any one try it."

"*Savile Row, March* 1873.

"You have heard me say, I think, how the truth of all
spiritual things, of all that is called dogmatic theology,
is in its being *spiritual truth*, true to the soul, and that, if
it has this, it has all the truth it can have or ought to
have; that to look for any other is a mistake; and that
no one intellectual form can be truer than another. The
highest expression of human thought in its utmost attainment is no more ' true ' than the very poorest and

lowest, all being alike altogether untrue, as being intellectual apprehensions of that which cannot . be intellectually apprehended. All are stories made up to
ourselves of things that are not, have not been, cannot be;
all are perfectly true, if they convey to man the *spiritual
truth* in the fullest way he can receive it; that is, if they
correspond to, and fulfil his knowledge and his moral
feeling.

"They become false as soon as ever, for the sake of
keeping a certain intellectual form, they do violence to
either of these—as soon as our knowledge is ignored or
moral sentiment coerced. The truth of theology is the
truth of a story; the truest truth, truth conveyed in
terms of things that are not. So we see the first stories
were of theology; that was the storyteller's earliest theme,
a prophecy perchance in this; and is it not therefore that the story takes such lead now in human interest, and absorbs so much of man's power? He is
learning the art of seeing truth the more true because in
terms of non-reality, of learning to recognise what that
true truth demands. And so shall we not discern that
the true 'story' for which all the others are but prepara-
tions, is the story of man's own life? the rest, fragments
of that?

"So it is visible, science must transform theology. God
has winked at the times of ignorance. Every statement
of spiritual truth must correspond absolutely to our knowledge. It must conform to all we know of physiology, to
all the needs which the physical expresses. What a
change is needed from the time when men did not know
how the mind depended upon the body! And so, too,
how men have made science antagonistic to religion, by
refusing to let its form change. . . .

"Of course, the reason of human history can be seen

only outside itself, it lies in its relations. This we have often spoken about. Then, as to thinking of humanity as ' one man.' I will tell you the difference between us; my feeling is a feeling of him, a perception or conscious-ness, like a sense-perception, not reasoned, not at all caring about being rational, but simply there. The being I mean by man is the being I perceive. I have not reasoned him out. I perceive him, nay, I love him, that is, her; for she is by no means a ' colossal man ' but a little, trembling, quivering, passion-driven woman, throbbing with uncom-prehended instincts, and afraid with timid regrets and sorrows for half-imaginary sins, which she repents of, but knows she will still commit, and does commit. I don't know about humanity as any ' colossal ' thing whatever; but that little restless woman thing I know, for she works in me, and keeps me in perpetual unrest. Would not the wave be quiet if it were not for the sea, which, when the spirit breathes upon it, can let no wave be still ?

"You are thinking of this ' one man ' with your intel-lect; there is no such thought-out ' one man ' any more than such one God. . . . And the idea of a ' colossal man ' is, above all, out of place, like thinking God is ' great,' because He fills all space. Those magnitudes, spiritual powers, and dominions are exactly not great, but too small ever to be found—too small for any microscope to reach them; ' he that would be greatest among you, let him be least,' is the very law of being. You are seeking a self man—the living among the dead. He is not here. He is risen."

"The real determining causes of man's history," Mr Hinton once said to me, "must of course lie outside itself. You could not give the history of so much as a stone as

long as you look only at the stone. You must know the
law of gravity and the motion of all celestial bodies, to
account for its weight; you must know the properties of
oxygen, and the laws of chemical reaction, to account for
the colour produced by the action of the air upon it. If it
be chalk, you must know the history of the earth through
ages of the past, the nature of organic life, and the órder
of its evolution from the inorganic; to account for its
hardness and constitution in general you must descend
into all the intricacies of molecular physics.* In the
same way the reason that the world is what it is, the
meaning of its sin and sorrow, must be extra-mundane.
We can of course only guess at it." Mr. Hinton believed
that in some way man is laying down his life for the
universe, consenting to death that he may reveal the
life of God as sacrifice. That man's fall and redemption
subserves some wider purpose is a thought with which
the readers of St. Paul are familiar. See especially Ephes.
i. 9, 10; iii. 9, 10.

He thus writes to a friend on his approaching retirement from practice :—

"Savile Row, July 18, 1873.

"I have been so happy often of late in looking forward to my life. What I want to do is so simple. I
want to say to people, 'Are we turning the moral power
God has already given us to its true account?' Without

---

* Compare Tennyson's well-known lines—
  "Flower in the crannied wall,
   I pluck you out of the crannies,
   Hold you here, root and all, in my hand,
   Little flower ;—but if I could understand
   What you are, root and all, and all in all,
   I should know what God and man is."

being better men or women, how much better our life might be. This is so continually before my eyes; and it flows like a new current of blood all through me. What hinders that men, now and here, should begin to have their regard on good, to take the absolute desire for it as their duty, their one and only right? This *easier* and better good stands ready for them, and they are ready, too, for it. It is of no use their trying to get better; they build their very good upon a wrong. The thing now to do is to correct that wrong; and it means not a harder, but an easier thing, possible to more and weaker people; instead of restraint of passion, a passion that does not need restraint. My heart beats so for it. And it is so strange. I am fifty, and it seems to me that my life is just beginning. I have more time for work (probably) than all the time I have ever had before; and I am younger than ever I have been besides."

"*Savile Row, July* 28, 1873.

"I wish you knew all my late thoughts; . . . they are the *same* as all the former ones—the very same over again, indeed. It strikes me so wonderfully sometimes how exactly the same thing they are; only the subjects altered. . . . You speak of luxury—could any thought be simpler or more sufficient than that *all* things that are for good are right to do, and nothing else?—that our desire must be on good always? Have you read 'Other's Needs'?"

The next letter is in answer to some inquiries as to the nature of the social changes that might come with a truer aim in human life. While holding to the essential permanence of the marriage tie, and being, therefore, opposed to divorce, Mr. Hinton considered that our mar-

riage laws were too much rigid and inflexible laws of the
letter, and needed to be made more fluent to the claims
of human good. But to questions of external order
Mr. Hinton was at heart profoundly indifferent. " Get
the true principles of human life recognised, and experience will teach us what is for service," he used to
say ; "set the living waters flowing, and they will make
their own channel." He never allowed that any one
differed from him who agreed with him as to principle,
and only differed as to practical application. On the
latter point, he emphatically recognised his fallibility, his
part being rather to discover than to apply.

" Savile Row, 1874.

"It is very interesting that you quote 'with what body
do they come?' You know that is one of my pas-
sages. I think, in using Paul's words to ask the question, you are using them in their true meaning, that
the spiritual body of man's emotions, passions, deeds, and
not this phenomenal flesh and blood, was his subject,
even as the resurrection is the raising up of man to
life. . . . But I confess I can't share the embarrassment
some of my best friends feel about this. What is human
life but emotions and convictions expressing themselves
in deeds and modes of living? I suppose, as it has
managed to be that before, it will go on being that. And
that is all I can even suppose to be wanted; new feelings and new thoughts will, as heretofore, go on to make
their own modes of operation. How has it got into
your head that they want predicting, much more pre-
arranging? How could that fail to be mischievous? Do
you propose to help a plant to grow? Is it not enough
to give it earth and water, and put it in the sun? It
is some curious wrinkle in your thought that wants

smoothing out. Pass your hands over it, as you would over a crumpled pocket-handkerchief, and see if it is not better. . . . Besides, I find, following the law of service (with endless mistakes, doubtless, I don't think anything of them; they are part of it) is not puzzling or hard at all, nor obscure, but exactly easy. It is always *coming* to you, as it were. And, indeed, it is nothing but the old familiar doing your best, than which I never had or felt the want of any other rule. . . . And even when following the law of service has seemed to me to mean diverging from former and from customary doing, I have found it not more hard, but enormously less so than I should have supposed. I am obliged to check myself, lest I should think social changes easier than they will turn out."

In 1873, Mr. Hinton was asked to give the inaugural lecture at Guy's, afterwards published, with one or two other essays, under the title of "The Place of the Physician," a title on which Sir William Gull wittily remarked to its author, "The place of the physician, by a surgeon? that is *nowhere.*"

But the longed-for day of deliverance had at last arrived. In March 1874, Mr. Hinton gave up practice and the large income he had at his control, to devote all his energies to the great objects of human good he had in view. But, alas! in order to effect his purpose, he had for the last year or two been working recklessly, throwing, as he himself said, the strength of ten men into his profession, and at the same time passing six or seven works simultaneously through the press, while piles of MSS. bear witness to the remorseless activity of his mind; and though the injury his brain received remained latent for a year and a half, there is no doubt the seeds of the

fatal malady which caused his premature death were
already sown.

He writes to his son :—

"Kentish Town, April 1, 1874.

"MY DEAREST HOW,—We have made the great change.
I trust in God that it will be for good. I think it was a
true desire for good that moved me to the resolve; and
nothing more encouraged me than the kind and generous
and loving way in which my children, as well as mamma,
entered into my hopes and aims, and chose less of this
world's advantages in order that those aims might be carried out. It *was* a trouble getting out of the house. I
could only feel one thing—a hope that I might never
have so much furniture again.

"As you may suppose, I feel the change. Already
the whole Savile Row life seems like a dream to me. It
is as if it had never been ; so much so, that even the
old Tottenham life seems nearer and realer. But perhaps
this is only temporary. But the feeling that has come is
not one of great depression, which I should have thought
natural—I only had a few hours of that—but one of
great seriousness and solemnity. The excitement of my
recent life has passed away, and I want to pause and
think, and be spoken to again by God, in quietness.
Then I have had a sort of unrooted baselessness of feeling, as if I had no place in the world, and especially a
feeling of total and utter impotence, as if I never had
been or should be able to do anything again. This has
been very strong, but it is passing away; and as I was
reading some of Matthew Browne's essays yesterday I
felt quite a passionate gladness come over me that my
business now was with human life.

"Willy will come to you to-morrow. After he has had

a little rest try and get him to work, and help him a little. You can do this in his natural philosophy. I believe he will get through. I tell him I believe in him; which, indeed, I always did and do. It is impossible to look in his face and not believe in him. Mamma has gone to grandmamma's at Bristol.—Your loving father,
"J. HINTON."

Mr. Hinton had suffered the loss of his father in 1873, as is already briefly alluded to in one of his letters; and now the sacred tie of so many years between mother and son was to be broken, and he was to lose his surviving parent. She died at the good old age of fourscore years, having peacefully bidden her beloved son "good-night" just before her eternal morning broke.

"Thanks, dearest mother," he writes, after a memorandum of the day of her death, "thanks to you now in heaven, thanks always, and boundless, for the reverence and respect for woman that you taught me, even if nothing were to come of it but my own delight and gladness and truer seeing of her loving heart."

His parting gift to his profession was his " Questions on Aural Surgery," and his " Atlas of the Ear," the latter a work of great labour, the drawings of which were executed by Mrs. Hinton, the originals being presented to Guy's Hospital. The whole work is the recognised text-book of the branch of the profession which Mr. Hinton had made his own, and formed a valuable advance in aural surgery.

CHAPTER XIV.

THE summer of 1874 was spent chiefly at Lulworth in Dorsetshire. Mrs. Hinton was at this time very much out of health, and needed absolute rest and quiet. So it was determined that she should winter with one of her children in the Azores, where, as has been already mentioned, Mr. Hinton had purchased a small property. Mr. Hinton acquiesced in what he felt was best for her, as securing her entire rest from all the exciting subjects that engrossed his own mind. Their home was therefore temporarily broken up.

"Kentish Town, 14th April 1874.

"MY DEAR HOW,—I am glad of your little note. You must send to me now all you write, because I shall have more time to enter into your pursuits, which I have long desired; and also you must give me some lifts in mathematics. I must attend to them a little. They are so interesting and so full of suggestiveness, I have been going on a little with Mrs. Boole in our desultory way, which nevertheless has its value, at least for me. I got a little inkling about the conic sections, and then we came on to the calculus. It is very jolly; and I find it quite like what I thought it. The four forms of it are such fun. The Fluxion (what I call the honest or nature-form) as plain as the day; the Infinitesimal, which keeps hold of the infinitely small quantities and neglects them (which roused Newton's ire even to madness, and no wonder); the refined Infinitesimal or Differential, which takes the ratio only; and La Grange's, which tries to get round the whole thing, but, as is said, doesn't quite. These are splendidly interesting, quite apart from mathematics; they are a study of human life; nor does one need to know anything more than algebraical notation to enjoy them—I won't say thoroughly, but exquisitely. And my ideas about a new teaching of mathematics become both clearer and more confirmed. I should say this way : What is taught in our schools (to boys) is not mathematics, but a little fraction of the *history* of mathematics, and not even *as a history.* It is just as if, in teaching astronomy, boys should not be taught anything of what Copernicus did, but trained just a little bit in the tracing on paper the apparent motions, and formulating them, and should simply hear of Copernicus as a man who did some wonderful thing which great astronomers could know about. That is exactly as our teaching of mathematics does in respect to Newton, and with just as good reason. What Newton did was simply what Copernicus did—to make the thought true to nature, putting aside the non-perception that infects our native vision, and makes us deal first with fictions of our own constructing. Now, I would have every child trained a little in the epicycles before it heard anything about what Copernicus did; and so in geometry. But of course the earth's motion is the beginning of astronomy; so is the fluxion of mathematics. And this should be our teaching of it: 'This is what Newton did for us : he revealed to us nature, and this is how it was done first; but the dead or fictitious mathematics came before, and must have come.' Then the lessons of it are infinite, for you see what Newton showed us was not—speaking of realities and true .

values—anything about magnitudes and spaces (much as
that is in one point of view, but it has no glory, by reason
of the glory that excelleth ; these were just the clay given
to create a statue in—anything will do) ; but what he did
was, to show us the everlasting art, the art of Life, of
letting go and holding on at once, of having in effect, of
raising from *things* into *powers*, from physical to spiritual.
This is what he taught us.   To look merely at the lines
and values is as if in a book one should look merely at
the letters.   It is his process, his act that has an infinite
value and significance.   That *is* being true to nature,
always and everywhere.

   "Then look at the dependent variables.   What it *is*, is
the relation of the external law to the law of the soul—
the variation of the former with the latter; the mutual
varying, indeed.   It is *Life* it teaches us.   And so it is
all through; the child must have these things put before
him quite afresh.

   " But I suppose, perhaps, it is not 'wise' of me to put
these thoughts before you now.   Only, I can't think of
that, because, you see, you are my dearest friend, whom I
want to know all about me. . . .   Your loving father,
                              " JAMES HINTON."

   "Mr. Hinton used often to remark," writes his
friend, Mrs. Boole,* "how curious it is to notice that,
whereas everybody thinks of geometry as if it were
true, the very type of absolute truth, many people
get an impression of something not quite true, not quite
satisfactory about all forms of fluxions and calculus
methods.   And this is natural.   The man who says,
" Here is a straight line, or circle, or ellipse, I am going
to investigate its properties," gives an impression of fixed-
ness and repose, which naturally convey a sense of truth

   * The widow of the well-known mathematician, Professor Boole.

and reality. He who says, 'There is a curve somewhere, and I am going to study this straight line which flies off from it at a tangent, and then that other straight line which diverges from it in some other direction, in order to find out where the curve would go, and how I am to trace its course,' gives to some minds the sense of bewilderment, of there being nothing to trust to, almost of being juggled with, and led off on a false track.

" But in reality it is Euclid who is apt to mislead and convey to those, whose attention has not been drawn to observe the contrary, the false impression that mathematical straight lines and circles are forms which exist in nature, whereas nothing that lives and grows moves in or contains a mathematical straight line or circle. In the calculus, straight lines are consciously and avowedly studied as fluxions or elements of more complicated forms which exist in nature, but which man's mind cannot grasp. A curve being the path of a point acted upon by two or more forces, and the human mind being able to follow the action of only one force at a time, we find the best way to study a curve is to divide it into its elements, and to consider, first, how the point would move if acted upon by one force only, then how it would move under the action of the other only. And the important difference, Mr. Hinton considered, between Newton and his rival imitators and appliers is, that they, looking only to get results, were content to say, or at least seemed to Newton to be saying, 'Go a little way wrong in this direction, then a little way wrong in that, you will get a zig-zag or polygon, which coincides with the curve at certain points; and if you make these points frequent enough, the difference between the zig-zag and the curve will be so slight that one may be taken for the other.'

" Mr. Hinton thought it only natural that Newton should

Y

be angry with those who suggested that this convenient method for getting immediate results.in mathematics was the same as, and could be substituted for, his own grand doctrine of fluxions. 'We must not neglect the very smallest errors,' Newton exclaims, meaning, as Mr. Hinton interprets him, 'A falsehood is not the less a falsehood for being *small.*' Not smallness but mutual counteraction of errors makes truth. Put both straight lines together from the very beginning—that is, from the very beginning of your tracing the effect of one force, remember that the other exists, and will have to be taken into account, and that any result you can get, until that is accounted for, will necessarily be false. 'Two wrongs can never make a right,' we often say. 'Two wrongs do lead us to discover a right,' Mr. Hinton said, 'on condition not of being so small that we are not much ashamed to call them right, but of our not mistaking either for the right, any more than we mistake the straight lines by which we come at the course of a curve for the curve itself, on condition of our remembering that the one is as necessary and true as a *process* and as false as a *final result* as the other, and endeavouring to put them together from the beginning. Our only hope, Mr. Hinton urged, of solving any important problem, lies in remembering that whatever a man can see and know can be only an element of the truth, the straight line which both is and is not in the curve; that man is being set to work out fluxions of the true right, which, when worked out, are not to be kept but used, as Newton taught us to let the straight line vanish, that we may have it in its effect The straight line has vanished, but we have a change of direction, and the resultant, the curve, remains."

Indeed, this was the one method Mr. Hinton traced

through nature, art, human life. In nature everything is fluxionised; she is perpetually letting go the straight line that she may secure the curve of her true orbit; sacrificing, in endless evolution, the lower form to the higher, which yet would not be without the lower. In art the same method may be traced: the "keeping" of a picture depends on the artist letting go some of the details, to have them in the effect of the whole. And in morality, in the highest moral act, self-sacrifice, do we not let right and justice vanish that we may have them in their effect, ceasing as an outward law, to be as the power of an inward life, the one principle which fulfils all law—love? Only in human life this method grows too painful to the self. In all ages man has wailed over this hard necessity that is on him, forbidding him to clutch and keep, suffering him only to have by losing, to keep by letting go, to possess by using, and bidding all else wither in his grasp—

" Entbehren soll'st du ! soll'st entbehren !
Das ist der ewige Gesang,
Der jedem an die Ohren klingt,
Den unser ganzes Leben lang
Uns heiser jede Stunde singt."

Hence man's resistance to this fluent order of nature, the tendency in all human life to stiffen into lifeless forms, and " good customs that corrupt the world," and the decay that relentlessly cleaves to his best and highest, too fondly grasped as ends, and not used as larger means.

The principle of the fluxion was accordingly the very key of all Mr. Hinton's thinking. He used to say that the secret of thinking is to treat all things in science, in religion, in morals, as the method of fluxions teaches us to treat curves. Our fixed rules are like the straight lines, whereas nature works in curves. And he believed

that what ailed mathematics itself is, that it keeps too
tight a grip on particular forms and modes of investigation, laying too much stress on forms that have once
been useful. "Nothing," Mr. Hinton urges, "is too precious to let go." But his letting go was the letting go
of the fluxion, the using utterly for a purpose, the ceasing
as an isolated thing to be as a living power—sacrifice, in
its highest and truest sense, without those adventitious
meanings which have so defaced the word.

On one occasion an intimate friend of his was fretting
somewhat at not being able to put a cross on the grave of a
relation because the rest of the family disliked it. "Don't
you see," he said to her, "that by giving up your own way,
you will be virtually putting a cross on the grave? You'll
have it in its effect. The one is but a stone cross, the
other is a true spiritual cross."

The law of service itself was not to be an end, but a
means. "Man," he held, "is not always consciously to
be thinking what is most for service, and trying to
pursue it; but through adopting that as his aim he will
have fulfilled the condition of being able to follow his
impulses, which then will reveal themselves truly as
guides to service infinitely beyond his power to see."

It was, doubtless, Mr. Hinton's intense realisation of
the method of the fluxion as the law of all life that
tended to make him the curiously selfless being he was.
Once I remarked to him, half laughingly, when he offered to
show me some of his MSS. on a subject I was thinking of
writing on myself, "But suppose I were unconsciously to
borrow some of your thoughts? I'll try not, but still I
might do so without knowing it." He looked at me
with a gentle surprise and said, "You are welcome to
take *any* of my thoughts. I would much rather you

should say them than myself." And it was no affectation in him which made him write in his journal, "I do not care—how can I care?—whether my thoughts are true or false. If they are not true, the truth must be better. It does not matter that they seem *to me* perfectly good. The truth, if they be not true, must be better still."

"I think of him pre-eminently," said one of his most intimate friends, "as the one man I have known who never tolerated selfishness or self-regard in any shape or under any disguise; who hunted them pitilessly out of every corner of life. Each thing was to be put aside as soon as it grew into a self form. And especially each thing which he himself had said was to be contradicted as soon as anybody tried to crystallise it into an excuse for selfish action, or for stagnation of thought, or especially for contempt of any class of thinkers. This constant flux and change of his point of view was perplexing to those who did not understand it. When once you saw what it meant, it became the most delightful element in his conversation. He always seemed to me to bring rest into the house with him, and just for the very reason that I could depend on his giving me the 'polar opposite' of my thought, whatever it might be, none the less so when my thought was the mere reflex of his talk on a former occasion.

"The severest lecture I remember getting was for having gas burning in a room which no one was using, 'wasting fire and light which the poor want,' he said. I tried to explain that the room would be wanted by and by, and I could not trust children to turn gas up and down. He interrupted me with, 'Oh yes; I know it is inconvenient;' but went on to explain the wickedness of one person wasting for their convenience what another needed for health and comfort."

But though he never tolerated selfishness of principle to all sorts of lapses, from failure, from forgetfulness, from weakness, from ignorance, he was absolutely tolerant. He used to say "that there is goodness enough in the world to save it over and over again; moral effort enough to effect six times over all that wants doing. Men are anxious enough to live up to a standard; it would be more to the purpose to alter their standard." Here again he would bring in his favourite idea of nutrition or stored-up force liberated in function. Nature has stored up moral force by setting people for ages to impossible and useless and self-centred tasks, till the habit of doing something else besides what one likes, has become strong enough for any purpose for which it can ever be wanted; and now the thing is to set it free to apply itself to true purposes. In this connection he often spoke of fashion as a great store-house of moral force. "It is vain to preach and write and talk," he used to say; "nothing would ever persuade men and women to leave of making themselves uncomfortable for fashion's sake, merely in order that they may be more comfortable. The habit of dressing not merely for one's comfort, for instance, has become ingrained and inveterate. But once show people that they can better serve others when more simply dressed, and then all the force of self-sacrifice, which has gone to make them dress outrageously, will flow into some other channel, and they will dress comfortably, as a matter of course."

The following extracts are from letters to one of his friends :—

"July 1874.

"I do not think you have yet clearly recognised what

you mean by ' right.' It would be well to take it on a
definite point. Take murder or killing. It would be
interesting if you were kind enough to make out clearly
here what is the right. I think you would find it a state
of the soul, not a literal or fleshy thing, and that this
state of soul is the true obedience to God's will, expressed
in its true revelation, the good of man. Is not this a
sufficient account of right in all cases ?

" I fancy there comes a confusion here, and much more
from what I don't say than from what I do; from my
taking for granted a thing I do not mean to controvert,
viz., that when there is self-regard, self-restraint may be,
is, must be, the road to a true regard. I take this for
granted; it is part of the position of the advance to the
correction of the premiss; it is involved in all I say,
which is meaningless without it. Nor do I believe that
any one who clearly felt and saw that the true aim was to
gain a true regard would ever have fancied that I omitted
it. People suppose I omit it because the idea ot self as
the centre being the evil to be escaped, has not been
clearly in their mind.

" The use of self-restraint *as a means* is a thing I have
no objection to lay any amount of stress on. It is one of
the keys to the ascetic ages, one of the reasons the whole
world has been ascetic. The self-restraint is the storing up
of the force to be used afterwards in making the correction of the premiss (the casting out of self-regard). One
of my complaints of our condition, especially in one
respect, is, that it puts aside most grossly and unnaturally
the natural demands for restraint, without fulfilling the
conditions. Here we are, and with what restraints of a
true kind ?

" There need be no misunderstanding between us here.

Self-restraint is a means through which the true right is gained. It is a lane leading to a house. What I complain of is, that we are not told to go through the lane into the house, but go and stay in that lane. And don't you see what comes of it to so very many is, *that they never enter the lane at all.* Nor shall we ever get them into the lane by any urging on them to go and stay there, only by bidding them hasten to the house.

"Another way of putting the same confusion may be this : We agree that service, true regard, is the true right. Now, it may truly be said, when self is the centre, then the thing that is service is self-restraint; as when a leg is broken the useful thing is not walking, which is the true right, but lying in bed, a false one made right by a false condition of the body. So that with a self-centred person the law of service means his self-restraint.

"This is my aim, to make this change : to cease consenting that self should be the centre, and then teaching the self-restraint that follows as the right; but to teach as the absolute and necessary right, never to be let go, or any substitute accepted, a true ruling response of the soul to good, which should give us true laws, laws that imply a true regard.

"I would seek more—seek more in respect to man's spiritual good. I say we don't try for enough.

"Now, dear friends, have I not Christ on my side? Did He bid us think that men shall always have self for their centre, and so have self-restraint for their right? and that God's will will never be done on earth as in heaven?

"I say let us not be content to go on trying to put away things we make wrong, but let us go deeper, and try to put away that feeling or state of soul which makes them wrong, which is simply to say, let us remember again that God's law is to love.

"And when I saw that this was our true duty, not to put things away, but to cease to make them evil, then I naturally perceived that the hopelessness of our attempts at putting them away had a new meaning; that it meant we were trying for too little, seeking a false good that never would or ought to be given to us; that the hopelessness of the failure was God's voice calling to us to seek more."

"*July* 1874.

"So you actually quote to me one of Ruskin's saddest sentences*—a sentence that you challenge me, as it were, to put beside this, 'Where the spirit of the Lord is, there is liberty.' Poor sad eyes! to which—though no eyes ever deserved it better—the vision of the joy has not been given, and in this life (one cannot but feel) never will be given. The pathos is infinite; but why quote it to me? I know what reverence is, and sometimes feel

---

* The sentence alluded to is from Ruskin's "Oxford Lectures on Art." After alluding to the good that came of the great masters' work, he says, "One thing more they taught of which nothing but evil ever comes or can come—liberty. By the discipline of five hundred years they had learned and inherited such power, that whereas all other painters could be right only with effort, they could be right with ease; the others right only under restraint, while they could be right, free. Tintoret's touch, Corregio's, Reynold's, Velasquez's, are free as air, and yet right. ' How very fine ! ' said everybody. Unquestionably very fine. What a grand discovery ! Here is the finest work done, and it is quite free. Let us be free also. What fine things shall we not do also ! With what results we know."

Which passage Mr. Hinton annotates thus :—" Consider that discipline of five hundred years; other men's not theirs; their own only adding a very little. So it is now; the discipline of the ages waits for its fruit. But it is most true that the reason and nature of the liberty need making clear. That is what I seek to do even for art as well as for life."

where it is due. I see the sadness of the man—nay, feel as if it were my own pain too—who sees and feels the sadness of the fall and failure, but not the assurance of the triumph; who, because by the hard destiny of his course, man's hands first grasp a shadow of good things to come, sees the mockery only of the type, and has no foretelling in his soul of the triumph that grows from it. True enough, men have grasped a false liberty, and art bears high, for all eyes to read, the lesson. *Thank God!*

"The true freedom will always corrupt until it can say and make intelligible, to men, 'This is my secret; the condition to be fulfilled is this.' It must explain as well as act, and act as well as explain.

"But where I feel you so absolutely one with me, and through art, is in this (which I feel to be the whole ques, tion), that the true ideal, the thought of the best right, the hope, and therewith the aim, lies not in the maintenance of the restrictions, but in the fulfilling the conditions of their passing. This is what I learnt from art, and what has enthroned it as the rule of my practical life. It has opened my eyes to the true aim. Now this is much less of a new light to a woman than it is to a man. But to us men, nevertheless, it is a turning from darkness to light, a whole new conception of life, a whole new revelation of possibilities of good in it. . . . It comes to us like a deliverance from self-seeking—a dull, leaden yoke that has crept over us, as far from being our will as stiffness is to a freezing man."

To his sister-in-law :—

"11 *Mitre Court Chambers, November* 1874.

"No one could have believed the things that I have

found. I am in a perpetual wonder. If the world had been made to amaze me, it could not have been a source of more boundless and endless wonder.* And it is so beautiful besides—at once a terror and a joy. There it is,—the taking up of man into that great life of nature's; he who thought himself the chief and highest. Oh me! it is a vision to have seen. But it won't let one go one's own way, nor avoid being a fool, nor be a person one can like, nor help giving perpetual pain. I shall be a dream or a vision people will think of with love; but I shall never be *liked* as a man, not by those that know me. Nature has taken me and used me, and she is welcome; but she ought to let me perish. What do *I* want to go on living for? I, who am but a power of seeing, having stripped myself of all else to purchase it, am already of the past. A sight *is* in having been."

"*London,* 1875.

"In respect to your feeling of the need of force to bring in a moral change, look at the history of early Christianity. The non-Jewish nations first and most readily accepted it—the people amongst whom you would say the force had not been. In the Jewish life there had been the tension; but when the new beginning came, then it was among those who had not shared in that tension that the new passion found its easiest acceptance. All do not have to do the same work. A tension is wanted to open men's eyes to a true way; but the truer way is also a more natural and easy way, and calls all to enter it. Does it remain hard to you to get the perfectly

---

* "All knowledge begins and ends with wonder; but the first wonder is the child of ignorance; the last wonder is the parent of adoration."—*S. T. Coleridge.*

clear perception and feeling of a growing life here, carried on by successive generations entering into the results of former labours, and not needing to repeat them, but to go on to fresh ones? If it is, tell me how, and I will look at it again.

"You see it took a long hard toil on the part of the Jew to bring in our thought of loving God—'anticipated,' I suppose, many times by poet and prophet, but only made a universal possession by Christ. But now we have the thought, is there any reason for not beginning with it? Any difficulty? We might do well to make every child understand how hard it was *to get it ;* even as I would teach every child a good deal more of how hard it was to get at the motion of the earth. Nay, it might even be well to make every child do for himself every chief correction of the premiss that man has achieved (and you see they are all easy; are all leaving off that which is more difficult, to take that which is less so, and therefore suitable for teaching a child to do). I should seek to come as near to that as possible if I were a teacher. But you see that does not affect what we were speaking of. The new beginning once attained, is the accomplished heritage of every child. From that, all the processes, disciplinary, and others, thereafter start. . . . It is man having his power, his force given him afresh.

" Think of astronomy; all the mental force with which man constructed, remembered, realised the epicycles, was given back to him when he said, ' I shall begin with the earth as moving.' And we have made stellar astronomy with the very same mental power that we should have had otherwise to put into keeping up the memory of the epicycles. It is like lifting a heavy weight, and placing it upon a shelf. While we are raising it, all our force is in that. We put it on the shelf, and all our force is given us again free for new doings. It is no more a tax upon us when it is on the shelf than when it was upon the ground. The new beginning is putting the weight upon a shelf. The raising is there still, but Nature does it then. All our strength is ready again for our tasks.

"Now, by the by, it is interesting to think of the great corrections of the premiss which man has done, and which a child of sixteen might be led through to do, each of them for himself. Let us try to enumerate some of them.

"I. Numeration and subtraction, &c. Putting 10 for 1111111111—a splendid achievement never surpassed, making position do for things. Then beginning to add or subtract from right to left.

"II. Leaving out dimensions from geometry: our definition of point and line.

"III. Earth's motion.

"IV. Unity of force.

"V. Mathematical fluxion, a fresh doing of geometry, another leaving out dimensions.

"This is a very scanty list, but it will do for a suggestion. Then there are other regions. There is that great one of art—that was a beginning whereby exactness ceases to be a duty. And then we come to the moral world. This, by the by, is what I mean by making the method of genius universal. For the person rightly called a genius is only a cunning little fellow, who has a knack of casting his eye on the beginning; and when he finds himself with a lot of nasty hard things to do or think, demonstrably 'right,' and yet coming somehow to wrong, with no way of making them really *fit*, looks round behind him to see how things are there, and finds—to his joy and gladness, and amazement, and sorrow, and distress, and to all the future's joy and gladness too, opening when he has overcome the sharpness of death, the dominion of joy to all who can share his vision, and that is every one in due time—finds that if he begins another way, those hard things, right with such a wrongness, need not be done at all.

"*Mitre Court*, 1875.

"That little note of M.'s is very interesting. I would point out, however, to this good girl, that in saying 'she cannot care so much for human good,' she is refusing God's command, and saying she cannot obey it. It is wonderful how we overlook this, take it for granted God's law cannot be obeyed, and proceed with no sense, not only of sin, but even of the fact that we are putting it aside, to bring in a substitute. At that I have felt, and still feel, an *amazement*. I wonder how I could have gone on so long—so unsuspecting of what I was doing—doing that. Surely we might at least recognise the fact in *words*, and say, as prefix to our other proposals, 'God's law to love cannot be obeyed.' We should then remember what we are doing. Do not even you a little bit forget this ? we are so trained to forget it even in our goodness; our very religion often means forgetting it, as we see in this child; do not you a little forget that saying we cannot have a passion for man, *is* saying we cannot obey God's law ? . . .

"Consider what hard things whole nations do. Is it really hard that people should truly ask and care what their fellows' lives are? Fancy one being thought an enthusiast for that ! . . .

"You see what makes the difference in my hopes from other men's ? It is just this: that I look forward to letting go things; that I propose, not only that men should care for their fellows, but that this should do alone. Don't you see the difference? Because men can't do two things that is no reason they cannot do one. And if other things are let go, that gives more force for the one that remains. . . .

"What do we mean by long? One hour is long for a butterfly; twenty years for a man. What is long for human life? I think the *visible* work of the last 2000 years has been visibly quickly done (besides all the work invisible as yet to us). Don't you feel that to recognise the bringing in of a true regard, as an end designed to be gained by man's experience, casts an exquisite light over history? What is there on any large scale that it does not take up into significance and reason? Well, what I hope for, and feel it is reasonable to expect, is, that every child in some 200 years will be taught the right, which is having his care on others, regarding himself as he truly is, as an instrument, not falsely as an end; not as an end either for being comfortable, or for being good. You see, in the other thought of right there is the same error as in self-indulgence; the self is put inaccurately as an end. And the change we would make is simply a correcting of the falsity to fact. We *are* instruments or means, and must, to be true to fact, so regard ourselves. In nature *nothing* is end; everything is means. The wrong in us is that to each of us self comes as an end—an error as much involved in seeking our own goodness as in seeking our own pleasure. I don't know any aspect of the thought that gives me more pleasure—at once delight to my intellect as beautiful, or hope to my soul as certain to be realised than this—that it is simply correcting a falsity to fact, simply saying our thought, our feeling, must be true. How can anything 'do' instead of truth;

how truth fail to rule ? Observe that what I say is not,
'We want a true regard.' All do really say that, or feel
it more or less distinctly. What I say is not, we must
have it, but *it will do alone*. We don't want morally
anything more. We may put all our force on gaining
that. . . .

"Is it hard to me—to any one—to think of my fellows' good, *if I try?* Harder than the other hard things
we do when we try ? Harder to cultivate and inflame
a passion—a passion natural to the human breast—than
to restrain one ? I only say, Turn the energy which you
devote to putting flames out into kindling flames. The
flames are all very well, and they don't want putting out;
we only want more of them. Of course you know it is
not harder, it is easier. We give it, at least all wise
people do, as an aid ; and when we want a person to
restrain his passions, what help is there so great as to say
to him, 'Think what mischief, and to how many, your
indulgence would be.' Nay, that you women do habitually do this so much more than men (men thinking so
much more of being good, you of helping others), is the
chief reason it is so much easier to you to avoid vice of
every sort. That is why mostly your practical life is so
much better than ours. You take the easier task, thinking of others instead of trying to restrain yourself. So
much is this the case, that Margaret and I used perpetually to misunderstand one another. She had no notion
of self-restraint, except thinking of others. The two
terms were to her identical. But they are not so to
men. All I want is that they should be so. I want
men's right made the same as women's. Is this a thing
to despair of ? "

To another friend he writes :—

"You ascribe to me thoughts the most entirely opposite to all I entertain. It really astonished me. I thought I had made you understand that the basis of my whole thought was that we had not interpreted God's law *stringently* enough (which law, I say, with you, if men sought of Him, He would give them strength to obey), but have consented that man should be impure in heart, and have substituted for it another law (which is not God's, but emphatically a commandment of men), viz., that having passions which are not good, they should restrain them. . . .

"You have lived in a dreamland. You have made up an idea of good and evil, of right and beauty, which belong to dreamland. . . . But the world is not dreamland, but better. Yes, better. And, above all, better in this; that the goodness it demands, and must and will have, is a better goodness than that of dreamland; and when you women wake, that is what you will find; that your vision of good and beauty has, in contact with facts—terrible as they may seem—to grow into a better one, infinitely better. That is what I feel. You know it. You think, and say, 'It is too good to come.' I say it is not; for not only 'God will give power to all who seek it, and obey His law,' but there is a power stored up in these facts, that are so hateful, to make it come. Here is the power to bring it, to bring the better good, surpassing dreamland, which you say cannot be.

"Did it never occur to you, knowing that God is ruler, and does according to His will, and makes the 'passion' of man to serve Him, did it never occur to you to ask, '*What has He suffered these evils for*'? Try if there be not some reason in my answer, 'To compel men to cast out and put away a hidden evil, that they

z

would never otherwise have even suspected, that evil being, that while life presents to them infinite questions of good and evil, they stand before it with their thought primarily fixed on the question of their own pleasure.

".It is to cure this evil in men that women have been sacrificed, and I say (with so much more than you can know present to my eye), that being sacrificed so is not cursed, but blessed. It is through woman and her pangs that man is to receive the life of the soul, as well as of the body. Man's life is their gift, who are sunk to hell without a chance; from their hands he shall be compelled to accept it. That is God's justice, His avenging. Shall He not avenge His own elect, His elect to sorrow and destruction?

"Try and keep this thought before you, and don't let any other get into its place as *being mine:* Men shall be compelled to take their thought off the question of their pleasure, and absolutely to enthrone their fellows' good, because women (insisting on saving their sisters) shall compel them to have a right, which *means* that their thought is absolutely on good, and not on their pleasure."

Elsewhere he writes, "I come and look at moral nature with eyes trained in looking at physical nature, and so I see that they are one. I do perceive anew this Nature whom I have known so long, and half-loved, and half-feared, and wholly served, she is the very angel that came and rolled away the stone of the grave where man had lain in death; and said to woman,—O God, it is too much!—to a redeemed harlot woman, 'Seek no more the living among the dead.' This is what I have seemed to see, that it is through lost women, and in their saving, that man's life shall be given him. . . . So when I read it was to a woman who had drunk that cup, that the angel said, 'He is risen; seek Him among the living,' awe seizes me, and I bless God who has made the world a miracle of wonder, and pray Him to remember that I am dust, and when He has given me as much as I can bear, to take another vessel, and seek Him out lips that the sight does not make dumb."

" South Wales, March 1875.

" MY DEAR CARRIE,—Looking as we passed at one of the self-acting machines where the loaded waggons, descending, drag the empty ones up, I thought, That is the principle I want to introduce into human life consciously, and as a method knowingly adopted—the method of our machinery, or use of nature's forces, the laying hold of the dynamic relations, and using the force of a thing falling to do our raising. I want to use the power of the fall of a thing that has been raised, consciously to have that in our thought and aim in man's moral life."

On the dynamic relations of evil, Mr. Hinton, as we see, laid great stress. It was to him an integral part of the process of correcting the premiss, by which man is educated in the true sense of the word, *i.e.*, made to educe for himself the true from the false, the right from the wrong, working out his results by a process of moral evolution. Evil in the world, he held, had its analogue in nutrition. In nutrition certain chemical elements are assimilated, and held in a state of tension, their tendency to combine being resisted in the organic matter. The force thus held ready for use is set free in the function, whether of muscular or nervous action, a chemical reaction taking place, which evolves heat and energy. Or, to take a far simpler analogy, evil is the raising of a heavy weight, which in its fall raises something else. In one of the great world-sores, slavery, we can see this process ever going on in one form or another; but perhaps it is most strikingly exemplified in the movements that have led to modern emancipation. Naturally the premiss was assumed, to begin with, that the stronger might impose his will on the weaker. Self-interest enjoined it; what was there so especially sacred in individual responsibility to forbid the stronger animal mastering the weaker? But slowly the selfish principle worked out its results of sorrow, degradation, cruelty, and licentiousness; the evil grew more and more intolerable; slowly the force gathered, till at last it needed but a touch to set it free, and, in the fall of slavery by its own weight of evil, to lift humanity for ever to the higher moral level that respects personal liberty, and recognises the brotherhood of man and the sanctity of individual responsibility.

May we not, therefore, believe, with Mr. Hinton, that that other great nameless world-sore, which eats like a cancer into the heart of our modern Christian and civilised society, with all its mystery of depravity, degradation, and disease,—may we not believe it a force stored up to impel man to recognise the evil of self as a basis of life, the impotence of mere self-restraint engrafted on such a basis—a force to lift him to a higher level of a purity which is love, a chastity which is service?

CHAPTER XV.

THE last letter in the preceding chapter, bearing the date of South Wales, was written during a brief sojourn among the miners of Merthyr Tydvil, on the occasion of the great strike, the causes of which he was anxious to investigate.

" Waiting for a Train, Berwick Station, May 1875.

"DEAR CARRIE,—Since our talk together I have wanted to write to you on one or two points. One thing is instructive to me, as to the way in which it happens that my processes of thought seem to me to excite a mistrust or feeling of inaccuracy or partialness, even (excuse me—I only say *seem*) in persons who so appreciate me, and enter into the results of my thinking as you do. I think I do see a reason, at any rate, one ' that I recognise as distinctly true in fact, and also as quite accounting for the phenomenon.

"It is what I can scarcely now help calling my fluxion method of thinking; that is, the plan which I am quite conscious of when I look into the workings of my mind, of laying aside part of the visible elements of a case, in order better to see the others. What makes this process right is, that the laying aside is *remembered;* and what makes it necessary is the complexity of facts, the presence in all of them, not only of many, but of counteracting or *balancing* elements, so that the results look simpler than they are, and the full extent of some of the things present, can be perceived only by getting rid, in thought, of the mixed-up influences of the others.

"The complexity of Nature—as I now judge, though I did not always know it—renders the process not less than essential to all true vision of her. You see how gravity is an instance of it; this is hidden by the tangential motion; it is only to be 'seen' by that being left out, and treated as if it were not for the time. I see it in art, too; indeed, I hold it to be a universal condition of true seeing; it alone can teach us how much there is, as, in order to see the oxygen in water, we must bid the hydrogen for the time to stand aside. I call it revealing by leaving out. Now, when this has been done, all persons, of course, can see it, by having it pointed out to them. But, you see, the only person who can see this *first* in any case, can discover it when it is not known, is a person who naturally tends to look that way or has been led to acquire the habit of doing so by long effort in vain to do without it. And you see how inevitably he will be misunderstood; that habit of laying aside in order to restore, that keeping in abeyance till the hidden things had been fully recognised—is sure to look like mere ignoring, mere putting away and oblivion, or even refusal, to those who have not the same tendency, or the same experience. Do not you see that misapprehension must come ? And the more natural that method is to any man, the more it comes to him as of course, and as the simple and natural and only method of seeing (which it is), the greater will be the difficulty to him to apprehend why he is misapprehended. Many, many things will be guessed or supposed by him as the reason his thoughts are misconceived, or not seen, before it occurs to him that his so natural and inevitable method of laying aside some elements for a time that others may be visible, is what is not understood. I have no doubt this accounts for what is often very, very provoking to others in me. When a thing is said in reference to a remark of mine, how I am apt to reply, 'Why do you say 'but' so and so? of course I include that.' Of course I do, but no doubt I have put it aside, in order to see the other thing I note; and this is visible, only through the laying aside for a time of the first.

"This is one thing I wanted to write to you. I am persuaded it is the source of a lot of mysterious difficulty. It is natural to some people to treat things in this way, to let go for revealing, holding all the while; less natural to others; but the former are a perpetual source of grief to the latter. It is easy to see how arbitrary, wanton, and vexatious they must look. But here is the good of it; nothing is wanted but that the case should be understood to put it all right. Let those who do it be aware that it wants explaining—those who don't do it understand that it wants doing sometimes, nevertheless, and be ready to recognise the process. So here is another help to peace we may hope to have gained. Do you not see that these two ways of looking—that which reveals by leaving out and then restores, and that which simply keeps hold of all answer to insight and onsight? The former is seeing that which is not apparent. And the force which brings it is the discontent with the apparent, the feeling that the apparent is not, and cannot be the true. That is how a man is forced—no one likes it—to that leaving out. It is just as hard and just as painful to the man who does it as it is to the man who won't do it—only he is driven to it by a pain also on the other side; it recognises what you will remember under the objectionable term 'positive denial,' that a thing practically not present, yet is truly present, and only seems not so by the presence of something else.

"Now, I think there is an illustration of all this in what we were talking about the other day; how far people are 'good,' and, if they are, how it is our practical life is so bad. . . . Now, first, here is the force. As I look at our life, taking it as it *appears*, I know I do not see it. I can't tell why; at least, not for 'reasons.' I doubt if I could give any adequate one; . . . but I feel that my sight of it is not knowledge, but ignorance. . . . An impression of absolute unreason and unreality is given to my mind. I don't care how accurately and completely all that is presented to me is formulated; that is not human life. It is a contradiction. So you see there is a compulsion on me, a necessity—the universal compulsion and necessity by which I believe all deeper seeing has come—to see human life differently, if I am to see it at all. That which is visible in it is not it. I must see more if I am to feel I see it. But that is, I must see some hidden thing, must recognise that some things that seem not there at all, are really there. . . .

"How shall this impossible apparent motion of human life be resolved into its true constituents? What is there that must be 'uncovered,' and seen to be truly there, though practically absent, before we can know it?

"Now, the fact that has arrested me in social life,— perhaps it is emphatically in modern social life, though perhaps not—is the discord between people and what they do; how such people can do such things. This is the problem. What I am perhaps more conscious of than most, is the evil of this good life. And this is, I suppose, the happy fruit of my sojourn in Whitechapel in my youth.

"Now, you know more or less my suggestions as to the

reasons of the discordance. But I don't want to go into them now. I don't feel that I do know them adequately; I am only just beginning my study of people; but I begin it in one respect advantageously, namely, with the clearest perception of my ignorance. . . . One point that interests me is, that the recognition of some force operating on people, and making their deeds not a true expression of *them*, is the same thing I have felt in other ways and often spoken of, namely, the recognition of man as one, and that the history, relations, and conditions of this one affect, and even largely determine, what the individuals are. You see that in this thought we do call in the question of the race, the meaning of its course and destiny, to make us understand the familiar doings of our fellows; and on quite other grounds I am sure it is only *so* that the individuals can be truly seen. It is the question I ask about men when I look at them, seeing as I do that what is presented to me as if it was, is a thing that cannot be—what force deflects their deeds ? . . .

" One may say the problem is, how came a society made up of such people, to have deliberately accepted putting self first, and for this world too ? Do you not see how this has come ? We will start from the classic or savage states, in which not the self, but the state or tribe, is first, *i.e.*, deliberately first with those who deliberately choose. With that intense religious life of Christianity and the consequent deepening of individual responsibility, there gradually came putting the self deliberately first; but then it was for another world and not for this—for heaven, not for greenhouses and carriages; and by means of all austerity and toil for the general good, not by means of high walls erected round every beautiful spot of land to keep off all eyes, but a few select ones. But then, having got self first for another world, this ' other world '

has been slipped away; the evidence would not stand;
the methods were mischievous; all sorts of causes combined, and slipped away the other world, and slipped
in this; and so landed poor man in this result, to which
I hold it impossible he should have been brought, except
by being thus betrayed into it—of deliberately putting
self first and yet not for another world, but for this. . . .
This could not have come except through the failure of
the old ascetic life, with self first for another life ; so that
came that this might follow, and this assuredly that
something else might follow. And what? When self
has been put first once for the other world, and then for
this world, what is next to come?

"Dear Carrie, it is assuredly true that some men and
women will be alive and remain to the coming of the
Lord ; the very last epoch of human life will be witnessed
by some eyes and hailed, or wailed (more likely at first)
by some hearts incredulous and incapable of believing
that they can be the witnesses of the last stage, the
triumph. Then assuredly, too, the last stage but one
will be witnessed by some eyes, and trembled at, and
mourned over, and disbelieved in by some weak and
troubled minds. Why should they not be yours and
mine ?

"Your loving brother,
"J. H."

The earlier part of the letter, alluding to Mr. Hinton's
habit of "thinking by leaving out," probably in great part
explains the fact of his so often producing the impression
of destructiveness, and exciting a feeling of dread and
distrust in the minds of those who did not understand
him. One was apt to feel at first as if one's most
cherished first principles were being slowly pulverised

by the energetic action of his mind, and were passing away from one's despairing clutch in an impalpable dust. It was only after one had got the clue to his mode of thinking, and had learned that the balancing fact, omitted in the processes of his thought, was carefully restored in the final conclusion, that one came to see how eminently constructive his mind was, and found one's self with quickened convictions, as if till then one had held the phenomenon of truth, and now grasped the reality.

As an instance of this peculiarity, he would often speak as though he thought that when man became a part of nature his individuality would be lost, there would be no more "I and thou;" that nature was truly living, and the organic creature only a special manifestation of the universal life, destined to be reabsorbed. This grieved one of his auditors, and he then proceeded to make his real meaning clear. He compared individual men to letters in a word, and God to the whole word. " A child sees the letters m, a, n, separately, and then sees the word 'man.' A man takes in first the word, then (if he looks) the letters. Now we say 'individuals and God in them.' Hereafter we shall say, ' God, and in this form.' "

The following letter is to Dr. Cassells of Glasgow :—

" *London,* 1875.

" MY DEAR CASSELLS,—I am very glad of your note. I do see the world with new eyes, and do feel it a joy, and long for others to see it with me, and to see it better. That would be better still, of course. I never expected that a man like you, with so much to do, would ever come to enter into my thoughts. It was certainly a good providence that brought us together. In the future we shall do much work together. I so want helpers, people who.can do what I can't; and I shall be most interested to see what you write. Another person's presentation is what is wanted almost most of all. . . .

"I've been working away, plodding hard at various things; and have exerted some influence indirectly on people engaged in various works. This is what I like best of all. I have been reading, amongst other things, Lewes's 'Problems of Life and Mind.' This is, you know, a thoroughly negative book, wanting to shut us up to the senses and immediate generalisations from them; but to me it has given an immense number of suggestions. Whole new regions have been opened by them. I have not published much because I feel so strongly the necessity of completing my knowledge and getting a better hold of the things I want to treat. I go on trying to learn, and my thoughts do expand and become larger and ever fuller. So I am not discontented.

"Yours sincerely,

"JAMES HINTON."

"*M. C. C.*, 1875.

DEAREST ELLICE,—I am very glad to hear that you are comfortably settled at Sark, and quite enjoy the thought of it, though I do wish it could have been at St. Michael's: all the other things would have been better for an intermission. I've quite discovered of late that some things can't be seen in a hurry, nor while you are in a hurry which some one is very apt to be. I should like to be with you, to tell you of a little thought I had on Saturday evening. There are two or three other later ones I've had the greatest pleasure from I'd like to tell you, but this is the last.

"A little girl of ten said to me, 'Do tell me about the

fluxion' (I'd been talking in her hearing about Newton's fluxions, which I don't at all understand, a great deal of it). So what do you think I did? Such a happy thought came to me. I told her plainly, so that she quite understood all I meant.

"I said (but I can only give you the barest notion, no notion at all in fact) 'Multiply me 17 by 3. So you know we get 3 times 7 is 21, 1 and carry 2; 3 times 1 is 3 and 2 is 5=51.' 'Now,' I said, 'do you see what you have done with that 2? You have put it down, and then rubbed it out; it was necessary to have it, but not to keep it. Now, a fluxion is this; it is a thing we need to have, but are not intended to hold; a thing we rightly make, but in order to unmake.' And indeed that is the whole point. But this simple case shows also perfectly how it comes, how the law of it comes upon our life. For you see our making 21, comes only from our taking the 7 of 17 by itself, isolating it from the 10. In the 3 times 17 there is no 21; we *make* the 21 simply by separating the 17 into 2 parts and taking one only first. That is (here is my word) the 21 is an isolation-right, a right or truth that comes by leaving out.'

"Now, all isolation-rights are fluxions in this sense; we have to do them, but in order that we may undo them.

"And this is the law of man's life, because nature is so great and rich that he is compelled to take her piecemeal, and in all things he makes for himself, by his inevitable leaving out at first, 'isolation-rights.'

"And the difficulty of his life—the difficulty above all others—is that these isolation-rights have got to be not kept, but used; not held as they come, but 'carried' on into another mode of being, which seems like their being lost.

"This is the pathos of man's life. He makes isolation-rights, and has not known the law of it and recognised its meaning.

"Now, this applies to all things. It is so pretty I can't show you even a fraction of its bearings. But you can think of many of them if you choose. Look at all our sciences. Are they not clearly enough, every one of them, *parts*—no more the whole than 7 is, not only of 17, but of a whole page full of figures? Each one of them, therefore, makes for itself an isolation-right or true, a truth which comes only by its being isolated, wants not holding, but to be lost, as the 2 of the 21 is lost in 5, when the one is taken in (*i.e.*, the 1 of the 17).

"And the very relation of the figures in numeration, whereby each term means not one, but many of those before it, comes to have a distinct significance all through our mental life.

"In fact, the world is so beautiful I don't know what to do; only, as you know, the condition of that joy is consenting to bear pain; and one scarcely dares to say one is happy, because it makes the pain confront one, and the words have lost their meaning ere they have passed one's lips.

"Look at this very fluxion; it is such joy to see it, such pain to have to live it. . . . Oh, me! I am happy and sorry; and just now I cannot see a bit whether that gladness I think is coming on the earth is coming or not.

"By the by, I expect to leave for St. Michael's on the 4th of August. If you have any of my letters by you—it does not matter else—I should like to take them to show Margaret. I know she'd like to see them. . . . I'm beginning to be always thinking about going to St. Michaels and being *at home* there. I'm not sure I shall be in a great hurry to come back.—Ever yours lovingly,

"JAMES HINTON."

Mr. Hinton's departure for St. Michael's having been unavoidably delayed till the end of the autumn, he came down to Brighton to be with me for a few days before setting sail for the Azores, from whence he was never to return. It seemed impossible to associate the thought of death with that exuberant vitality. Never had his intellect been more brilliant. To talk to him was, to use a quaint simile of Oliver Holmes, like shaking hands with Briareus. Metaphysics, science, poetry, art, insoluble human problems, ethics, books, heaven, hell, life, death, passed in endless procession before me as he talked, now clapping his hands with boyish glee at some new light that had occurred to him, and exclaiming triumphantly, "Now, isn't that pretty—intellectually pretty, I mean?" and now speaking of desecrated womanhood, and the hope of its redemption in the future, with an intensity of feeling that seemed like the

> " Tides of the whole great world's anguish
> Forced through the channels of a single heart."

Feeling the great world-evils, and especially the wrongs of women, as his own, it was no wonder he once said, "I haven't had much pain of any particular sort in my life, but I feel as if life itself were chiefly pain to me."

Those lines of Browning of one risen from the dead always seemed to me to describe him best in the keenness of his spiritual vision, and a certain strangeness that belonged to him. His "thread of life" ever seemed to

> " Run across some vast distracting orb
> Of glory on either side that meagre thread,
> Which, conscious of, he must not enter yet—
> The spiritual life around the earthly life !
> The law of that is known to him as this ;
> His heart and brain move there, his feet stay here.

So is the man perplext with impulses
Sudden to start off crosswise, not straight on,
Proclaiming what is Right and Wrong across,
And not along, this black thread through the blaze. . . .
And oft the man's soul springs into his face."

Once or twice I urged him to work up some of his numerous MSS. for publication. "Well, you see," he would reply, "the activity of my brain must die down. I shan't be able to go on producing much longer, and then will be the time to work up old materials, and get them into shape. There's immense longevity in my family; I shall probably live till I am eighty."

"What!" I exclaimed; "do you look forward to such an undesirable thing as living till you are eighty?"

"Oh, I think I can do," was the characteristic answer, with a slight shrug of the shoulders.

His attitude towards death and questions of a future world, the "light hand" with which he touched the subject—whether his own death or another's—was most peculiar. His manner in speaking of it was as far as possible from frivolity or flippancy; and yet it was almost equally far from our ordinary conventional solemnity. There was something Socratic about it, and reminded one irresistibly of the "Crito" and "Phædo." If any one spoke of the dogma of everlasting punishment, for instance, to which he was much opposed, he never answered indignantly. He would sometimes say, "Yes; if a cannon-ball hits a sinner on the head, he goes to hell for ever without a chance of mending; but if it had happened to hit him on the knee, he would have had a bad illness; and might have been converted, and be finally saved. So everlasting perdition is a matter of measurement of an iron ball going a few feet higher or lower.

Several times when he was with me he complained of

having suffered from sleeplessness and depression, but knowing the severe strain that had been on him, it did not excite any apprehension in my mind, more especially as he was suffering much anxiety with regard to his affairs in the Azores, fearing lest his absorption in the great interest of mankind had made him in any measure careless of what was due to Mrs. Hinton's comfort. The bad symptoms, however, increased after he left me, and those who devotedly tended him during the last few weeks he was in town were aware that he was very ill. Still, when he set sail with his eldest daughter for St. Michaels, we hoped the best from change of scene and quiet, and above all, reunion with Mrs. Hinton. But the shock, on arriving, of finding his worst fears realised about his property necessarily deepened the melancholy that had settled upon him.

He writes to a sister-in-law :—

" It is so sad to me that I have lost the power of helping those who need worldly aid. I wanted to give the aid of thought and knowledge instead, which indeed are better when they are true. But now how I feel the trial it is not to have means to help! But I feel also that God may have given me more than I have lost—the very wisdom I sought, the very sobriety and humility which alone could make my thoughts truly and perfectly helpful. I have no doubt of them, except as all my soul seems thrown into doubt; and I want and wish to hold nothing certain that I have thought, but to have all made better."

And again :—

" I have tried for too much, and failed; but yet perhaps in that, my failure, God is giving me more even than I tried for. He has opened my eyes, at least a little, though I am blind and foolish still, no doubt. I will try and be wiser, and look more, and care more what others feel."

And in his last letter to his son :—

"But, How, there is a wrong, an intense wrong, in our society running all through our life, and it will be made · righter some day. I dashed myself against it; but it is not one man's strength that can move it. It was too much for my brain; but it is by the failure of some that others succeed, and through my very foolishness, perhaps, there shall come a better success to others, perhaps more than any cleverness or wisdom of mine could have wrought. And I hope I have learnt, too, to be wiser. We have not come to the end; though I am so exhausted, that I seem scarcely able to believe in anything more before me."

At first it seemed as if our hopes would be realized, and that with rest and care he would recover. He grew better, and talked of returning with his wife and daughters.

The blow fell with awful suddenness at the last. Acute inflammation of the brain declared itself, and after a few days' intense suffering, in which he knew no one, he entered into his rest on the 16th of December 1875.

He sleeps among the unfamiliar orange-trees, alone with his God, in the churchyard of the little English Church at Ponta Delgada, in that far island of the West, far, far away from all who loved him on earth, whose hearts can but cry, "He is not there; he is risen."

God's ways are not our ways. We have to remember that

" The perfect circle of eternity
Is but a crooked line in time."

Looking at the goodly stones he had amassed, but which now want the master-hand to raise them from an aimless heap into a fair temple of truth, with that unity of plan for head and heart which is the one want of modern thought, we can but bow to His inscrutable will whose way is in the bitter unfathomable sea, and His paths in the deep waters, and whose footsteps are not known, but who yet leads His people like a flock.

But there are some on this earth to whom to have known and loved James Hinton has given to all life a diviner meaning; and who now live to carry on his work for the world, for that human good which he loved with a passion that found no equal even in the sum of all other desires.

PRINTED BY BALLANTYNE, HANSON AND CO.
EDINBURGH AND LONDON

A LIST OF

KEGAN PAUL, TRENCH & CO.'S
PUBLICATIONS.

1, *Paternoster Square,*
London.

A LIST OF

KEGAN PAUL, TRENCH & CO.'S PUBLICATIONS.

———❧———

CONTENTS.

	PAGE		PAGE
GENERAL LITERATURE.	. 2	MILITARY WORKS. .	. 31
PARCHMENT LIBRARY .	. 19	POETRY. . . .	. 32
PULPIT COMMENTARY .	. 21	WORKS OF FICTION .	. 39
INTERNATIONAL SCIENTIFIC		BOOKS FOR THE YOUNG	. 40
SERIES . . .	. 28		

———————

GENERAL LITERATURE.

ADAMSON, H. T., B.D.—The Truth as it is in Jesus. Crown 8vo, 8s. 6d.

The Three Sevens. Crown 8vo, 5s. 6d.

The Millennium ; or, The Mystery of God Finished. Crown 8vo, 6s.

A. K. H. B. — From a Quiet Place. A Volume of Sermons. Crown 8vo, 5s.

ALLEN, Rev. R., M.A.—Abraham : his Life, Times, and Travels, 3800 years ago. With Map. Second Edition. Post 8vo, 6s.

ALLIES, T. W., M.A.—Per Crucem ad Lucem. The Result of a Life. 2 vols. Demy 8vo, 25s.

A Life's Decision. Crown 8vo, 7s. 6d.

AMOS, Professor Sheldon.—The History and Principles of the Civil Law of Rome. An aid to the Study of Scientific and Comparative Jurisprudence. Demy 8vo. 16s.

ANDERDON, Rev. W. H.—Fasti Apostolici ; a Chronology of the Years between the Ascension of our Lord and the Martyrdom of SS. Peter and Paul. Second Edition. Enlarged. Square 8vo, 5s.

Evenings with the Saints. Crown 8vo, 5s.

ANDERSON, David.—"Scenes" in the Commons. Crown 8vo, 5*s.*

ARMSTRONG, Richard A., B.A.—Latter-Day Teachers. Six Lectures. Small crown 8vo, 2*s.* 6*d.*

AUBERTIN, J. J.—A Flight to Mexico. With Seven full-page Illustrations and a Railway Map of Mexico. Crown 8vo, 7*s.* 6*d.*

BADGER, George Percy, D.C.L.—An English-Arabic Lexicon. In which the equivalent for English Words and Idiomatic Sentences are rendered into literary and colloquial Arabic. Royal 4to, 80*s.*

BAGEHOT, Walter. — The English Constitution. New and Revised Edition. Crown 8vo, 7*s.* 6*d.*

Lombard Street. A Description of the Money Market. Eighth Edition. Crown 8vo, 7*s.* 6*d.*

Essays on Parliamentary Reform. Crown 8vo, 5*s.*

Some Articles on the Depreciation of Silver, and Topics connected with it. Demy 8vo, 5*s.*

BAGENAL, Philip H.—The American-Irish and their Influence on Irish Politics. Crown 8vo, 5*s.*

BAGOT, Alan, C.E.—Accidents in Mines: their Causes and Prevention. Crown 8vo, 6*s.*

The Principles of Colliery Ventilation. Second Edition, greatly enlarged. Crown 8vo, 5*s.*

BAKER, Sir Sherston, Bart.—The Laws relating to Quarantine. Crown 8vo, 12*s.* 6*d.*

BALDWIN, Capt. J. H.—The Large and Small Game of Bengal and the North-Western Provinces of India. With 20 Illustrations. New and Cheaper Edition. Small 4to, 10*s.* 6*d.*

BALLIN, Ada S. and F. L.—A Hebrew Grammar. With Exercises selected from the Bible. Crown 8vo, 7*s.* 6*d.*

BARCLAY, Edgar.—Mountain Life in Algeria. With numerous Illustrations by Photogravure. Crown 4to, 16*s.*

BARLOW, James H.—The Ultimatum of Pessimism. An Ethical Study. Demy 8vo, 6*s.*

BARNES, William.—Outlines of Redecraft (Logic). With English Wording. Crown 8vo, 3*s.*

BAUR, Ferdinand, Dr. Ph.—A Philological Introduction to Greek and Latin for Students. Translated and adapted from the German, by C. KEGAN PAUL, M.A., and E. D. STONE, M.A. Third Edition. Crown 8vo, 6*s.*

BELLARS, Rev. W.—The Testimony of Conscience to the Truth and Divine Origin of the Christian Revelation. Burney Prize Essay. Small crown 8vo, 3*s.* 6*d.*

BELLINGHAM, Henry, M.P.—Social Aspects of Catholicism and Protestantism in their Civil Bearing upon Nations. Translated and adapted from the French of M. le BARON DE HAULLEVILLE. With a preface by His Eminence CARDINAL MANNING. Second and Cheaper Edition. Crown 8vo, 3s. 6d.

BELLINGHAM, H. Belsches Graham.—Ups and Downs of Spanish Travel. Second Edition. Crown 8vo, 5s.

BENN, Alfred W.—The Greek Philosophers. 2 vols. Demy 8vo, 28s.

BENT, J. Theodore.—Genoa: How the Republic Rose and Fell. With 18 Illustrations. Demy 8vo, 18s.

BLACKLEY, Rev. W. S.—Essays on Pauperism. 16mo. Cloth, 1s. 6d. ; sewed, 1s.

BLECKLEY, Henry. — Socrates and the Athenians: An Apology. Crown 8vo, 2s. 6d.

BLOOMFIELD, The Lady.—Reminiscences of Court and Diplomatic Life. With 3 Portraits and 6 Illustrations. Sixth Edition. 2 vols., 8vo, cloth, 28s.

   *** New and Cheaper Edition. With Frontispiece. Crown 8vo, 6s.

BLUNT, The Ven. Archdeacon.—The Divine Patriot, and other Sermons. Preached in Scarborough and in Cannes. New and Cheaper Edition. Crown 8vo, 4s. 6d. .

BLUNT, Wilfred S.—The Future of Islam. Crown 8vo, 6s.

BOOLE, Mary.—Symbolical Methods of Study. Crown 8vo, 5s.

BOUVERIE-PUSEY, S. E. B.—Permanence and Evolution. An Inquiry into the Supposed Mutability of Animal Types. Crown 8vo, 5s.

BOWEN, H. C., M.A.—Studies in English. For the use of Modern Schools. Seventh Thousand. Small crown 8vo, 1s. 6d.

   English Grammar for Beginners. Fcap. 8vo, 1s.

BRADLEY, F. H.—The Principles of Logic. Demy 8vo, 16s.

BRIDGETT, Rev. T. E.—History of the Holy Eucharist in Great Britain. 2 vols. Demy 8vo, 18s.

BRODRICK, the Hon. G. C.—Political Studies. Demy 8vo, 14s.

BROOKE, Rev. S. A.—Life and Letters of the Late Rev. F. W. Robertson, M.A. Edited by.

   I. Uniform with Robertson's Sermons. 2 vols. With Steel Portrait. 7s. 6d.
   II. Library Edition. With Portrait. 8vo, 12s.
   III. A Popular Edition. In 1 vol., 8vo, 6s.

BROOKE, *Rev. S. A.—Continued.*

The Fight of Faith. Sermons preached on various occasions. Fifth Edition. Crown 8vo, 7s. 6d.

The Spirit of the Christian Life. New and Cheaper Edition. Crown 8vo, 5s.

Theology in the English Poets.—Cowper, Coleridge, Wordsworth, and Burns. Fifth and Cheaper Edition. Post 8vo, 5s.

Christ in Modern Life. Sixteenth and Cheaper Edition. Crown 8vo, 5s.

Sermons. First Series. Thirteenth and Cheaper Edition. Crown 8vo, 5s.

Sermons. Second Series. Sixth and Cheaper Edition. Crown 8vo, 5s.

BROWN, *Rev. J. Baldwin, B.A.*—**The Higher Life.** Its Reality, Experience, and Destiny. Sixth Edition. Crown 8vo, 5s.

Doctrine of Annihilation in the Light of the Gospel of Love. Five Discourses. Fourth Edition. Crown 8vo, 2s. 6d.

The Christian Policy of Life. A Book for Young Men of Business. Third Edition. Crown 8vo, 3s. 6d.

BROWN, *S. Borton, B.A.*—**The Fire Baptism of all Flesh;** or, The Coming Spiritual Crisis of the Dispensation. Crown 8vo, 6s.

BROWN, *Horatio F.*—**Life on the Lagoons.** With two Illustrations and Map. Crown 8vo, 6s.

BROWNBILL, *John.*—**Principles of English Canon Law.** Part I. General Introduction. Crown 8vo, 6s.

BROWNE, *W. R.*—**The Inspiration of the New Testament.** With a Preface by the Rev. J. P. NORRIS, D.D. Fcap. 8vo, 2s. 6d.

BURDETT, *Henry C.*—**Hints in Sickness—Where to Go and What to Do.** Crown 8vo, 1s. 6d.

BURTON, *Mrs. Richard.*—**The Inner Life of Syria, Palestine, and the Holy Land.** Cheaper Edition in one volume. Large post 8vo. 7s. 6d.

BUSBECQ, *Ogier Ghiselin de.*—**His Life and Letters.** By CHARLES THORNTON FORSTER, M.A., and F. H. BLACKBURNE DANIELL, M.A. 2 vols. With Frontispieces. Demy 8vo, 24s.

CARPENTER, *W. B., LL.D., M.D., F.R.S., etc.*—**The Principles of Mental Physiology.** With their Applications to the Training and Discipline of the Mind, and the Study of its Morbid Conditions. Illustrated. Sixth Edition. 8vo, 12s.

Catholic Dictionary. Containing some account of the Doctrine, Discipline, Rites, Ceremonies, Councils, and Religious Orders of the Catholic Church. By WILLIAM E. ADDIS and THOMAS ARNOLD, M.A. Second Edition. Demy 8vo, 21s.

CERVANTES.—Journey to Parnassus. Spanish Text, with Translation into English Tercets, Preface, and Illustrative Notes, by JAMES Y. GIBSON. Crown 8vo, 12s.

CHEYNE, Rev. T. K.—The Prophecies of Isaiah. Translated with Critical Notes and Dissertations. 2 vols. Third Edition. Demy 8vo, 25s.

CLAIRAUT. — Elements of Geometry. Translated by Dr. KAINES. With 145 Figures. Crown 8vo, 4s. 6d.

CLAYDEN, P. W.—England under Lord Beaconsfield. The Political History of the Last Six Years, from the end of 1873 to the beginning of 1880. Second Edition, with Index and continuation to March, 1880. Demy 8vo, 16s.

Samuel Sharpe. Egyptologist and Translator of the Bible. Crown 8vo, 6s.

CLIFFORD, Samuel.—What Think Ye of the Christ? Crown 8vo, 6s.

CLODD, Edward, F.R.A.S.—The Childhood of the World : a Simple Account of Man in Early Times. Seventh Edition. Crown 8vo, 3s.
A Special Edition for Schools. 1s.

The Childhood of Religions. Including a Simple Account of the Birth and Growth of Myths and Legends. Eighth Thousand. Crown 8vo, 5s.
A Special Edition for Schools. 1s. 6d.

Jesus of Nazareth. With a brief sketch of Jewish History to the Time of His Birth. Small crown 8vo, 6s.

COGHLAN, J. Cole, D.D.—The Modern Pharisee and other Sermons. Edited by the Very Rev. H. H. DICKINSON, D.D., Dean of Chapel Royal, Dublin. New and Cheaper Edition. Crown 8vo, 7s. 6d.

COLERIDGE, Sara.—Memoir and Letters of Sara Coleridge. Edited by her Daughter. With Index. Cheap Edition. With Portrait. 7s. 6d.

Collects Exemplified. Being Illustrations from the Old and New Testaments of the Collects for the Sundays after Trinity. By the Author of "A Commentary on the Epistles and Gospels." Edited by the Rev. JOSEPH JACKSON. Crown 8vo, 5s.

CONNELL, A. K.—Discontent and Danger in India. Small crown 8vo, 3s. 6d.

The Economic Revolution of India. Crown 8vo, 4s. 6d.

CORY, William.—A Guide to Modern English History. Part I. —MDCCCXV.-MDCCCXXX. Demy 8vo, 9s. Part II.— MDCCCXXX.-MDCCCXXXV., 15s.

COTTERILL, H. B.—An Introduction to the Study of Poetry. Crown 8vo, 7s. 6d.

COX, Rev. Sir George W., M.A., Bart.—A History of Greece from the Earliest Period to the end of the Persian War. New Edition. 2 vols. Demy 8vo, 36s.

The Mythology of the Aryan Nations. New Edition. Demy 8vo, 16s.

Tales of Ancient Greece. New Edition. Small crown 8vo, 6s.

A Manual of Mythology in the form of Question and Answer. New Edition. Fcap. 8vo, 3s.

An Introduction to the Science of Comparative Mythology and Folk-Lore. Second Edition. Crown 8vo. 7s. 6d.

COX, Rev. Sir G. W., M.A., Bart., and JONES, Eustace Hinton.—Popular Romances of the Middle Ages. Third Edition, in 1 vol. Crown 8vo, 6s.

COX, Rev. Samuel, D.D.—Salvator Mundi; or, Is Christ the Saviour of all Men? Eighth Edition. Crown 8vo, 5s.

The Genesis of Evil, and other Sermons, mainly expository. Third Edition. Crown 8vo, 6s.

A Commentary on the Book of Job. With a Translation. Demy 8vo, 15s.

The Larger Hope. A Sequel to "Salvator Mundi." 16mo, 1s.

CRAVEN, Mrs.—A Year's Meditations. Crown 8vo, 6s.

CRAWFURD, Oswald.—Portugal, Old and New. With Illustrations and Maps. New and Cheaper Edition. Crown 8vo, 6s.

CROZIER, John Beattie, M.B.—The Religion of the Future. Crown 8vo, 6s.

DANIELL, Clarmont.—The Gold Treasure of India. An Inquiry into its Amount, the Cause of its Accumulation, and the Proper Means of using it as Money. Crown 8vo, 5s.

Darkness and Dawn : the Peaceful Birth of a New Age. Small crown 8vo, 2s. 6d.

DAVIDSON, Rev. Samuel, D.D., LL.D.—Canon of the Bible : Its Formation, History, and Fluctuations. Third and Revised Edition. Small crown 8vo, 5s.

The Doctrine of Last Things contained in the New Testament compared with the Notions of the Jews and the Statements of Church Creeds. Small crown 8vo, 3s. 6d.

DAVIDSON, Thomas.—The Parthenon Frieze, and other Essays. Crown 8vo, 6s.

DAWSON, Geo., M.A. Prayers, with a Discourse on Prayer. Edited by his Wife. First Series. Eighth Edition. Crown 8vo, 6s.

Prayers, with a Discourse on Prayer. Edited by GEORGE ST. CLAIR. Second Series. Crown 8vo, 6s.

DAWSON, Geo., M.A.—continued.

Sermons on Disputed Points and Special Occasions.
Edited by his Wife. Fourth Edition. Crown 8vo, 6s.

Sermons on Daily Life and Duty. Edited by his Wife.
Fourth Edition. Crown 8vo, 6s.

The Authentic Gospel, and other Sermons. Edited by
GEORGE ST. CLAIR. Third Edition. Crown 8vo, 6s.

Three Books of God : Nature, History, and Scripture.
Sermons edited by GEORGE ST. CLAIR. Crown 8vo, 6s.

DE JONCOURT, Madame Marie.—**Wholesome Cookery.** Second
Edition. Crown 8vo, 3s. 6d.

DE LONG, Lieut. Com. G. W.—**The Voyage of the Jeannette.**
The Ship and Ice Journals of. Edited by his Wife, EMMA
DE LONG. With Portraits, Maps, and many Illustrations on
wood and stone. 2 vols. Demy 8vo, 36s.

DESPREZ, Philip S., B.D.—**Daniel and John ;** or, The Apocalypse
of the Old and that of the New Testament. Demy 8vo, 12s.

DEVEREUX, W. Cope, R.N., F.R.G.S.—**Fair Italy, the Riviera,
and Monte Carlo.** Comprising a Tour through North and
South Italy and Sicily, with a short account of Malta. Crown
8vo, 6s.

DOWDEN, Edward, LL.D.—**Shakspere :** a Critical Study of his
Mind and Art. Seventh Edition. Post 8vo, 12s.

Studies in Literature, 1789–1877. Third Edition. Large
post 8vo, 6s.

DUFFIELD, A. J.—**Don Quixote : his Critics and Commentators.** With a brief account of the minor works of MIGUEL DE
CERVANTES SAAVEDRA, and a statement of the aim and end of
the greatest of them all. A handy book for general readers.
Crown 8vo, 3s. 6d.

DU MONCEL, Count.—**The Telephone, the Microphone, and
the Phonograph.** With 74 Illustrations. Second Edition.
Small crown 8vo, 5s.

DURUY, Victor.—**History of Rome and the Roman People.**
Edited by Prof. MAHAFFY. With nearly 3000 Illustrations. 4to.
Vol. I. in 2 parts, 30s.

EDGEWORTH, F. Y.—**Mathematical Psychics.** An Essay on
the Application of Mathematics to Social Science. Demy 8vo,
7s. 6d.

**Educational Code of the Prussian Nation, in its Present
Form.** In accordance with the Decisions of the Common Pro-
vincial Law, and with those of Recent Legislation. Crown 8vo,
2s. 6d.

Education Library. Edited by PHILIP MAGNUS :—

An Introduction to the History of Educational Theories. By OSCAR BROWNING, M.A. Second Edition. 3*s.* 6*d.*

Old Greek Education. By the Rev. Prof. MAHAFFY, M.A. Second Edition. 3*s.* 6*d.*

School Management. Including a general view of the work of Education, Organization and Discipline. By JOSEPH LANDON. Third Edition. 6*s.*

Eighteenth Century Essays. Selected and Edited by AUSTIN DOBSON. With a Miniature Frontispiece by R. Caldecott. Parchment Library Edition, 6*s.* ; vellum, 7*s.* 6*d.*

ELSDALE, Henry.—Studies in Tennyson's Idylls. Crown 8vo, 5*s.*

ELYOT, Sir Thomas.—The Boke named the Gouernour. Edited from the First Edition of 1531 by HENRY HERBERT STEPHEN CROFT, M.A., Barrister-at-Law. With Portraits of Sir Thomas and Lady Elyot, copied by permission of her Majesty from Holbein's Original Drawings at Windsor Castle. 2 vols. Fcap. 4to, 50*s.*

Enoch the Prophet. The Book of. Archbishop LAURENCE'S Translation, with an Introduction by the Author of "The Evolution of Christianity." Crown 8vo, 5*s.*

Eranus. A Collection of Exercises in the Alcaic and Sapphic Metres. Edited by F. W. CORNISH, Assistant Master at Eton. Second Edition. Crown 8vo, 2*s.*

EVANS, Mark.—The Story of Our Father's Love, told to Children. Sixth and Cheaper Edition. With Four Illustrations. Fcap. 8vo, 1*s.* 6*d.*

A Book of Common Prayer and Worship for Household Use, compiled exclusively from the Holy Scriptures. Second Edition. Fcap. 8vo, 1*s.*

The Gospel of Home Life. Crown 8vo, 4*s.* 6*d.*

The King's Story-Book. In Three Parts. Fcap. 8vo, 1*s.* 6*d.* each.

** Parts I. and II. with Eight Illustrations and Two Picture Maps, now ready.

" Fan Kwae " at Canton before Treaty Days 1825-1844. By an old Resident. With Frontispiece. Crown 8vo, 5*s.*

FLECKER, Rev. Eliezer.—Scripture Onomatology. Being Critical Notes on the Septuagint and other Versions. Second Edition. Crown 8vo, 3*s.* 6*d.*

FLOREDICE, W. H.—A Month among the Mere Irish. Small crown 8vo, 5*s.*

FOWLE, Rev. T. W.—The Divine Legation of Christ. Crown 8vo, 7s.

FULLER, Rev. Morris.—The Lord's Day ; or, Christian Sunday. Its Unity, History, Philosophy, and Perpetual Obligation. Sermons. Demy 8vo, 10s. 6d.

GARDINER, Samuel R., and J. BASS MULLINGER, M.A.—Introduction to the Study of English History. Second Edition. Large crown 8vo, 9s.

GARDNER, Dorsey.—Quatre Bras, Ligny, and Waterloo. A Narrative of the Campaign in Belgium, 1815. With Maps and Plans. Demy 8vo, 16s.

Genesis in Advance of Present Science. A Critical Investigation of Chapters I.-IX. By a Septuagenarian Beneficed Presbyter. Demy 8vo. 10s. 6d.

GENNA, E.—Irresponsible Philanthropists. Being some Chapters on the Employment of Gentlewomen. Small crown 8vo, 2s. 6d.

GEORGE, Henry.—Progress and Poverty : An Inquiry into the Causes of Industrial Depressions, and of Increase of Want with Increase of Wealth. The Remedy. Fifth Library Edition. Post 8vo, 7s. 6d. Cabinet Edition. Crown 8vo, 2s. 6d. Also a Cheap Edition. Limp cloth, 1s. 6d. Paper covers, 1s.

Social Problems. Fourth Thousand. Crown 8vo, 5s. Cheap Edition. Sewed, 1s.

GIBSON, James Y.—Journey to Parnassus. Composed by MIGUEL DE CERVANTES SAAVEDRA. Spanish Text, with Translation into English Tercets, Preface, and Illustrative Notes, by. Crown 8vo, 12s.

Glossary of Terms and Phrases. Edited by the Rev. H. PERCY SMITH and others. Medium 8vo, 12s.

GLOVER, F., M.A.—Exempla Latina. A First Construing Book, with Short Notes, Lexicon, and an Introduction to the Analysis of Sentences. Second Edition. Fcap. 8vo, 2s.

GOLDSMID, Sir Francis Henry, Bart., Q.C., M.P.—Memoir of. With Portrait. Second Edition, Revised. Crown 8vo, 6s.

GOODENOUGH, Commodore J. G.—Memoir of, with Extracts from his Letters and Journals. Edited by his Widow. With Steel Engraved Portrait. Third Edition. Crown 8vo, 5s.

GOSSE, Edmund W.—Studies in the Literature of Northern Europe. With a Frontispiece designed and etched by Alma Tadema. New and Cheaper Edition. Large crown 8vo, 6s.

Seventeenth Century Studies. A Contribution to the History of English Poetry. Demy 8vo, 10s. 6d.

GOULD, Rev. S. Baring, M.A.—Germany, Present and Past. New and Cheaper Edition. Large crown 8vo, 7s. 6d.

GOWAN, Major Walter E.—A. Ivanoff's Russian Grammar. (16th Edition.) Translated, enlarged, and arranged for use of Students of the Russian Language. Demy 8vo, 6s.

GOWER, Lord Ronald. My Reminiscences. Second Edition. 2 vols. With Frontispieces. Demy 8vo, 30s.

** Also a Cheap Edition. With Portraits. Large crown 8vo, 7s. 6d.

GRAHAM, William, M.A.—The Creed of Science, Religious, Moral, and Social. Second Edition, Revised. Crown 8vo, 6s.

GRIFFITH, Thomas, A.M.—The Gospel of the Divine Life : a Study of the Fourth Evangelist. Demy 8vo, 14s.

GRIMLEY, Rev. H. N., M.A.—Tremadoc Sermons, chiefly on the Spiritual Body, the Unseen World, and the Divine Humanity. Fourth Edition. Crown 8vo, 6s.

G. S. B.—A Study of the Prologue and Epilogue in English Literature from Shakespeare to Dryden. Crown 8vo, 5s.

GUSTAFSON, A.—The Foundation of Death. Crown 8vo.

HAECKEL, Prof. Ernst.—The History of Creation. Translation revised by Professor E. RAY LANKESTER, M.A., F.R.S. With Coloured Plates and Genealogical Trees of the various groups of both Plants and Animals. 2 vols. Third Edition. Post 8vo, 32s.

The History of the Evolution of Man. With numerous Illustrations. 2 vols. Post 8vo, 32s.

A Visit to Ceylon. Post 8vo, 7s. 6d.

Freedom in Science and Teaching. With a Prefatory Note by T. H. HUXLEY, F.R.S. Crown 8vo, 5s.

HALF-CROWN SERIES :—

A Lost Love. By ANNA C. OGLE [Ashford Owen].

Sister Dora : a Biography. By MARGARET LONSDALE.

True Words for Brave Men : a Book for Soldiers and Sailors. By the late CHARLES KINGSLEY.

Notes of Travel : being Extracts from the Journals of Count VON MOLTKE.

English Sonnets. Collected and Arranged by J. DENNIS.

London Lyrics. By F. LOCKER.

Home Songs for Quiet Hours. By the Rev. Canon R. H. BAYNES.

HARROP, Robert.—Bolingbroke. A Political Study and Criticism. Demy 8vo, 14s.

HART, Rev. J. W. T.—The Autobiography of Judas Iscariot. A Character Study. Crown 8vo, 3s. 6d.

HAWEIS, Rev. H. R., M.A.—**Current Coin.** Materialism—The Devil—Crime—Drunkenness—Pauperism—Emotion—Recreation —The Sabbath. Fifth and Cheaper Edition. Crown 8vo, 5*s.* '

Arrows in the Air. Fifth and Cheaper Edition. Crown 8vo, 5*s.*

Speech in Season. Fifth and Cheaper Edition. Crown 8vo, 5*s.*

Thoughts for the Times. Thirteenth and Cheaper Edition. Crown 8vo, 5*s.*

Unsectarian Family Prayers. New and Cheaper Edition. Fcap. 8vo, 1*s.* 6*d.*

HAWKINS, Edwards Comerford.—**Spirit and Form.** Sermons preached in the Parish Church of Leatherhead. Crown 8vo, 6*s.*

HAWTHORNE, Nathaniel.—**Works.** Complete in Twelve Volumes. Large post 8vo, 7*s.* 6*d.* each volume.

VOL. I. TWICE-TOLD TALES.
    II. MOSSES FROM AN OLD MANSE.
    III. THE HOUSE OF THE SEVEN GABLES, AND THE SNOW IMAGE.
    IV. THE WONDERBOOK, TANGLEWOOD TALES, AND GRANDFATHER'S CHAIR.
    V. THE SCARLET LETTER, AND THE BLITHEDALE ROMANCE.
    VI. THE MARBLE FAUN. [Transformation.]
    VII.⎱
    VIII.⎰ OUR OLD HOME, AND ENGLISH NOTE-BOOKS.
    IX. AMERICAN NOTE-BOOKS.
    X. FRENCH AND ITALIAN NOTE-BOOKS.
    XI. SEPTIMIUS FELTON, THE DOLLIVER ROMANCE, FANSHAWE, AND, IN AN APPENDIX, THE ANCESTRAL FOOTSTEP.
    XII. TALES AND ESSAYS, AND OTHER PAPERS, WITH A BIOGRAPHICAL SKETCH OF HAWTHORNE.

HAYES, A. A., Junr.—**New Colorado, and the Santa Fé Trail.** With Map and 60 Illustrations. Square 8vo, 9*s.*

HENNESSY, Sir John Pope.—**Ralegh in Ireland.** With his Letters on Irish Affairs and some Contemporary Documents. Large crown 8vo, printed on hand-made paper, parchment, 10*s.* 6*d.*

HENRY, Philip.—**Diaries and Letters of.** Edited by MATTHEW HENRY LEE, M.A. Large crown 8vo, 7*s.* 6*d.*

HIDE, Albert.—**The Age to Come.** Small crown 8vo, 2*s.* 6*d.*

HIME, Major H. W. L., R.A.—**Wagnerism : A Protest.** Crown 8vo, 2*s.* 6*d.*

HINTON, J.—**Life and Letters.** Edited by ELLICE HOPKINS, with an Introduction by Sir W. W. GULL, Bart., and Portrait engraved on Steel by C. H. Jeens. Fourth Edition. Crown 8vo, 8*s.* 6*d.*

Philosophy and Religion. Second Edition. Crown 8vo, 5*s.*

The Law Breaker. Crown 8vo.

HINTON, J.—continued.
The Mystery of Pain. New Edition. Fcap. 8vo, 1s.

Hodson of Hodson's Horse ; or, Twelve Years of a Soldier's Life
in India. Being extracts from the Letters of the late Major
W. S. R. Hodson. With a Vindication from the Attack of Mr.
Bosworth Smith. Edited by his brother, G. H. HODSON, M.A.
Fourth Edition. Large crown 8vo, 5s.

HOLTHAM, E. G.—Eight Years in Japan, 1873-1881. Work,
Travel, and Recreation. With three Maps. Large crown 8vo, 9s.

HOOPER, Mary.—Little Dinners : How to Serve them with
Elegance and Economy. Eighteenth Edition. Crown
8vo, 2s. 6d.

Cookery for Invalids, Persons of Delicate Digestion,
and Children. Third Edition. Crown 8vo, 2s. 6d.

Every-Day Meals. Being Economical and Wholesome Recipes
for Breakfast, Luncheon, and Supper. Fifth Edition. Crown
8vo, 2s. 6d.

HOPKINS, Ellice.—Life and Letters of James Hinton, with an
Introduction by Sir W. W. GULL, Bart., and Portrait engraved
on Steel by C. H. Jeens. Fourth Edition. Crown 8vo, 8s. 6d.

Work amongst Working Men. Fifth Edition. Crown
8vo, 3s. 6d.

HOSPITALIER, E.—The Modern Applications of Electricity.
Translated and Enlarged by JULIUS MAIER, Ph.D. 2 vols.
Second Edition, Revised, with many additions and numerous
Illustrations. Demy 8vo, 12s. 6d. each volume.
    VOL. I.—Electric Generators, Electric Light.
    VOL. II.—Telephone : Various Applications : Electrical
    Transmission of Energy.

Household Readings on Prophecy. By. a Layman. Small
crown 8vo, 3s. 6d.

HUGHES, Henry.—The Redemption of the World. Crown 8vo,
3s. 6d.

HUNTINGFORD, Rev. E., D.C.L.—The Apocalypse. With a
Commentary and Introductory Essay. Demy 8vo, 5s.

HUTTON, Arthur, M.A.—The Anglican Ministry : Its Nature
and Value in relation to the Catholic Priesthood. With a Preface
by His Eminence CARDINAL NEWMAN. Demy 8vo, 14s.

HUTTON, Rev. C. F.—Unconscious Testimony ; or, The Silent
Witness of the Hebrew to the Truth of the Historical Scriptures.
Crown 8vo, 2s. 6d.

HYNDMAN, H. M.—The Historical Basis of Socialism in
England. Large crown 8vo, 8s. 6d.

IM THURN, Everard F.—Among the Indians of Guiana. Being Sketches, chiefly anthropologic, from the Interior of British Guiana. With 53 Illustrations and a Map. Demy 8vo, 18*s.*

Jaunt in a Junk : A Ten Days' Cruise in Indian Seas. Large crown 8vo, 7*s.* 6*d.*

JENKINS, E., and RAYMOND, J.—The Architect's Legal Handbook. Third Edition, Revised. Crown 8vo, 6*s.*

JENNINGS, Mrs. Vaughan.—Rahel : Her Life and Letters. Large post 8vo, 7*s.* 6*d.*

JERVIS, Rev. W. Henley.— The Gallican Church and the Revolution. A Sequel to the History of the Church of France, from the Concordat of Bologna to the Revolution. Demy 8vo, 18*s.*

JOEL, L.—A Consul's Manual and Shipowner's and Shipmaster's Practical Guide in their Transactions Abroad. With Definitions of Nautical, Mercantile, and Legal Terms ; a Glossary of Mercantile Terms in English, French, German, Italian, and Spanish ; Tables of the Money, Weights, and Measures of the Principal Commercial Nations and their Equivalents in British Standards; and Forms of Consular and Notarial Acts. Demy 8vo, 12*s.*

JOHNSTONE, C. F., M.A.—Historical Abstracts : being Outlines of the History of some of the less known States of Europe. Crown 8vo, 7*s.* 6*d.*

JOLLY, William, F.R.S.E., etc.—The Life of John Duncan, Scotch Weaver and Botanist. With Sketches of his Friends and Notices of his Times. Second Edition. Large crown 8vo, with etched portrait, 9*s.*

JONES, C. A.—The Foreign Freaks of Five Friends. With 30 Illustrations. Crown 8vo, 6*s.*

JOYCE, P. W., LL.D., etc.—Old Celtic Romances. Translated from the Gaelic. Crown 8vo, 7*s.* 6*d.*

JOYNES, J. L.—The Adventures of a Tourist in Ireland. Second edition. Small crown 8vo, 2*s.* 6*d.*

KAUFMANN, Rev. M., B.A.—Socialism : its Nature, its Dangers, and its Remedies considered. Crown 8vo, 7*s.* 6*d.*

Utopias ; or, Schemes of Social Improvement, from Sir Thomas More to Karl Marx. Crown 8vo, 5*s.*

KAY, David, F.R.G.S.—Education and Educators. Crown 8vo, 7*s.* 6*d.*

KAY, Joseph.—Free Trade in Land. Edited by his Widow. With Preface by the Right Hon. JOHN BRIGHT, M.P. Seventh Edition. Crown 8vo, 5*s.*

KEMPIS, Thomas à.—Of the Imitation of Christ. Parchment Library Edition.—Parchment or cloth, 6*s.* ; vellum, 7*s.* 6*d.* The Red Line Edition, fcap. 8vo, red edges, 2*s.* 6*d.* The Cabinet Edition, small 8vo, cloth limp, 1*s.* ; cloth boards, red edges, 1*s.* 6*d.* The Miniature Edition, red edges, 32mo, 1*s.*

*** All the above Editions may be had in various extra bindings.

KENT, C.—Corona Catholica ad Petri successoris Pedes Oblata: De Summi Pontificis Leonis XIII. Assumptione Epigramma. In Quinquaginta Linguis. Fcap. 4to, 15*s.*

KETTLEWELL, Rev. S.—Thomas à Kempis and the Brothers of Common Life. 2 vols. With Frontispieces. Demy 8vo, 30*s.*

KIDD, Joseph, M.D.—The Laws of Therapeutics ; or, the Science and Art of Medicine. Second Edition. Crown 8vo, 6*s.*

KINGSFORD, Anna, M.D.—The Perfect Way in Diet. A Treatise advocating a Return to the Natural and Ancient Food of our Race. Small crown 8vo, 2*s.*

KINGSLEY, Charles, M.A.—Letters and Memories of his Life. Edited by his Wife. With two Steel Engraved Portraits, and Vignettes on Wood. Fourteenth Cabinet Edition. 2 vols. Crown 8vo, 12*s.*

*** Also a People's Edition, in one volume. With Portrait. Crown 8vo, 6*s.*

All Saints' Day, and other Sermons. Edited by the Rev. W. HARRISON. Third Edition. Crown 8vo, 7*s.* 6*d.*

True Words for Brave Men. A Book for Soldiers' and Sailors' Libraries. Tenth Edition. Crown 8vo, 2*s.* 6*d.*

KNOX, Alexander A.—The New Playground ; or, Wanderings in Algeria. New and cheaper edition. Large crown 8vo, 6*s.*

LANDON, Joseph.—School Management ; Including a General View of the Work of Education, Organization, and Discipline. Third Edition. Crown 8vo, 6*s.*

LAURIE, S. S.—The Training of Teachers, and other Educational Papers. Crown 8vo, 7*s.* 6*d.*

LEE, Rev. F. G., D.C.L.—The Other World ; or, Glimpses of the Supernatural. 2 vols. A New Edition. Crown 8vo, 15*s.*

Letters from a Young Emigrant in Manitoba. Second Edition. Small crown 8vo, 3*s.* 6*d.*

LEWIS, Edward Dillon.—A Draft Code of Criminal Law and Procedure. Demy 8vo, 21*s.*

LILLIE, Arthur, M.R.A.S.—The Popular Life of Buddha. Containing an Answer to the Hibbert Lectures of 1881. With Illustrations. Crown 8vo, 6*s.*

LLOYD, Walter.—The Hope of the World : An Essay on Universal Redemption. Crown 8vo, 5*s.*

LONSDALE, Margaret.—Sister Dora : a Biography. With Portrait. Twenty-seventh Edition. Crown 8vo, 2*s.* 6*d.*

LOUNSBURY, Thomas R.—James Fenimore Cooper. Crown 8vo, 5*s.*

LOWDER, Charles.—A Biography. By the Author of "St. Teresa." New and Cheaper Edition. Crown 8vo. With Portrait. 3*s.* 6*d.*

LYTTON, Edward Bulwer, Lord.—Life, Letters and Literary Remains. By his Son, the EARL OF LYTTON. With Portraits, Illustrations and Facsimiles. Demy 8vo. Vols. I. and II., 32*s.*

MACAULAY, G. C.—Francis Beaumont : A Critical Study. Crown 8vo, 5*s.*

MAC CALLUM, M. W.—Studies in Low German and High German Literature. Crown 8vo, 6*s.*

MACDONALD, George. — Donal Grant. A New Novel. 3 vols. Crown 8vo, 31*s.* 6*d.*

MACHIAVELLI, Niccolò. — Life and Times. By Prof. Villari. Translated by Linda Villari. 4 vols. Large post, 8vo, 48*s.*

MACHIAVELLI, Niccolò.—Discourses on the First Decade of Titus Livius. Translated from the Italian by NINIAN HILL THOMSON, M.A. Large crown 8vo, 12*s.*

The Prince. Translated from the Italian by N. H. T. Small crown 8vo, printed on hand-made paper, bevelled boards, 6*s.*

MACKENZIE, Alexander.—How India is Governed. Being an Account of England's Work in India. Small crown 8vo, 2*s.*

MACNAUGHT, Rev. John.—Cœna Domini : An Essay on the Lord's Supper, its Primitive Institution, Apostolic Uses, and Subsequent History. Demy 8vo, 14*s.*

MACWALTER, Rev. G. S.—Life of Antonio Rosmini Serbati (Founder of the Institute of Charity). 2 vols. Demy 8vo.
[Vol. I. now ready, price 12*s.*

MAGNUS, Mrs.—About the Jews since Bible Times. From the Babylonian Exile till the English Exodus. Small crown 8vo, 6*s.*

MAIR, R. S., M.D., F.R.C.S.E.—The Medical Guide for Anglo-Indians. Being a Compendium of Advice to Europeans in India, relating to the Preservation and Regulation of Health. With a Supplement on the Management of Children in India. Second Edition. Crown 8vo, limp cloth, 3*s.* 6*d.*

MALDEN, Henry Elliot.—Vienna, 1683. The History and Conse-quences of the Defeat of the Turks before Vienna, September 12th, 1683, by John Sobieski, King of Poland, and Charles Leopold, Duke of Lorraine. Crown 8vo, 4*s.* 6*d.*

Many Voices. A volume of Extracts from the Religious Writers of Christendom from the First to the Sixteenth Century. With Biographical Sketches. Crown 8vo, cloth extra, red edges, 6*s.*

MARKHAM, Capt. Albert Hastings, R.N.—The Great Frozen Sea : A Personal Narrative of the Voyage of the *Alert* during the Arctic Expedition of 1875-6. With 6 Full-page Illustrations, 2 Maps, and 27 Woodcuts. Sixth and Cheaper Edition. Crown 8vo, 6*s*.

A Polar Reconnaissance : being the Voyage of the *Isbjörn* to Novaya Zemlya in 1879. With 10 Illustrations. Demy 8vo, 16*s*.

Marriage and Maternity ; or, Scripture Wives and Mothers. Small crown 8vo, 4*s*. 6*d*.

MARTINEAU, Gertrude.—Outline Lessons on Morals. Small crown 8vo, 3*s*. 6*d*.

MAUDSLEY, H., M.D.—Body and Will. Being an Essay concerning Will, in its Metaphysical, Physiological, and Pathological Aspects. 8vo, 12*s*.

McGRATH, Terence.—Pictures from Ireland. New and Cheaper Edition. Crown 8vo, 2*s*.

MEREDITH, M.A.—Theotokos, the Example for Woman. Dedicated, by permission, to Lady Agnes Wood. Revised by the Venerable Archdeacon DENISON. 32mo, limp cloth, 1*s*. 6*d*.

MILLER, Edward.—The History and Doctrines of Irvingism ; or, The so-called Catholic and Apostolic Church. 2 vols. Large post 8vo, 25*s*.

The Church in Relation to the State. Large crown 8vo, 7*s*. 6*d*.

MINCHIN, J. G.—Bulgaria since the War : Notes of a Tour in the Autumn of 1879. Small crown 8vo, 3*s*. 6*d*.

MITCHELL, Lucy M.—A History of Ancient Sculpture. With numerous Illustrations, including 6 Plates in Phototype. Super royal 8vo, 42*s*.

Selections from Ancient Sculpture. Being a Portfolio containing Reproductions in Phototype of 36 Masterpieces of Ancient Art to illustrate Mrs. Mitchell's " History of Ancient Sculpture." 18*s*.

MITFORD, Bertram.—Through the Zulu Country. Its Battle-fields and its People. With five Illustrations. Demy 8vo, 14*s*.

MOCKLER, E.—A Grammar of the Baloochee Language, as it is spoken in Makran (Ancient Gedrosia), in the Persia-Arabic and Roman characters. Fcap. 8vo, 5*s*.

MOLESWORTH, Rev. W. Nassau, M.A.—History of the Church of England from 1660. Large crown 8vo, 7*s*. 6*d*.

MORELL, J. R.—Euclid Simplified in Method and Language. Being a Manual of Geometry. Compiled from the most important French Works, approved by the University of Paris and the Minister of Public Instruction. Fcap. 8vo, 2*s*. 6*d*.

C

MORRIS, George.—The Duality of all Divine Truth in our Lord Jesus Christ. For God's Self-manifestation in the Impartation of the Divine Nature to Man. Large crown 8vo, 7s. 6d.

MORSE, E. S., Ph.D.—First Book of Zoology. With numerous Illustrations. New and Cheaper Edition. Crown 8vo, 2s. 6d.

MURPHY, John Nicholas.—The Chair of Peter; or, The Papacy considered in its Institution, Development, and Organization, and in the Benefits which for over Eighteen Centuries it has conferred on Mankind. Demy 8vo, 18s.

My Ducats and My Daughter. A New Novel. 3 vols. Crown 8vo, 31s. 6d.

NELSON, J. H., M.A.—A Prospectus of the Scientific Study of the Hindû Law. Demy 8vo, 9s.

NEWMAN, Cardinal.—Characteristics from the Writings of. Being Selections from his various Works. Arranged with the Author's personal Approval. Sixth Edition. With Portrait. Crown 8vo, 6s.

*** A Portrait of Cardinal Newman, mounted for framing, can be had, 2s. 6d.

NEWMAN, Francis William.—Essays on Diet. Small crown 8vo, cloth limp, 2s.

New Truth and the Old Faith: Are they Incompatible? By a Scientific Layman. Demy 8vo, 10s. 6d.

New Werther. By Loki. Small crown 8vo, 2s. 6d.

NICHOLSON, Edward Byron.—The Gospel according to the Hebrews. Its Fragments Translated and Annotated, with a Critical Analysis of the External and Internal Evidence relating to it. Demy 8vo, 9s. 6d.

A New Commentary on the Gospel according to Matthew. Demy 8vo, 12s.

NICOLS, Arthur, F.G.S., F.R.G.S.—Chapters from the Physical History of the Earth: an Introduction to Geology and Palæontology. With numerous Illustrations. Crown 8vo, 5s.

NOPS, Marianne.—Class Lessons on Euclid. Part I. containing the First Two Books of the Elements. Crown 8vo, 2s. 6d.

Notes on St. Paul's Epistle to the Galatians. For Readers of the Authorized Version or the Original Greek. Demy 8vo, 2s. 6d.

Nuces: Exercises on the Syntax of the Public School Latin Primer. New Edition in Three Parts. Crown 8vo, each 1s. *** The Three Parts can also be had bound together, 3s.

OATES, Frank, F.R.G.S.—Matabele Land and the Victoria Falls. A Naturalist's Wanderings in the Interior of South Africa. Edited by C. G. Oates, B.A. With numerous Illustrations and 4 Maps. Demy 8vo, 21s.

OGLE, W., M.D., F.R.C.P.—Aristotle on the Parts of Animals. Translated, with Introduction and Notes. Royal 8vo, 12s. 6d.

O'HAGAN, Lord, K.P. — Occasional Papers and Addresses. Large crown 8vo, 7s. 6d.

OKEN, Lorenz, Life of. By ALEXANDER ECKER. With Explanatory Notes, Selections from Oken's Correspondence, and Portrait of the Professor. From the German by ALFRED TULK. Crown 8vo, 6s.

O'MEARA, Kathleen.—Frederic Ozanam, Professor of the Sorbonne : His Life and Work. Second Edition. Crown 8vo, 7s. 6d.

Henri Perreyve and his Counsels to the Sick. Small crown 8vo, 5s.

OSBORNE, Rev. W. A.—The Revised Version of the New Testament. A Critical Commentary, with Notes upon the Text. Crown 8vo, 5s.

OTTLEY, H. Bickersteth.—The Great Dilemma. Christ His Own Witness or His Own Accuser. Six Lectures. Second Edition. Crown 8vo, 3s. 6d.

Our Public Schools—Eton, Harrow, Winchester, Rugby, Westminster, Marlborough, The Charterhouse. Crown 8vo, 6s.

OWEN, F. M.—John Keats : a Study. Crown 8vo, 6s.

Across the Hills. Small crown 8vo, 1s. 6d.

OWEN, Rev. Robert, B.D.—Sanctorale Catholicum ; or, Book of Saints. With Notes, Critical, Exegetical, and Historical. Demy 8vo, 18s.

OXENHAM, Rev. F. Nutcombe.—What is the Truth as to Everlasting Punishment. Part II. Being an Historical Inquiry into the Witness and Weight of certain Anti-Origenist Councils. Crown 8vo, 2s. 6d.

OXONIENSIS. — Romanism, Protestantism, Anglicanism. Being a Layman's View of some questions of the Day. Together with Remarks on Dr. Littledale's " Plain Reasons against joining the Church of Rome." Crown 8vo, 3s. 6d.

PALMER, the late William.—Notes of a Visit to Russia in 1840-1841. Selected and arranged by JOHN H. CARDINAL NEWMAN, with portrait. Crown 8vo, 8s. 6d.

Early Christian Symbolism. A Series of Compositions from Fresco Paintings, Glasses, and Sculptured Sarcophagi. Edited by the Rev. Provost NORTHCOTE, D.D., and the Rev. Canon BROWNLOW, M.A. In 8 Parts, each with 4 Plates. Folio, 5s. coloured ; 3s. plain.

Parchment Library. Choicely Printed on hand-made paper, limp parchment antique or cloth, 6s. ; vellum, 7s. 6d. each volume.

The Book of Psalms. Translated by the Rev. T. K. CHEYNE, M.A.

Parchment Library—*continued.*

The Vicar of Wakefield. With Preface and Notes by AUSTIN DOBSON.

English Comic Dramatists. Edited by OSWALD CRAWFURD.

English Lyrics.

The Sonnets of John Milton. Edited by MARK PATTISON. With Portrait after Vertue.

Poems by Alfred Tennyson. 2 vols. With miniature frontispieces by W. B. Richmond.

French Lyrics. Selected and Annotated by GEORGE SAINTSBURY. With a miniature frontispiece designed and etched by H. G. Glindoni.

Fables by Mr. John Gay. With Memoir by AUSTIN DOBSON, and an etched portrait from an unfinished Oil Sketch by Sir Godfrey Kneller.

Select Letters of Percy Bysshe Shelley. Edited, with an Introduction, by RICHARD GARNETT.

The Christian Year. Thoughts in Verse for the Sundays and Holy Days throughout the Year. With Miniature Portrait of the Rev. J. Keble, after a Drawing by G. Richmond, R.A.

Shakspere's Works. Complete in Twelve Volumes.

Eighteenth Century Essays. Selected and Edited by AUSTIN DOBSON. With a Miniature Frontispiece by R. Caldecott.

Q. Horati Flacci Opera. Edited by F. A. CORNISH, Assistant Master at Eton. With a Frontispiece after a design by L. Alma Tadema, etched by Leopold Lowenstam.

Edgar Allan Poe's Poems. With an Essay on his Poetry by ANDREW LANG, and a Frontispiece by Linley Sambourne.

Shakspere's Sonnets. Edited by EDWARD DOWDEN. With a Frontispiece etched by Leopold Lowenstam, after the Death Mask.

English Odes. Selected by EDMUND W. GOSSE. With Frontispiece on India paper by Hamo Thornycroft, A.R.A.

Of the Imitation of Christ. By THOMAS À KEMPIS. A revised Translation. With Frontispiece on India paper, from a Design by W. B. Richmond.

Tennyson's The Princess: a Medley. With a Miniature Frontispiece by H. M. Paget, and a Tailpiece in Outline by Gordon Browne.

Poems: Selected from PERCY BYSSHE SHELLEY. Dedicated to Lady Shelley. With a Preface by RICHARD GARNETT and a Miniature Frontispiece.

Tennyson's In Memoriam. With a Miniature Portrait in *eau-forte* by Le Rat, after a Photograph by the late Mrs. Cameron.

*** The above volumes may also be had in a variety of leather bindings.

PARSLOE, Joseph.—**Our Railways.** Sketches, Historical and Descriptive. With Practical Information as to Fares and Rates, etc., and a Chapter on Railway Reform. Crown 8vo, 6s.

PAUL, Alexander.—**Short Parliaments.** A History of the National Demand for frequent General Elections. Small crown 8vo, 3s. 6d.

PAUL, C. Kegan.—**Biographical Sketches,** Printed on hand-made paper, bound in buckram. Second Edition. Crown 8vo, 7s. 6d.

PEARSON, Rev. S.—**Week-day Living.** A Book for Young Men and Women. Second Edition. Crown 8vo, 5s.

PESCHEL, Dr. Oscar.—**The Races of Man and their Geographical Distribution.** Second Edition. Large crown 8vo, 9s.

PETERS, F. H.—**The Nicomachean Ethics of Aristotle.** Translated by. Crown 8vo, 6s.

PHIPSON, E.—**The Animal Lore of Shakspeare's Time.** Including Quadrupeds, Birds, Reptiles, Fish and Insects. Large post 8vo, 9s.

PIDGEON, D.—**An Engineer's Holiday ;** or, Notes of a Round Trip from Long. 0° to 0°. New and Cheaper Edition. Large crown 8vo, 7s. 6d.

POPE, J. Buckingham. — **Railway Rates and Radical Rule.** Trade Questions as Election Tests. Crown 8vo, 2s. 6d.

PRICE, Prof. Bonamy. — **Chapters on Practical Political Economy.** Being the Substance of Lectures delivered before the University of Oxford. New and Cheaper Edition. Large post 8vo, 5s.

Pulpit Commentary, The. (Old Testament Series.) Edited by the Rev. J. S. EXELL, M.A., and the Rev. Canon H. D. M. SPENCE.

Genesis. By the Rev. T. WHITELAW, M.A. With Homilies by the Very Rev. J. F. MONTGOMERY, D.D., Rev. Prof. R. A. REDFORD, M.A., LL.B., Rev. F. HASTINGS, Rev. W. ROBERTS, M.A. An Introduction to the Study of the Old Testament by the Venerable Archdeacon FARRAR, D.D., F.R.S.; and Introductions to the Pentateuch by the Right Rev. H. COTTERILL, D.D., and Rev. T. WHITELAW, M.A. Eighth Edition. 1 vol., 15s.

Exodus. By the Rev. Canon RAWLINSON. With Homilies by Rev. J. ORR, Rev. D. YOUNG, B.A., Rev. C. A. GOODHART, Rev. J. URQUHART, and the Rev. H. T. ROBJOHNS. Fourth Edition. 2 vols., 18s.

Leviticus. By the Rev. Prebendary MEYRICK, M.A. With Introductions by the Rev. R. COLLINS, Rev. Professor A. CAVE, and Homilies by Rev. Prof. REDFORD, LL.B., Rev. J. A. MACDONALD, Rev. W. CLARKSON, B.A., Rev. S. R. ALDRIDGE, LL.B., and Rev. McCHEYNE EDGAR. Fourth Edition. 15s.

Pulpit Commentary, The—*continued.*

Numbers. By the Rev. R. WINTERBOTHAM, LL.B. With Homilies by the Rev. Professor W. BINNIE, D.D., Rev. E. S. PROUT, M.A., Rev. D. YOUNG, Rev. J. WAITE, and an Introduction by the Rev. THOMAS WHITELAW, M.A. Fourth Edition. 15*s.*

Deuteronomy. By the Rev. W. L. ALEXANDER, D.D. With Homilies by Rev. C. CLEMANCE, D.D., Rev. J. ORR, B.D., Rev. R. M. EDGAR, M.A., Rev. D. DAVIES, M.A. Third edition. 15*s.*

Joshua. By Rev. J. J. LIAS, M.A. With Homilies by Rev. S. R. ALDRIDGE, LL.B., Rev. R. GLOVER, REV. E. DE PRESSENSÉ, D.D., Rev. J. WAITE, B.A., Rev. W. F. ADENEY, M.A.; and an Introduction by the Rev. A. PLUMMER, M.A. Fifth Edition. 12*s.* 6*d.*

Judges and Ruth. By the Bishop of Bath and Wells, and Rev. J. MORRISON, D.D. With Homilies by Rev. A. F. MUIR, M.A., Rev. W. F. ADENEY, M.A., Rev. W. M. STATHAM, and Rev. Professor J. THOMSON, M.A. Fourth Edition. 10*s.* 6*d.*

1 Samuel. By the Very Rev. R. P. SMITH, D.D. With Homilies by Rev. DONALD FRASER, D.D., Rev. Prof. CHAPMAN, and Rev. B. DALE. Sixth Edition. 15*s.*

1 Kings. By the Rev. JOSEPH HAMMOND, LL.B. With Homilies by the Rev. E. DE PRESSENSÉ, D.D., Rev. J. WAITE, B.A., Rev. A. ROWLAND, LL.B., Rev. J. A. MACDONALD, and Rev. J. URQUHART. Fourth Edition. 15*s.*

Ezra, Nehemiah, and Esther. By Rev. Canon G. RAWLINSON, M.A. With Homilies by Rev. Prof. J. R. THOMSON, M.A., Rev. Prof. R. A. REDFORD, LL.B., M.A., Rev. W. S. LEWIS, M.A., Rev. J. A. MACDONALD, Rev. A. MACKENNAL, B.A., Rev. W. CLARKSON, B.A., Rev. F. HASTINGS, Rev. W. DINWIDDIE, LL.B., Rev. Prof. ROWLANDS, B.A., Rev. G. WOOD, B.A., Rev. Prof. P. C. BARKER, M.A., LL.B., and the Rev. J. S. EXELL, M.A. Sixth Edition. 1 vol., 12*s.* 6*d.*

Jeremiah. By the Rev. T. K. CHEYNE, M.A. With Homilies by the Rev. W. F. ADENEY, M.A., Rev. A. F. MUIR, M.A., Rev. S. CONWAY, B.A., Rev. J. WAITE, B.A., and Rev. D. YOUNG, B.A. Vol. I., 15s.

Pulpit Commentary, The. (New Testament Series.)

St. Mark. By Very Rev. E. BICKERSTETH, D.D., Dean of Lichfield. With Homilies by Rev. Prof. THOMSON, M.A., Rev. Prof. GIVEN, M.A., Rev. Prof. JOHNSON, M.A., Rev. A. ROWLAND, B.A., LL.B., Rev. A. MUIR, and Rev. R. GREEN. 2 vols. Fourth Edition. 21*s.*

The Acts of the Apostles. By the Bishop of Bath and Wells. With Homilies by Rev. Prof. P. C. BARKER, M.A., LL.B., Rev. Prof. E. JOHNSON, M.A., Rev. Prof. R. A. REDFORD, M.A., Rev. R. TUCK, B.A., Rev. W. CLARKSON, B.A. 2 vols., 21*s.*

Pulpit Commentary, The—*continued.*
    1 Corinthians. By the Ven. Archdeacon FARRAR, D.D. With Homilies by Rev. Ex-Chancellor LIPSCOMB, LL.D., Rev. DAVID THOMAS, D.D., Rev. D. FRASER, D.D., Rev. Prof. J. R. THOMSON, M.A., Rev. J. WAITE, B.A., Rev. R. TUCK, B.A., Rev. E. HURNDALL, M.A., and Rev. H. BREMNER, B.D. Price 15*s.*

PUSEY, Dr.—**Sermons for the Church's Seasons from Advent to Trinity.** Selected from the Published Sermons of the late EDWARD BOUVERIE PUSEY, D.D. Crown 8vo, 5*s.*

QUILTER, Harry.—**" The Academy," 1872–1882.** 1*s.*

RADCLIFFE, Frank R. Y.—**The New Politicus.** Small crown 8vo, 2*s.* 6*d.*

RANKE, Leopold von.—**Universal History.** The oldest Historical Group of Nations and the Greeks. Edited by G. W. PROTHERO. Demy 8vo, 16*s.*

Realities of the Future Life. Small crown 8vo, 1*s.* 6*d.*

RENDELL, J. M.—**Concise Handbook of the Island of Madeira.** With Plan of Funchal and Map of the Island. Fcap. 8vo, 1*s.* 6*d.*

REYNOLDS, Rev. J. W.—**The Supernatural in Nature.** A Verification by Free Use of Science. Third Edition, Revised and Enlarged. Demy 8vo, 14*s.*

    The Mystery of Miracles. Third and Enlarged Edition. Crown 8vo, 6*s.*

    The Mystery of the Universe; Our Common Faith. Demy 8vo, 14*s.*

RIBOT, Prof. Th.—**Heredity:** A Psychological Study on its Phenomena, its Laws, its Causes, and its Consequences. Second Edition. Large crown 8vo, 9*s.*

ROBERTSON, The late Rev. F. W., M.A.—**Life and Letters of.** Edited by the Rev. STOPFORD BROOKE, M.A.
    I. Two Vols., uniform with the Sermons. With Steel Portrait. Crown 8vo, 7*s.* 6*d.*
    II. Library Edition, in Demy 8vo, with Portrait. 12*s.*
    III. A Popular Edition, in 1 vol. Crown 8vo, 6*s.*

    Sermons. Four Series. Small crown 8vo, 3*s.* 6*d.* each.

    The Human Race, and other Sermons. Preached at Cheltenham, Oxford, and Brighton. New and Cheaper Edition. Small crown 8vo, 3*s.* 6*d.*

    Notes on Genesis. New and Cheaper Edition. Small crown 8vo, 3*s.* 6*d.*

    Expository Lectures on St. Paul's Epistles to the Corinthians. A New Edition. Small crown 8vo, 5*s.*

    Lectures and Addresses, with other Literary Remains. A New Edition, Small crown 8vo, 5*s.*

ROBERTSON, The late Rev. F. W., M.A.—continued.

An Analysis of Mr. Tennyson's "In Memoriam." (Dedicated by Permission to the Poet-Laureate.) Fcap. 8vo, 2s.

The Education of the Human Race. Translated from the German of GOTTHOLD EPHRAIM LESSING. Fcap. 8vo, 2s. 6d.

The above Works can also be had, bound in half morocco.

*** A Portrait of the late Rev. F. W. Robertson, mounted for framing, can be had, 2s. 6d.

ROMANES, G. J. — **Mental Evolution in Animals.** With a Posthumous Essay on Instinct by CHARLES DARWIN, F.R.S. Demy 8vo, 12s.

ROSMINI SERBATI, A., Founder of the Institute of Charity. **Life.** By G. STUART MACWALTER. 2 vols. 8vo.
[Vol. I. now ready, 12s.

Rosmini's Origin of Ideas. Translated from the Fifth Italian Edition of the Nuovo Saggio *Sull' origine delle idee.* 3 vols. Demy 8vo, cloth. [Vols. I. and II. now ready, 16s. each.

Rosmini's Philosophical System. Translated, with a Sketch of the Author's Life, Bibliography, Introduction, and Notes by THOMAS DAVIDSON. Demy 8vo, 16s.

RULE, Martin, M.A. — **The Life and Times of St. Anselm, Archbishop of Canterbury and Primate of the Britains.** 2 vols. Demy 8vo, 32s.

SALVATOR, Archduke Ludwig.—**Levkosia, the Capital of Cyprus.** Crown 4to, 10s. 6d.

SAMUEL, Sydney M.—**Jewish Life in the East.** Small crown 8vo, 3s. 6d.

SAYCE, Rev. Archibald Henry.—**Introduction to the Science of Language.** 2 vols. Second Edition. Large post 8vo, 21s.

Scientific Layman. The New Truth and the Old Faith: are they Incompatible? Demy 8vo, 10s. 6d.

SCOONES, W. Baptiste.—**Four Centuries of English Letters:** A Selection of 350 Letters by 150 Writers, from the Period of the Paston Letters to the Present Time. Third Edition. Large crown 8vo, 6s.

SHILLITO, Rev. Joseph.—**Womanhood:** its Duties, Temptations, and Privileges. A Book for Young Women. Third Edition. Crown 8vo, 3s. 6d.

SHIPLEY, Rev. Orby, M.A.—**Principles of the Faith in Relation to Sin.** Topics for Thought in Times of Retreat. Eleven Addresses delivered during a Retreat of Three Days to Persons living in the World. Demy 8vo, 12s.

Sister Augustine, Superior of the Sisters of Charity at the St. Johannis Hospital at Bonn. Authorised Translation by HANS THARAU, from the German "Memorials of AMALIE VON LASAULX." Cheap Edition. Large crown 8vo, 4s. 6d.

SKINNER, James.—A Memoir. By the Author of "Charles Lowder." With a Preface by the Rev. Canon CARTER, and Portrait. Large crown, 7s. 6d.

SMITH, Edward, M.D., LL.B., F.R.S.—Tubercular Consumption in its Early and Remediable Stages. Second Edition. Crown 8vo, 6s.

SPEDDING, James.—Reviews and Discussions, Literary, Political, and Historical not relating to Bacon. Demy 8vo, 12s. 6d.

Evenings with a Reviewer; or, Bacon and Macaulay. With a Prefatory Notice by G. S. VENABLES, Q.C. 2 vols. Demy 8vo, 18s.

STAPFER, Paul.—Shakspeare and Classical Antiquity: Greek and Latin Antiquity as presented in Shakspeare's Plays. Translated by EMILY J. CAREY. Large post 8vo, 12s.

STEVENSON, Rev. W. F.—Hymns for the Church and Home. Selected and Edited by the Rev. W. FLEMING STEVENSON. The Hymn Book consists of Three Parts :—I. For Public Worship.—II. For Family and Private Worship.—III. For Children.

*** Published in various forms and prices, the latter ranging from 8d. to 6s.

Stray Papers on Education, and Scenes from School Life. By B. H. Second Edition. Small crown 8vo, 3s. 6d.

STREATFEILD, Rev. G. S., M.A.—Lincolnshire and the Danes. Large crown 8vo, 7s. 6d.

STRECKER-WISLICENUS.—Organic Chemistry. Translated and Edited, with Extensive Additions, by W. R. HODGKINSON, Ph.D., and A. J. GREENAWAY, F.I.C. Demy 8vo, 21s.

Study of the Prologue and Epilogue in English Literature. From Shakespeare to Dryden. By G. S. B. Crown 8vo, 5s.

SULLY, James, M.A.—Pessimism : a History and a Criticism. Second Edition. Demy 8vo, 14s.

SWEDENBORG, Eman.—De Cultu et Amore Dei ubi Agitur de Telluris ortu, Paradiso et Vivario, tum de Primogeniti Seu Adami Nativitate Infantla, et Amore. Crown 8vo, 6s.

SYME, David.—Representative Government in England. Its Faults and Failures. Second Edition. Large crown 8vo, 6s.

TAYLOR, Rev. Isaac.—The Alphabet. An Account of the Origin and Development of Letters. With numerous Tables and Facsimiles. 2 vols. Demy 8vo, 36s.

TAYLOR, Sedley. — Profit Sharing between Capital and Labour. To which is added a Memorandum on the Industrial Partnership at the Whitwood Collieries, by ARCHIBALD and HENRY BRIGGS, with remarks by SEDLEY TAYLOR. Crown 8vo, 2s. 6d.

Thirty Thousand Thoughts. Edited by the Rev. CANON SPENCE, Rev. J. S. EXELL, Rev. CHARLES NEIL, and Rev. JACOB STEPHENSON. 6 vols. Super royal 8vo.
[Vols. I. and II. now ready, 16s. each.

THOM, J. Hamilton. — Laws of Life after the Mind of Christ. Second Edition. Crown 8vo, 7s. 6d.

THOMSON, J. Turnbull. — Social Problems ; or, An Inquiry into the Laws of Influence. With Diagrams. Demy 8vo, 10s. 6d.

TIDMAN, Paul F. — Gold and Silver Money. Part I.—A Plain Statement. Part II.—Objections Answered. Third Edition. Crown 8vo, 1s.

TIPPLE, Rev. S. A. — Sunday Mornings at Norwood. Prayers and Sermons. Crown 8vo, 6s.

TODHUNTER, Dr. J. — A Study of Shelley. Crown 8vo, 7s.

TREMENHEERE, Hugh Seymour, C.B. — A Manual of the Principles of Government, as set forth by the Authorities of Ancient and Modern Times. New and Enlarged Edition. Crown 8vo, 3s. 6d.

TUKE, Daniel Hack, M.D., F.R.C.P. — Chapters in the History of the Insane in the British Isles. With 4 Illustrations. Large crown 8vo, 12s.

TWINING, Louisa. — Workhouse Visiting and Management during Twenty-Five Years. Small crown 8vo, 2s.

TYLER, J. — The Mystery of Being: or, What Do We Know ? Small crown 8vo, 3s. 6d.

UPTON, Major R. D. — Gleanings from the Desert of Arabia. Large post 8vo, 10s. 6d.

VACUUS VIATOR. — Flying South. Recollections of France and its Littoral. Small crown 8vo, 3s. 6d.

VAUGHAN, H. Halford. — New Readings and Renderings of Shakespeare's Tragedies. 2 vols. Demy 8vo, 25s.

VILLARI, Professor. — Niccolò Machiavelli and his Times. Translated by Linda Villari. 4 vols. Large post 8vo, 48s.

VILLIERS, The Right Hon. C. P. — Free Trade Speeches of. With Political Memoir. Edited by a Member of the Cobden Club. 2 vols. With Portrait. Demy 8vo, 25s.
*** People's Edition. 1 vol. Crown 8vo, limp cloth, 2s. 6d.

VOGT, Lieut.-Col. Hermann. — The Egyptian War of 1882. A translation. With Map and Plans. Large crown 8vo, 6s.

VOLCKXSOM, E. W. v.—Catechism of Elementary Modern Chemistry. Small crown 8vo, 3*s.*

VYNER, Lady Mary.—Every Day a Portion. Adapted from the Bible and the Prayer Book, for the Private Devotion of those living in Widowhood. Collected and Edited by Lady Mary Vyner, Square crown 8vo, 5*s.*

WALDSTEIN, Charles, Ph.D.—The Balance of Emotion and Intellect; an Introductory Essay to the Study of Philosophy. Crown 8vo, 6*s.*

WALLER, Rev. C. B.—The Apocalypse, reviewed under the Light of the Doctrine of the Unfolding Ages, and the Restitution of All Things. Demy 8vo, 12*s.*

WALPOLE, Chas. George.—History of Ireland from the Earliest Times to the Union with Great Britain. With 5 Maps and Appendices. Crown 8vo, 10*s.* 6*d.*

WALSHE, Walter Hayle, M.D.—Dramatic Singing Physiologically Estimated. Crown 8vo, 3*s.* 6*d.*

WARD, William George, Ph.D.—Essays on the Philosophy of Theism. Edited, with an Introduction, by WILFRID WARD. 2 vols. Demy 8vo, 21*s.*

WEDDERBURN, Sir David, Bart., M.P.—Life of. Compiled from his Journals and Writings by his sister, Mrs. E. H. PERCIVAL. With etched Portrait, and facsimiles of Pencil Sketches. Demy 8vo, 14*s.*

WEDMORE, Frederick.—The Masters of Genre Painting. With Sixteen Illustrations. Post 8vo, 7*s.* 6*d.*

WHEWELL, William, D.D.—His Life and Selections from his Correspondence. By Mrs. STAIR DOUGLAS. With a Portrait from a Painting by Samuel Laurence. Demy 8vo, 21*s.*

WHITNEY, Prof. William Dwight. — Essentials of English Grammar, for the Use of Schools. Second Edition. Crown 8vo, 3*s.* 6*d.*

WILLIAMS, Rowland, D.D.—Psalms, Litanies, Counsels, and Collects for Devout Persons. Edited by his Widow. New and Popular Edition. Crown 8vo, 3*s.* 6*d.*

Stray Thoughts Collected from the Writings of the late Rowland Williams, D.D. Edited by his Widow. Crown 8vo, 3*s.* 6*d.*

WILSON, Sir Erasmus. — The Recent Archaic Discovery of Egyptian Mummies at Thebes. A Lecture. Crown 8vo, 1*s.* 6*d.*

WILSON, Lieut.-Col. C. T. — The Duke of Berwick, Marshal of France, 1702-1734. Demy 8vo, 15*s.*

WILSON, Mrs. R. F.—The Christian Brothers. Their Origin and Work. With a Sketch of the Life of their Founder, the Ven. JEAN BAPTISTE, de la Salle. Crown 8vo, 6*s.*

WOLTMANN, Dr. Alfred, and WOERMANN, Dr. Karl.—History
of Painting. Edited by SIDNEY COLVIN. Vol. I. Painting
in Antiquity and the Middle Ages. With numerous Illustrations.
Medium 8vo, 28s. ; bevelled boards, gilt leaves, 30s.

Word was Made Flesh. Short Family Readings on the Epistles for
each Sunday of the Christian Year. Demy 8vo, 10s. 6d.

WREN, Sir Christopher.—His Family and His Times. With
Original Letters, and a Discourse on Architecture hitherto un-
published. By LUCY PHILLIMORE. Demy 8vo, 10s. 6d.

YOUMANS, Eliza A.—First Book of Botany. Designed to
Cultivate the Observing Powers of Children. With 300
Engravings. New and Cheaper Edition. Crown 8vo, 2s. 6d.

YOUMANS, Edward L., M.D.—A Class Book of Chemistry, on
the Basis of the New System. With 200 Illustrations. Crown
8vo, 5s.

THE INTERNATIONAL SCIENTIFIC SERIES.

I. Forms of Water: a Familiar Exposition of the Origin and
Phenomena of Glaciers. By J. Tyndall, LL.D., F.R.S. With
25 Illustrations. Eighth Edition. Crown 8vo, 5s.

II. Physics and Politics; or, Thoughts on the Application of the
Principles of "Natural Selection" and "Inheritance" to Political
Society. By Walter Bagehot. Sixth Edition. Crown 8vo, 4s.

III. Foods. By Edward Smith, M.D., LL.B., F.R.S. With numerous
Illustrations. Eighth Edition. Crown 8vo, 5s.

IV. Mind and Body: the Theories of their Relation. By Alexander
Bain, LL.D. With Four Illustrations. Seventh Edition. Crown
8vo, 4s.

V. The Study of Sociology. By Herbert Spencer. Eleventh
Edition. Crown 8vo, 5s.

VI. On the Conservation of Energy. By Balfour Stewart, M.A.,
LL.D., F.R.S. With 14 Illustrations. Sixth Edition. Crown
8vo, 5s.

VII. Animal Locomotion; or Walking, Swimming, and Flying. By
J. B. Pettigrew, M.D., F.R.S., etc. With 130 Illustrations.
Third Edition. Crown 8vo, 5s.

VIII. Responsibility in Mental Disease. By Henry Maudsley,
M.D. Fourth Edition. Crown 8vo, 5s.

IX. The New Chemistry. By Professor J. P. Cooke. With 31
Illustrations. Seventh Edition. Crown 8vo, 5s.

X. **The Science of Law.** By Professor Sheldon Amos. Fifth Edition. Crown 8vo, 5*s.*

XI. **Animal Mechanism** : a Treatise on Terrestrial and Aerial Loco-motion. By Professor E. J. Marey. With 117 Illustrations. Third Edition. Crown 8vo, 5*s.*

XII. **The Doctrine of Descent and Darwinism.** By Professor Oscar Schmidt. With 26 Illustrations. Fifth Edition. Crown 8vo, 5*s.*

XIII. **The History of the Conflict between Religion and Science.** By J. W. Draper, M.D., LL.D. Eighteenth Edition. Crown 8vo, 5*s.*

XIV. **Fungi :** their Nature, Influences, Uses, etc. By M. C. Cooke, M.D., LL.D. Edited by the Rev. M. J. Berkeley, M.A., F.L.S. With numerous Illustrations. Third Edition. Crown 8vo, 5*s.*

XV. **The Chemical Effects of Light and Photography.** By Dr. Hermann Vogel. Translation thoroughly Revised. With 100 Illustrations. Fourth Edition. Crown 8vo, 5*s.*

XVI. **The Life and Growth of Language.** By Professor William Dwight Whitney. Fourth Edition. Crown 8vo, 5*s.*

XVII. **Money and the Mechanism of Exchange.** By W. Stanley Jevons, M.A., F.R.S. Sixth Edition. Crown 8vo, 5*s.*

XVIII. **The Nature of Light.** With a General Account of Physical Optics. By Dr. Eugene Lommel. With 188 Illustrations and a Table of Spectra in Chromo-lithography. Third Edition. Crown 8vo, 5*s.*

XIX. **Animal Parasites and Messmates.** By Monsieur Van Beneden. With 83 Illustrations. Third Edition. Crown 8vo, 5*s.*

XX. **Fermentation.** By Professor Schützenberger. With 28 Illus-trations. Fourth Edition. Crown 8vo, 5*s.*

XXI. **The Five Senses of Man.** By Professor Bernstein. With 91 Illustrations. Fourth Edition. Crown 8vo, 5*s.*

XXII. **The Theory of Sound in its Relation to Music.** By Pro-fessor Pietro Blaserna. With numerous Illustrations. Third Edition. Crown 8vo, 5*s.*

XXIII. **Studies in Spectrum Analysis.** By J. Norman Lockyer, F.R.S. With six photographic Illustrations of Spectra, and numerous engravings on Wood. Third Edition. Crown 8vo, 6*s. 6d.*

XXIV. **A History of the Growth of the Steam Engine.** By Professor R. H. Thurston. With numerous Illustrations. Third Edition. Crown 8vo, 6*s. 6d.*

XXV. **Education as a Science.** By Alexander Bain, LL.D. Fourth Edition. Crown 8vo, 5*s.*

XXVI. **The Human Species.** By Professor A. de Quatrefages. Third Edition. Crown 8vo, 5s.

XXVII. **Modern Chromatics.** With Applications to Art and Industry. By Ogden N. Rood. With 130 original Illustrations. Second Edition. Crown 8vo, 5s.

XXVIII. **The Crayfish :** an Introduction to the Study of Zoology. By Professor T. H. Huxley. With 82 Illustrations. Third Edition. Crown 8vo, 5s.

XXIX. **The Brain as an Organ of Mind.** By H. Charlton Bastian, M.D. With numerous Illustrations. Third Edition. Crown 8vo, 5s.

XXX. **The Atomic Theory.** By Prof. Wurtz. Translated by G. Cleminshaw, F.C.S. Third Edition. Crown 8vo, 5s.

XXXI. **The Natural Conditions of Existence as they affect Animal Life.** By Karl Semper. With 2 Maps and 106 Woodcuts. Third Edition. Crown 8vo, 5s.

XXXII. **General Physiology of Muscles and Nerves.** By Prof. J. Rosenthal. Third Edition. With Illustrations. Crown 8vo, 5s.

XXXIII. **Sight :** an Exposition of the Principles of Monocular and Binocular Vision. By Joseph le Conte, LL.D. Second Edition. With 132 Illustrations. Crown 8vo, 5s.

XXXIV. **Illusions :** a Psychological Study. By James Sully. Second Edition. Crown 8vo, 5s.

XXXV. **Volcanoes : what they are and what they teach.** By Professor J. W. Judd, F.R.S. With 92 Illustrations on Wood. Second Edition. Crown 8vo, 5s.

XXXVI. **Suicide :** an Essay in Comparative Moral Statistics. By Prof. E. Morselli. Second Edition. With Diagrams. Crown 8vo, 5s.

XXXVII. **The Brain and its Functions.** By J. Luys. With Illustrations. Second Edition. Crown 8vo, 5s.

XXXVIII. **Myth and Science :** an Essay. By Tito Vignoli. Second Edition. Crown 8vo, 5s.

XXXIX. **The Sun.** By Professor Young. With Illustrations. Second Edition. Crown 8vo, 5s.

XL. **Ants, Bees, and Wasps :** a Record of Observations on the Habits of the Social Hymenoptera. By Sir John Lubbock, Bart., M.P. With 5 Chromo-lithographic Illustrations. Sixth Edition. Crown 8vo, 5s.

XLI. **Animal Intelligence.** By G. J. Romanes, LL.D., F.R.S. Third Edition. Crown 8vo, 5s.

XLII. The Concepts and Theories of Modern Physics. By J. B. Stallo. Second Edition. Crown 8vo, 5s.

XLIII. Diseases of the Memory; An Essay in the Positive Psychology. By Prof. Th. Ribot. Second Edition. Crown 8vo, 5s.

XLIV. Man before Metals. By N. Joly, with 148 Illustrations. Third Edition. Crown 8vo, 5s.

XLV. The Science of Politics. By Prof. Sheldon Amos. Second Edition. Crown 8vo, 5s.

XLVI. Elementary Meteorology. By Robert H. Scott. Second Edition. With Numerous Illustrations. Crown 8vo, 5s.

XLVII. The Organs of Speech and their Application in the Formation of Articulate Sounds. By Georg Hermann Von Meyer. With 47 Woodcuts. Crown 8vo, 5s.

XLVIII. Fallacies. A View of Logic from the Practical Side. By Alfred Sidgwick. Crown 8vo, 5s.

MILITARY WORKS.

BARRINGTON, Capt. J. T.—England on the Defensive; or, the Problem of Invasion Critically Examined. Large crown 8vo, with Map, 7s. 6d.

BRACKENBURY, Col. C. B., R.A. — Military Handbooks for Regimental Officers.

I. Military Sketching and Reconnaissance. By Col. F. J. Hutchison and Major H. G. MacGregor. Fourth Edition. With 15 Plates. Small crown 8vo, 4s.

II. The Elements of Modern Tactics Practically applied to English Formations. By Lieut.-Col. Wilkinson Shaw. Fourth Edition. With 25 Plates and Maps. Small crown 8vo, 9s.

III. Field Artillery. Its Equipment, Organization and Tactics. By Major Sisson C. Pratt, R.A. With 12 Plates. Second Edition. Small crown 8vo, 6s.

IV. The Elements of Military Administration. First Part: Permanent System of Administration. By Major J. W. Buxton. Small crown 8vo. 7s. 6d.

V. Military Law: Its Procedure and Practice. By Major Sisson C. Pratt, R.A. Second Edition. Small crown 8vo, 4s. 6d.

BROOKE, Major, C. K.—A System of Field Training. Small crown 8vo, cloth limp, 2s.

CLERY, C., Lieut.-Col.—Minor Tactics. With 26 Maps and Plans. Sixth and Cheaper Edition, Revised. Crown 8vo, 9s.

COLVILE, Lieut.-Col. C. F.—Military Tribunals. Sewed, 2s. 6d.

CRAUFURD, Lieut. H.J.—Suggestions for the Military Training of a Company of Infantry. Crown 8vo, 1s. 6d.

HARRISON, Lieut.-Col. R.—The Officer's Memorandum Book for Peace and War. Third Edition. Oblong 32mo, roan, with pencil, 3s. 6d.

Notes on Cavalry Tactics, Organisation, etc. By a Cavalry Officer. With Diagrams. Demy 8vo, 12s.

PARR, Capt. H. Hallam, C.M.G.—The Dress, Horses, and Equipment of Infantry and Staff Officers. Crown 8vo, 1s.

SCHAW, Col. H.—The Defence and Attack of Positions and Localities. Second Edition, Revised and Corrected. Crown 8vo, 3s. 6d.

SHADWELL, Maj.-Gen., C.B.—Mountain Warfare. Illustrated by the Campaign of 1799 in Switzerland. Being a Translation of the Swiss Narrative compiled from the Works of the Archduke Charles, Jomini, and others. Also of Notes by General H. Dufour on the Campaign of the Valtelline in 1635. With Appendix, Maps, and Introductory Remarks. Demy 8vo, 16s.

WILKINSON, H. Spenser, Capt. 20th Lancashire R.V. — Citizen Soldiers. Essays towards the Improvement of the Volunteer Force. Crown 8vo, 2s. 6d.

POETRY.

ADAM OF ST. VICTOR.—The Liturgical Poetry of Adam of St. Victor. From the text of GAUTIER. With Translations into English in the Original Metres, and Short Explanatory Notes, by DIGBY S. WRANGHAM, M.A. 3 vols. Crown 8vo, printed on hand-made paper, boards, 21s.

AUCHMUTY, A. C.—Poems of English Heroism : From Brunanburh to Lucknow; from Athelstan to Albert. Small crown 8vo, 1s. 6d.

AVIA.—The Odyssey of Homer. Done into English Verse by. Fcap. 4to, 15s.

BANKS, Mrs. G. L.—Ripples and Breakers: Poems. Square 8vo, 5s.

BARING, T. C., M.A., M.P. — The Scheme of Epicurus. A Rendering into English Verse of the Unfinished Poem of Lucretius, entitled "De Rerum Naturâ" ("The Nature of Things"). Fcap. 4to.

BARNES, *William.*—Poems of Rural Life, in the Dorset Dialect. New Edition, complete in one vol. Crown 8vo, 8s. 6d.

BAYNES, *Rev. Canon H. R.*—Home Songs for Quiet Hours. Fourth and Cheaper Edition. Fcap. 8vo, cloth, 2s. 6d.
•⁎• This may also be had handsomely bound in morocco with gilt edges.

BENDALL, *Gerard.*—Musa Silvestris. 16mo, 1s. 6d.

BEVINGTON, *L. S.*—Key Notes. Small crown 8vo, 5s.

BILLSON, *C. J.*—The Acharnians of Aristophanes. Crown 8vo, 3s. 6d.

BLUNT, *Wilfrid Scawen.* — The Wind and the Whirlwind. Demy 8vo, 1s. 6d.

BOWEN, *H. C., M.A.*—Simple English Poems. English Literature for Junior Classes. In Four Parts. Parts I., II., and III., 6d. each, and Part IV., 1s. Complete, 3s.

BRASHER, *Alfred.*—Sophia ; or, the Viceroy of Valencia. A Comedy in Five Acts, founded on a Story in Scarron. Small crown 8vo, 2s. 6d.

BRYANT, *W. C.*—Poems. Cheap Edition, with Frontispiece. Small crown 8vo, 3s. 6d.

BYRNNE, *E. Fairfax.*—Milicent : a Poem. Small crown 8vo, 6s.

CAILLARD, *Emma Marie.*—Charlotte Corday, and other Poems. Small crown 8vo, 3s. 6d.

Calderon's Dramas : the Wonder-Working Magician — Life is a Dream—the Purgatory of St. Patrick. Translated by DENIS FLORENCE MACCARTHY. Post 8vo, 10s.

Camoens Lusiads. — Portuguese Text, with Translation by J. J. AUBERTIN. Second Edition. 2 vols. Crown 8vo, 12s.

CAMPBELL, *Lewis.*—Sophocles. The Seven Plays in English Verse. Crown 8vo, 7s. 6d.

Castilian Brothers (The), Chateaubriant, Waldemar : Three Tragedies ; and The Rose of Sicily : a Drama. By the Author of " Ginevra," etc. Crown 8vo, 6s.

Chronicles of Christopher Columbus. A Poem in 12 Cantos. By M. D. C. Crown 8vo, 7s. 6d.

CLARKE, *Mary Cowden.* — Honey from the Weed. Verses. Crown 8vo, 7s.

Cosmo de Medici ; The False One ; Agramont and Beaumont : Three Tragedies ; and The Deformed : a Dramatic Sketch. By the Author of " Ginevra," etc., etc. Crown 8vo, 5s.

D

COXHEAD, Ethel.—Birds and Babies. Imp. 16mo. With 33 Illustrations. Gilt, 2s. 6d.

David Rizzio, Bothwell, and the Witch Lady: Three Tragedies. By the author of " Ginevra," etc. Crown 8vo, 6s. .

DAVIE, G. S., M.D.—The Garden of Fragrance. Being a complete translation of the Bostán of Sádi from the original Persian into English Verse. Crown 8vo, 7s. 6d.

DAVIES, T. Hart.—Catullus. Translated into English Verse. Crown 8vo, 6s.

DENNIS, J.—English Sonnets. Collected and Arranged by. Small crown 8vo, 2s. 6d.

DE VERE, Aubrey.—Poetical Works.
  I. THE SEARCH AFTER PROSERPINE, etc. 6s.
  II. THE LEGENDS OF ST. PATRICK, etc. 6s.
  III. ALEXANDER THE GREAT, etc. 6s.

  The Foray of Queen Meave, and other Legends of Ireland's Heroic Age. Small crown 8vo, 5s.

  Legends of the Saxon Saints. Small crown 8vo, 6s.

DILLON, Arthur.—River Songs and other Poems. With 13 autotype Illustrations from designs by Margery May. Fcap. 4to, cloth extra, gilt leaves, 10s. 6d.

DOBELL, Mrs. Horace.—Ethelstone, Eveline, and other Poems. Crown 8vo, 6s.

DOBSON, Austin.—Old World Idylls and other Poems. Third Edition. 18mo, cloth extra, gilt tops, 6s.

DOMET, Alfred.—Ranolf and Amohia. A Dream of Two Lives. New Edition, Revised. 2 vols. Crown 8vo, 12s.

Dorothy : a Country Story in Elegiac Verse. With Preface. Demy 8vo, 5s.

DOWDEN, Edward, LL.D.—Shakspere's Sonnets. With Introduction and Notes. Large post 8vo, 7s. 6d.

DUTT, Toru.—A Sheaf Gleaned in French Fields. New Edition. Demy 8vo, 10s. 6d.

EDMONDS, E. W.—Hesperas. Rhythm and Rhyme. Crown 8vo, 4s.

ELDRYTH, Maud.—Margaret, and other Poems. Small crown 8vo, 3s. 6d.

  All Soul's Eve, " No God,"and other Poems. Fcap. 8vo, 3s. 6d.

ELLIOTT, Ebenezer, The Corn Law Rhymer.—Poems. Edited by his son, the Rev. EDWIN ELLIOTT, of St. John's, Antigua. 2 vols. Crown 8vo, 18s.

English Odes. Selected, with a Critical Introduction by EDMUND W. GOSSE, and a miniature frontispiece by Hamo Thornycroft, A.R.A. Elzevir 8vo, limp parchment antique, or cloth, 6s. ; vellum, 7s. 6d.

English Verse. Edited by W. J. LINTON and R. H. STODDARD. 5 vols. Crown 8vo, cloth, 5s. each.
I. CHAUCER TO BURNS.
II. TRANSLATIONS.
III. LYRICS OF THE NINETEENTH CENTURY.
IV. DRAMATIC SCENES AND CHARACTERS.
V. BALLADS AND ROMANCES.

EVANS, Anne.—**Poems and Music.** With Memorial Preface by ANN THACKERAY RITCHIE. Large crown 8vo, 7s.

GOSSE, Edmund W.—**New Poems.** Crown 8vo, 7s. 6d.

GRAHAM, William. **Two Fancies,** and other Poems. Crown 8vo, 5s.

GRINDROD, Charles. **Plays from English History.** Crown 8vo, 7s. 6d.

The Stranger's Story, and his Poem, The Lament of Love : An Episode of the Malvern Hills. Small crown 8vo, 2s. 6d.

GURNEY, Rev. Alfred.—**The Vision of the Eucharist,** and other Poems. Crown 8vo, 5s.

HELLON, H. G.—**Daphnis :** a Pastoral Poem. Small crown 8vo, 3s. 6d.

HENRY, Daniel, Junr.—**Under a Fool's Cap.** Songs. Crown 8vo, cloth, bevelled boards, 5s.

Herman Waldgrave : a Life's Drama. By the Author of "Ginevra," etc. Crown 8vo, 6s.

HICKEY, E. H.—**A Sculptor,** and other Poems. Small crown 8vo, 5s.

HONEYWOOD, Patty.—**Poems.** Dedicated (by permission) to Lord Wolseley, G.C.B., etc. Small crown 8vo, 2s. 6d.

INGHAM, Sarson, C. J.—**Cædmon's Vision, and other Poems.** Small crown 8vo, 5s.

JENKINS, Rev. Canon.—**Alfonso Petrucci,** Cardinal and Conspirator: an Historical Tragedy in Five Acts. Small crown 8vo, 3s. 6d.

JOHNSON, Ernle S. W.—**Ilaria,** and other Poems. Small crown 8vo, 3s. 6d.

KEATS, John.—**Poetical Works.** Edited by W. T. ARNOLD. Large crown 8vo, choicely printed on hand-made paper, with Portrait in *eau-forte.* Parchment, 12s. ; vellum, 15s.

KING, Edward.—**Echoes from the Orient.** With Miscellaneous Poems. Small crown 8vo, 3s. 6d.

KING, Mrs. Hamilton.—**The Disciples.** Sixth Edition, with Portrait and Notes. Crown 8vo, 5s.

A Book of Dreams. Crown 8vo, 3s. 6d.

KNOX, The Hon. Mrs. O. N.—**Four Pictures from a Life,** and other Poems. Small crown 8vo, 3s. 6d.

LANG, A.—XXXII Ballades in Blue China. Elzevir 8vo, parchment, 5s.

LAWSON, Right Hon. Mr. Justice.—Hymni Usitati Latine Redditi : with other Verses. Small 8vo, parchment, 5s.

Lessings Nathan the Wise. Translated by EUSTACE K. CORBETT. Crown 8vo, 6s.

Life Thoughts. Small crown 8vo, 2s. 6d.

Living English Poets MDCCCLXXXII. With Frontispiece by Walter Crane. Second Edition. Large crown 8vo. Printed on hand-made paper. Parchment, 12s. ; vellum, 15s.

LOCKER, F.—London Lyrics. A New and Cheaper Edition. Small crown 8vo, 2s. 6d.

Love in Idleness. A Volume of Poems. With an etching by W. B. Scott. Small crown 8vo, 5s.

Love Sonnets of Proteus. With Frontispiece by the Author. Elzevir 8vo, 5s.

LUMSDEN, Lieut.-Col. H. W.—Beowulf : an Old English Poem. Translated into Modern Rhymes. Second and Revised Edition. Small crown 8vo, 5s.

Lyre and Star. Poems by the Author of "Ginevra," etc. Crown 8vo, 5s.

MAGNUSSON, Eirikr, M.A., and PALMER, E. H., M.A.—Johan Ludvig Runeberg's Lyrical Songs, Idylls, and Epigrams. Fcap. 8vo, 5s.

M.D.C.—Chronicles of Christopher Columbus. A Poem in Twelve Cantos. Crown 8vo, 7s. 6d.

MEREDITH, Owen [The Earl of Lytton].—Lucile. New Edition. With 32 Illustrations. 16mo, 3s. 6d. Cloth extra, gilt edges, 4s. 6d.

MORRIS, Lewis.—Poetical Works of. New and Cheaper Editions, with Portrait. Complete in 3 vols., 5s. each.

> Vol. I. contains "Songs of Two Worlds." Ninth Edition. Vol. II. contains "The Epic of Hades." Seventeenth Edition. Vol. III. contains "Gwen" and "The Ode of Life." Fifth Edition.

> The Epic of Hades. With 16 Autotype Illustrations, after the Drawings of the late George R. Chapman. 4to, cloth extra, gilt leaves, 21s.

> The Epic of Hades. Presentation Edition. 4to, cloth extra, gilt leaves, 10s. 6d.

> Songs Unsung. Fourth Edition. Fcap. 8vo, 6s.

MORSHEAD, E. D. A.—The House of Atreus. Being the Agamemnon, Libation-Bearers, and Furies of Æschylus. Translated into English Verse. Crown 8vo, 7s.

> The Suppliant Maidens of Æschylus. Crown 8vo, 3s. 6d.

NADEN, Constance W.—Songs and Sonnets of Spring Time. Small crown 8vo, 5*s.*

NEWELL, E. J.—The Sorrows of Simona and Lyrical Verses. Small crown 8vo, 3*s.* 6*d.*

NOEL, The Hon. Roden. — A Little Child's Monument. Third Edition. Small crown 8vo, 3*s.* 6*d.*

The Red Flag, and other Poems. New Edition. Small crown 8vo, 6*s.*

O'HAGAN, John.—The Song of Roland. Translated into English Verse. New and Cheaper Edition. Crown 8vo, 5*s.*

PFEIFFER, Emily.—The Rhyme of the Lady of the Lock, and How it Grew. Small crown 8vo, 3*s.* 6*d.*

Gerard's Monument, and other Poems. Second Edition. Crown 8vo, 6*s.*

Under the Aspens : Lyrical and Dramatic. With Portrait. Crown 8vo, 6*s.*

PIATT, J. J.—Idyls and Lyrics of the Ohio Valley. Crown 8vo, 5*s.*

POE, Edgar Allan.—Poems. With an Essay on his Poetry by ANDREW LANG, and a Frontispiece by Linley Sambourne. Parchment Library Edition.—Parchment or cloth, 6*s.* ; vellum, 7*s.* 6*d.*

RAFFALOVICH, Mark André. — Cyril and Lionel, and other Poems. A volume of Sentimental Studies. Small crown 8vo, 3*s.* 6*d.*

Rare Poems of the 16th and 17th Centuries. Edited W. J. LINTON. Crown 8vo, 5*s.*

RHOADES, James.—The Georgics of Virgil. Translated into English Verse. Small crown 8vo, 5*s.*

ROBINSON, A. Mary F.—A Handful of Honeysuckle. Fcap. 8vo, 3*s.* 6*d.*

The Crowned Hippolytus. Translated from Euripides. With New Poems. Small crown 8vo, 5*s.*

Schiller's Mary Stuart. German Text, with English Translation on opposite page by LEEDHAM WHITE. Crown 8vo, 6*s.*

SCOTT, George F. E.—Theodora and other Poems. Small crown 8vo, 3*s.* 6*d.*

SEAL, W. H.—Ione, and other Poems. Crown 8vo, gilt tops, 5*s.*

SELKIRK, J. B.—Poems. Crown 8vo, 7*s.* 6*d.*

Shakspere's Sonnets. Edited by EDWARD DOWDEN. With a Frontispiece etched by Leopold Lowenstam, after the Death Mask. Parchment Library Edition.—Parchment or cloth, 6*s.* ; vellum, 7*s.* 6*d.*

Shakspere's Works. Complete in 12 Volumes. Parchment Library Edition.—Parchment or cloth, 6s. each; vellum, 7s. 6d. each.

SHAW, W. F., M.A.—Juvenal, Persius, Martial, and Catullus. An Experiment in Translation. Crown 8vo, 5s.

SHELLEY, Percy Bysshe.—Poems Selected from. Dedicated to Lady Shelley. With Preface by RICHARD GARNETT. Parchment Library Edition.—Parchment or cloth, 6s. ; vellum, 7s. 6d.

Six Ballads about King Arthur. Crown 8vo, cloth extra, gilt edges, 3s. 6d.

SKINNER, H. J.—The Lily of the Lyn, and other Poems. Small crown 8vo, 3s. 6d.

SLADEN, Douglas B.—Frithjof and Ingebjorg, and other Poems. Small crown 8vo, 5s.

SMITH, J. W. Gilbart.—The Loves of Vandyck. A Tale of Genoa. Small crown 8vo, 2s. 6d.

Sophocles: The Seven Plays in English Verse. Translated by LEWIS CAMPBELL. Crown 8vo, 7s. 6d.

SPICER, Henry.—Haska : a Drama in Three Acts (as represented at the Theatre Royal, Drury Lane, March 10th, 1877). Third Edition. Crown 8vo, 3s. 6d.

TAYLOR, Sir H.—Works. Complete in Five Volumes. Crown 8vo, 30s.

> Philip Van Artevelde. Fcap. 8vo, 3s. 6d.
>
> The Virgin Widow, etc. Fcap. 8vo, 3s. 6d.
>
> The Statesman. Fcap. 8vo, 3s. 6d.

TAYLOR, Augustus.—Poems. Fcap. 8vo, 5s.

Tennyson Birthday Book, The. Edited by EMILY SHAKESPEAR. 32mo, limp, 2s. ; cloth extra, 3s.

> **** A superior Edition, printed in red and black, on antique paper, specially prepared. Small crown 8vo, extra, gilt leaves, 5s. ; and in various calf and morocco bindings.

THORNTON, L. M.—The Son of Shelomith. Small crown 8vo, 3s. 6d.

TODHUNTER, Dr. J.—Laürella, and other Poems. Crown 8vo, 6s. 6d.

> Forest Songs. Small crown 8vo, 3s. 6d.
>
> The True Tragedy of Rienzi : a Drama. 3s. 6d.
>
> Alcestis : a Dramatic Poem. Extra fcap. 8vo, 5s.

WALTERS, Sophia Lydia.—A Dreamer's Sketch Book. With 21 Illustrations by Percival Skelton, R. P. Leitch, W. H. J. Boot, and T. R. Pritchett. Engraved by J. D. Cooper. Fcap. 4to, 12s. 6d.

WATTS, Alaric Alfred and Anna Mary Howitt.—Aurora. A Medley of Verse. Fcap. 8vo, bevelled boards, 5s.

WEBSTER, *Augusta.*—In a Day : a Drama. Small crown 8vo, 2*s.* 6*d.*
Disguises : a Drama. Small crown 8vo, 5*s.*

Wet Days. By a Farmer. Small crown 8vo, 6*s.*

WILLIAMS, J.—A Story of Three Years, and other Poems. Small crown 8vo, 3*s.* 6*d.*

Wordsworth Birthday Book, The. Edited by ADELAIDE and VIOLET WORDSWORTH. 32mo, limp cloth, 1*s.* 6*d.* ; cloth extra, 2*s.*

YOUNGS, Ella Sharpe.—Paphus, and other Poems. Small crown 8vo, 3*s.* 6*d.*

WORKS OF FICTION IN ONE VOLUME.

BANKS, Mrs. G. L.—God's Providence House. New Edition. Crown 8vo, 3*s.* 6*d.*

INGELOW, Jean.—Off the Skelligs : a Novel. With Frontispiece. Second Edition. Crown 8vo, 6*s.*

MACDONALD, G.—Castle Warlock. A Novel. New and Cheaper Edition. Crown 8vo, 6*s.*

Malcolm. With Portrait of the Author engraved on Steel. Sixth Edition. Crown 8vo, 6*s.*

The Marquis of Lossie. Fifth Edition. With Frontispiece. Crown 8vo, 6*s.*

St. George and St. Michael. Fourth Edition. With Frontispiece. Crown 8vo, 6*s.*

PALGRAVE, W. Gifford.—Hermann Agha : an Eastern Narrative. Third Edition. Crown 8vo, 6*s.*

SHAW, Flora L.—Castle Blair ; a Story of Youthful Days. New and Cheaper Edition. Crown 8vo, 3*s.* 6*d.*

STRETTON, Hesba.—Through a Needle's Eye : a Story. New and Cheaper Edition, with Frontispiece. Crown 8vo, 6*s.*

TAYLOR, Col. Meadows, C.S.I., M.R.I.A.—Seeta : a Novel. New and Cheaper Edition. With Frontispiece. Crown 8vo, 6*s.*

Tippoo Sultaun : a Tale of the Mysore War. New Edition, with Frontispiece. Crown 8vo, 6*s.*

Ralph Darnell. New and Cheaper Edition. With Frontispiece. Crown 8vo, 6*s.*

A Noble Queen. New and Cheaper Edition. With Frontispiece. Crown 8vo, 6*s.*

The Confessions of a Thug. Crown 8vo, 6*s.*

Tara : a Mahratta Tale. Crown 8vo, 6*s.*

Within Sound of the Sea. New and Cheaper Edition, with Frontispiece. Crown 8vo, 6*s.*

BOOKS FOR THE YOUNG.

Brave Men's Footsteps. A Book of Example and Anecdote for Young People. By the Editor of "Men who have Risen." With 4 Illustrations by C. Doyle. Eighth Edition. Crown 8vo, 3s. 6d

COXHEAD, Ethel.—**Birds and Babies.** Imp. 16mo. With 33 Illustrations. Cloth gilt, 2s. 6d.

DAVIES, G. Christopher.—**Rambles and Adventures of our School Field Club.** With 4 Illustrations. New and Cheaper Edition. Crown 8vo, 3s. 6d.

EDMONDS, Herbert.—**Well Spent Lives;** a Series of Modern Biographies. New and Cheaper Edition. Crown 8vo, 3s. 6d.

EVANS, Mark.—**The Story of our Father's Love,** told to Children. Sixth and Cheaper Edition of Theology for Children. With 4 Illustrations. Fcap. 8vo, 1s. 6d.

JOHNSON, Virginia W.—**The Catskill Fairies.** Illustrated by Alfred Fredericks. 5s.

MAC KENNA, S. J.—**Plucky Fellows.** A Book for Boys. With 6 Illustrations. Fifth Edition. Crown 8vo, 3s. 6d.

REANEY, Mrs. G. S.—**Waking and Working;** or, From Girlhood to Womanhood. New and Cheaper Edition. With a Frontispiece. Crown 8vo, 3s. 6d.

Blessing and Blessed: a Sketch of Girl Life. New and Cheaper Edition. Crown 8vo, 3s. 6d.

Rose Gurney's Discovery. A Book for Girls. Dedicated to their Mothers. Crown 8vo, 3s. 6d.

English Girls: Their Place and Power. With Preface by the Rev. R. W. Dale. Fourth Edition. Fcap. 8vo, 2s. 6d.

Just Anyone, and other Stories. Three Illustrations. Royal 16mo, 1s. 6d.

Sunbeam Willie, and other Stories. Three Illustrations. Royal 16mo, 1s. 6d.

Sunshine Jenny, and other Stories. Three Illustrations. Royal 16mo, 1s. 6d.

STOCKTON, Frank R.—**A Jolly Fellowship.** With 20 Illustrations. Crown 8vo, 5s.

STORR, Francis, and TURNER, Hawes.—**Canterbury Chimes;** or, Chaucer Tales re-told to Children. With 6 Illustrations from the Ellesmere MS. Third Edition. Fcap. 8vo, 3s. 6d.

STRETTON, Hesba.—**David Lloyd's Last Will.** With 4 Illustrations. New Edition. Royal 16mo, 2s. 6d.

Tales from Ariosto Re-told for Children. By a Lady. With 3 Illustrations. Crown 8vo, 4s. 6d.

WHITAKER, Florence.—**Christy's Inheritance.** A London Story. Illustrated. Royal 16mo, 1s. 6d.

PRINTED BY WILLIAM CLOWES AND SONS, LIMITED, LONDON AND BECCLES.

www.ingramcontent.com/pod-product-compliance
Lightning Source LLC
Chambersburg PA
CBHW021336110726
47900CB00005B/1494